Vera

W9-AAA-312

Advance Praise for *The Last Platoon*

"Among the many virtues Bing West brings to any military/political enterprise is that he knows his shit from the level of the grunt in the foxhole to the SecDef in the Situation Room. He has been there. He has done that. Every page of *The Last Platoon* radiates authenticity, whether it's the chaos and carnage of a firefight in Afghanistan or the kitchen-table back-and-forth between a Marine husband and wife on the eve of a deployment. And the man can write! If you've only read Bing West's non-fiction (which is universally five-star), you will sit back with satisfaction seeing that he doesn't drop a step shifting into the realm of the novel. *The Last Platoon* reads like a cinematic thriller with nonstop action and conflict, but it is also informed on every page by the maturity and depth of understanding of a Marine combat officer, a war journalist, and a former assistant Secretary of Defense, who has been in the tall grass for decades and has seen and done it all. *The Last Platoon* is dark because its subject matter—the folly and arrogance of those at the strategic level and the price in blood that young men and women have to pay at the tactical—is grim and permanent. I read it in one sitting, and I will read it again."

—STEVEN PRESSFIELD, Bestselling Author of *Gates of Fire* and *The Legend of Bagger Vance*

"Bing West knows combat, the Corps, and the infantry. He is also a masterful storyteller. In *The Last Platoon* he gives us a raw, passionate feel for what warriors go through on the ground and the price they pay in blood to try to accomplish ill-thought-out missions."

—GENERAL ANTHONY C. ZINNI, USMC (Retired)

"Combat veteran, historian, and front-line war correspondent Bing West writes a graphic odyssey into the tragic absurdity of the Americans' twenty years in Afghanistan—a gripping paean to those brave men who fought there and survived the ordeal with dignity."

—VICTOR DAVIS HANSON, Author of *Carnage and Culture* and *The Second World Wars*

"Bing West is one of America's great combat writers. He knows what it is like to be out on the pointy end because he has 'been there and done that.' In *The Last Platoon*, West tells the story of our Nation's Warriors with the hard, tough, factual clarity. A team of individuals, overcoming their fears, works together to accomplish a tough mission, which becomes intertwined with politics, international relations, and the complexity of the Washington process. But that's what war is, right? Thanks Bing for reminding us of what it is to serve well and honorably in battle."

—GENERAL ROBERT B. NELLER, USMC (Retired)
37th Commandant of the Marine Corps

"I rarely read fiction books, but when Bing West writes one I know that it will be a page turner. This one is no exception! Bing knows his subject matter like no one else does and writes in a way that draws you in as if you were there. Once I started it, I couldn't put it down until it was finished. I highly recommend this book!"

—MAJOR GENERAL RAY "E-TOOL" SMITH, USMC (Retired),
Navy Cross recipient, Hue City, 1968

ALSO BY BING WEST

Small Unit Action in Vietnam, Summer 1966

The Village

Naval Forces and Western Security (ed.)

The Pepperdogs: A Novel

The March Up:
Taking Baghdad with the United States Marines
(with Major General Ray Smith)

No True Glory:
A Frontline Account of the Battle for Fallujah

The Strongest Tribe:
War, Politics, and the End Game in Iraq

The Wrong War:
Grit, Strategy, and the Way Out of Afghanistan

Into the Fire: A Firsthand Account
of the Most Extraordinary Battle of the Afghan War
(with Sergeant Dakota Meyer)

One Million Steps:
A Marine Platoon at War

Call Sign Chaos: Learning to Lead
(with General Jim Mattis)

THE LAST
PLATOON

THE LAST PLATOON

A Novel of the
Afghanistan War

BING WEST

BOMBARDIER
BOOKS

A BOMBARDIER BOOKS BOOK
An Imprint of Post Hill Press

The Last Platoon:
A Novel of the Afghanistan War
© 2020 by Bing West
All Rights Reserved

ISBN: 978-1-64293-673-5
ISBN (eBook): 978-1-64293-674-2

Cover art by Cody Corcoran
Interior design and composition, Greg Johnson, Textbook Perfect

BOMBARDIER
BOOKS

Post Hill
PRESS

Post Hill Press
New York • Nashville
posthillpress.com

Published in the United States of America

*In doing what we ought we deserve no praise,
because it is our duty.*

—AUGUSTINE

CONTENTS

DAY 6 APRIL 11

DAY 7 APRIL 12

MAJOR CHARACTERS

CIA Director Webster	President Dinard	National Security Advisor Armsted

Secretary of Defense Towns	Chairman of Joint Chiefs Admiral Michaels

US Forces Afghanistan General Gretman	Marine Forces Central Command Lieutenant General Killian

CIA Team	Helmand Task Force	Afghan Brigade
Richards	Colonel Coffman	Colonel Ishaq
Eagan	*Eagle Six*	Lieutenant Ibril
Stovell		Advisor: Captain
Tic		Golstern

Executive Officer: **Major Barnes** *Eagle Five*
Artillery: **Captain Lasswell** *Bear Six*
Medical: **Doctor Zarest**
Intel: **Staff Sergeant Ahmed**
Security Platoon: **Captain Diego Cruz** *Wolf Six*
Platoon Sergeant: **Staff Sergeant Sullivan** *Wolf Five*
1st Squad: **Sergeant Denton** *Wolf One*
2nd Squad: **Sergeant McGowan** *Wolf Two*
3rd Squad: **Sergeant Binns** *Wolf Three*
Sniper: **Sergeant Ashford** *Winmag*
Forward Observer: **Sergeant Doyle** *Badger Two*
Engineer: **Corporal Wolfe**
Terp: **Mohamed**

OPPOSITION MAJOR CHARACTERS
Taliban Commander **Zar**
Drug Dealer **"The Persian"**
Pakistani Commander **Colonel Balroop**
Taliban Emir **Imam Sadr**
Prominent Farmer **Nantush**
Vietnamese Sapper **Quat**
And **one million poppy growers**

Time

This novel takes place over seven days.

The time in Afghanistan is 8½ hours in front of Washington, DC.

For example, when it is 5:30 P.M. in Afghanistan, it is 9:00 A.M. in Washington.

Prelude

A Decade Ago

The Marines were walking in single file across a farm field that lay bare and muddy on a dreary winter day. To a civilian observer, they looked like a scraggly bunch of tired teenagers, ambling along with no place to go and all the time in the world to get there. Scudding gray clouds spat sleet into their faces, and frozen poppy stalks snapped beneath their feet. Slender sheens of ice covered the irrigation ditches, and after hours of trudging through soggy fields and wading across frigid creeks, their shabby cammies were dripping and brown water sloshed from their boots. Only their weapons looked clean and burnished, the black lacquer rubbed off by months of hard use.

From a distance, it was hard to tell them apart. The only oddity was a thin whip antenna bobbing high on the back of a stocky grunt in the middle of the column. As he had on his previous tours, Lieutenant Diego Cruz carried his own radio. Snipers usually tried to pick off the radio operator. He wasn't showing off; it was his way of sharing in the danger.

1

Cruz had logged the highest number of patrols in the platoon, and was proud of his people. Seven months earlier, fifty grunts, fit and cocky, had deployed to Helmand Province. Since then, they had lost five killed and seventeen wounded, including five amps. But the troops hadn't slacked off, and they rarely bitched.

Their base, if it could be called that, consisted of an abandoned farm compound with thick mud walls and a rusty hand pump that tapped into a deep well. A mile of poppy fields and irrigation ditches separated them from their company headquarters. Cruz liked the isolation. It gave him the time to wring out the immature impulses of newly minted Marines and shape them into alert, lethal grunts. With no access to the internet and sleeping in caves hacked out of the walls, they had grown close to each other, even as their numbers dropped week by week.

Located at the bottom of Afghanistan, Helmand was a vast, flat expanse of dusty desert and tired hills. One major river snaked through the province, bringing ample water from the snowfields far to the north. Most of the Pashtun tribal people lived and farmed along its fertile banks.

Officially, the platoon was protecting the farmers from the Taliban. In violent Helmand, however, the farmers ignored the Marines or ran away when approached. Cruz didn't dwell on the irony. If a senior officer had ever asked his opinion about why they were in Helmand, he would have said he had no idea. No farmer's heart would be won and no farmer's son would fight for the government in Kabul, somewhere on the other side of the moon. The way Cruz saw it, his job was to kill Taliban by out-thinking and outmaneuvering them. That left fewer of them to blow up his Marines. Each patrol was an invitation to a gunfight, nothing more.

After two hundred days under Cruz's care, the young grunts had adopted his stoicism. They trudged along silently. Walking across the open fields invited a sniper's bullet, while staying on the paths along the canal banks risked tripping buried explosives. It was a game of scissors versus stone, risk a bullet in the face or shrapnel in the testicles. Sooner or later, some Taliban would shoot at them, and it would be game on.

The Marine at point, Corporal Blake Hanley, was sweeping his VMR metal detector back and forth like a beachcomber searching for coins in the sand. Hanley concentrated on the ground in front of him, rarely looking up. Behind him, Lance Corporal Hector Sanchez kept his eyes on the tangles of birch and junipers where a sniper might lurk. In his left hand, he held a can of shaving cream, occasionally squirting a dab to mark the cleared passage. The grunts behind him were looking in different directions, each scanning a separate quadrant. None spoke, and no birds twittered. The only sounds were the hissing of their handheld radios and the slurping of their water-filled boots.

When Hanley reached an irrigation canal, he stopped to check the digital map on his iPad tablet. The GPS downlink showed the patrol route running across the canal. The stream wasn't wide, but the brown water was flowing steadily. The villagers had cut down a scrub oak to provide a path across. Hanley turned to Sanchez and shook his head, pointing at the tree trunk.

"I don't like using it," Hanley said.

"Bro, my toes are numb," Sanchez said. "I don't want to wade across no creek."

For Sanchez, that was a long sentence. Back at patrol base, he could sit by the cooking fires for an hour without speaking, letting Hanley prattle on. Sanchez knew how to butcher and cook a goat, while Hanley bartered choice MRE food items for both of them. Inside the squad cave, they slept in adjoining bags. As a team, in the past seven months they had uncovered thirty-eight IEDs and killed four Taliban.

While the two bickered about whether to wade the freezing creek, Cruz signaled the others to take a knee. In the field behind them, a farmer in a ragged jacket was hacking away, clearing a small space for each poppy plant. To Cruz, he looked nervous, but that wasn't unusual. Americans were bullet magnets.

Hanley and Sanchez glanced from their lieutenant to the farmer, who was scratching the dirt with his hoe. He seemed to smile at them.

"Gross," Sanchez said. "Dude's got only one front tooth."

"That means he's old," Hanley said. "Most die before their teeth fall out."

"You don't know that," Sanchez said. "You born a bullshitter."

"Read it in Wikipedia," Hanley said.

"That proves what I'm saying," Sanchez said. "We got no internet. We both know it all comes out your ass."

The farmer was scratching vigorously with his hoe, all the time shaking his head back and forth.

"Snaggle Tooth's acting weird, bro," Hanley said, "like he's signaling us or something."

Sanchez responded by shouldering his rifle to look through the scope. That caused the startled farmer to drop his hoe and scuttle hastily toward his dun-colored compound on the far side of the field.

"Show's over, man," Sanchez said. "Now can we stop grab-assing and beat feet? I can't feel my toes."

Hanley resumed sweeping the hard-packed earth leading to the crude footbridge. Sanchez let out a sigh of relief and fell in behind him. *WHAM!* The ground heaved up when Hanley's foot hit the buried pressure plate. He evaporated in a curtain of thick dust, while Sanchez was bowled over and thrown into the canal.

Several feet behind them, the pressure wave rocked Cruz. Mud, pebbles, and bits of flesh slapped against his face, snapping his head back. For a few seconds, the force of the concussion blocked out all hearing and speech. Then, even while the black cloud hung like a shroud over the stunned Marines, Cruz was screaming orders.

"Freeze!" he shouted. "No one steps outside the shaving cream! Corpsman up!"

Hanley was lying facedown next to the tree trunk. Sanchez had regained his footing in the chest-deep canal and, covered in mud, was frantically clawing up the slick bank. Cruz reached down and with a heave jerked him out of the water. From back in the file, a Marine scrambled up with the backup metal detector and began sweeping forward.

Inside thirty seconds, the corpsman, Navy HM3 Stebbins, was kneeling beside Hanley. He was unconscious, his right leg below the knee ripped off, blood pulsing out in steady spurts. Stebbins tore open a tourniquet, wrapped it around the gushing thigh, and twisted the knob, cinching hard. Sanchez stumbled over, sat down in the gore, and cradled Hanley in his arms, murmuring to him. Stebbins jerked open his aid bag, pulled out a morphine syrette, and plunged the needle into Hanley's thigh.

Cruz called for a medevac and deployed the Marines to guard the landing zone. This was the interval when any local Taliban would try to sneak in. But no shot was fired, and no person moved in the barren fields.

Sanchez and Stebbins tended to Hanley, while Cruz kept checking his watch. Ten minutes passed. Fifteen.

"We need that fucking bird!" Stebbins yelled.

Hanley was semiconscious and breathing hoarsely, his thigh ballooning like a giant sausage swelling over a fire.

"Can you stabilize him a little longer?" Cruz said. "Bird's five mikes out."

Sanchez was holding Hanley's hand, rocking his body back and forth. Hanley's gray face had a faint bluish tinge. Stebbins slid over next to Cruz.

"His pulse is fading," he whispered. "He's hemorrhaging internally. Organs all messed up. He's closing down."

Hanley slipped from life without saying a word as two Hueys roared in from the southwest. One hovered overhead while the other flared into the field. The body was quickly placed on board, with a Marine handing the crew chief Hanley's right boot, the foot intact inside.

After the choppers left, Cruz called in the perimeter guards. Once back at their outpost, he'd have to spend two hours laboring over this, his sixth letter on the deployment. He was thinking how to phrase it. Painlessly? No, he'd used that in the last letter. Dear Ms. Hanley, Brad felt no pain. Yes, that sounded better. Once he wrote the first line, all he had to do was compose five more sentences. He hadn't thought in Spanish for years, and talking in English was no problem. But he froze each time he had to write to the parents or the wife. The words never came out right. He rewrote each letter, over and over again.

He pushed away the thought and looked around to gather the troops. Sanchez was standing on the embankment, head down and cammies soggy with blood. Hanley's helmet and torn armored vest lay nearby in the mud. Sanchez grabbed the helmet and hurled it into the brown waters. He looked furiously around. A few feet away lay the hoe dropped by the farmer. He grabbed it and swung viciously at the mounds of poppy. Cruz left him alone for several seconds before speaking.

"Let's form up, Sanchez," Cruz said.

Covered with blood and mud, Sanchez was swaying from side to side. Rivulets of tears ran down his filthy face. He glared and pointed at the walled compound on the far side of the field.

"That fucking farmer knew," he said. "He lives right there. What the fuck we waiting for, Lieutenant?"

Cruz had sensed something like that was coming. Time and again, he had to cope with the rage of the survivors.

"We don't know he did it," he said. "We're not snuffing some farmer who's scared shitless."

"They blow away Hanley," Sanchez said, "and we walk? They kill us and we don't kill them? We should fucking burn his place so it don't happen again!"

"And put our whole battalion in the shit?" Cruz said. "No. This is over."

Sanchez raised the hoe high above his head, opened his hips, and swung fiercely. The iron blade buried deep into the earth, and the pole splintered. He hurled the broken handle into the creek.

"This country sucks," he yelled. "It sucks all to hell!"

Day 1

APRIL 6

1

The Night Watchman

The San Diego courtroom looked as austere as a jail cell. The judge on the raised podium, her graying hair tied back in a bun, was briskly sorting through papers. She habitually settled the guilty pleas in the morning before court opened. A few family members were shifting uncomfortably on narrow wooden benches. Off to one side, the bailiff was shooing the guards to their assigned places. With manacles on his hands and feet, the prisoner in an orange jump suit stood erect, head bowed as though in shame. He was solidly built, with a military-style crew cut, a swollen right eye, and bandages across his cheek.

"Mr. Sanchez," the judge said, "I've read the letters written on your behalf. In view of your military service, I have agreed to hear from your former commanding officer."

She gestured at the Marine sitting in the front bench. Captain Diego Cruz got to his feet, his broad chest stretching the seams of his crisp khaki shirt with four rows of colored ribbons. His eyes seemed strangely soft in a face stern and unyielding.

"Captain, Mr. Sanchez pleaded guilty," the judge said. "And he has three prior convictions, all drug related."

She held up a few handwritten letters.

"What can you add to these appeals?" she said.

"Sanchez fell apart, Your Honor," Cruz said. "He didn't intend to harm anyone, only himself."

The judge had expected to hear a booming voice, but Cruz spoke with a high-pitched, lilting cadence. Surprised, she shook her head as she looked down at her papers.

"He drunkenly stormed into a 7-Eleven with a rifle," she said, "and opened fire! Life imprisonment is the guideline for attempted murder."

The public defender who had requested Cruz's presence had warned him to be brief. The judge had a full docket and a brusque manner.

"Your Honor," Cruz said, "he fired into the ceiling. I think he wanted the police to kill him. I've seen Sanchez make a head shot at five hundred meters. If he wanted to smoke someone, he would've done it."

"He's misguided?" she said. "The war made him do it? That's the excuse you're offering?"

Cruz hesitated to find the right words.

"No, Sanchez deserves punishment," he said. "He got sick of his life and dove off the deep end. But when he was in my platoon, he obeyed orders, didn't flinch, and took care of his brothers. He's not a punk criminal."

The judge looked at him quizzically.

"Not a criminal?" she said. "We're in San Diego, Captain, not on some battlefield. The past has no bearing on his actions."

Cruz felt the anger surge inside him like an electric current. *How do you know?* he thought. *You weren't out there.* He almost blurted it out. Then he thought of Jenny's warnings and amended his reply.

"Sanchez came home carrying a heavy load, Your Honor," he said quietly. "He hasn't cut it loose."

The judge leaned forward to appraise his hard face. Cruz returned her stare without blinking.

"In your laconic way, Captain," she said, "I believe you're telling me something."

AFTER LEAVING THE COURTROOM, Cruz drove to the Marine Corps Recruit Depot near the downtown airport. On the enormous grinder, a 180-man company of trim recruits was marching past the reviewing stands to the cheers of their proud parents. The band was playing John Philip Sousa's "Pass In Review," the snappy tune echoing off the stucco walls of the beige Spanish-style buildings with their domed walkways and terra-cotta roofs.

Unnoticed, Cruz stood behind a group of captains watching the ceremony. Two years ago, he had been a series officer training recruits like those he was now watching. He had loved that job, supervising the drill instructors who in thirteen arduous weeks turned green teenagers into fledgling Marines. Then last year, he was assigned to the admin staff, where his discomfit with paperwork and lack of proper syntax became all too evident. On his fitness report, he was rated "average," a failing grade.

The list for promotion to major had been posted on the internet last night. Of the five captains eligible for promotion, four had been picked up. Cruz was the one left off the list. Despite his Bronze Star and Purple Heart, he would remain a captain, to be reevaluated next year.

When the parade ended, the other captains turned around to greet him with the usual smattering of "bros," quick pats on the shoulder, and a few knuckle-knocks to celebrate having the rest of the day off. Cruz mumbled short replies and forced a halfway grin that looked like it was chiseled in stone. For a few minutes, they stood around awkwardly, none wanting to bring up the subject.

"I better hit the books," Cruz finally said. "I got an afternoon class."

He walked away, feeling isolated and alone, shut off from friends who were now his superiors. His work schedule allowed flextime to work on his master's at San Diego State. He liked the art appreciation class. Maybe that would distract him.

When he arrived at the classroom, he sat in his usual seat in the rear tier. The professor was clicking through the Impressionist Period. The screen showed a painting of two women strolling through a field of blazing scarlet flowers under an azure sky.

"Notice," the professor said, "how the sky sheds light upon the poppies."

Cruz slightly shook his head just as the professor happened to look in his direction. He rarely spoke in class, and she remembered his name only because on each Friday he wore his uniform.

"Mr. Cruz," she said, "you disapprove of Monet?"

Surprised, Cruz blurted out what he had been thinking.

"I didn't know," he said, "there were corn poppies in France."

"Corn?"

"Imitation. The petals on real poppies have softer shades," he said. "Their sap looks like fried bacon or cow dung. Monet wouldn't paint that."

A few in the class snickered. Caught off guard, the professor responded defensively.

"Monet lived in Paris, Mr. Cruz," she said, "not in some Third World country. Your reference to fauna is not relevant."

With a wave of her hand, she clicked on the next slide.

Not relevant, Cruz thought. *Meaning you think I'm out of place in your classroom. You're right. Damned if I know anymore where I belong.*

FOLLOWING CLASS, CRUZ PICKED UP his four-year-old, Josh, at the prekindergarten school on base and drove through a quiet neighborhood to his neat bungalow. Josh was strapped in the infant seat in the back, and Cruz absentmindedly mumbled a few replies to his son's perky questions. When he lifted Josh to the ground, his son clung to his leg. Surprised, Cruz looked down.

"Daddy's sad," Josh said.

Cruz dropped to one knee, hiding his tears as he hugged his son. *I haven't taken care of you*, he thought. *I didn't make the grade.*

"No, no," he said. "Daddy's not sad. Now let's get you into the pool!"

Soon, Josh was splashing merrily in the rubber wading pool in the backyard. Cruz sat in a beach chair, tapping a beer bottle against his front teeth, trying not to drink or think. He forced his mind to remain blank. Around five, Navy Lieutenant Jennifer Cruz arrived home from the nearby naval base at Point Mugu. After she changed out of her uniform, they sat in the backyard sipping beers.

"Add any names to the list?" Cruz said.

"Yep," Jennifer said. "One O'Brien and a John Smith."

It was their standard joke. Jennifer ran an intel team on the 3rd Fleet staff, providing a threat folder for each ship sailing to the Gulf. The Secretary of the Navy, a defeated governor, had criticized the folders as racial profiling, composed of only Muslim names. Since then, every folder included a few Caucasians, selected randomly from the FBI Most Wanted list.

Cruz nodded in a distracted way.

"Why the glum face?" she asked. "How'd court go?"

"Sanchez got seven years." he said. "The public defender said that was light."

"Did you mention the phone calls?" she said. "You've tried to settle him down, what, eight or ten times?"

"That was between Sanchez and me," Cruz said. "The 7-Eleven stunt was different. I did tell the judge he was mission reliable."

She looked down at her hands before speaking carefully.

"We're back to that again?" she said. "You have to stop comparing everything to performance in the field. You put people off."

That isn't the half of it, Cruz thought. All day he had been mulling how to tell her he'd been passed over. When he didn't respond, Jennifer gently kicked at his foot.

"Earth calling Silent Sam," she said. "Anyone home up there?"

He smiled a grimace and didn't answer.

"OK, next question," she said. "How'd class go?"

"I told the professor that Monet didn't paint real poppies" he said. "That irritated her."

Jennifer drew in a breath.

"In one day, you've angered a judge and a teacher. That's above quota, even for you. But stop brooding. Cheer up! You're taking Josh and me to the beach tomorrow, and we have that barbeque on Sunday."

Having played on the women's soccer team at Cal State, Jennifer shared Cruz's compulsion to stay in shape. By far the better long-distance runner, she chattered merrily on their weekend ten-mile runs as Cruz plodded along, adding an occasional "uh-huh." Where she was bubbly, he was terse. Small talk didn't come easily to him, and she organized their social life.

Jennifer was self-confident and Josh was a joy. Cruz felt he was the miserable failure. As he was brooding, his cell phone rang. Seeing the number came from on base, he answered formally.

"Captain Cruz."

"Cruz, Inchon Six here," Lieutenant General Paul Killian said. "I have a bit of problem you might help with."

Cruz walked inside to take notes. Inchon Six had been Killian's radio call sign in Afghanistan. Back then, he had accompanied Cruz on several patrols. In the five years since, Cruz had spoken to Killian only a few times at review parades. Now the general was the Marine deputy commander at the Central Command, with headquarters in Tampa, Florida. On the phone, his manner was still preemptory.

"Standing by to copy, sir," he said.

"I'm sending an artillery battery back into Helmand," Killian said. "A temporary op. The security platoon commander has come down with an appendicitis, and I'd like you to replace him."

Cruz felt he'd been punched in the gut. He was a captain, yet the general wanted him to take a lieutenant's job. A platoon? He'd done that twice. He blurted out his hurt.

"A security platoon, sir?" he said in a strained voice. "You want me to babysit arty tubes? Check the wire twice a day?"

"Captain, take a deep breath and listen," Killian said in very much a general's voice. "I saw the major's list. In my opinion, you slipped on a banana peel. You're not cut out for admin duty. Now open your ears. Commanding this platoon puts distance between you and that fitrep. Once you're evaluated in your natural environment, you'll make major. Are you clear on what I'm offering?"

Cruz calmed down and gathered himself. All he had to do was check guard posts and he'd be rated "Outstanding." It might look absurd—being rated first in a field of one—but it would help with the next promotion board. Killian was extending a lifeline.

"I understand, sir," he said.

"Took you long enough to get the message," Killian said crisply. "And stow that talk about babysitting. Hell, I'm stuck in the Pentagon doing liaison work for this op. At least you'll get your boots dirty. Are you in?"

"When, sir?" Cruz said.

"That's a slight problem," Killian said. "It's wheels-up in twelve hours. Not much time. Want to talk to your wife and call me back?"

Cruz didn't hesitate. This was his way out.

"I'd be glad to take the platoon, sir."

"Good. Take this down and get your ass in gear."

After writing down the details, Cruz hung up and walked outside. Jennifer, her back to him, was wrapping Josh in a towel. She didn't say a word.

"I'm making a short hop to Helmand," he said apologetically. "The general…"

She whirled around and cut him off.

"Helmand! That horrid place?" she said. "The general calls and all of a sudden our lives change? You're shipping off again, thinking only of yourself? We were sitting right here and you never even looked at us. What's the matter with you?"

She was trembling with anger, and Josh had buried his head against her legs.

"It's not a real deployment," he said, "only a week of checking lines for an arty battery."

Jennifer flared up.

"Do you know how absurd that sounds?" she said. "You're going over with artillery, and you expect me to believe there'll be no trauma? Something happens every damn time."

The prior deployments had taken their toll on her, the calls from the command centers, the vales of tears, and the trips to Balboa Hospital where those with missing limbs comforted those who came to console them.

"Someone has to take care of those kids," Cruz said. "I doubt any of them have been there before."

Cruz knew how flimsy that sounded. Jennifer wasn't buying it.

"The troops? Weren't four deployments enough? I thought that was behind you. What about Josh and me and…"

She almost let it slip that she was pregnant. She stopped talking, determined not to heap on guilt. Her husband had to make up his own mind.

Cruz felt penned in, his thoughts churning. It was stupid to tell Killian yes before talking it through with Jenny. *Fuck*, he thought. *I've messed up royally.*

"You're right, babe," he said. "I was selfish. I'll tell the general no."

Jennifer studied his square, stoic face.

"I don't mean to whine," she said. "Before you call, look me in the eye and tell me why you said yes in the first place."

Cruz looked down at the floor for a few seconds.

"Hey, buster," Jennifer said, "don't wimp out. I'm waiting for your answer."

Cruz let his hurt burst out.

"I'm a thirty-four-year-old captain," he said, "prior enlisted, a mustang with a state college degree. You know I hate my job on the admin staff."

Jennifer smiled wryly.

"So you were flattered the general called?"

Cruz nodded.

"He was out there with me," he said. "So yeah, I felt good he called."

"At last, the truth," she said softly. "It's an ego trip."

Her disappointment in him hit home. Cruz let his depression burst to the surface.

"The truth is we're not fighting anymore and I'm not needed. In a few years I'll be lucky to teach Spanish in some high school."

Jennifer drew back in disbelief.

"You're twenty years beyond that," she said. "You didn't learn English until you were ten, and now you're working on your MA. You don't speak Spanish even to Josh. People say your diction's more from Boston than Bogota. The Marine Corps is your career. What's gotten into you?"

Cruz wanted to crawl inside himself and disappear. He drew a breath and let it out, the words strangling him.

"The list for major was posted. I didn't make it."

Jennifer stood still for a moment. Then she reached out, tears welling in her eyes.

"Oh, baby, I'm so sorry. You worked so hard. This is absolutely unfair. No wonder you're upset! There has to be a mistake."

Cruz shook his head.

"I suck at admin," he said. "Colonel Tobin counseled me about it. I didn't tell you."

Jenny flared into full defense mood.

"Tobin has the IQ of a file cabinet," she said. "He wouldn't hack it on my staff."

"He signed my last fitness report," Cruz said. "I'm the one who didn't hack it."

He felt deflated. He'd let down Jenny and Josh, but didn't want to lose them. He'd call the general and say no. As he picked up his cell phone, Jennifer touched his arm.

"The general called to help? That's what this is all about, isn't it?"

Cruz thought back on Killian's words.

"He did say the deployment would be a plus," Cruz said. "But I should've talked it over with you. Forget I mentioned it. I'm not going."

Jennifer dabbed at her eyes and tried to smile.

"Put that phone away," she said. "I want you to go. It's a chance to show what you're good at. But honey, you have to improve your technique for telling people bad news. Now give me a hug. And, I expect a tasteful present by way of apology."

As she buried her face into his chest, Josh mimicked the gesture by wrapping his arms around Cruz's knee. Cruz felt a sense of relief and a tinge of hope. The general had handed him a mission he could perform in his sleep.

"This op's so short," he said, "that I'll be back before I'm gone."

Jennifer picked up Josh and hugged him tight. She knew no deployment was ever short. Some like Sanchez would come back messed up. They'd call late at night, drunk or high, and Cruz would try to straighten them out. She shook it off.

"No wild stuff over there," she said. "You've had your wars. Don't try to impress anyone. Promise there'll be no last hoorah. Remember what really counts. We need you back."

"No pain on this op, Jen," Cruz said. "My job is to make sure the sentries stay awake. I'm just the night watchman."

2

Mission Approval

Secretary of Defense Michael Towns had a few minutes to reflect during the short drive to the White House. Eight months into the top job at the Pentagon, he still couldn't predict what President Dinard would do next. The only habit of POTUS was no habit. A creature of impulse, he agreed one day and reversed direction the next. This was the third time Towns thought this decision was firm, only to be summoned at the last minute. Glancing at his talking points, he could think of nothing new to add. This meeting seemed gratuitous; a short phone call would have sufficed.

When he entered the Situation Room in in the basement level of the West Wing, he was again struck by its tiny size. Over the terms of seven presidents, the room had never been enlarged. That a dozen principals had to squeeze around the rectangular mahogany table gave intimacy to discussions among the most powerful persons in the world. On this breezy April afternoon, there was ample room because President Paul Thomas Dinard liked small, short business meetings.

Only the Chairman of the Joint Chiefs of Staff and the National Security Advisor were waiting. Towns had barely exchanged pleasantries when POTUS walked in. Gesturing for them to remain sitting, he theatrically strode to the electronic screen showing a large map of Afghanistan. A blue symbol near the bottom of the map was blinking on and off.

"That's Helmand Province?" he said. "It looks like the end of the earth. You sure about this, Professor?"

Towns disliked the title. While his PhD in astrophysics from MIT impressed POTUS, Towns took pride in how he had built a world-class company specializing in miniature satellites. Before every launch, he ensured that two separate teams had examined the risks. Although he hadn't served in the military, he had double-checked this operation in the same thorough manner. If he showed the slightest hesitation, POTUS would cancel the operation.

"The Taliban are close to capturing the provincial capital, sir," he said. "The task force can prevent that."

The president sat down at the head of the table and pressed his fingertips together.

"Our country beat the coronarvirus in nine months," he said. "That was tough, but I got it done. You Pentagon guys have been stuck in Afghanistan for twenty years! What's this going to cost me?"

Dinard saw himself as the CEO of the world's largest business. In his mind, the federal budget was his budget.

"Our request for Afghanistan is seventy-five billion," Towns said. "The task force doesn't cost extra. I'm testifying before the Senate tomorrow."

"Don't give those pricks an opening," Dinard said.

By long-standing tradition, the Pentagon avoided domestic politics. Unlike other cabinet members, the Secretary of Defense did not participate in political campaigns. Dinard resented that. He couldn't understand why the generals didn't openly support him. The troops were the opposite. They loved it when he visited, flocking around him to take selfies, laughing at his quips. *Hell*, he thought, *the brass should take a lesson from the troops, God bless 'em!*

He waited several seconds, determined to elicit some token of loyalty from his Secretary of Defense. Finally, Towns nodded in agreement.

"I'll be careful, sir," Towns said.

Satisfied Towns was in line, Dinard looked down at his briefing notes. Tapping the paper for emphasis, he pointed at Admiral Bernard Michaels, Chairman of the Joint Chiefs of Staff.

"Admiral, you sure we have to send troops?" he said. "We can't just bomb the bastards?"

The trim four-star, sitting erect in his uniform with six rows of campaign ribbons and no combat experience, was an accomplished bureaucrat, thoughtful, reserved, and confident. He rarely smiled and spoke as solemnly as a prophet. His staff referred to him as Moses. He'd been over this ground in two previous meetings and kept his reply short.

"I've checked with our commanders, sir," Michaels said. "Air support is too episodic. Artillery will provide the Afghan soldiers with covering fire twenty-four hours a day. They won't get to the provincial capital without it."

Towns sensed an opening to appeal to the president's vanity.

"Sir, the Taliban promised to reduce the violence. Instead, they're trying to capture a major city. They're breaking the deal they cut with you."

"You see it that way, Security Advisor?" Dinard said.

The National Security Advisor, sitting in a wingback chair, bobbed his head. An extroverted retired Air Force officer of enormous girth and bellowing laugh, Richard Armsted had parlayed his bonhomie into a mega lobbying firm before joining the administration. He possessed a courtesan's sense of flattery, effortlessly adjusting to Dinard's erratic moods. To keep him in his place, Dinard called him "Security Advisor." Armsted was the third to have that title.

"You're right to teach the Taliban a lesson, Mr. President," Armsted said.

Pleased to be judged correct, Dinard turned to Towns.

"OK, Professor, but don't get sucked in deeper," Dinard said.

Towns nodded. As Secretary of Defense, he saw his job as preparing for the high tech wars sure to come in the 21st century. His task was to wean the services off vestigial habits, like building aircraft carriers that could be sunk by cheap drones. To Towns, Islamist crazies were not the main enemy. Afghanistan was a tiny part of the Pentagon's budget.

"We're sending a small force, Mr. President," Towns said, "with a strictly limited mission, the same as we're doing in Syria and Africa."

"Let's hope it doesn't go south," Armsted rumbled in a voice sounding like a trombone.

His tone put Towns on guard. POTUS didn't touch liquor, but did imbibe pleasure in pitting his appointees against each other. As National Security Advisor, Armsted popped in and out of the Oval Office several times a day, rarely providing Towns with any feedback.

"You know something we don't?" Towns said.

"Helmand's a long way from anywhere, that's all," Armsted said. "Not to be a nitpicker, Admiral, but to open that road to the capital, what's the distance?"

"Twenty miles," Michaels said.

"That's not much," Armsted said. "That should take less than a week, right? I mean, even Afghan soldiers can walk three miles a day. Hell, I do that on the treadmill in an hour."

The gratuitous remark seemed deliberately challenging. Towns tried to deflect it.

"We don't place a time limit on our objective," he snapped. "The enemy gets a vote."

The press lauded Towns for his epigrams, but their pedantry irritated POTUS. He leaned forward, assuming the scowl that had delighted his reality TV audiences. It was time to deliver a hard business truth.

"Professor," Dinard said, "I need a number, not a philosophy."

Towns flushed, but knew better than to reply. Dinard turned to the Chairman of the Joint Chiefs.

"Admiral, before I agree to a project, my engineers give me a completion date," he said. "What's yours?"

Admiral Michaels tried to balance his answer.

"A week seems reasonble, sir," he said. "But as the Secretary said, we shouldn't limit…"

Dinard cut him off with a thumbs-up gesture. Here was something concrete to grasp.

"Excellent!" he beamed. "Get it done. One week!"

POTUS extended his arms, dispensing a farewell benediction. Armsted bobbed in agreement, his massive frame shaking the sturdy Doyle chair. The meeting was over. Towns walked out sensing that more than one deal had just been struck. POTUS had the maddening habit of disapproving while approving. Dinard had agreed to launch the mission, and then set a deadline for withdrawal.

Armsted remained behind, waiting silently while Dinard drummed his fingers and scowled.

"Security Advisor, that was good work on your part," Dinard said. "They're not going to string me along."

"I'm sure that's not their intent, sir," Armsted said. "It's the military mindset at work. They believe that conditions on the ground are more important than deadlines."

"I don't care what they believe. I want that task force out of there in a week."

3

The Wild Ox

The tan Toyota Hilux sped down the center of the two-lane dirt road, forcing donkeys, tractors, and worn-out cars to give way. The thick, unkempt black beard of the driver identified him as a mujahideen, an everyday sight in Helmand, a province controlled by the Taliban. His plump passenger with smooth cheeks and a trim beard wore the tightly bound black turban common among mullahs.

"We'll collect from twenty farms today," the mujahideen said, "starting with the largest."

Mullah Khan was tapping the screen of his iPad.

"That will please the shura," the mullah said. "We're behind schedule, Zar."

"Don't provoke me, Persian," Zar said. "The shura told me to help you, not to listen to your whining. It's you who's working too slowly, not me."

They passed an abandoned police station, a scruffy, unpainted concrete building surrounded by a decaying dirt berm and a tangle of rusty barbed wire. Near the sagging main gate, the drooping leaves of the marijuana plants begged for water under the hot sun. They rode in truculent silence for several more minutes until Zar's cell phone rang. He answered with a grunt, listened, and smiled.

Rounding the next bend, Zar saw a van and two motorbikes parked off the road. Two Talibs in Levi's, T-shirts, and Skechers, with AKs strapped over their shoulders, were rummaging through thin plastic shopping bags. The portly driver stood next to his van, looking at the ground. A woman in a full black burka was squatting in the thin shade of the van. Her husband, wearing work boots and a red-checked turban, stood beside her, clutching the hand of a frightened ten-year-old boy. A few feet away, two young men were kneeling in the dirt, their arms tied behind them.

Zar pulled over and got out. As usual he was wearing a white Western shirt, an affectation that displayed the girth of his chest. Even at a distance, he wanted everyone to recognize the new Taliban chieftain.

"Well done!" he shouted.

The young Talibs smiled and bowed slightly. The Persian looked at the dejected prisoners.

"Do they work for the Baloch?" he said. "Are they buying poppy?"

"Persian, with you everything's money," Zar snorted. "No, they're army deserters."

He picked up a broken tree branch, walked behind the two men, drew back the stick, and swung down. *Thwack!* With a gasp, one of the prisoners pitched forward and lay groaning, his face in the dust.

"You're *askars*, aren't you?" Zar shouted. "You defied the Prophet! You are *takfir!*"

Thwack! Thwack! The long tail of Zar's turban swayed in rhythm with his strikes. With each blow to his ribs and kidneys, the prisoner screamed.

"We did nothing wrong," he shrieked. "We sold our bullets to the mujahideen in the market. We want to go home. I am Pashto, like you."

"Do the other *askars* want to leave Lashkar?"

The soldier nodded.

"We haven't been paid in two months," he said. "The people avoid us."

Zar kicked the other prisoner once, twice.

"Where were you going?"

"Turerah."

His voice sounded soft and dull, without hope. Zar could barely understand the word.

"Turerah? That's Tajik! You don't even speak Pashto. You're a puppet paid by Kabul!"

From several kilometers to the north, they heard the deep bark of a PKM machine gun, followed by a sharp explosion. The two Talibs exchanged an excited glance.

"You'll get your chance," Zar said. "Soon people will know you fight under Zar."

Zar's forehead was indented with an ugly black callous from touching the ground in prayer five times daily for thirty years. He was proud that the scab marked him as a pious man. But while other Taliban gangs were fighting, he had to help this Persian. He felt this assignment from the shura was beneath the dignity a true warrior of Allah. As he tapped his scab, an idea came to him.

He knew the mullahs in the *rahbari shura*, safe in Pakistan, called him *araia unbzat*, the Wild Ox. Well, how could he be smart? He'd never been to school. But he was the best wrestler in Helmand. And so what if he couldn't control his temper? No one insulted him twice.

He dimly connected two ideas. The shura had entrusted the Persian to him. Now he would demonstrate his total dedication to Allah. When the shura saw that, they would appoint him as the emir, the absolute ruler of Helmand.

He strode to his pickup and pulled out his small white battle flag, with its jihadist fealty verse inscribed in black Arabic symbols: *"I bear witness that there is no deity other than Allah and that Muhammad is his servant and Messenger."* After smoothing it into a long strip and wrapping it around his head as a bandanna, he gestured at the older of the two Taliban guards.

"In battle, half of victory lies in the enemy's fear of you," he said. "Bring over your camera."

In a baldric slung over his right shoulder, he carried a curved *saif* with an engraved ebony handle. Zar drew out his sword and held it aloft, the razor edge of the blade glinting.

"Like you, I pray five times each day," the frightened Pashtun prisoner pleaded. "There is no god but Allah!"

"Ask his mercy," Zar said, "when you see him."

He rolled up his sleeves, straddled the soldier, and jerked him up so that his face pointed at the camera.

"Turn on the camera," he said.

Zar waited until he saw the small red light flick on.

"This is the fate of all *takfir*," he shouted. "Allahu Akbar!"

With one powerful slice, Zar slit the prisoner's throat. As the blood spurted out, he jerked back the severed neck so that the wound gaped open like a second mouth, garish and vermillion. He set to work as he did with a sheep, hacking deeply, snapping the spinal cord and twisting off the severed head. Dropping the body, he smiled wolfishly at Mullah Khan.

"Hey, Persian, you're related to Tajiks, right?"

Mullah Khan, his face drained of color, struggled to answer.

"I am as Pashtun as you, a Mashwani descended from Umra Khan, the Napoleon of Afghanistan."

Zar shook his head.

"That was a century ago," he said. "You fled to Iran. Watch. This is how a Pashtun mujahideen deals with Tajiks."

Zar reached for the other prisoner, who snarled and lunged forward, trying to head-butt him. Startled, Zar stumbled back, losing his balance. Realizing he looked foolish on camera, he jumped on the prisoner and drove the knife deep into his neck. The blood spurted upward like red water from a fountain. After a few spastic kicks, the Tajik sagged and the stream of blood subsided into a trickle. Zar hacked and hacked at the tendons until a small vertebra snapped. He grabbed an ear to wrest the head free, but it stubbornly clung to the body by a clump of skin. Another backhand slice and the head popped loose.

Zar rose erect, blood-smeared hands raised holding the heads by their hair for a closing frame shot, red rivulets splatting into the dirt. Feeling the thick, rich blood splattered across his face and shirt, Zar sensed—no, he knew—this was his moment. It had been fifteen years since Zarqawi had beheaded an americani in Iraq and ten years since al-Baghdadi had burned alive a Jordanian pilot in Syria. Now the world was witnessing Allah's protector in Helmand. Zar too would be a legend.

In the background, the Persian stood stock-still, stunned by the savagery. The camera continued to record the scene.

"Behold the wrath of Allah!" Zar yelled. "We drove Alexander the Great from our land, and the Russkis, and the americani! No one can seize Helmand from us!"

Zar threw aside the two heads.

"This is the fate of all invaders!" he said. "The dogs eat them!"

To give time for Zar's blood lust to subside, the Persian bowed and backed away. He tried to calm himself by estimating the profits he would soon gain. But he felt a deep unease. Why had the shura entrusted $100 million to this blood-soaked illiterate intent on resurrecting a ninth-century caliphate, one dripping head after another?

4

Shakedown

Nantush squatted next to an irrigation ditch, idly poking a stick at goat turds, pushing them downstream toward his neighbor's melon patch. From inside the compound, he heard his wife yelling at the little ones to herd the cows out to graze. He looked at his fields where the long-stemmed poppy bulbs were bursting open in a profusion of scarlet, pink, white, and purple. His older sons and daughters shuffled past him, fiddling with their cloth poppy sacks and short, sharp knives. He watched as they entered the nearest field and began to lance the side of each egg-shaped bulb.

Every slice was razor thin, deep enough for the sap to ooze out. Over the next few days, the sun would bake the resin into muddy blisters, and the laborers would return to snip off each teardrop of pure black opium. Like thousands of other farmers, Nantush hired *nishtgars*—migrant laborers who were mostly Taliban. They slept on the ground in makeshift lean-tos, rising each morning to collect the raw opium, one snippet after another. Nantush could see the wisps of their breakfast fires out in the farther fields.

He leaned his back against the hard compound wall of baked mud and straw. In early April, southern Helmand Province was hot but bearable. Despite his torn brown tunic and soiled turban, he looked vaguely like a Western tourist catching the sun's rays, content in his moment of comfort. He daydreamed of his wealth from this poppy harvest—a color television, a new tractor, and a Honda motorcycle.

He dozed until he heard the whine of a car engine. A tan Hilux was jouncing up the tractor path to his compound. As the pickup braked to a stop, Nantush stumbled forward. He tried to hide his shock when he saw the blood smeared over Zar's shirt and face.

"*Salam alekim*," Zar said more in command than in greeting, "all are blessed who worship Allah."

"Allahu Akbar," Nantush stammered. "Zar Mohammad is always welcome at my farm."

Standing a head taller than Nantush, Zar gazed around benevolently, despite looking like a butcher who had hacked to pieces a panicky goat.

"If I am welcome," he said, "why did you turn aside my guest yesterday? He traveled far to buy your crop."

Nantush fidgeted and bowed toward the plump young man wearing soft leather boots and carrying an iPad.

"Yesterday," Nantush stammered, "we were negotiating…"

"Then continue," Zar said.

Without a word, the Persian brushed by Nantush, strode into the field, plucked a lanced poppy and squinted at the sap, like a jeweler pricing a diamond. He adjusted his iPad, took a close-up photo of the bud, and snapped pictures of the surrounding fields. He walked back, nodding his approval.

"You'll have a good harvest, Nantush," he said, speaking Pashto with an Iranian accent. "Let's settle on eighty dollars a pound for your poppy. Or do you prefer rupees?"

"The Baloch pays in dollars," Nantush said.

Zar, his beard matted with blood, bent his head toward Nantush.

"The Baloch is not coming this year," Zar said. "The Persian is now the buyer."

The workers had straggled in, some carrying AKs, others unarmed. Their tunics and hands were stained an ugly brown from the opium sap. Including family members of all ages, dozens now formed an outer circle to listen to the haggling. To Zar's satisfaction, several were whispering on their cell phones. News of the beheadings and of this poppy sale would flash across the district. He ignored the onlookers, rolling his prayer beads as though he were a feudal lord visiting a serf.

The Persian finished tapping his iPad.

"Nantush, you have twenty *jeribs*?" the Persian said. "I'll offer sixteen thousand for your harvest. That's more than the Baloch ever paid."

Nantush stroked his beard, playing for time. The Baloch from Pakistan had remained during the bad times when the Marines patrolled the Green Zone. Now this Persian had arrived, offering a higher price.

When Nantush did not reply, The Persian tried a different approach.

"All right," he said, "I'll give you seven thousand now for half, before you harvest the poppy. I'm taking all the risk. If a *haroum* ruins your crop, I get no poppy and you keep my money."

It was a shrewd offer, appealing to every farmer's instinct to hedge against bad weather. Nantush hesitated. What if this Persian didn't come back next year? Then the Baloch would refuse to buy his crop.

"Perhaps if we held a *jirga*…" Nantush said.

That broke it for Zar. No stupid farmer would embarrass him in front of his own fighters.

"A *jirga*?" he roared. "You don't need other farmers to decide for you. You are a *malik*! Others follow you. Sell half or all of your harvest now! Make up your mind! One or the other."

Nantush stumbled back.

"Half, half," he stuttered.

The Persian opened a camel-skin valise and pulled out wrapped packets of hundred-dollar bills. With a salesman's smile, he handed Nantush the money.

"May Allah bless your crop," he said. "Soon you will be rich."

A murmur of awe at the size of the cash bundle rippled through the crowd. For a moment, Nantush felt proud. Like his father and the generations before him, he had toiled without complaint throughout his life. None of them, though, had the wealth now visited upon him. Perhaps this Persian, who smelled faintly of perfume, was bringing good fortune.

"Your price is fair, honorable preacher," Nantush said.

This display of deference ignited the anger in Zar. He, not the dainty foreigner, had arranged this. He deserved the credit. He held out his hand.

"Pay the *usher*," he said. "We Taliban protect you."

Nantush's good humor drained away.

"How much?"

"Seven percent," he said. "One thousand dollars."

Nantush blinked, but he dared not speak. One thousand was 13 percent, twice the *usher*. Zar could barely add. Perhaps the Persian would correct the error. A few seconds of silence passed.

"Now!" Zar shouted.

Nantush gave him one thousand dollars. Without a word, Zar walked to his pickup, threw the money in the back seat, and got behind the wheel. The Persian hopped into the passenger seat and they drove away.

"That didn't go well," the Persian said. "I was hoping to buy Nantush's whole harvest. Instead, you overcharged him."

Zar slammed on the brakes and raised his fist.

"Persian, don't tell me how to deal with my people!" Zar yelled. "This is my province, not yours."

The frightened Persian blurted out the *shahadah* to appease him.

"There is no God but Allah," he stammered, *"and Muhammad is his messenger."*

Zar banged his fist against the steering wheel, still wanting to strike him.

"For your community is a single community," the Persian hurried on, "and I am your Lord, so worship me."

For a moment, Zar was again the goat herder's skinny son, barefoot in turd-strewn dust, listening awestruck as a plump mullah quoted the Qur'an. He shook his head and resumed driving. It was unfair of Allah that this Persian, afraid of sword and blood, should be so quick with sums and words.

5

Welcome on Board

The runway apron was bright under the lights of the tractors trundling the artillery tubes toward the KC-130s. Even from a distance, Colonel Hal Coffman knew that the stocky Marine approaching him was Cruz. He was carrying a worn ruck over his right shoulder, and his rumpled cammies were faded. *Typical Killian pick*, Coffman mused. *A field jock.* Like Cruz, Coffman had been a sergeant prior to becoming an officer. Unlike Cruz, Coffman saw himself as a future general. He knew how to handle the enlisted men, how to direct a staff, how to entertain with flair, and how to look ahead.

"Welcome on board, Captain," Coffman said, returning Cruz's salute. "I believe in being direct. I told General Killian I didn't want someone new joining us at the last minute. Strangers don't fight well together. I'm sure you agree."

Cruz knew he was being tested.

"Agreed, sir, but we're all Marines."

"Exactly the sentiment of the old man. He said you knew the area."

"I did years ago, sir."

"That's what I mean. That was past history. Anyway, I lost the argument and here you are. Don't take it personally. Your platoon sergeant knows the routine. Let him run things while you snap in. I look forward to telling General Killian you did a fine job."

There it is, Cruz thought. *I play by his rules and come out looking good.*

In Cruz's eyes, bird colonels in their midforties fell into three categories. A few—especially those commanding infantry regiments or air squadrons—were the front-runners to make brigadier general. They tended to be fretful but self-confident. Most of the others were hard working and relaxed, comfortable in a career nearing its end, appreciative of a well-deserved pension after decades of service that entailed moving their families a dozen times. Lastly, there were a few still nakedly ambitious, smart or driven enough to snare important staff jobs, hoping to distinguish themselves. That included Coffman.

"Aye-aye, sir," Cruz said.

"Good! Use my cabin to get up to speed. The XO will see to it."

Cruz had intended to meet with the security platoon but knew not to object. Coffman beckoned to a slight major with a round face and tortoiseshell glasses.

"I'm Major Barnes," he said in a neutral tone.

He guided Cruz to the lead aircraft. They walked up the ramp, skirting past the lashed-down cargo. Like the troops in sixty other countries, they were flying in a Hercules C-130, designed eighty years ago and still the workhorse of armies around the globe. A large metal box filled the forward end of the bay. When they entered, Cruz took in the small conference table, the neat bunk, the computer desk, the reading lights, and the small couch. Only generals rated such a command cubicle.

"The colonel has clout," Cruz said.

Barnes nodded and held out an iPad.

"Here's the op order."

Cruz tapped the screen a few times, noting that the document ran for 250 pages.

"*War and Peace* is shorter than this. We invading Pakistan?"

Barnes kept a straight face.

"We're on a short time leash," he said. "Colonel Coffman takes this command very seriously. He's General Killian's chief of staff, something to keep in mind."

With a half smile, Barnes left and Cruz sat down to study the op order. The mission was simple. The Marines would provide artillery support to a thousand-man brigade of the Afghan National Army. The ANA in turn would break the Taliban's grip on the highway leading to Lashkar Gah, the capital of Helmand. Every detail was covered in depth—personnel, operations, communications, logistics, etc. Cruz's job was to guard the perimeter of the small artillery base. He was taking notes when Coffman opened the door.

"It's take-off time," he said. "You read in?"

"Yes, sir," Cruz said. "The op order's very thorough."

"It better be. The SecDef's watching this one," Coffman said. "Grab a seat out there and buckle up."

Cruz walked out into the cavernous bay where a hundred Marines were jammed into the narrow web seats, their bulging packs lashed in the center of the bay. A small Marine with the twin bars of captain rank gestured to the seat next to her. After he cinched in, she extended her hand.

"Jean Lasswell," she said. "I'm the battery commander."

She had wide-set eyes and an open, confident manner. With her firm handshake and thin, almost emaciated cheeks, Cruz assumed she was a runner and could probably smoke him.

"Diego Cruz, security platoon."

"Ah, General Killian's draft pick has arrived," she said. "We all feel more secure with Rolling Thunder on deck. RT himself."

She said it with a clear smile and the right amount of light sarcasm.

"Let's bury that RT bullshit," Cruz said.

Lasswell grinned and shook her head.

"You can't hide from Google. That story about you pursuing the Taliban for two days without a break? After that, the troops called you *Rolling Thunder*."

To show she meant no offense, she rolled out the r, *rrrrrr*.

"That was years ago," Cruz said. "What's this about SecDef being in the loop?"

"The colonel worked for him," Lasswell said. "He likes to remind people of that."

"The old boys' club at work."

Lasswell laughed.

"It goes deeper. An Army general in Kabul controls us. But the word is he's letting General Killian stay in touch with the good Colonel Coffman."

Cruz looked quizzically at her.

"Coffman's a cannon cocker?"

"Nope, he's admin," she said. "Whip smart. He snagged this task force kind of as an award. I'm jacked he selected me."

"I don't feel those warm vibes," Cruz said.

Lasswell gave Cruz a halfway nod and gestured toward Coffman's cabin.

"The colonel refers to us as his hand-picked team," she said. "He didn't pick you."

"Good to be loved," Cruz said.

"This is my first combat deployment," she said. "Same for my Marines. What counts with us is that you've been there."

The engines were coughing and spinning up. She unwrapped her earplugs.

"Going to be a long, noisy trip," she said.

Day 2

APRIL 7

6

First to Fall

Following two refueling stops, the task force landed after dark at Kandahar Airport in southern Afghanistan. Everyone set about assigned tasks, with Cruz the outsider looking on. One Marine bustled up and saluted hastily.

"Staff Sergeant Sullivan, sir," he said. "I'm shitload busy right now. OK if I put off briefing you until we're on the objective?"

In his battle rattle, helmet tucked low and the tarmac lights throwing long shadows, Sullivan looked imposing. With his jaw thrust forward and no warmth in his tone, he seemed to be giving an order.

"Go to it, Staff Sergeant."

At two in the morning, the first wave of helicopters touched down on a field seven miles from the provincial capital. After the grunts secured the perimeter, a CH-53, its massive three engines thumping, lowered a small dozer slung beneath its fuselage. Another dozer and two backhoes followed. Next to land were the artillery tubes. Each was thirty feet long, its nine-thousand-pound bulk evenly distributed between the chassis and the barrel, enabling a dozen Marines to roll it into position.

IN THE MIDDLE OF THE NIGHT, the pulsing throbs of engines pushed Nantush awake. He propped up on one elbow, thinking this was a pelting rainstorm. But no, the noise was pounding straight down on the roof. Helicopters—a raid! The devils in black dropping from ropes, the blinding lights…

Sharia was sitting up beside him, clinging to his hand. The children, the children! Pulling on his man dress, Nantush ran barefoot down the corridor, banging on door after door, pushing the servants and groggy children downstairs. The throb receded and settled into a deep, steady drum out in the fields to the west. While Sharia herded the women and children into the living room, Nantush yelled at his sons and workers to stay inside the compound walls and, above all, to not shoot at the helicopters!

For the next hour, the men paced around the courtyard and peered out at the blackness, listening to the sounds of the dozers. Nantush climbed to the roof and peered out at the dust and the clamor. He realized this wasn't a raid. The americanis were digging in and tearing up his land. Why were they here? What if they burned his fields? The agitated workers were shaking their AKs in the air, vowing *jihad!* and jabbering on their cell phones. Nantush rushed down the outside stairway.

"If anyone shoots from my compound," he yelled, "he will never again work in this district!"

A KILOMETER TO THE WEST, the Marines were systematically clearing an acre of poppy and undergrowth. While scooping out a bunker, a dozer clawed up a dry patch of bush, raising a great billow of dirt. Operators and diggers stopped their labors and closed their eyes until the dirt settled. The calm was pierced by a loud, startled "AHH!" followed by a terrified "ARRGH!" and an agonizing "YIEE!," shrill and pitiful.

"Help me! Help! Help!"

Marines grabbed their weapons and crouched low, waiting for whatever predator to leap out of the blackness. Beams of flashlights with red filters stabbed and bobbed through the dust like the clashing red swords of unseen warriors. Squad leaders were yelling back and forth.

"What the fuck? Who's screaming?"

"Who's been hit? If you need help, sound off!"

Supported by two comrades, a husky Marine hobbled out of the dust cloud.

"Jacobs's been bitten. Corpsman up! Get the doc!"

For a few seconds, Jacobs stood bewildered in the glare of a dozen flashlights. Then he sat down, pawing at his leg and whimpering in fear. He started to tremble and fell on his back. Two corpsmen snapped together a fold-up litter, lifted him onto it, and cut open his right trouser. The task force doctor, Navy Commander Herbert Zarest, rushed up and wiped the blood from Jacobs's calf. Deep sets of dual puncture wounds showed how swiftly the snake had struck, again and again.

"Get that compression bandage around his leg," Zarest said. "Prop it up! Call a priority medevac."

Captain Lasswell was hovering near the wounded Marine.

"Was the snake killed?" Zarest asked.

"No, sir," Lasswell said.

"Damn, I need to call in the correct serum."

Cruz turned to Lasswell.

"How about showing me," he said, "where the snake was."

They walked over to where a half-dozen Marines were standing well back from a tangle of brush. Cruz took a machete and stepped forward.

"Shine some white light over here," he said.

"We're in blackout condition," a voice said.

"Not now we're not," Cruz said.

A Marine clicked off the red filter on his flashlight. With the bright light behind him, Cruz whacked at a thick bush and drew back a few feet. No movement or hiss. He waded deeper into the thicket and whacked again. Lasswell watched for a moment, then put on a pair of leather gloves and joined him. Soon two Marines joined her, with others shining more lights.

"Keep a circle," Cruz yelled. "When that snake bolts, pound it! Pound it and pound it! Don't let it coil!"

He flailed at some loose branches and again warily stepped back. This time a snake twisted and slithered past Cruz, its long eel-like body looping rapidly back and forth. He struck down, slicing off its tail. The snake never turned or slowed down. The Marine holding the light behind Cruz leaped back.

"Stay on it!" Cruz yelled. "Crush it!"

The Marine ran after the snake, the beam of the flashlight bobbing wildly, catching, losing, then again shining on the writhing in the dirt. A Marine with a shovel ran forward and swung the flat of the blade down again and again. Cruz rushed up, knelt down, and sliced off its head.

"Good work," he said.

A dozen white lights illuminated the scene. From behind the group, Coffman's voice rang out, sharp with anger.

"What the hell? Who authorized this idiocy?"

"I did, sir," Cruz said. "The doctor wants to identify the snake."

"And I want my orders followed," Coffman said. "Turn off those lights! You're exposing us to a mortar attack."

Inside a few seconds, every white light was turned off.

"I estimated the risk of mortars as low, Colonel," Cruz said.

"That was my call to make," Coffman said, "not yours, Captain." Before he could say anything else, Lasswell spoke up.

"Colonel," Lasswell said, "Commander Zarest's really worried about Corporal Jacobs."

Coffman was about to reprimand her, then thought better of it, conscious that several troops were listening. One was holding the mangled snakehead.

"Everyone back to work," he said. "Give that damn thing to the doctor."

Cruz trotted over to where Zarest was attending to Corporal Jacobs.

"It's a saw-tooth viper," Zarest said. "That's what I was afraid of. Jacobs is vomiting, explosive diarrhea, constant seepage from the punctures. No coagulation."

Shortly later, a CH-53 thundered in, its sixteen thousand pounds of thrust hurling brush and dirt into the air. Jacobs was carried on board, and the chopper quickly left. Lasswell walked over to where Cruz was talking with Zarest.

"We got him out in forty-five minutes," Lasswell said. "That's good, right?"

"I don't know," Zarest said. "We put a liter of saline into him, but he's bleeding internally. That can cause brain hemorrhage."

As Zarest walked away, Lasswell turned to Cruz.

"I should call his parents," she said. "He's a good kid, quiet, strong. He's been accepted at Ohio State."

When Cruz didn't reply, Lasswell raised a hand, distracted and uncertain.

"You've been through this," she said. "Any pointers?"

"Don't call his parents," he said. "You can't answer medical questions. Your job now is to stamp out bullshit rumors about great white sharks and ten-foot snakes. Keep your people focused."

"A viper," she said. "We fly halfway around the world to blow up terrorists, and we're attacked by a snake."

"Lots of vipers here," Cruz said. "Cobras too. Afghanistan's a paradise. It grows on you."

7

Do Your Job, Captain

At five in the morning, construction stopped and the Marines assumed a defensive position called "stand-to," a nineteenth-century British precaution against surprise attacks at sunup. Cruz walked over to the east side of the perimeter, where Staff Sergeant Sullivan was sitting in a fighting hole alongside a radio operator.

"The engineers scooped out one for you, sir," Sullivan said, pointing several yards away. "Catch up to you later."

As the razor edge of the sun appeared, Cruz sat on the edge of his hole and aligned his photomap with the contours of the tree lines and fields. The flat countryside was broken only by a few gentle inclines and small hummocks. From a distance, the mud walls of the compounds seemed white, clean, and sparkling. Fed by the snowmelts from the faraway Himalayas, the Helmand River provided nutrient-rich water for the poppy fields. Purple, burgundy, and white poppies swayed in the slight breeze.

Myrtle stands of spring corn contrasted with the darker hues of the tree lines, and the tussocks of fescue where sheep had grazed were as smooth and spongy as putting greens. Cruz had read that people played golf because green is the most soothing color. Maybe a resort lay in Helmand's future. But to Cruz, the pastoral setting pulsed with a hostility that clung to the land like the morning mist. With a grunt's eye for terrain, he viewed the landscapes as angles and planes for bullets. Wanting to apprise the fields of fire from each sentry position, he beckoned to Sullivan.

"Let's walk the lines, Staff Sergeant," he said. "The op order calls for twelve four-man fighting bunkers. They all set in?"

"Yes, sir," Sullivan said. "I also have a two-man sniper team and a few engineers."

"A static defense," Cruz said, "behind the concertina?"

"Beyond the wire," Sullivan said, "it's up to the Afghan army to provide security."

The bunkers were chest-deep craters clawed out by the backhoes. They walked from one to the next, with Cruz talking to each Marine. He had shaped and fought alongside hundreds like them. Seventy-five percent of the Marine Corps turned over every four years. Cruz had gone through the entire cycle, from his own recruit training to the battlefields and then back to the recruit depot to train new Marines. Without knowing one name, he knew every member of the platoon, how they thought, and what they feared. He knew how they would respond before they did.

What he didn't know was how to get through to Sullivan. The platoon sergeant had an easy, too-friendly manner with his troops. At each bunker, he joked about the living quarters for the grunts compared to the tents for the cannon-cockers. He introduced Cruz in the same polite, patronizing way.

"Devil dogs, say hello to Captain Cruz. He's filling in for a week or so."

Most of the platoon was friendly, some nervous, and all alert. They reminded Cruz of young Labrador retrievers, energetic and desirous to please. The exception was Sergeant Matt McGowan. When Sullivan and Cruz approached the leader of the 2nd Squad, he was hacking away at the undergrowth. He had taken off his helmet and armor, and sweat from his bald-shaved head was pouring down his thin face. He was working a plug of tobacco tucked into his cheek, with the brown spittle dripping down his chin. He scarcely acknowledged Cruz.

"Hey, sir," he said in an offhanded way before turning back to Sullivan.

"This ain't sound, Staff Sergeant," he said, gesturing at the scrub brush. "I can't tie in my left and right lateral limits. Huge fucking gaps."

He showed them his notebook, with a crude sketch of his fields of fire.

"We got radar," Sullivan said. "You don't have to see everything. Now put your battle rattle back on."

McGowan squirted brown saliva through a gap in his front teeth.

"I told you this'd be unsat," he said in a heavy Texas accent. "We've been here five hours and already evac'd one brother. Whole fucking land's a snake pit."

"McGowan," Sullivan said, "STFU, not another word."

Sullivan glanced at his watch.

"We're due at the staff meeting, sir."

As they walked back, Sullivan vented.

"McGowan's a fucking know-it-all," he muttered. "Always mouthing off. Two NJPs."

"Prior push?"

"Yes, sir. He was at Shorab when it was overrun. Got the Silver Star and a bust in rank. Knows his stuff. Doesn't know his place."

"He has a point about the lines," Cruz said.

"My platoon's solid, sir," Sullivan said. "Me and Lieutenant Reynolds trained these devil dogs hard. No new joins in my platoon."

Except me, Cruz thought. *I'm the short-timer, the temporary help.*

48

They reached a large tent staked down inside a chest-high dirt revetment. The canvas sides were rolled up, letting in a humid breeze. In one corner, four operators were monitoring a bank of laptop computers, radios, and video feeds displayed on three flat screens. Sullivan and Cruz pulled up folding chairs next to Lasswell and several NCOs. Colonel Coffman was sitting at the head of the table, the thick op order in front of him.

Back at Pendleton, each morning Coffman got up at five, jogged for an hour, showered, put on his pressed uniform, and kissed his wife (no children) goodbye. His first meeting began promptly at 0730, and he remained in his office until 1900 (7:00 p.m.). His staff considered him exacting, fair, and humorless. He didn't seem to need affection, relaxation, or friendship. A disciplined man, he expected the same in others.

"Open for business, Captain?" he asked brusquely. "Guns up?"

"Cocked and standing by to receive fire missions, sir," Lasswell said.

"Perimeter in shape?" Coffman said, looking at Cruz.

The dozers had pushed up a berm around the square perimeter, with the dozen bunkers spaced evenly apart. Inside the perimeter, separate berms had been scooped out for the four guns, plus an ammo pit. The artillery crews slept in tents inside their berms. A revetment also enclosed the tent holding the ops center. The security platoon had its own tent near the ops center, used to hold meetings and stow gear. For the duration of the mission, the platoon would eat, sleep, and keep watch in the twelve bunkers along the perimeter, just inside the ring of barbed wire.

"We've set in, sir," Cruz said. "But, um, we're stretched thin. I need more Marines."

Coffman tapped the op order. It was his personal Pelmanism; he could recall every detail filed under every appendix. He had left nothing to chance, yet here was a superannuated captain criticizing that thorough planning.

Firebase Bastion

Bunkers 1   2   3

12	Ammo pit	Latrines	4
	Gun pit #2	Gun pit #3	
11	Gun pit #1	Gun pit #4	5
10	Platoon tent	Op Center	6

9   8   7

"Captain, I told General Killian I could do this job with three hundred and fifty Marines," Coffman said. "The general told the Chairman of the Joint Chiefs, who told the Secretary of Defense, who told the president. My command does not include extra Marines."

To drive home his point, Coffman turned to Sullivan.

"How many rehearsals did you run, Staff Sergeant?"

"Six, sir," Sullivan said.

"And the Red Team, how many times did they get through your defenses?"

"Not once, sir. That LADAR is awesome."

Coffman looked at Cruz.

"Four laser detection and ranging devices, Captain," Coffman said. "Plus, million-dollar drones, a pair of electronic telescopes on fifty-foot hydraulic lifts for twenty-four-hour surveillance, and ELINT. Now, given all that high tech, can you execute with the fifty-four Marines in your platoon? Or are you too concerned about snakes?"

Cruz saw it in a flash. First the ass-chewing about the flashlights and now this lecture. Coffman had pegged him as a spy for General Killian. He had opened up his mouth without thinking. A bad fitness report would doom him. He backed off.

"I'll ensure the perimeter is secure, sir."

Having put Cruz in his place, Coffman changed his tone.

"Of course you will," he said amiably. "Here at Firebase Bastion, we pack one hell of a punch. Do your part, Captain, and everything will be fine."

As Coffman moved on to the next subject, Cruz sat ramrod straight, hoping no one noticed his flushed face.

8

Added Mission

Secretary of Defense Mike Towns had driven over to the West Wing with Admiral Michaels, a gesture symbolizing the closeness between the Secretary and the Chairman of the Joint Chiefs. Two meetings with POTUS inside two days was unusual. Now both sat in the Oval Office, neither smiling at the Director of Central Intelligence sitting next to them.

"This popped up," DCI James Webster whispered apologetically. "Too sensitive to send through channels."

Both Towns and Michaels were wary of Webster, a tall, thin man in his seventies with a wizened face and a shy manner. A denizen of Washington, the DCI had served in three administrations, and his agency had consistently disagreed with the Pentagon's annual optimistic assessment of Afghanistan.

POTUS was sitting behind his massive desk built from the oak timbers of the nineteenth-century English Arctic explorer, HMS

Resolute. On the wall to his left hung the gilded portrait of President Andrew Jackson, his flinty eyes turned toward the *Resolute* desk. *One populist autocrat,* Towns thought, *approving of another.* Dinard rested his forearms on the buffed desktop and nodded at Webster.

"OK, Yoda," he said, "you're on."

Webster held up a photo of Zar, holding two dripping heads. A blue halo encircled the face of the Persian, hovering in the background.

"This video was posted on the internet an hour ago, sir," Webster said. "The ghoul is named Zar Mohammad. Quite rabid."

"He looks like a cannibal," Dinard said. "You going to zap him?"

"We'll drone him eventually, sir. Right now, we're interested in the one circled in blue. He's an Iranian smuggler, linked to the Republican Guard."

The president was paying attention. He liked solving puzzles. Much as he loathed *The Times*, each Sunday he labored over the *Times* crossword.

"What's he doing in Afghanistan?" he said. "Real estate speculation?"

Webster waited until the wry smiles and Armsted's sycophantic chuckle had faded.

"You're close, Mr. President," he said. "Your sanctions have crimped the Republican Guard. They're looking for other sources."

Webster pointed to a map of the Middle East, using a laser pointer to trace a route.

"Most of the world's heroin," he said, "moves from Afghanistan south into Pakistan, then west through Iran up into Europe. Opium and heroin account for half of Afghanistan's gross domestic product, about three billion dollars a year."

POTUS held up his hand and pointed at the Chairman of the Joint Chiefs, Admiral Michaels.

"Admiral, that's why it's stupid to stay in Afghanistan," Dinard said. "They're selling poison, and our soldiers put up with it."

Accustomed to Dinard's hectoring, Michaels appeared unfazed.

"Interdicting the poppy trade wasn't part of our strategy, sir," Michaels said. "Our goal was to win over the farmers, not antagonize them."

"You didn't succeed, did you?" Dinard said.

As the admiral flushed red, Dinard turned back to the Director of Central Intelligence.

"DCI, hurry it up. What's your point?"

"Iran is back in the heroin trade, Mr. President," he said. "A losing competitor came to us and identified the Iranian buyer. Intercepts place him close to that Marine firebase. If we capture him with heroin, we can show him on every TV network."

"I get it!" Dinard said. "Thousands of Americans dying from opioids, and Iran is involved. What do you think, Security Advisor?"

Armsted nodded vigorously.

"That's why I brought this to you, sir. It's time sensitive."

POTUS looked back at Webster.

"What do you want, Yoda?"

"Sir, I'd like to send a team to that firebase," the DCI said. "If they locate where the buyer is, we can execute a raid to capture him."

"Professor, how's this strike you?"

At the Pentagon, Towns encouraged initiative, provided it was nestled inside a sensible plan. Ad hoc impulsiveness irritated him. Even though he was accustomed to the president's whimsies, this one seemed too fuzzy. He tried to refuse without appearing negative or narrow-minded.

"The Republican Guard caused the deaths of hundreds of our troops in Iraq, sir," he said. "They're terrorists. But this is too sudden. The Marines arrived yesterday and today we're changing their mission?"

"No, Mike," Webster said. "I'm adding only a recon."

Towns and Admiral Michaels exchanged a glance.

"Two separate ops," Michaels said, "with two reporting chains?"

"Admiral, I agree that won't work," Webster said. "My team will only snoop. To make it easy, I'll send in only a few operatives from my Special Activities Group."

"Even if they've served in the military," Towns said, "you're still adding a second mission on one small base."

There was silence for a few seconds as POTUS drummed his fingers.

"I like it!" he said. "The doofus before me dithered. I don't. There's a big payoff if I connect Iran to the drug trade. DCI, send in your team."

9

A Temporary Setback

Colonel Avi Balroop lived in a three-bedroom condo in the senior officers' enclave barricaded behind the concrete walls enclosing Pakistan's heavily-guarded airfield in Quetta. Only nine miles east of the Afghan border, the polyglot city of Quetta provided the space and tolerance for one million Pashtun, Baloch, and Punjabi tribesmen to live in hovels, middle-class suburbs, and palaces while indulging in baccarat, treason, horse racing, subversion, polo, assassination, cricket, smuggling, camel auctions, and bomb making.

When Balroop heard his cell phone ringing before dawn, he didn't pick up. One minute later, the phone rang again six times and no more. He dressed in jogging clothes and trotted at an easy pace along a path through patches of shrubbery. In the gray light, his vague shadow blended into the bushes. He stopped to retrieve a hidden cell phone and dialed a number.

"Yes?"

"The coyotes are back."

"Coyotes? You're sure?"

"Yes, yes! They howled all night. No other sound like that."

Balroop ran back to his house, showered, apologized to his wife for skipping breakfast, and rushed to ISI headquarters inside the airport. The Inter-Services Intelligence was under constant attack from enemies, external and internal. His division operated from a one-story building marked by a cluster of antennas encased behind concrete barriers next to the flight tower. The long runways and expansive tarmacs made impossible any covert approach.

For over half a century, ISI had concocted plots, subversion, and terrorist raids against India, Pakistan's strong enemy to the east. Afghanistan to the west was, in ISI's view, a rebellious collection of illiterate tribes. To prevent India from gaining a foothold there, the ISI sheltered the Taliban inside Pakistan. Once America gave up on Afghanistan, Pakistan would help the Taliban take over the government. This simple plan required only a few decades of patience, combined with an instinct to deceive all foreigners.

Sitting in his modest office, Balroop was not surprised when his general walked in without knocking. Gesturing furiously with his cigarette, the general immediately got to the point.

"Colonel, you're the action officer for Helmand. You did advise the Taliban not to increase the military pressure?"

"Yes, sir, but they disagreed. They wanted a clear victory to show they're going to take every city, including Kabul."

"Instead they drew the Americans back in. The Taliban have no brains!"

"Apparently, it's a temporary base, sir," Balroop said. "A negotiating gambit to force the Talibs to stick to their agreement."

"That base has suddenly popped up at the end of the harvest season! How do we protect our thirty million?"

The ISI plucked the highest achievers from the two-hundred-thousand-man army. At the age of forty, Balroop was chosen because he adapted quickly.

"We may have to settle for a bit less, sir," he said. "But I do have a way of driving out the Americans."

For the next thirty minutes, Balroop laid out his plan, step-by-step. When he proposed his solution, the general was impressed and wary.

"Daring," he said, "but it depends on the weather."

"Exactly. The Pashto call it 'The Wind of 120 Days,'" Balroop said. "The chances of a few strong storms are one hundred percent. Our meteorologist reports that one is forming now. We need to get everything in place."

"All right," the general said. "I'll clear it with Islamabad. No written reports and don't use the internet. Not one Pakistani is to cross the border, including you. This can never be traced back to us. Never."

BALROOP SPENT THE MORNING dispatching and receiving couriers from the Quetta shura, the council of Taliban elders who lived in middle-class compounds on the city's outskirts. By noon, he was prepared for his visitor. Through a corner window, he watched as two Pakistani jeeps escorted a black SUV into the parking lot. Minutes later, Mullah Khan entered Balroop's office, dabbing his forehead with a white linen handkerchief. His cheeks glowed with perspiration.

"Six hours jouncing in that damn Cadillac," he said. "And the air-conditioning didn't work!"

Iranian mullahs had long ago shed the appearance of pious modesty. Their preference for American status symbols amused Balroop. Usually the urbane Mullah Khan prefaced negotiations with a droll quip. Not this time. As soon as they were alone, he burst out.

"Balroop, this is a disaster!" he said. "I paid for the harvest, and now we can't ship it. The Americans have drones, cameras, spies, helicopters, all near the mosque!"

Balroop pretended to be unfazed.

"No reason to be upset," he said. "The Taliban overreached. They thought they could goad the Americans into leaving faster. A tactical mistake."

"Tactical? They're idiots!"

"I'm meeting with the shura. I know how to take care of this."

"I can't move the product. That kills our profits! We have to adjust our agreement."

The mullah had taken out his iPad, clutching it like a pacifier while pecking at the screen.

"I persuaded the Republican Guard to put in the fifteen million," he said. "So the Guard takes the first fifty. That's fair."

Balroop's face hardened. If he broached this with his general, his career was over.

"Fair? I don't hear you offering to reduce your four percent. Let me remind you: the heroin comes out through our part of Baluchistan. Without us, you get nothing."

The threat by the self-assured Pakistani enraged the mullah.

"America has cut off aid to your country," he said, his voice trembling in anger. "China gives you nothing. And now the ISI makes an enemy of the Islamic Republic of Iran?"

Balroop had anticipated pushback and was ready with a counter.

"America is squeezing Iran harder than us," he said. "We stick to our agreement. You provide the cash and we deliver the security."

"You call Zar 'security'?" the mullah said. "That lunatic thinks Allah is talking to him. He beheads people! He calls me 'the Persian,' when I am Pashtun. Security? I'm here talking with you because those damned Marines are back!"

"Not for long," Balroop said. "I know what to do. Once Americans bleed, they leave. But the Republican Guard has to pledge a few dozen 107s to Haqqani."

The Persian snorted his disbelief.

"Haqqani! He's like Zar, a demon!" the Persian said. "He'll launch those missiles at Kabul. The markings will point back to Iran. You shelter him, so give him your own missiles."

Balroop laughed.

"You're the open enemy of America," he said. "Our relationship is…more complicated."

The Persian held his tongue. His complaint about Haqqani was achieving nothing. Recriminations were excuses for failures.

"What does Haqqani contribute in exchange?"

"It's best your Iranian bosses not know until things fall into place."

"You don't trust us?"

Balroop couldn't resist a jibe.

"Why risk a leak?" he said. "What if you're captured?"

The Persian twitched, almost dropping his iPad. Balroop laughed.

"All you have to know is that America doesn't learn from past mistakes."

"You ISI people, speaking in riddles," the Persian said angrily, "running your own state within a state."

"And the Republican Guards you work for? Are they any different?" Balroop said. "Look, your uncle the general delivers a few missiles, and we get the assets to drive out the Americans."

"Has the Quetta shura agreed to this?" he said.

"I'll deal with the Taliban after you agree to the missiles," Balroop said.

The Persian sipped his tea. As a Sunni Pashtun, he had not prospered in Shiite Iran by being obstinate. The art of negotiating was compromise.

"I can persuade my uncle," he said, "if he receives the first twenty-five million."

Pleased that the Persian had reverted to haggling, Balroop smiled. He didn't need a calculator to do the math. Even after Iran and the Taliban took their cuts, Balroop could still deliver thirty million dollars to the ISI.

"Always the accountant," he said, "hedging so you come out ahead. All right, I think I can sell your adjustment."

"And you'll persuade the Quetta shura?" the Persian said. "There can be no resentments. I don't want that maniac Zar hacking off my head!"

The Persian's eyes were so wide with fear that Balroop almost laughed.

"The Taliban need you," Balroop said. "You're the man with the gold. Oh, one smaller matter. What are you carrying on this trip, two or three million?"

"I have about a million left," the Persian said. "I've bought most harvests, but not all."

"Put aside three hundred thousand dollars," Balroop said. "You'll know when to pay it. Both our futures depend on it. Be patient for a few days."

"A few days? That quick?"

"It won't be long. So keep that three hundred thousand dollars close at hand."

10

Contact

Shortly before noon, Colonel Coffman climbed atop a steep earthen berm and proudly surveyed Firebase Bastion. In front of the bunkers along the perimeter, work crews were staking in coils of razor wire, an added precaution to the laser beams of the LADAR scopes monitoring each side of the square encampment. Looking at the defenses, he was confident no Marine would be killed on his base. Instead, they'd exact a bloody toll on their enemy, while living like field Marines. Piss tubes, crappers, MREs, tepid bottled water, no showers, no cots, no cell phones—expeditionary to the core! When it was over, he'd write a classic article for the *Marine Corps Gazette*.

Satisfied, he entered the ops center tent and glanced at the console displays. One screen was monitoring the feed from a UAV. It showed in sharp detail a column of seven vehicles skirt around an armored bulldozer and depart the encampment of the Afghan National Army, six miles to the northeast.

"XO," Coffman said, "is that the ANA, finally on the move?"

"Affirmative, sir," Major Barnes said. "Heading to our pos. I dispatched two drones to scout for them."

INSIDE NANTUSH'S COMPOUND, anxiety had given way to curiosity. Women, children, and workers had secured vantage points on the roof, peering at the clouds of dust and listening to growl of engines to the west. A courier raced up on his motorcycle and, full of self-importance, took Nantush aside and whispered a message. Nantush then called together the agitated workers.

"Go back into the fields," he said. "And no one is to shoot at the Americans! I don't want my home destroyed."

Nantush knew his workers would obey him. Few of them owned even one *jerib* of land, and none had a steady job. In his view, most lacked ambition and came from the lower subtribes. It annoyed him that his eldest son, Ala, called them mujahideen—Fighters of God. Over the past three harvest seasons, Ala had sweated alongside them. Around the fires at night, smoking hash and sipping scalding herb tea, they had bragged about their battles, how Itzek had set in the IED, how Ahmed had downed the helicopter with his RPG. Thanks be to Allah!

As the workers returned to the fields, Ala scurried to a shed, where he unwrapped from an oily cloth the AK his father had given him last month on his sixteenth birthday. He had dry-fired it hundreds of times, sighting in on imaginary infidels. He fished into a meal sack and pulled out a magazine loaded with nine bullets he had filched from his father's neglected and rusty AK. Unseen, he slipped out the compound wall and onto a path that led to a small rise two fields west of the compound. Imitating what he had seen on television, he built an amateurish sniper's hide, twisting together vines and branches before wedging the rifle barrel into the crook of a small tree.

He crouched low, peering at the dust raised by the noisy machines grinding away several hundred meters to the west. Squinting through the saplings, he could see the outlines of black artillery tubes and occasionally glimpsed the americani, tiny figures that popped up and down. He tried to sight in, but his hands shook. He sat down, breathing heavily. Four or five times, he repeated standing up and sighting in. Gradually his heartbeat slowed. But no americani stood still long enough for him to get a sight picture.

Finally, he aimed at the top of an artillery tube jutting above a berm. When he jerked the trigger, he was surprised how loud the shot sounded. He ducked, convinced he had been spotted. When nothing happened, he peeked out. The americani camp was still noisy and dusty. No one had noticed. This time, he carefully sighted in, drew a breath, and fired twice more, squeezing instead of jerking the trigger. He heard a slight *ping!* Yes! He had hit something!

INSIDE THE OPS CENTER, the intel, fire control, and perimeter security sections each had a bank of consoles to monitor. Cruz and Sullivan were sitting in a corner, making small changes before posting the watch assignments for the next day. There was the sharp *crack!* of air snapping shut after a bullet zipped through the tent. Several Marines dove into the dirt. Two more shots followed, neither hitting the tent.

"Corpsman! Corpsman up!"

The shouting came from an artillery pit where most of the Marines had sought shelter or were crouched over, not sure what to do. A few had continued with their chores, trying to appear unfazed. Coffman rushed out of his office in the rear of the ops center.

"Casualty report!" he shouted.

"No one's hit, sir. One twisted ankle."

"Location of the sniper?" Coffman yelled.

An operator watching a video screen spoke up.

"Nothing showing on the downlink, sir," he shouted. "Thermals can't pick up anything under the tree lines."

Ignoring Cruz, Sullivan leaped up and strode over to Coffman.

"Take the QRF out, sir?" Sullivan said. "I think the azimuth of the shooter is about zero seven zero."

The question startled Cruz. Sullivan was acting as though he commanded the security platoon. Coffman too was caught off guard. He had no combat time, no way of judging the risk of being lured into an ambush. But if he did nothing, he'd look weak.

"Launch the Quick Reaction Force, Staff Sergeant," he said. "God knows you've rehearsed this enough."

Sullivan rushed outside, where Sergeant Trey Denton was waiting with 1st Squad, the designated QRF. . On the photo map on his iPad, Sullivan pointed to a tree line. Denton nodded and quickly briefed his squad. Each Marine was told his sector of fire, radio call signs, and rally points. Cruz noticed Denton's rhythm: read the written order, look at the Marines, point at the map, and glance at Sullivan for approval. Denton was a steady man who knew his way up.

It had been thirty minutes since the three shots. The video from the UAV showed harvesters still in the fields, normal patterns of life inside the scattered farm compounds, and vehicles and motorcyclists on the roads. It was as though the shots had never been fired.

Sullivan lined the grunts up for one final inspection, the grins gone, their expressions determined. After the radio check, Cruz took Sullivan aside and spoke quietly.

"Stay in visual range of the base. The shooter can't be more than a click out. I'll be up on the net."

Sullivan's face tightened.

"Roger, I got that," he said. "Departing the wire, sir."

Cruz watched as the patrol wended its way through the fields, alternately bobbing into sight before plunging into another fold in the foliage. He resented being cut out. But on balance, the incident wasn't a big deal. The UAVs overhead would detect any large group of fighters sneaking toward the firebase. The odds were high that some local show-off, after firing a few random rounds, had already run away.

11

Marine Down

Cruz watched the patrol cross a footbridge and disappear into the undergrowth on the other side. Sergeant McGowan was standing beside him, working a wad of tobacco in his cheek.

"Should've waded across, not taken the risk," McGowan said.

"Have 2nd Squad on deck," Cruz said. "You're on five mikes alert..."

"Standing by, sir," McGowan said. "Semper Gumby."

"Know why Gumby is always flexible?" Cruz said. "Because Gumby is a clay toy. You keep dipping that split, your lungs will be clay."

SULLIVAN'S PATROL WAS PROCEEDING SLOWLY. Lance Corporal Nick Mason, the engineer at point, kept his eyes down, watching the dials as he swept his mine detector back and forth. Behind him, a Marine squirted the shaving cream for the others to follow. From farther back in the file, Sullivan occasionally pointed for a slight change in direction.

"Check out those goats, Denton," Sullivan said in a relaxed tone. "Maybe we bring one back for dinner."

"I'd prefer a sheep, Staff Sergeant," Denton said.

"I don't trust what you'd do with a sheep," Sullivan said.

He was enjoying himself. It was good to be outside the wire, a combat leader respected by the colonel, in charge of his platoon while Captain Cruz was sitting back in the ops center.

Several meters ahead, Mason had stopped at the edge of a small marsh marked by tangles of soggy hassocks and spindly reeds. An irrigation canal separated them from a thick stand of trees and undergrowth on the far bank. Sullivan gestured to cross the canal. Holding the mine detector above his head, Mason waded out a few feet before sinking up to his waist. As he scrambled back, Sullivan walked forward. It had now been an hour since the last shot had been fired.

"The shooter's gone," he said. "We'll cut across this low spot and work our way back to base."

The muddy depression in front of them was about fifty meters wide, with high, dry ground on the far side. Sopping wet, Mason started across the spit, followed by PFC Michael Tadcomb with the can of shaving cream. Sullivan and Denton slid in behind the lead pair. With ten other Marines strung out behind them, they sloshed forward in the sedge. The mud, thick as wet cement, tugged at their boots. After several steps, the muck had reached to their knees, then to their thighs. Each Marine had to slowly pull up one leg after another, trying not to lose a boot in the sucking ooze.

"We're going to stink for the rest of the deployment," Tadcomb muttered.

ALA WAS CROUCHED IN HIS HIDE on the other side of the canal, his heart fluttering. *There! Kafirs!* So close he could hit them with a stone. He aimed in.

TADCOMB WAS LEANING FORWARD, right arm upraised to keep his rifle clean, when the bullet hit him under his armpit. At the sound of the shot, Sullivan twisted around, thinking a Marine had fired an accidental round. Tadcomb was facedown in the mud. Adrenaline surging, Sullivan grabbed him by the armored vest and pulled him up. Denton bulled forward and together they dragged Tadcomb forward across the spit.

"Cover! Cover!" Denton was screaming.

The Marine behind him froze, unsure whether to go forward or back. *Crack!* A bullet whipped by his face. He flinched and fell, bumping into the Marine behind him and setting off a chain reaction. Inside a few seconds, the ten Marines had scrambled back up the bank they had just left. Once on solid ground, they fired short, aimless bursts at the leaves, trees, and sky.

ALA WAS CONFUSED. The Marines had stampeded so suddenly, most running back and a few forward. Now they all were hidden in the bushes, shouting back and forth. He couldn't pick out a single figure to shoot. A few bullets snapped over his head so high that he wasn't afraid. Instead, he was anxious to fire again. He had shot one infidel, and he had four bullets left. To escape, the infidels would have to wade back across the mud pit. He settled down to wait.

Sullivan and Denton dragged Tadcomb into a tangle of underbrush. Breathing hoarsely, they lay on either side of him. Mason, the engineer, was lying down a few feet away. He started to rise to his knees.

"Stay the fuck down!" Sullivan shouted.

"Shit, shit, shit," Mason stuttered. "We're cut off!"

"Shut the fuck up and help me."

Together they stripped off Tadcomb's armor. Sullivan looked at his rib cage, so filthy with mud that the dark blood seemed to be only trickling out. Tadcomb's eyes were closed, and his slim chest was heaving. Sullivan fumbled for his compression bandage.

"See an exit wound?" he asked Mason.

"No, nothing."

"Maybe the bullet ricocheted off his armor. Might not be too bad."

A few feet away, Denton was listening to his intra-squad radio. Other radios were squawking, a chaos of words and static. He pressed the button attached to his left lapel and yelled into his voice mic.

"Everyone shut up! Wolf One-Three, you have eyes on the sniper?"

On the other side of the marsh, Lance Corporal Ed Thomas was lying in thick foliage, the other nine Marines spread out around him. None could see through the undergrowth. A few Marines were shooting at nothing.

"Negative," Thomas said. "Can't see shit. He's on the other side of the canal, damn close. Want us to close on you? Over."

Denton looked at Sullivan, who shook his head. Denton pressed his talk button.

"Wolf One-Three, hold where you are. Stay under cover."

BACK AT THE FIREBASE A KILOMETER AWAY, Cruz had watched the overhead video that showed the patrol splitting into two groups, both now hidden beneath the foliage. Sullivan's voice came up on the net in the ops center.

"Eagle Three, this is Wolf Five. Have one WIA critic. Sniper has us pinned down. Our pos is 962 355. Over."

Cruz looked at Coffman, who nodded. Cruz squeezed the push-to-talk button.

"Wolf Five, this is Wolf Six. QRF on the way."

McGowan was waiting outside, his keyed up squad behind him.

"This fucking country never changes, sir," Mac said. "We're good to go."

The point man held up his mine detector. Cruz shook his head.

"No time for that. Follow the shaving cream."

The patrol set off briskly, half trotting and half walking at a quick shuffle. Cruz had inserted an earbud and was talking with Sullivan.

"Bullet in his chest," Sullivan said. "He's breathing, but we're pinned down."

"Call smoke," Cruz said into his throat mic. "We're ten mikes out."

The reaction squad held to a fast pace. Within a few minutes they reached Thomas and the other Marines on the bank.

"There," Thomas said, pointing across the mud flat. "Sergeant Sullivan's stuck on the other side. The sniper has us zeroed in. We tried to get across twice, and he fired both times."

Through his earbud, Cruz heard Sullivan fumbling to call in a fire mission. The sniper could be anywhere in the dense green tangle of bushes and trees on the far side of the canal, not sixty meters away. A small drone was hovering a few feet above the canal, but the operators back at the ops center could not pick out the shooter.

Cruz adjusted his binoculars with its laser range finder and centered the red reticle. He saw no one. He didn't expect to. Usually it was like this, with no target visible. He spoke into his throat mic, contacting the fire direction center and not bothering with a lengthy format.

"Badger Six, this is Wolf Six. Give me one Willie Peter. Sniper at 962 368. I'm giving you a quick polar. Target is one five zero meters from my pos, niner five magnetic."

Coffman interrupted, coming up on the net. "Wolf Six, this is Eagle Six Actual. Do you have PID?"

The standing regulation was clear: do not shoot unless you have PID—positive identification of the enemy.

"Eagle Six," Cruz radioed. "Am requesting Willie Peter to conceal friendly movement."

Willie Peter—white phosphorous—was a chemical that burned, emitting a large billow of white smoke. Coffman did not reply, his silence signaling consent.

The next transmission from the ops center was, "Wolf Six, shot out." A few seconds later, Cruz heard the metallic thunk of the shell leaving the tube back at base. After a pause, the ops center radioed "Splash." Cruz heard the slight sound of a newspaper being ripped, followed by a dull thump. He watched as white smoke swirled from the tree line.

"Drop five zero and give me four Willie Pete."

Cruz waited fifteen seconds for the smoke to thicken on the other side of the canal. Then he led four Marines across the mud and flopped down next to Sullivan. Tadcomb was lying on his back, gulping air in rapid, shallow breaths. His lips were a faint blue. The entrance wound in his lower ribs was covered with a compression bandage. When he inhaled, air filled the chest cavity, preventing his lungs from expanding. As his heart strained to suck oxygen from his bloodstream, he was slowly strangling.

"What the fuck," Cruz said. "Why didn't you stick him?"

"I didn't want to kill him," Sullivan stammered.

"He's suffocating! Doc, get that needle into him."

Navy Corpsman Third Class Bushnell had slipped on latex gloves and unwrapped the nine-gauge needle catheter. With his left hand, he probed Tadcomb's chest to locate the intercostal space between the second and third ribs. With his right hand, he pushed the needle in a full two inches, drawing a hiss as the trapped air shot out. Bushnell dropped his head to listen to Tadcomb's breathing.

"Got it!" he said. "That eased the pressure."

He plucked out the needle and slapped on an occlusive bandage, carefully sealing the adhesive edges so no air could seep in.

Cruz showed no emotion, instead turning his attention to the far bank of the canal where the white smoke lay like a lazy fog. He was operating with no conscious thought. Suppressing the sniper was as automatic to him as a golfer selecting a club to hit out of the rough. He called again for mortars.

"Badger Six, give me an open sheaf of HE on the coordinates where you dropped the smoke."

"Wolf Six, this is Badger Six. I assume you have PID."

There it was again, the ritualistic question about positive identification of an enemy demanding a ritualistic answer.

"Affirmative," Cruz replied.

A husky Marine with a florid face rushed up and flopped down beside Cruz.

"Sir, I'm the JTAC, Sergeant Doyle," he blurted out. "I'm supposed to be doing this."

A Joint Terminal Attack Controller was qualified to call in mortars, artillery, and air. Cruz appraised Doyle's determined expression.

"Doyle, you got Killswitch on your tablet?"

"That and more, sir. I'll make the adjustments."

Within two minutes, both heard "shot out" from the ops center, followed twenty seconds later by "splash."

WHILE THE MORTAR SHELLS WERE STILL HAMMERING DOWN, four Marines carried Tadcomb, strapped to a foldable litter, across the mud flat. As they stumbled forward, they sank to their knees and hoisted the litter poles up to their shoulders. After everyone was across and deep inside the bush, Cruz stopped to regroup.

"Gear check," he said.

Denton and McGowan inspected their squads, checking each man for his rifle, radio, and night-vision pouch.

"We got Tadcomb's M27," Denton said. "We're missing his hand-held. My bad. I'll go back."

Cruz tensed. Crossing the bog had cost one Marine. But he couldn't let the Talibs recover an encrypted radio. He thought of going back himself and dismissed the idea. That would finish Denton in the eyes of his squad.

"You're right," he said. "It was your bad, Sergeant. Take care of it."

With two other Marines, Denton slogged across the mire. A few minutes later, he came up on the platoon net.

"Wolf Six, I found it."

As Denton was wading back, he lurched and twisted his leg. Limping badly, he hobbled up to Cruz and showed him the 152 handheld.

"Good," Cruz said. "You OK?"

"No biggie, sir. Fucking mud."

Cruz arranged the two squads in a single file. Without saying a word, Sullivan hefted a litter pole onto his shoulder. They carried Tadcomb at a fast pace across two fields before his weight slowed them down. At the next irrigation creek, Cruz discarded Tadcomb's armor and helmet in the waist-deep muddy waters.

"Take the magazines," he said. "Dump the rest. No sense lugging extra weight. No one'll find them."

When the first shell had exploded with a dull crump behind him, Ala had flopped to the ground and wiggled behind a stout tree trunk. As the shells burst nearer, he curled into a fetal position, placing one arm over his head. He never thought of crawling forward to take another shot. Instead, he feared the Americans would come looking for him. He lay there, rapidly repeating "Allahu Akbar, Allahu Akbar," thinking only of running back to the compound after the shelling stopped. He had killed an americani. Yes! He had seen the *kafir* fall! Ala was scared and agog, anticipating the approval of his father and the envy of the workers. He was now a mujahideen, a true warrior of Islam.

12

Two Holy Warriors

As he drove south, Zar heard the mortar explosions behind him. They sounded close to Nantush's farmlands, but he paid them no attention. He stopped in Yaget, a cluster of storefronts on the outskirts of Lashkar Gah. Most were unpainted gray concrete shops, few larger than one room, offering bright scarves, long shovels, plastic toys, patched-up tires, and dozens of items with price points below five dollars.

Zar parked in the rear of a shop with the rusted skeleton of a Nissan on the roof and a tractor with a broken axle blocking most of the driveway. Inside, a boy was holding a light behind a man hunched under the hood of a car. They both straightened when Zar entered. The man's face was a patchwork of scars that drew his lips up in a perpetual sneer. The empty left sleeve of his greasy *kameez* was pinned to his tunic. He nudged the boy, who murmured a frightened "*salam alekim*" and left.

Zar stood in the shadows, shaking his head as he looked at the junk strewn across the hard-packed dirt floor—deflated tractor tires, a twisted truck engine, dented car fenders, a torn mattress with its box springs sticking up like corn stalks. In a corner, a flat-screen Samsung TV was blaring. Zar squinted at the image of a seductive woman sipping wine.

"Tulus," he said, "you watch filth. Infidel pornography."

Tulus knew Zar's wife watched the same channel. He wiped sweat from his face and batted away the accusation.

"The *kafirs* call that soap, like washing hair," he said. "It's how I learn americani."

Whenever the crafty province chief met with American advisers, he had Tulus interpret, knowing the crippled mechanic would later report to the Taliban. Tulus turned off the TV and gestured toward a teapot. Zar shook his head.

"Business seems slow," Zar said in a bargaining mode.

Tulus gestured vaguely with his right hand.

"I do what I can alone," he said, slurring each syllable. "Is the tunnel leaking again?"

"No, your repairs were good," Zar said. "I have another job for you. The americani are back. I don't want them leaving their base."

"You think they would go to the mosque?"

"Not if we sow mines to rip them apart."

Tulus glanced appraisingly at Zar and hobbled over to a rusted tractor engine decaying in the dirt. Using two small pneumatic jacks, he pumped up one end of the engine and scraped at the dirt with a hand pick to reveal a metal ring. He attached a short rope, and gestured to Zar to help. Together they slid back an iron plate and climbed down a wooden ladder. Handing a flashlight to Zar, Tulus tugged aside dusty tarps covering several sacks of ammonium nitrate fertilizer with Pakistani markings. Empty yellow plastic jugs were strewn in a damp corner.

"I have enough diesel fuel and blasting caps," Tulus said, "to mix ten jugs."

Zar reached down and picked up two short pieces of wood, taped together and held apart by a few slices of sponge. A thin electric wire was taped on the inside of each piece. He squeezed the pieces together until the two wires touched, then relaxed his grip and squinted at Tulus through the small gap between the two boards.

"Of course you will set them in," Zar said.

Both men were experts at rigging improvised explosive devices, or IEDs. Dig a small hole for the jug and insert into the fertilizer a blasting cap attached to a wire glued to one piece of wood. Several feet away, bury a small battery with a wire attached to another piece of wood. Place the two pieces together, held apart by a few bits of sponge, and cover them with dirt. When a foot pressed the boards and wires together, a spark would leap from the battery to the blasting cap, setting off ten pounds of nitrate that ripped apart legs, testicles, and intestines.

"I prepare the explosives," Tulus said. "That's all. Your men attach the batteries and bury them."

"The farmers know you," Zar said. "You repair their tractors. My *majid* are brave but don't have your experience. I need you to go with them."

Tulus's abrupt laugh sounded like a cough.

"And I needed my left arm. I won't go out there, not after the last time."

Zar sharply snapped the boards together and Tulus stumbled back.

"I'm your commander," he said. "You will do..."

Zar sucked in his breath and stopped. How many times had Abra laid her hand on his arm and softly entreated him to hold back. *My husband, you frighten people. There's no need to do that. They know your might. Do not chase them away.*

Zar regained control, stopped talking, and shone the flashlight around the small cave.

"Ten isn't enough."

"I can mix more for two thousand rupees each."

Zar looked at him sharply, then shrugged. He wasn't paying with his own money.

"Agreed. I'll buy as many as you can build. Hire other workers."

Tulus's eyes widened.

"I'll have twenty tomorrow," he said. "More after that. Our mines will pen in the infidels. But something more will be needed to drive them out. Perhaps you should call the shura…"

Zar slapped him across the face, the backhand blow unleashing more power than intended. Tulus staggered back, falling on his crippled shoulder. Zar sighed, lifting his arm as though exasperated by its strength. He reached down to help Tulus, who crabbed away, wiping the blood from his split lip.

"It's not my fault that I tapped you," Zar said. "You must watch your tongue. We are both holy warriors. We are brothers."

Tulus, staring at the dirt in front of his bleeding face, refused to look up.

"And brother," he muttered, "we must both obey the shura."

Zar was puzzled. It seemed an odd thing for Tulus to say.

"Indeed we do obey," Zar said. "The shura guides us to victory."

13

Cruz Takes Command

It took the patrol less than thirty minutes to reach the base. Coffman was waiting at the wire. He ignored Cruz, fell in step with the four Marines carrying the litter and placed his hand softly on Tadcomb's shoulder.

"We got you, son," he shouted. "I'm right here with you. You'll be fine. Medevac's inbound. You hang on tight!"

To Cruz, it looked like the colonel was imitating what he'd seen in war films. Yet at the same time, he seemed genuinely concerned. Then it struck him that Coffman had never comforted a wounded, scared grunt. He didn't know how to act. This was all new to him.

When they reached the med tent, Commander Zarest pushed the Marines aside and examined Tadcomb.

"What dose did you give him?"

"Five milligrams, sir," Bushnell said.

"He's stable," Zarest said. "Good job with that needle. Now everyone out."

Once outside, Coffman wheeled on Sullivan.

"Staff Sergeant," he said. "WTF? What were you doing out there?"

The dozen Marines within earshot exchanged glances. Sullivan grimaced.

"Sir, I…"

"Excuse me, Colonel," Cruz broke in. "When I got there, the platoon sergeant had everyone under cover. That mud was like glue."

Coffman hesitated. He looked at the two Marines, both sopping wet from sweat, cammies caked with mud. He was aware of others watching them, and of his own clean uniform.

"No more incidents like this," he said, waving a finger. "Get your shit together and clean up."

As Coffman walked back to the med tent, Cruz turned to the patrol.

"Devil dogs, now you know what Helmand's all about," he said. "T-man gets off the first shots. It's how you react once under fire that counts."

He picked out the pinkish face of Doyle, who was bobbing his head up and down, listening to some silent beat.

"Good job adjusting mortars."

Doyle smiled widely, baring back his lips to show crooked and overgrown incisors.

"Mad Dog bites again," Sergeant McGowan said.

Doyle growled to the delight of the grunts. Playing along, Cruz leaned forward for a closer look.

"Yep, I agree," he said. "Sergeant Doyle, those are the ugliest teeth I've ever seen."

"Grrr," Doyle replied to general laughter.

"All right," Cruz said. "Assemble in the platoon tent for the debrief."

Sullivan lagged behind as the others moved off.

"Thanks for the hus, skipper," he said.

"Hold fast for a few mikes," Cruz said. "Not to second guess, but why didn't you send a pos for the mortars to hit?"

"My laser was just picking up trees," Sullivan said.

"That's all you needed," Cruz said.

"Not the way I saw it, sir," he said. "Rules of engagement are clear. I had no target."

Cruz let out a sigh. After years without combat, peacetime attitudes had crept in.

"Look, Staff Sergeant," he said. "In Nawa, your battalion took only a few casualties. Me? I had a platoon in Sangin. On my first patrol, the point man was veering toward a compound. I got a bad feeling, but I didn't want to be pushy and I kept my mouth shut. A few seconds later, *bam!*, he's a screaming double amp. That didn't happen again on my watch."

"I don't get where you're going, sir," Sullivan said. "Maybe I kinda made a mistake. No one's perfect."

"There's a learning curve in combat," he said. "We're here for only a few days. Not enough time to smooth things out."

"What're you driving at, sir?"

"You and I are dividing responsibilities. The wounded Marine, he with you long?"

"Tad? Yeah, about a year. This was his first deployment. Never bitched. Expert qual on the range. Thinks the Vikings are a lock for the Super Bowl."

"Married?"

"Nah, he's twenty, not old enough to drink."

Cruz revised his opinion. Sullivan was ambitious, thin-skinned, and lacked tactical sense. But he cared about his men.

"Write his parents."

"Sir? We don't have access to email."

"Mail the letter when you get back. His family will hang on to it forever."

"My spelling stinks."

"It's not what you write. It's that you cared enough to try. Now here's how we'll operate. You take care of admin, police the lines, and stay close to the troops. I look after the tactics and stuff outside the wire."

Sullivan was shaken.

"You're putting me on the shelf?"

"The platoon is yours, long-term."

"The op plan has the ANA running the patrols."

"Fine. If the Afghan soldiers carry the load, it'll be a short, dull week for us. Now let's get to the debrief."

When they walked into the platoon tent, the men were sitting in the dirt in a semicircle. A glum Sullivan took a knee, while Cruz remained standing. He looked at the earnest young faces, waiting to be told what to do and willing to do it.

"Devil dogs, your brother's been evaced," Cruz said. "He's on his way home."

Cruz extended his hand, palm open.

"See my fingers? You can break them like twigs."

He clenched his fingers into a fist and cocked his arm as though to throw a punch.

"Want to try now?"

The Marines laughed and shook their heads.

"We fight as a fist, together," Cruz said. "Now, let's start the debrief and sort out what we did right and where we can do better. I expect everyone to speak up."

Cruz paused, letting the platoon absorb the fact that he had taken command.

14

Not an Eight-Thousand-Mile Screwdriver

Coffman remained in the med tent for half an hour, lightly touching Tadcomb's arm and talking occasionally in a low voice to Commander Zarest. In his detached way, Coffman did care for the troops. While in college, he had seen the film *Full Metal Jacket*. He had admired the demanding drill instructor, but the senior officers in the movie had appeared weak to him. Instead of becoming a lawyer, Coffman decided he would lead Marines.

He wanted to be an infantry officer but during training tore a rotator cuff and ended up in administration. He knew Helmand was his moment to shine. He had chosen Barnes so that the staff back at headquarters would hear firsthand about the mission. He had selected Lasswell because her female presence guaranteed favorable media coverage.

It was midafternoon when he walked through the ops center back into his tiny office. He slept in the dirt without an air mattress, surrounded by a wooden footlocker crammed with files, two folding chairs, and a collapsible table holding a computer. A washbasin was tied to the rear flap of the tent, while a double flap of canvas separated the front entrance from the ops center. Before he clicked on the secure video link, he made sure the camera angle captured his spartan style. He was quickly patched through to General Killian.

"Coffman here, sir. Sorry it took a few minutes to call back. I was with a wounded devil dog."

In World War I, the Germans had called them "Höllenhunde," or devil dogs, and the nickname had stuck.

Killian wasted no time with preliminaries.

"I read the message," Killian said. "Your Marine OK?"

"He's stable, General. His patrol was pushing back a sniper."

"Good. Don't let those pricks get close. Is Cruz on top of it?"

There it was again. The old warhorse trotting out his favorite pony.

"I'm sure Cruz will be fine," Coffman said, "once he gets his feet under him."

"Don't sugarcoat it," Killian said. "If he's not doing his job, relieve him and turn in a report when you get back."

Killian's tone was abrupt, even testy. Coffman knew he'd pushed too far. Any report would show Cruz had gone to the aid of the patrol. Coffman changed the subject.

"We're all adapting, sir. We have a full plate, yet I've received a sitrep that a spook team is inbound."

"That's why I called," Killian said. "The agency wants to track a drug buyer operating near your base."

"Sir? I don't have the manpower to support—"

"Hal, you're not the first to feel overburdened," Killian said. "Both times I deployed to Helmand, Spec Ops sent me dozens of BOLOs and choppered in whenever they felt like it."

Intel shops routinely posted BOLOs (Be On Lookout), mug shots of wild-eyed, thickly bearded terrorists or descriptions of battered cars allegedly packed with explosives.

"Sir, this sitrep is vague as smoke," Coffman said. "The command in Kabul provided no instructions."

"Don't be a pain in the ass," Killian said. "These spooks carry heavy clout."

"So, uh, the SecDef is in on this?"

"I'm surprised he didn't call you personally," Killian said.

Months earlier, after reading SecDef Towns's glowing fitrep of Coffman, Killian had selected him as his chief of staff. But Coffman's clumsy display of ambition bothered him.

"You'll help them," Killian continued, "as long as it doesn't interfere with your mission. Got that?"

"Aye-aye, sir," Coffman said. "And, uh, this sniper attack? It won't happen again. I'm bringing in Afghan soldiers to conduct the local patrols. Do you think that's sensible?"

There was a moment's silence.

"Let me spell it out, Hal," Killian said. "I'm not in your direct chain of command over there. I'll keep you clued in, but General Gretman in Kabul is your operational boss. I'm not an eight-thousand-mile screwdriver. Good night, Hal."

Catching the general's arm's-length tone, Coffman modified his response.

"I'll adjust to the situation," he said. "Good night, sir."

As Coffman hung up, he caught a reflection on the screen of his office. It looked austere and expeditionary. Too bad Killian hadn't noticed.

15

Unusual Spooks

Half an hour later, a V-22 Osprey came in from the north. When the thirty-thousand-pound aircraft was over the landing zone, the four engines pivoted vertically and the craft dropped straight down, hurling dust and pebbles at gale speed. As Tadcomb was placed on board, four men hopped out. Coffman had remained in his office. When the sounds of the departing aircraft faded away, he called out to Barnes in the ops center.

"Send in their team chief, Major," he said.

A few minutes later, there was a soft rap on a tent pole and a tall, solid man with no insignia walked in.

"Hi," he said, "I'm John Richards."

Dressed in standard-issue cammies, Richards had bland features. He projected an ambiguous presence, an agreeable man but not memorable. A casual acquaintance might assume he was an unassuming fortyish middle manager, satisfied with his position in life.

Coffman was determined to keep this formal and short. After shaking hands, he gestured for Richards to sit in a folding metal chair.

"Mr. Richards, it's a tight fit on this base," Coffman said. "But I'll try to support you."

"That's appreciated, Colonel," Richards said. "We're just three Americans plus a terp. We've brought our own gear, except for chow and water."

When they walked out to the ops center, only one other civilian was there, squinting at the screen streaming video from a UAV eight thousand feet above.

"Oh hi, Colonel," he said, casually extending his hand. "Stovell here. I'm impressed with your downlink. Five hundred mps, I'd estimate."

Coffman refused to shake hands, offended by the offhanded assumption of equality. Stovell shrugged. He was wearing a custom-made khaki shooting jacket with zippered pockets and cartridge loops, the name patch discreetly stitched in small type. Despite a trim cut that revealed no rotund girth, his face seemed slightly doughy. A stern personal trainer made Stovell sweat daily to hold down the weight brought on by his nightly $200 bottle of wine. Coffman stood motionless for several seconds before making the recognition.

"Stovell Industries," Coffman said. "Of course! You've designed some of our best simulations."

"You're confusing me with my skilled engineers," Stovell said. "My programming days are far behind me."

Venture capitalist J. Busby Stovell was a maze of contradictions, alternately seeking and hiding from publicity. In the '90s, while serving as a Marine corporal, Stovell was involved in an epic firefight in Serbia. His clever use of the internet had saved his recon team, and the press had raved about his digital genius. After his tour, backed by Silicon Valley, he wrote code designing quirky holograms, bringing virtual reality into every home, offering all shapes and voices. A two-year-old could wave his hand and a cuddly puppy would do a somersault. Stovell created entertaining alternate worlds in a bubble. He secured a copyright for the source code and generously shared profits with anyone who added an imaginative app. As his corporation expanded, he developed artificial intelligence products for the military. Stovell was the digital age successor to Bill Gates. His psychiatrist chided him for affecting three personas—inquisitive geek, brilliant chief executive, and quixotic patriot.

Coffman tried to make up for his gaffe in not shaking hands. There was always a consulting job to be considered after retirement.

"Well, gentlemen," he said affably. "I must say, you're unusual, even for spooks. Welcome to Firebase Bastion."

Assuming Coffman had loosened up, Richards put forward his request in a casual manner, "OK if we accompany your next patrol?"

Coffman frowned.

"I have none planned," he said. "My staff, however, will assist you here on base."

"Actually, Colonel, we have to get outside the base," Richards said, "to triangulate on our target."

"That's not possible," Coffman said. "The ANA is expected to provide local security and your small team obviously can't go out with the Afghans. The risk is too high."

"Maybe you can lend us a squad for a few hours each day?"

"There seems to be a misunderstanding," Coffman said. "I've been assured that your presence won't interfere with my mission. We running skintight. I didn't deploy with an extra squad. In fact, I didn't bring one extra Marine."

Having established his rules, Coffman closed on an avuncular note.

"The ANA colonel is due here now," he said. "You're welcome to sit in on our coordination brief."

16

We Don't Pick Targets

It was midafternoon when the small Afghan convoy led by an up-armored Humvee turned off the main road and headed to the base. It took the six vehicles another ten minutes to bounce across the irrigation ditches and park outside the revetment. A few dozen Afghan soldiers hopped out of Toyota pickups and sought the thin shade of nearby scrub bushes. After a sentry peeled back a strand of concertina wire, a handful of Afghans and Americans in battle rattle walked into the command tent.

A slender Afghan colonel with a trim black mustache strode up to Coffman and bowed before extending his hand. Like many senior Afghans who had dealt with Americans for two decades, he spoke fluent English.

"Colonel Ishaq, sir," he said formally. "I apologize for being late. After your drones left, we took harassing fire that slowed us down."

"No harm done," Coffman said. "Sorry I had to pull back the drones, but I needed eyes to cover our medevac. Now you can take over the local security."

Ishaq nodded without enthusiasm.

"We've been fighting very hard," Ishaq said. "Many losses. But I have brought a platoon, very experienced, for you."

When Coffman didn't immediately reply, Cruz spoke up.

"One platoon won't hack it, sir. In Sangin, we deployed three platoons to—"

Coffman tapped the table.

"No war stories, Captain. I decide how to protect my task force."

Cruz retreated into silence.

"Perhaps we can divide the perimeter," Ishaq said.

Coffman's face tightened. These slipshod Afghans were disrupting a month of solid planning.

"We protect our own perimeter, Colonel," Coffman said. "The fields are your responsibility."

"Of course," Ishaq said. "Every day, my *askars* will patrol the dangerous sector to the west, away from the road."

"And to the east?" Coffman said.

Ishaq spread his hands.

"My *askars* can alternate their routes," he said, "one day to the west and the next to the east. That's all I can spare. Kabul calls every day, demanding I get to Lashkar."

Coffman dropped his diplomat's tone.

"Without my artillery," he said, "you won't get there. You're to provide all local security."

Ishaq resented being reprimanded publicly but knew he had no choice.

"I can send more," he said, "in a day or two. I cannot tell you how much your artillery means to my soldiers. My adviser said you will destroy every target."

Ishaq's flattery mollified Coffman, who gestured to proceed. Ishaq beckoned toward a short, burly American with a full brown beard. He stepped forward and nodded respectfully at Coffman.

"Captain Matt Golstern, sir. I have the SF team with the brigade."

"Special Forces do fine work, Captain," Coffman said. "How about a quick review to ensure we're all on the same page?"

Golstern walked over to a large computer screen showing a photo-map and pointed at Route 11, leading to Lashkar Gah.

"We have three Afghan Joint Fires Observers," he said. "Each JFO has digital binos and a computer tablet. When he identifies a target, he transmits the data. Your artillery then fires, killing the bad guys, and Colonel Ishaq's *askars* move down the highway."

He held up a palm-size tablet connected to his handheld radio.

"We have requests on call right now."

Coffman looked over at the fire direction cell monitoring a bank of computers. The ops chief, headphones in his ears, nodded.

"Good," Coffman said. "Gentlemen, let's witness our inauguration."

The officers walked outside and climbed a revetment overlooking the four gun pits. Attached to each artillery tube was a touch-screen computer. Supported by a digital radio, the crew chief plugged in the firing data sent from the ops center. The loader inserted a bronze-green shell containing a GPS chip, twenty-five pounds of TNT, and seventy pounds of high-fragmentation steel. Each shell could hit a pinpoint target fifteen miles away.

The first lanyard was pulled. *BAM!* The howitzer bucked in its carriage, sending up a billow of dust. In quick succession the other three guns fired. *BAM, BAM, BAM.* At ten thousand feet, the rockets kicked in and the shells rolled across the sky in a display of vermillion red that looked like the Greek gods were bowling. The crews whooped with delight.

Several feet behind Coffman, Lasswell shook her head, smiled, and spoke in a soft voice to Cruz and Golstern.

"I never cease," she said, "to admire the blood lust lurking in the breast of every Marine."

Coffman glanced back at the junior officers.

"Remind me," he said, "how many shells on hand, Captain?"

"Eight hundred, sir," Lasswell said.

"Excellent. We're not taking any home with us."

★ ★ ★

EARLIER THAT DAY BACK AT THE ANA POSITION, the senior Afghan Joint Fires Observer—call sign Eagle Claw One—had climbed into the turret of his Humvee and focused his binoculars on a stand of scrub pines. He aligned the laser reticle on the trunk of a tall tree, clicked a button, and read the range: 760 meters. He waited several seconds and repeated the procedure. 767 meters. Close enough. Two sightings were required for the computer to confirm the GPS coordinates of a target. On a tablet attached to his digital radio, he tapped in the fire request form labeled in both English and Arabic.

The day before, someone had shot at the ANA convoy from those pine trees. Eagle Claw One had no idea whether the shooter was still out there. He entered the coordinates of the trees, marking them as an "enemy position." How many shells should he request? Umm, why not four in an open sheaf? That would spray shrapnel across two hundred meters. Might get lucky and hit a Taliban. After completing the form, he hit Send and adjusted his binoculars to watch.

Two miles away, Specialist Brian Noonan had the comm watch for the twelve-man Special Forces team. When Eagle Claw One's request popped up on his computer, he had forwarded it without written comment to the task force ops center where Coffman was presiding. Now, three hours later, the ops center was asking if the mission was still valid. Noonan queried Eagle Claw One, who replied yes. Noonan had his doubts. *The T-man hadn't moved in three hours?* But there was no harm in lobbing a few shells to raise morale among the weary Afghan soldiers.

Eagle Claw One and Noonan were both looking at their screens when the words SHOT OUT popped up. Forty seconds later, the screen read SPLASH. Eagle Claw One, his binoculars locked on the pine trees, heard a whoosh. The shell exploded within ten meters of the grid coordinates, releasing thousands of chunks of molten shrapnel. Eagle Claw One heard a deep, low *CRUUM*. In rapid succession, three more shells exploded, sending up columns of dirt and smoke. He adjusted his binoculars. As the smoke cleared, no animal or man staggered out from the pines. He looked down at his tablet, tapped the menu, and chose: TARGET DESTROYED. Estimate of Damage: UNK. Unknown.

Next, it was Eagle Claw Two's turn. His target was a shed with a rusty tin roof inside an abandoned compound. Yesterday, he had seen a tan Toyota creep out, only to duck back inside when the noise of a drone became distinct. He watched as three 155mm shells were fired. The shed buckled under their combined impact, and the tin roof collapsed. The shrapnel ripped apart the engine and chassis of the Toyota being prepared for use by a suicide bomber. Eagle Claw Two had no way of knowing that. Estimate of damage: UNK.

The third mission struck a poppy field recently harvested and empty of workers. The previous afternoon, five Talibs had ambled across, casually carrying over their shoulders their AKs by their barrels. It was a gesture of scorn toward the *askars* who dared not leave the highway. In the morning, Eagle Claw Three had glassed the field and seen nothing. But he didn't want to be left out when the 155s began firing. On his tablet, he selected as the target: ENEMY ON THE MOVE. After all, he had seen Taliban on the move sixteen hours earlier. After four shells exploded in a neat line along the far edge of the field, Eagle Claw Three tapped the menu on the screen: TARGET DESTROYED. Estimate of damage: UNK.

A few sheep had wandered from their herd grazing on the far side of the field. An eight-year-old boy and his little sister, switches in hand, had slipped through the undergrowth to drive them back. Too small to be seen above the poppy stalks, they were in the field when the first shell exploded, ripping apart the girl. The boy, farther away, was tossed against a tree and when he tried to stand, his knees buckled and he fell on his face, bleeding from his nose and ears.

LASSWELL AND CRUZ HAD REMAINED on top of the berm to watch the fire missions.

"I just heard from the doc," she said. "Corporal Jacobs suffered no brain damage from that viper bite, thank God."

She pointed toward Captain Golstern, who was sauntering over to them, munching on a fruit bar. His dust-caked cammies were frayed, and his beard hadn't been combed in days.

"I think our Special Forces amigo," Lasswell said, "has had his ticket punched too many times."

"Commenting on my superior military appearance?" Golstern said affably.

"We're standing downwind," Cruz said. "How long you been with the brigade?"

"Three months, one to go."

"Many TICs?" Cruz asked.

"Nothing serious. The usual rope-a-dope. IEDs, snipers. There's never heavy shit when you draw Ishaq. His brigade avoids meat grinder work. My team calls him Slick."

"What's your rate of advance down the highway?" Cruz said.

Golstern looked embarrassed.

"Five hundred meters a day. The *askars* stop every car at a distance. They don't want to risk being hit by a suicide bomber. We crawl along, then halt at noon to let the dozers push up a barrier for the night."

"Better pick up the pace," Lasswell said. "We're supposed to be out of here inside a week."

Golstern hesitated, and then decided to speak bluntly.

"Kabul's working up a full-court press to extend your stay," he said.

"Neva hoppon, mon," Lasswell drawled. "President not crazee."

Two tubes barked, and they watched the red arcs speed downrange.

"Bro, I don't mean to be a pain," Cruz said, "but that Afghan platoon you're dropping off? I'm parking them outside my lines. I'm not having a green on blue. Losing one Marine that way on my last tour was enough."

Golstern held up his hands in mock surrender.

"No dispute here," Golstern said. "The platoon leader's solid, but he doesn't know who might be an assassin."

He glanced at his watch.

"Time for me to join the herd and collect Ishaq."

Together they walked back to the operations tent. Coffman and Ishaq were standing off to one side, letting the watch officer handle things. Major Barnes hurried over to Golstern.

"Your team," he said, "has reported a civilian cas."

Golstern picked up a mic.

"What's going on, Brian?"

"A tractor pulled up," Noonan said over the speakerphone, "with two kids. One's totally mashed. From the pieces, we think it's a girl. The other's a boy, about ten, faint pulse, clammy skin, smashed-in face. He's projectile vomiting. I'd guess his skull's fractured. The farmer's screaming that our arty did it. I need a priority medevac Cat C."

Golstern held the mic up and looked down at the dirt, inviting a response from the Marines. Frowning deeply, Coffman strode forward.

"Those children may have tripped an IED," he said.

Colonel Ishaq stayed in the background and shrugged. Maybe, maybe not. Not getting any support, Coffman took a different tack.

"Who's responsible for each fire mission, Captain Lasswell?"

The Marines had gone over this repeatedly. Coffman was establishing the public record.

"A qualified Afghan, sir," she said. "We're strictly in support."

Coffman looked at Golstern.

"Same applies to me, sir," he said. "My team monitors the fire net. So does the ops center in Kabul. We don't interfere unless something's definitely wrong."

"Did anyone detect anything wrong with those fire missions?" Coffman asked loudly.

When no one answered, Coffman turned to Ishaq.

"Colonel, I can't request a bird all the way from Kandahar," he said. "This isn't our responsibility. We don't pick targets."

Ishaq shook his head.

"My Humvees cannot get through the Taliban," he said. "His family can try to drive the boy to the hospital. An unfortunate situation, beyond our control."

Off to one side, Golstern whispered to Cruz.

That's how Slick operates," he said. "Everything slides off him."

17

Tajiks Die in Helmand

Ishaq beckoned to one of the Afghans who had followed him into the ops center. A thin soldier stepped forward, eyes slack with fatigue, a full black mustache drooping down his tired face.

"Colonel," Ishaq said, "this is Lieutenant Ibril. His platoon is staying with you."

Coffman did not return the man's salute, instead gesturing toward Cruz.

"The captain," Coffman said brusquely, "will show you where to set in."

Ibril nodded blankly and followed Cruz out of the tent. Ibril's *askars* were waiting outside the perimeter gate. Without a word, they picked up their packs and fell in behind the two officers.

"Been in Helmand long?" Cruz asked.

"Eleven months," Ibril said.

"Long time in a shitty place," Cruz said.

Ibril glanced back at his haggard soldiers. Some looked too young to shave; others had thin mustaches, or had grown short, scruffy beards. Only a few wore helmets, and most hadn't bothered to wipe the grime from their faces. Many had the Mongol features common among northern tribes.

"We're Tajiks," Ibril said. "I started with fifty. Now I have thirty. A few more leave every day."

He seemed indifferent to the desertion. *This guy's beat*, Cruz thought.

"You're five hundred miles from home," Cruz said. "How they manage that?"

Ibril shrugged.

"They dress as civilians and pay for rides. They don't speak good Pashto. The Alikozai betray them. Foolish boys. Tajiks die in Helmand."

In single file they walked to the west side of the base. About seventy meters beyond the wire, scrub growth marked the edge of an irrigation ditch.

"Set up on the far side of the ditch," Cruz said. "We'll meet once a day. The ops center will coordinate your patrols. Captain Golstern is sending you his terp, Mohamed."

"Mohamed the terp," Ibril said in a mocking tone. "He is your spy?"

"He's qualified to call for fire," Cruz said tightly. "You're not. You want to leave the wire without artillery support?"

Ibril nodded slightly, accepting the offer.

"He can join us," he said. "We leave wire once a day, OK?"

It wasn't possible for one patrol to protect all sides of the perimeter. But Cruz could see Ibril was burned out, beyond caring about the opinions of the American advisers who came and went with the seasons.

"All right, take the west side tomorrow," Cruz said. "Anything you need?"

Ibril thought for a moment…a good night's sleep, the back pay owed his troops, replacements, hope.

"Water," he said, "batteries, NVGs."

"No night-vision goggles. The other stuff, fine."

Cruz looked back at the double strands of concertina surrounding the Marine perimeter.

"Here's the deal," he said. "I'll give you ten coils of wire to place around your pos. See that panel?"

He pointed to a flat, square olive-colored panel staked chest-high.

"That's laser radar. Any movement near our lines after dark gets popped. Tell your *askars*, anyone crossing that ditch dies. I'll send over MREs and three hundred in cash."

Ibril brightened a bit.

"I'll buy melons and goats," he said.

It took an hour to work out the lateral limits for their sectors, deconfliction procedures, radio frequencies, call signs, and patrol routes. When they were finished, Cruz thought about telling Ibril not to smoke too much *tshar*, the local hashish. He decided against it. No sense looking naive.

18

Planting Death

The afternoon shadows were falling when two dusty pickups sped through the open gate of Nantush's compound, scattering chickens, children, goats, and cows. Zar leaped out, carrying his prayer rug with its elaborate crimson stitching. Workers were clustered at the well, washing off the opium tar that blackened their hands and soiled their tunics. They hastily grabbed their shabby rugs and knelt behind Zar for the *maghrib*, or sunset prayer. As they finished, Ala slid into the front rank, proudly clutching his AK. When a worker patted him on the shoulder, he grinned shyly and bobbed his head, hoping Zar would notice.

"Is it true?" Zar said.

"Yes, I saw the *kafir* fall," Ala said. "Right over there, across the canal."

Zar frowned. A few hours earlier, he had seen an aircraft drop straight out of the sky and take off the same way, too fast for any RPG to hit. So an americani had been hit. The boy was telling the truth.

"Allahu Akbar!" Zar shouted. "A good start."

From the backs of the pickups, men were unloading plastic yellow jugs. Zar turned to Nantush.

"I must hurry," Zar said. "I have ten farms to visit. After dark, plant these mines near the footbridges and along the canals."

Nantush had a glum, confused look on his face.

"Don't worry," Zar said. "Guides will take the workers safely to the fields."

He turned to the workers.

"In Kabul," he shouted, "they scrape off their fingernails to make twenty dollars in a month. You earn that in a day. If the americani stay, you will have nothing. We Alikozai rule Helmand. With Allah's blessings, we will drive out the *kafirs*!"

An approving murmur swept through the crowd. Amidst shouts of "Allahu Akbar," Zar climbed into one of the pickups and drove away. As the workers stored the jugs, Nantush, his face contorted with anger, took Ala aside.

"See what you started."

"The mujahideen fight for Allah," Ala said. "To be a martyr, a *shaheed*—"

Nantush slapped Ala across the face, stunning him into silence.

"Never say that! A *shaheed* is a nobody. He blows himself up because his family needs money. You are *dawlat*. You have wealth and will inherit twelve *jeribs*. I have built the largest farm in the district. You will not throw that away."

"The Taliban praise me," Ala muttered.

"They are day laborers with no land," Nantush said, raising his finger for emphasis. "They fill you with stories of jihad because they have nothing else. If you die, your mother will cry forever."

"Zar flew to Mecca. He is hajj, and Alikozai like us."

"Yes, and he owns fifteen *jeribs*, a refrigerator, and a TV. When he visits Pakistan, he watches cricket and drinks liquor."

Ala looked down, scuffing at the dirt.

"Go help with the mines," Nantush said. "Make sure none are hidden inside our walls. And do not touch the wires!"

AT THE FIREBASE ONE KILOMETER TO THE WEST, a UAV operator had noticed the two pickups and zoomed in on Nantush's compound. On the wide screen, Barnes counted the jugs being unloaded.

"That could be a resupply of tractor fuel," he said. "Corporal Fuentes, when does tilling for the next season begin?"

"June, sir."

"So what do you suppose," Barnes said, "is in those pretty yellow jugs?"

"Send a patrol to find out?" Fuentes suggested.

"And have the good colonel kick my ass?"

Fuentes and the other computer operators laughed.

"Take a still shot of those jugs," Barnes said. "We'll show it at tonight's update."

19

Barter or Blackmail

The security platoon ate, slept, and kept watch in four-man teams inside the dozen bunkers ringing the perimeter. They used their large tent near the ops center only for meetings and storing gear. The CIA team had pitched a smaller tent alongside. In late afternoon, Richards walked into the platoon tent, where Cruz was checking the duty roster.

"Skipper," Richards said, "can you show me around the perimeter?"

Cruz guessed Richards was pushing fifty, and he talked with casual authority. His diffident tone was not an act. Richards was a modest leader, open to collaboration. Calm and unfazed in close combat, he had risen rapidly inside the close-knit Special Activities branch of the CIA. Once they were alone, he got to the point.

"We have an ELINT vector on our target," he said. "We have to get outside the wire. Using resection, we might pin down where he is."

"ANA's handling the patrols," Cruz said.

"I saw the route posting," Richards said. "The Afghans are going west tomorrow."

He gestured at the tree lines dense with green conifers and heavy undergrowth.

"Your east flank is open," he said.

Cruz sidestepped a direct response.

"You were at the meeting," he said. "Once more ANA arrive, they'll fill in."

Richards appraised him.

"That will take a day or two," Richards said. "In the meantime, you're exposed."

Cruz stopped walking as anger surged through him.

"You a colonel on attached duty, sir? An Omega?"

Richards smiled and shook his head.

"I was a sergeant in Force Recon," he said. "I shifted over to the company a long time ago."

"The CIA doesn't tell a Marine how to do his job," Cruz said. "I know what has to be done."

Richards smiled tolerantly.

"But you can't do your job, can you?" he said. "Coffman shut you down in that meeting. He seems to be allergic to you. You need an ally, a friend inside the royal court."

"That won't work," Cruz said. "The XO isn't on my wave length."

Richards laughed.

"An apt phrase," he said. "What if I told you we've monitored two calls in the last half hour? One was a snuffy blabbering about that snake bite."

Cruz had worked enough spec ops to admire the wizardry of the agency.

"You know I'm not cleared for that stuff," Cruz said. "Why are you breaking opsec?"

"Only a hypothetical," Richards said. "But what if the other call was to Pendleton, an officer keeping his boss back home informed?"

"If you mean Major Barnes," Cruz said, "what a weasel."

Richards looked amused.

"No, he's looking after his career," he said. "Hell, inside the Beltway, he'd be promoted. He broke an admin regulation. Other units allow cell phones, Snapchat, whatever. Troops even do homework with their kids over Skype."

"Where are you taking this?"

"Intercepts of our target point east," Richards said. "My team has to get out that way. So do you. Suppose we help Barnes avoid trouble? Then he helps us. Does that sound sensible?"

"Sounds like blackmail," Cruz said. "Turn him in."

"Then I'd also have to name the snuffy who called his wife," Richards said. "That makes me a rat and my team will get zero cooperation. My way is better."

"Barnes broke the rules," Cruz said.

Richards seemed surprised.

"You have what, sixteen years in the Corps? You've dealt with lots of shit off the books. What's really bothering you about listening to my workaround?"

Cruz knew he was temporizing, not wanting to risk blowback from Coffman if Richards's plan went awry.

"Nothing," he said. "All right, I'll listen. What do you have in mind?"

"A solution that helps us both," Richards said. "Don't look it as blackmail. Call it barter. Barnes will get the credit, and we get on with our jobs."

★ ★ ★

HALF AN HOUR LATER, Cruz walked into the ops center and beckoned to Barnes. Once they were outside, Cruz steered him away from the tent.

"Something bothering you, Captain?" Barnes said. "And by the way, good work today bringing in that wounded Marine."

Cruz ignored the patronizing tone.

"Major, the CIA team's been testing their spook gear," he said. "Richards asked me if cell phones were permitted on base."

Barnes stiffened, the color draining from his cheeks.

"Of course they're not. You know that."

Cruz hurried on.

"Some idiot's been talking to his girlfriend. I've bumped into this before, when I was training recruits. Millennials feel too damn entitled."

"Has Richards identified the user?" Barnes said.

"No," Cruz said, "and he doesn't want to blow relations with the troops by being a snitch. I think there's a simple fix."

"Really?" Barnes said. "What's your suggestion?"

"If the colonel announces that the spooks are listening to every call," Cruz said, "that'll end it, unless that snuffy has a single-digit IQ. We don't have to turn the whole base upside down and piss everyone off."

Barnes laughed in nervous relief.

"I like it!" he said. "Occam's razor, the simplest path is the best."

"There's, uh, one other thing. That CIA team wants to get a fix on their target off to the east."

"You heard the colonel. The ANA's taking care of patrolling. We stay buttoned up."

Cruz shook his head.

"Our east flank is open," he said. "The colonel will fry me if we lose anyone here on base."

Barnes smiled, confident now that he was back on his own solid bureaucratic ground.

"You really want this, don't you? OK, I'll do what I can in the ops meeting."

He pointed his finger at Cruz.

"But when I raise the topic, you don't say a word."

20

Reappraisal

When Cruz entered the ops tent for the evening brief, Lasswell was waiting.

"Barnes told me you want to patrol," she said. "He asked for my support with the colonel. I'm all for it."

"Appreciated," Cruz said. "You can't defend a castle from inside the drawbridge. It's just a matter of tactics. Nothing personal between me and the colonel."

Lasswell widened her eyes.

"Hello, Earth calling moon," she said. "This is totally personal! To the colonel, you're the problem. He's a clever manager, sensitive about who he never was. You remind him of what he hasn't done."

"Come on, he could care less about me. I'm the temporary help."

Lasswell shook her head in exasperation.

"You're here because you and General Killian fought the war together," she said. "Coffman never deployed. When you mentioned

Sangin, that was like saying, 'I fought on Iwo Jima in 1945, while you sat on your ass in the States.' You cut his pride. Let Barnes and me take the lead on this, OK?"

They sat down at the folding table. Coffman kept his meetings brief and on point. He let Barnes, as XO, step through the agenda, checking on the weather, personnel, and a dozen other items essential for managing the organization. When he reached the communications section, he stopped and looked at Coffman.

"Before we deployed," Coffman said, "I said there'd be no cell phones or other personal digital devices. This isn't a state troopers' barracks. We're never off duty. So if Lance Corporal No Brains calls his sweetie, it'll be intercepted and he'll face a court-martial. Pass that word."

Coffman sat back, pleased with himself. A messy situation, neatly dispatched. Barnes moved on to the next subject. Toward the end of the meeting, he showed the picture of the yellow jugs unloaded at the compound a kilometer east of the firebase.

"This happened about three hours ago, sir," Barnes said. "Taliban traffic on the ICOM net has increased. They're on the prowl."

"Tell the ANA," Coffman said, "to search that farm."

"They only have enough men for one patrol a day, sir," Barnes said. "With the Taliban planting IEDs, they have to move slowly. They can't cover to the east."

Barnes paused, letting Lasswell pitch in.

"If we take fire again," she said, "my men are exposed. A few patrols like you sent out this morning, Colonel, seem good insurance."

Her tone was neutral. The sun will rise, the wind will blow, the snipers will come, her artillery crew will be hit and the mission disrupted. She glanced into middle space, resuming the camouflage of the deferential subordinate.

"It would increase security, sir," Barnes said, "if Captain Cruz occasionally patrolled to the east. Richards's team has volunteered to help."

Coffman didn't snap back. He was thinking about his conversation with Killian. An occasional patrol would help his standing with the general. He looked at Cruz.

"What do you have in mind, Captain? Keep it short."

Cruz pointed on the map to a canal a kilometer to the east.

"If we patrol out one click to that canal, sir," he said, "we keep the muj beyond sniper range."

"All right," Coffman said. "Now, let's move on. Our mission is to provide fire support. Let's keep focus on that."

When the meeting concluded, Cruz walked over to Lasswell.

"Thanks for bailing me out," Cruz said.

"Purely selfish on my part," Lasswell said. "I've done my service time. My future includes a high-tech job, a loving husband, three adorable kids, and a beach house. Defending the ramparts against sword-wielding maniacs, I leave to you."

It was twilight when Cruz returned to the platoon tent. The squad leaders were waiting, sprawled in the dirt, swapping items from their MRE packets. Sergeant Denton was sitting with his left leg fully extended, his rifle resting on a rough cane.

"We're cleared to patrol tomorrow," Cruz said. "Break out your maps and tablets."

Cruz had invited the CIA team to attend the meeting. He gestured toward them.

"Mr. Richards and his team will be joining us," Cruz said. "They're known as Other Government Agency, OGA, as in CIA."

Everyone grinned.

"Third Squad's up tomorrow," Cruz said. "Sergeant Binns, why don't you lead us through the op order?"

With his lips pursed as he squinted through his black-rimmed military-issue glasses, Sergeant Oliver Binns looked like a teacher perpetually disappointed by the behavior of his students.

"First, I need to know," Binns said, "how many CIA are coming with me?"

"Four," Richards said. "Stovell and I will trade off carrying the ruck that contains our computer. With us will be Tic, our terp, and Eagan, our shooter. We're all prior enlisted. We won't be any bother."

Binns opened up his notebook.

"OK," he said. "Let's go through the patrol brief."

21

Hunters of Gunmen

Cruz had assumed the full CIA team wanted to hear the brief. But Binns hadn't plodded through five sentences before Eagan gulped down a handful of Skittles and popped to his feet.

"Gonna check sight data," he said to no one in particular, "before we lose the light."

Eagan was wearing expensive shooting glasses with a faint yellowish tint. A V-shaped face squeezed his features together and his eyes flickered restlessly, as though charged by an alternating electric current. Short and overly muscular, his head seemed too small for his thick shoulders. He reminded Cruz of a badger or wolf, a predator constantly scanning for danger and prey.

Eagan walked back to his tent, opened his gun bag, and took out a long rifle with a polished mahogany stock inlaid with the date 8 June 1999. From an aluminum case, he extracted a telescopic sight with three lenses and five dials on the right side. After attaching the scope to the barrel, he climbed to the top of a nearby revetment. He screwed into the rifle's underside a slender steel rod with three extendable legs on the bottom. Standing upright, he pushed the tripod into the dirt, tugged the rifle butt into his shoulder, and peered at the distant fields. He pressed a side button as though taking a picture, shifted the rifle slightly, squinted, and clicked again.

Several Marines were watching this procedure. A thin black Marine nudged his companion.

"Lamont, is that him?" Sergeant Colin Ashford said.

Sergeant Brian Lamont, who had a reddish complexion and startling blue eyes, wasn't sure.

"He's got that hawk face I remember from *Soldier of Fortune*," Lamont said. "But, Ash, that dude's fucking old, maybe forty."

"Maybe he's a photographer," a third Marine quipped. "We'll be on Fox or CNN."

"Don't talk like a motard," Lamont said. "That's a boss HOG."

The Marine looked mystified. Lamont tugged at his rune, a bullet with a hole in its center dangling from a leather thong around his neck.

"Ashford and me, we're HOGs. Hunters of Gunmen, boot. Every sniper carries a bullet with his name on it. That way, he won't get shot 'cause he's carrying the bullet destined to snuff him."

Lamont pointed toward Eagan.

"You think he's taking pictures for CNN? Hell no! He's plotting aim points, getting set for his next kill."

When Ashford picked up his rifle, Lamont did the same. Together they walked up the revetment and stopped a few feet below Eagan.

"That's a cool stock," Ashford said. "What you shoot?"

"Six point five polymer," Eagan said. "Hollow point."

"We're 0317s too. We got Mark 13s with Nightforce scopes," Ashford said, holding up his rifle. "Solid hits at a thousand meters with 300 Win Mag hard point."

"No targets here that far out," Eagan said. "Terrain's not that open."

Eager to agree, both Marines nodded.

"Never seen a scope like that," Ashford said.

Eagan smiled wryly.

"These software chips will put us HOGs out of business," he said. "I click on the target and the computer calculates windage, drift, humidity, and gravity. Once the computer locks in, it follows the target even if it moves. See for yourself."

Ashford squinted through the scope.

"Shit," Ashford said. "I can count the hairs on a goat's ass. What's this package cost?"

"One hundred K for rifle and scope."

"Oh man," Lamont said, "the Corps will never spring for that."

The two Marines took turns looking through the scope. Lamont stroked the inscription on the stock.

"1999. You win that year?"

"Tricky crosswind," Eagan growled. "Gave the home boys an advantage. I took second."

"Sounds like ancient history," Ashford said.

When Eagan's face tightened, Ashford stumbled back.

"My bad," he mumbled.

Three seconds of silence, then Eagan grinned.

"OK, wise ass, this your first time downrange?" he said.

Lamont and Ashford shifted uneasily.

"We got one pump each," Lamont said. "No shooting time, though."

"It kind of sucks," Ashford said. "The Green Machine not snoop'n and poop'n like it used to."

"Going out tomorrow?"

Both nodded enthusiastically.

"We're attached," Lamont said. "Any advice would be appreciated."

"Not in my job description," Eagan said, shaking his head. "I don't want to get cross with your patrol leader."

The Marines exchanged a disappointed look.

"How many rounds you carrying?" Eagan said.

"Hundred each."

Eagan looked at them sharply.

"Uh, two hundred?"

"Sounds better. What's your call sign?"

"Winmag."

"Should've guessed," Eagan said, walking off the revetment. "See you on the firing line."

"Think we'll get into some shit tomorrow?" Lamont said.

"What'd you hear today?"

INSIDE THE PLATOON TENT, Binns was droning on. Cruz was only half listening as he wrestled with what role he would play. He didn't know these NCOs. As the temporary commander, he should let the squad leaders do their jobs and stay out of their way. If he pushed, he'd be resented. Don't run the show. Let them go out, get shot at a little bit, earn their Combat Action Ribbons, and tell war stories when they got back home. Plus, he owed his family to return in one piece. Another reason to stay in the background.

It took fifty minutes for Binns to wind down. By then, Cruz had a sense for how the squad leader would react outside the wire. *Thorough*, Cruz thought, *but plodding*.

"That wraps it up," Cruz said. "And Sergeant Binns, I'll tag along in the morning. Need to stretch my legs."

He kept his tone conversational and offhand, but Binns wasn't having it. He looked startled, then offended.

"Sir, I can handle my own patrol," Binns blurted out. "You heard me go over our immediate action drills, and my countersniper plan. I'm no boot."

Out here, you're a boot, Cruz thought. *The whole platoon is.* Binns was walking the line of insubordination, but Cruz didn't want him sulking. He decided to deflect the resentment with banter.

"The OGA are our guests," he said. "I'm going because I'm the host. You're the patrol leader, Sergeant."

As long as you do it right.

Day 3

APRIL 8

22

The Green Zone

At midnight, Cruz set out to check the lines. He heard the mosquito buzz of a drone overhead, its muffler removed to remind the enemy they were being watched. He walked slowly so the sentries could see the infrared strobe attached to his body armor, and in the bunkers he kept his conversations low in order not to disturb those asleep a few feet away.

His last stop was inside the ops tent, where he stood behind a UAV operator. The thermal image on a large screen showed three men shoveling in a ditch. They could be farmers working at night to escape the day's heat.

"This is the fourth group I've spotted," the operator said. "They know the UAV's watching them. One guy mooned us."

"Setting in IEDs?" Cruz said.

"Or clearing out weeds," the operator said. "They're playing Whack-A-Mole. They know the rules. We can't kill 'em for working for a living."

Cruz returned to his tent and had barely dozed off when he was awakened by a wailing siren. Across the base, Marines scrambled into trenches, but nothing happened. No explosions, only a few faint crumping sounds.

The Taliban had hastily fired several shells from a single mortar tube. The shells were instantly detected by counter-mortar radar. Even before they exploded outside the perimeter, a computer calculation of the launch point had been sent to the artillery and mortar crews.

As Cruz reached the ops tent, he heard the sharp reports of outgoing shells. The thermal screen showed two black figures crumbled in a field. Farther away, a dark smudge from an exploding shell blossomed and faded. A dozen Marines were laughing and exchanging high fives.

Cruz walked over to Lasswell.

"That was fast," Cruz said. "How'd you get permission to fire?"

"No one's ever court-martialed an algorithm," she said. "Once we had the point of origin, we fired. Lobbing mortars at us is a sucker's game. They'd be crazy to try it again."

★ ★ ★

CRUZ WENT BACK TO SLEEP. At first light, he met Richards and Binns inside the ops center. Two Pashto-speaking Marines with headsets were listening to the local radio chatter.

"What're you picking up?" Cruz said.

Sergeant Ishmel Ahmed, born in Kandahar and now living in Laguna Beach, was short, slightly overweight, and in his late twenties. His tortoiseshell eyeglasses and long-stemmed pipe gave him an academic look that was reinforced by his deliberate speaking cadence. Ahmed walked to the photomap and swept his hand to the right.

"Most ICOM and VHF traffic is coming from the east," he said. "A few Talib bands of four to six, typical stuff."

"Pakistan on the line?"

"Most definitely," Ahmed said, affecting the clipped Pakistani accent. "All the usual partridge in a pear tree code-word garbage. They are most upset with our presence, *sahib*."

Cruz turned to Richards.

"Do you have any questions?"

"Have you heard Farsi accents?" Richards said.

Ahmed's eyes widened.

"Ah-ha! A CIA plot afoot!" he said.

"Share and share alike," Richards said. "My team helps you, you help us."

"We haven't heard any Iranians," Ahmed said. "Only locals bitching that the Americanis will spoil the harvest. We're as welcome as cholera."

That provided an opening for Binns. *The captain thinks he's so fucking smart*, Binns thought, *but he's bungled this one.*

"Sir, we don't have a terp," Binns said. "We can't talk to the hajjis. So we'll get no info?"

Cruz caught the accusatory tone. He looked at Ahmed, who recoiled.

"I don't make house calls," Ahmed said. "Those are animals out there."

"My terp will translate for all of us," Richards said.

"Fine," Cruz said. "Let's get started."

On the far bank of the Helmand River five kilometers northwest of the base, Zar lived in a spacious compound shaded by a grove of olive trees. The four guard posts on the compound wall sat atop decaying mounds of sandbags. Only one sentry dozed at his post. The fighting had ceased years ago.

The main house was tastefully furnished. Hand-knotted red Isfahan rugs covered the aromatic cedar floors, a fifty-five-inch TV provided entertainment, and a french-door Samsung refrigerator held cold tea and ice cream. To smother its noise, the twenty-kilowatt Kohler generator was tucked against the outside wall of the compound, while at the opposite end a small room housed a huge clay oven where servants prepared the meals. Large yellow sunflowers and rose bushes lined the path from the guest quarters to the main house.

Inside the comfortable guesthouse on the other side of the courtyard, Zar sat sipping morning tea opposite the fretful Persian. In the distance they heard the occasional boom of the Americani artillery fire. A map was spread out on the rug between them. The Persian was poring over names and numbers in a black notebook.

"I have to visit at least fifteen farms today," he said in a challenging tone.

Zar pointed at the camel-skin valise.

"How much is left?"

"About a million."

"Good."

"No, it's bad," the Persian said. "The Baloch are saying we can't move our heroin. If the Americanis find the lab, we're finished."

"All Baloch are liars," Zar said. "You attend to the buying. I'll take care of the infidels."

The Persian glumly shook his head.

"Last night didn't end well for your mortar crew," he said. "I felt the Americani shells shaking the earth. They're strong."

"Don't talk about what you don't know," Zar snapped. "Even as we speak, my brave warriors are preparing to slaughter them."

My warriors? the Persian thought. *This idiot is taking action on his own? I hope Balroop hurries with his plan.*

121

★ ★ ★

CRUZ STOOD OFF TO ONE SIDE as Binns aligned the seventeen-man patrol. All wore Kevlar vests and midcut helmets with ear cups, wireless headsets, and boom mics. Clipped to the nape of every vest was a small antenna that broadcast its location. Most carried the M27 automatic rifle with a suppressor, a thirty-round magazine, laser-sighting tools, and a Leupold variable-power scope, permitting every rifleman to hit an enemy skull at six hundred meters. In addition, the patrol included a two-man 7.62mm machine-gun crew, two 40mm grenadiers, and two snipers. Adding up the weight of the armor, weapon, ammo, and hydration packs, each Marine was carrying about eighty pounds.

Cruz thought the grunts looked like sixteenth-century French knights, cloaked in heavy armor yet lacking horses. Walking in eighty-degree temperatures was an exertion; jogging was torment; sprinting was out of the question. Every step of the way, the patrol's location was tracked at the ops center, allowing the mortars to continuously adjust their aim points. Massive amounts of explosives waited on call to incinerate or blast apart any enemy. The age-old tactic of fire and maneuver to close with the enemy had morphed into applying an accurate, intense volume of fire, followed by more fire.

At point was an engineer, Corporal Atsa Wolfe, a Navajo with a broad bronze face and unruffled manner. Rifle slung across his back, he was fiddling with the dials and headset attached to his PSS-14 mine detector. Behind him stood Sergeant Ashford, sniper rifle cradled in his arms.

"I keep you from being blown up, bro," Wolfe said, "and you keep the shooters away from me."

"I've been waiting four years for this, Wolfe," Ashford said. "I got you covered."

The CIA team had slipped into the middle of the column. Richards was carrying a standard automatic weapon, and Eagan had slung over his shoulder his sniper rifle with the monstrous sight. Stovell, in his Abercrombie-tailored utilities, had no weapon. Instead he was carrying a stiff-sided knapsack with a zippered front and a miniature satellite dish.

The fourth member of the team was wearing US Army Ranger cammies that hung loosely on his slender frame. Clean-shaven and grinning hugely, he playfully patted Stovell on the head and stood behind him in the column. It took Cruz a few seconds to realize this was Tic, the interpreter. Since this wasn't the time for introductions, without speaking Cruz quietly joined the line, rifle in hand and on his back a compact digital radio with a three-foot whip antenna.

Seeing this, Binns drew Cruz aside.

"Excuse me, sir," he said tensely, "but I don't want you carrying that radio. It'll draw fire. I got all the freqs covered. And another thing—outside the wire my Marines call you Cruz. The Talibs know the word for captain."

"I carry my own comms, Sergeant," Cruz said quietly, "and my own rank. Tell the devil dogs to call me *Captain* Cruz. I want the muj to know I'm coming for them."

Binns sucked in a breath.

"Sir, this is my patrol. You're making me look bad."

Bad beats dead, Cruz thought. But he'd pushed this far enough. He looked at Binns and said nothing.

"So that's how it is," Binns said to show his defiance.

"That's how it is."

As he cleared the wire with the sun full in his eyes, one sniff told him he was in some backcountry. He smiled. He shouldn't call it "backcountry," but it was true. Whether deployed in the farmlands of Colombia, the Philippines, Iraq, or Afghanistan, the smell was the same. He breathed in the mixture of wood cooking fires, smoldering garbage pits, and shit decaying in the damp earth. In any backcountry, the same families talked to each other daily, decade after decade. Within a small community, the first rule was to take care of your own and not piss off your neighbors. This was the Green Zone, miles of flat fields, acres of tall corn and still more acres of brilliant poppy bulbs, green tree lines, deep canals and shallow ditches, thick-walled compounds, and sullen tribal clans. Taliban territory. If the Marines stayed for a hundred years and spent a trillion dollars, that wouldn't change. Cruz accepted the hostility as he did the wood smoke, a fact of life.

Six hundred meters east of the firebase, Hassan squatted in the warm, thick foliage, safe from the thermal imagery that relied upon a significant temperature difference between the heat of a human body and the surroundings. When Hassan had fought the Marines years ago, he had learned to shoot from the far side of irrigation ditches and use the tree lines to escape. Now the Marines were back, and Zar had selected Hassan to conduct the first strike.

Together with porn and snuff videos, the Taliban watched Hollywood war films and copied American techniques. Hassan had watched *Platoon* four times, memorizing how Sergeant Elias had inspected his squad before each patrol, correcting the slightest errors. Now Hassan lined up his five fighters. None wore a helmet or an armored vest. Speed was their advantage. Shoot and scoot.

The oldest, Alam Shah, stood first in line, his teeth yellow from neglect, military fatigues baggy and his *shalwar kameez* shirt soiled from not washing his left hand after wiping his ass. Slow thinking and stubborn, he was Hassan's older cousin. Hassan tapped at a rust spot on Alam's SKS rifle. Alam shrugged and continued to chew a mouthful of sunflower seeds.

Following him came tall Ajbar, cradling his glistening PKM machine gun, his *kufiya* turban tightly wound. When Hassan moved up in rank, he wanted Ajbar to be his successor. But he feared Zar or the Quetta shura would choose Alam. Replacements and promotions were based upon family ties and clan loyalties.

Ibir, a teenager from Hassan's village, was next in line. He was grasping the stock of an RPG, or rocket-propelled grenade launcher that looked like a rifle with a giant onion bulb at the end of the barrel.

Behind them, Ala was fidgeting like an restive puppy. Hassan planned to keep the son of Nantush, a wealthy khan, out of the fight. Last in line was Yakoz, an itinerant worker from Farah Province, grinning absently under his threadbare *pakul*, the flat gray woolen Pashtun cap. He carried the sturdy AK-47, with magazines stuffed into a Soviet-style green chest harness.

Hassan watched the firebase, stroking his thick beard as he swept his binoculars back and forth. An hour after daybreak, he saw a line of figures exit the wire, heading south. He gestured to his companions and they slipped down an irrigation ditch. They paused in the ditch to take off their sandals and put on the Skechers dangling from their shoulders. Then they set off to intercept the American patrol.

THE MARINES PLODDED ALONG at a slow pace, with Wolfe moving the mine detector back and forth like a pendulum, his eyes focused on the ground, looking for wires or scuff marks. They would head southeast until reaching the wide canal about a kilometer away, then turn north and meander back to base. With a UAV buzzing overhead as a scout, the ops center was monitoring the route. Cruz hoped that any lurking Taliban would have the sense to fall back and avoid being trapped. That way, he'd protect the base and return to Pendleton without writing a single letter.

He swept his gaze across the flat terrain. Tall, thick mud walls, sun-bleached to a light brown, encased one-story farmhouses scattered randomly across the fields. Straight lines of verdant trees and underbrush marked the main irrigation sluices running from the canal to the east. He viewed the countryside as a maze of traps and escape routes for the muj. Stands of beeches with dark, heavy leaves provided concealment from thermals and overhead cameras. Disease spores infected the hardy hybrid trees on the banks of the ditches. As their limbs rotted, thick vines snaked from one tree to the next, weaving an impassable tangle. The Talibs knew every opening and back trail, enabling them to slip down a ditch and minutes later pop up in some scrub growth a quarter of a mile away.

On this warm April morning, the emerald-green fields were ablaze with poppy bulbs in white, ruby, and regal purple colors. Small bands of laborers were moving among the poppy rows, grim bearded men with whipcord sinews, accustomed to walking ten or more miles each day with a long, easy gait. They wore shapeless long-sleeved shirts that draped down to their knees, baggy pants, and sandals. Every boy or man was a watcher, a dicker, an informant eager to report the route the infidels were taking.

The patrol cut through a long field where three men and two boys were lancing tiny slits in the bulbs. Their soiled *dishdashas* were splotched with dabs of the dung-colored opium tar, and their hands were black from dropping the poppy resin into their small sacks. They sullenly ignored the few courteous *salaam*s from the Marines. One pointed at the plants crushed under the boots of the Marines and shouted angrily. In response, Ashford grinned and squirted another dab of the pastel-orange Silly String he was using to mark the route for those following.

Upon reaching a row of columnar junipers dense with the green growth of spring, Wolfe stopped. On his tablet, the patrol route was superimposed in red over a digital photomap. Although the route ran straight ahead, Wolfe turned slightly left. Binns called a halt and darted up.

"Wolfe, the fuck you going?"

Wolfe pointed to hoof marks in the mud.

"Following the sheep," he said casually. "Same general direction."

"No," Binns said. "Stay on the GPS track. Go through the bush. You got the ECM on, right?"

"Yeah," Wolfe snapped. "But Sergeant, don't tell me how to do my job. We have sheep back on my reservation. I can spot any cover-up of an IED and move faster."

"Hell yes," Ashford chimed in. "Why hack through this shit when we don't have to? Wolfe knows the drill."

"Ashford, shut the fuck up," Binns said. "Wolfe, we're not following sheep. Get back on track."

Cruz didn't intervene. He felt old. He had witnessed hundreds of such disputes on patrols. Wolfe was probably correct, but Binns had the rank and responsibility.

The patrol moved ahead, breaking brush and hacking at vines, plunging into a chilly chest-deep creek, scrambling in sopping cammies up the far bank, following the Silly String through more broken scrub before stomping across another field ablaze with bulbs of brilliant magenta and deep burgundy. Again a small band of laborers refused to respond to polite *salaam*s. The patrol wound through the next tree line, across the next field, and the next.

Most fields were about an acre, the size of a football field. Rows of tangled trees and thick shrubs clung to the edges of the irrigation ditches and larger canals. Scattered haphazardly amongst the fields were walled compounds. Inside each, three or four adobe or cement one-story buildings with flat roofs sheltered a dozen or more members of an extended family. A few courtyards boasted shade trees with bark tough enough to survive the nibbling of the goats, sheep, and cows herded inside each night. Some compounds boasted a refrigerator, and most had television sets. Electric power was provided via a single strand of heavy wire, supported by short, thick poles running across the fields from one compound to the next. The government in Kabul provided the dams, generators, and the transmission wire, while the Taliban collected a thin tax of a few dollars per month from each farmer. Entrepreneurs from India had delivered cheap cell phone service and for the first time in eight years, the Taliban had ordered the service shut down at night because the americanis had returned.

As the Marines passed, children ran out to gawk, while the older boys and men peeked over the walls. The Marines were using their telescopic sights as spyglasses. When a man's head popped up over a wall, an exasperated Marine sighted in and mockingly yelled, "Bang, bang, you're dead, motherfucker."

"Knock that shit off," Binns yelled.

By midmorning, the sun was searing and the Marines were sweating profusely. Cruz checked the time. In the past hour, they had covered half a mile. At that turtle pace, they'd finish the route in eight hours. Each Marine was carrying a CamelBak holding six quarts. They'd be out of water before returning to base. They had hydrated well the night before, so he wasn't too concerned.

Half an hour later, they struck a stream too deep to wade across. Binns called a halt to let Wolfe and Ashford search for a fording point. The Marines knelt or sat in line, none venturing outside the lane marked by the string. As they had crossed the fields, Tic the terp had sauntered along like a tourist, greeting the lancers in Pashto, waving with a map in his hand, and occasionally scribbling a note. Some *nishtgars* had looked startled, while others had laughed.

Now Tic, squatting on his haunches near Lamont at the rear of the column, was waving at some workers, who were yelling back angrily. One threw a rock at Tic, who wagged his finger and seemed to repeat what he had said.

"What's that about?" Lamont said.

"They're asking why we're here," Tic said. "I tell him to burn their poppy."

"You don't have to jerk them around," Lamont said.

"It's my job," Tic said.

Lamont gestured with his sniper rifle toward the laborers bent over in the fields.

"Whoa. I thought you were one of them," Lamont said. "You American?"

"I'm whatever Stovell wants me to be," Tic said.

Lamont walked into the bushes and unzipped his fly. He had barely begun to pee when a clod of dirt hit him in the back. He whirled around to face two boys who were chucking more clods at him and shaking their fists.

"They're telling you to squat," Tic said, laughing. "A *mal* doesn't piss standing up. Not to worry. Eagan will pop them for you."

Eagan idly gave Tic the finger and continued to glass the tree lines. Tic laughed and walked away.

"That's one strange dude," Lamont said.

"That fucker's a lot smarter than you or me," Eagan said. "Paid more too."

"What's he really do?" Lamont said.

"Like he told you, he screws with their minds."

Taking advantage of the halt, Stovell had unzipped his pack and taken out a computer that roamed the radio frequencies. Through relays, the intercepted data flowed to a cryptology center back in Virginia. From there, vectors and clues were sent by text and voice back to Stovell.

"Fort Meade identified one short burst from our target," Stovell said. "He's about three miles northwest of here, using Silent Circle encryption."

Richards was kneeling a few feet away.

"Can Meade break it?" he said.

Stovell shrugged. "You want Langley to assign a high priority?"

"Let's save that chip for later," Richards said. "How you coming, Tic?"

Tic, who had spread out his map, grinned.

"The lancers think I'm working for the Baloch. I'm warning them they'd better get paid now."

He poked his finger at a few dots along their patrol route.

"I told them the Marines plan to spray the poppy. Most workers laugh. They don't care because their poppy's been bought. The guys who threw rocks? They're upset because their harvest hasn't been sold yet. That means our target hasn't finished buying around here."

He put away the map as Cruz and Binns came up.

"Op center's picking up heavy ICOM chatter," Cruz said. "Dickers reporting our route."

"Sergeant Ahmed says he's hearing crap about crows and kites and bags of flour," Binns said. "The Talibs have eyes on."

Binns moved off and Cruz stayed with the CIA team. With Stovell shielding him from the workers in the fields, Tic dug a small hole with his knife, inserted a black metal disk that looked like a hockey puck, and filled in the dirt.

"A pressure plate," Richards said. "We get a radio signal if someone steps on it. It gives us direction of movement."

Tic was again yelling at the laborers.

"Stirring them up? Cruz said.

"Correct. Get them worried about selling their poppy," Stovell said. "Our target might come up on the net and talk too long."

"I don't want you to endanger my people," Cruz said.

Stovell pointed at the patrol route outlined in blue on Cruz's handheld display.

"Skipper, you know you're going to get hit," he said. "Our team makes no difference."

Cruz kept his eyes fixed on the laborers.

"I hate the Green Zone," Cruz said. "Lost too many good devil dogs in these fields. We thought we could change those people, win them over."

"Did you really believe that?" Stovell said.

"The generals believed it," Cruz said. "I'm just a grunt."

"Democracy was never the future for these tribes," Stovell said. "We're antibodies in this culture. You were sent on a fool's errand."

"We should be careful what we say," Cruz said. "The troops might get the wrong idea."

Stovell smiled.

"In Helmand, heroin rules," Stovell said. "Our generals know that. So does every grunt after his first patrol. Still we fight on, year after year."

"Yet you're here, and you don't have to be."

Taking no offense, Stovell laughed.

"I find the chase challenging," he said. "Don't forget—I was a corporal before my corporate days. John Richards was a staff sergeant back then."

"And Eagan?"

"He's why I'm still in one piece."

23

A Deadly Engagement

Wolfe and Ashford returned from their recon, cammies dripping and water sloshing from their boots.

"We can cross a hundred meters upstream," Wolfe said.

The patrol followed the squirts of Silly String along the bank to a spot where a herd of sheep had trampled down the underbrush. In brown, slow-flowing water up to their knees, the Marines waded across. When he reached the edge of the next field, Wolfe abruptly stopped. The warning needle on the metal detector had jumped into the red, and the warning buzz was screeching like a zipper being jerked back and forth. He knelt and gently probed with his hunting knife until he exposed a nine-volt battery the size of a cigarette pack, with a thin wire attached to its positive pole.

He snipped the wire and carefully followed it through the damp dirt for several feet to the wooden pressure plate wrapped in plastic. He lay down flat and peered at the slight opening between the two thin boards. He looked up at Binns, who was standing nervously several feet away.

"Carbon rods," he said. "They don't emit a metallic signature. We got lucky to find the battery."

He traced a wire from the boards to a nearby pile of leaves. Brushing them gently aside, he uncovered a dirty yellow plastic jug filled with blue ammonium nitrate. The wire led inside the open top of the jug.

"A directional charge," he yelled genially, "pointed toward the path."

Binns jumped back.

"We'll call the engineer detachment," he said, "to blow it."

That automatic response worried Cruz; Binns wasn't thinking.

"We don't have the time," Cruz said. "We have to push."

Annoyed at being contradicted, Binns glared at Cruz.

"I don't want to wait around here," Wolfe said. "Blasting caps are frisky mothers. Let's get off this trail and cut through the field."

Binns had the sense not to argue further. He gestured at Lamont.

"Lamont, we'll be exposed out there. You fall back to the rear and keep eyes behind us."

As Wolfe swept toward the middle of the field, Ashford squirted a large X near the IED and followed in trace. Eagan moved up and fell in behind him. When Ashford looked at him, Eagan tapped his scope. Contact likely.

HASSAN WAS WATCHING FROM A TREE LINE when the Marines discovered the IED. Now the infidels were walking across an open field, with no place to hide! He wagged his finger at Ajbar, who was eagerly clutching his PKM. Young Ibir had shoved a rocket into the nose of his RPG. Hassan flapped his hand for them to wait. He would take the first shot. He couldn't see the americanis if he lay down flat, so he squatted on his haunches, squinted through the wavering iron sights of his AK, and squeezed off the first burst. *Whack, whack, whack.* The solid 7.62 rounds snapped out, quickly joined by Ajbar's PKM, firing with the slow, heavy percussion of a sledgehammer. The Marines went flat so fast that Hassan wasn't sure if he had hit one.

★ ★ ★

WHEN THE ROUNDS CRACKED BY HIS EAR, Wolfe dove headfirst into the poppy plants. Ashford and Eagan did the same.

"Get rounds downrange," Eagan was yelling. "Eleven o'clock."

"I can't see shit!" Ashford shouted.

"Makes no difference," Eagan yelled. "No friendlies out there. Shoot!"

Wolfe and Ashford responded. Lying prone a few Marines farther down the line, Cruz jerked at Binns's boot.

"Move the pig up to Eagan," he shouted.

"I want to keep the machine gun here, sir," Binns yelled back. "It's my fucking squad!"

"Eagan has the azimuth!" Cruz said.

"All right, all right!" Binns yelled. "Curtis, gun up! And crawl, goddamn it, don't stand!"

"What'll you make, Eagan?" Cruz yelled.

Eagan had swung his rifle in the direction of the incoming rounds and read the compass heading on the scope.

"Three ten magnetic," he read. "Four hundred meters to that tree line!"

Binns and Cruz were looking at the spot on their iPads, while Sergeant Mad Dog Doyle was talking with the mortar crew chief back at base.

"Jimenez," Binns shouted, "get your thumper up here!"

A thickset Marine ran up with his Mark 320 grenade launcher. *Pop!* A 40mm shell the size of a baseball arced out over the field and four seconds later exploded among the trees. *Pop. Pop. Pop.* A few feet away, Mad Dog Doyle was calling in a fire mission.

Hassan knew better than to stay where he was. His men were shooting blind and return rounds were cracking by, none yet close to their position. It was time to fall back before being fixed and pounded.

BACK AT THE OPS CENTER, Coffman had grabbed the mic from the watch officer. He knew he should stay off the net and not distract the patrol leader. *Thunk.* The first shell had left a mortar tube. Coffman knew he had no role to play. *Damn it!* He had to know what was going on.

"Wolf Six, this is Eagle Six actual. Sitrep, over."

Cruz had stayed out of the fight, letting Binns command his squad. The M240 machine gun was hammering out short, steady bursts, the sound reverberating off the ground. The grenade launcher was thunking in an easy rhythm.

"Eagle Six, this is Wolf Six," Cruz said into his boom mic. "Wait one, out."

Coffman's frustration boiled over.

"Wolf Six, don't tell me to wait! What is your situation? Over."

In the ops center, Marines glanced at each other.

"Eagle Six, this is Wolf Six," Cruz radioed. "We are exchanging fire. No friendly cas. Over."

"Wolf Six, good. But damn it, keep me informed."

Doyle was crouching, head above the poppies, calling a correction to the mortar pit. Eagan had attached the steel rod to his sniper rifle, stuck the supporting tripod into the ground, and was glassing the tree line.

"They're hauling ass," Eagan said. "Keep putting rounds into the bush."

★ ★ ★

HASSAN WAS GRABBING AT HIS FIGHTERS, shoving at them to run deeper into the woods, put more trees between them and the Marines. Young Ibir, though, couldn't abide running away without firing one of his beloved rockets. He stepped out of the underbrush, the RPG pointed skyward, and settled the butt into his shoulder for a quick shot.

Wolfe yipped and pointed. Ashford aligned on the target and snapped off one shot. The bullet hit Ibir center chest. First T-man down.

"Yes!" Ashford shouted.

Eagan had adjusted his scope to scan deeper into the tree line. The three lenses on the sight refracted light to distinguish movement against the stationary background. The computer identified a blur lasting one-hundredth of a second and calculated the location, allowing the twenty-power lens to focus in. The computer then slewed in front of the target until finding an opening among the trees wide enough, about three feet, to allow the 6.5mm Creedmoor to cover 1,200 feet in half a second.

Lugging his PKM, a muj was blundering so awkwardly through the bush that Eagan thought he could have found him without the computer. He had set the trigger on automatic. He did nothing but hold steady and absorb the recoil. The round hit Ajbar in the back, pushing him forward into the dirt. Second T-man down.

Eagan worked the bolt and continued scanning.

ALA, THE ELDEST SON OF NANTUSH, was the next to fall, because he didn't know what to do. Was he supposed to run away or help Ajbar? He ran a few steps back and paused, an easy target. The bullet struck him in the neck.

HASSAN HAD TAKEN COVER behind a thick oak. He lay there for a few seconds, breathing hard, trying to think. Ibir, then Ajbar, and now Ala struck down in what…a few seconds? That couldn't be. He rose to one knee and looked carefully about. The first hollow point shattered his right shoulder and lodged in his chest cavity. The second ripped through his ass.

His piercing scream reached Alam Shah, who was safely hiding in a gully. Without hesitating, he ran back and reached down to aid his younger cousin. A bullet smacked into his cheek. Fifth T-man down.

That left Yakoz, the itinerant worker. After exiting the far side of the tree line, he ran pell-mell across the next field and slipped into a deep drainage ditch. He lay there for several minutes, gasping. When no one joined him, he wondered what he would tell Zar, who was sure to beat him. He hid his AK, and climbed out of the ditch. It was seventy kilometers to Farah Province, but he had enough money to pay for a motorcycle ride. The sole surviving mujahideen headed home.

EAGAN KEPT SCANNING, but the computer detected no further movement in the tree line. It had been four minutes since the last incoming round. The outgoing rate of fire from the patrol had slackened to occasional short bursts. Mad Dog Doyle wasn't sure whether to call for more mortar rounds. He looked from Binns to Cruz, uncertain which of them was in charge.

"Continue the mission?" he said.

Cruz didn't reply, deferring to Binns. The sergeant held up his hand, listening for a moment.

"Cease fire!" he shouted into his mic.

The Marines stood up and looked around, grinning and softly yelling, "Yeah! Yeah!" The first firefight for the squad. Combat Action Ribbons for everyone. No friendly casualties. Enemy down. All right!

"We lit those fuckers up!" Mad Dog Doyle shouted.

"You heard the bronze gong, didn't you, Sergeant?" a bemused Stovell said.

"What the fuck you talking about?" Doyle said, hastily adding a "sir."

"Homer," Stovell said, "wrote that warriors hear imaginary drums in battle."

"When was that?"

"Three thousand years ago."

"I wasn't born back then."

Up at point, Ashford was grinning hugely. He raised his sniper rifle triumphantly and looked back down the line to Lamont.

"Tango down!" he yelled. "In the black!"

"Bro!" Lamont shouted back.

Running forward to congratulate his friend, he lurched slightly outside the Silly String. *WHAM!* The earth heaved up in a black mushroom of smoke as the tremor from the explosion shook the ground. Lamont flew several feet in the air and landed in a crumbled mess, helmet knocked off, armored torso bent at an odd angle, tiny red bits of his leg dripping from the faces of stunned Marines. The percussion slammed into their eardrums and for a few seconds sealed the grunts in a tomb of silence. It was broken by Lamont's moans that quickly mounted into a piercing wail.

"My leg!" he screamed. "My leg!"

Cruz was trying to clear the ringing in his head when he saw Corpsman Ronnie Thomas running up the line of frozen Marines.

"Hold! Don't go out there!" Cruz yelled. "Wolfe, do a sweep!"

Wolfe stumbled past Cruz, paused to suck in a breath, then turned outboard into the shroud of gray smoke. He swept the metal detector back and forth, quickly covering the short distance to Lamont. Corpsman Thomas was right behind him, fumbling to tear the plastic covering off a tourniquet. Lamont was sitting upright, weight balanced on his outstretched arms and hands, looking in horror at the gushing stump where his right leg had been. Thomas knelt down and frantically adjusted the wide black strap around the stump. He twisted hard on the knob to cinch the strap tight and stop the spurting blood. Lamont shrieked in fresh pain.

Binns was looking around absently, tapping his helmet, his brain concussed, unable to make sense of what was happening. Cruz had bent over, opening his mouth to emit sharp yawns, forcing air to clear his ear canals. Mad Dog was tugging at his armored vest.

"Sir, it's Eagle Six," Doyle said.

Cruz pressed his voice mic.

"Eagle Six, this is Wolf Six. We have one critic. Over."

"Wolf Six," Coffman said. "Medevac's on the way. Get that patrol back here!"

"Eagle Six, I repeat. Cas is critic. Recommend Lima Zebra here."

A moment's pause before Coffman came back on the net.

"The zone's not secure. We're talking about a V-22."

We're talking about a fucking life, Cruz thought.

"Eagle Six, zone will be secure in ten mikes."

He switched off. Binns and Eagan had gathered around him.

"Set up over-watch from three points," he said. "One fire team with Eagan to search the bodies. Binns, take the second team with Wolfe and clear an LZ to the west. Third team, cover our backs with the 240."

As they turned away, Lamont let out another piercing cry. Ashford pivoted to run to him. Eagan seized him by the collar and jerked him around.

"Stay focused," he said. "Your job's with Wolfe. He's exposed without you."

Ashford fell in behind Wolfe and the fire teams dispersed, leaving Corpsman Thomas cradling Lamont in his arms, rocking back and forth, waiting for the morphine to grab hold. Doyle hunkered down so that the corpsman could shout into his mic.

"Talkin' to aid station," Mad Dog whispered to Cruz.

Lamont's right leg had swollen balloon-size, straining the stitching of his trouser. Thomas looked up, his face white and lips quivering.

"How critic, Doc?" Cruz said.

"Femoral's cut," Thomas said. "The tourniquet's so tight the blood has nowhere to go. Come on, sir!"

Cruz checked the time. Ten minutes had passed.

"Fifteen mikes out."

Cruz moved away and checked his iPad. Blue dots showed where the fire teams were set up in over-watch positions.

Lamont moaned again. Doyle was holding him now, crooning to him.

"I got you, bro. We got you."

"Arrgh fuck, I was an asshole, goin' with you to Tijuana."

"Sush, it's all right, man. That don't mean nothin'."

Thomas was holding up the saline packet, ferociously concentrating on the drip into Lamont's arm.

"It's not all right," Lamont said. "Aww Jesus, I was a shit. I can't die like this."

Binns was kneeling, his head almost touching the ground. He had grasped Lamont's hand and was softly praying. Lamont's back was arcing in spasms, and the sepulchral blue tint had spread from his lips to his cheeks.

"You tell Amy I love…"

"Tell her yourself, bro," Doyle said. "Big bird coming all for you. Wheee. You're going home."

"You think so?"

Lamont's breathing was rasping and gargled.

"Brother, I know so."

Over the next several seconds, Lamont eased away. Thomas put down the IV packet and closed Lamont's eyes. Mad Dog gently detached himself from the body, while Binns frantically looked around for a poncho liner or something to cover the body. It was the fifth time Cruz had witnessed a young Marine slowly die. Each time, in that last, liminal moment he had heard a final profession of love, not anger.

"Sergeant Binns," he said, "inform base that we have one angel."

A few minutes later, the V-22 streaked in from the northeast at seven thousand feet, its twin engines pivoting vertical directly over the purple smoke popped to mark the LZ. The aircraft dropped straight down, the four-thousand-horsepower thrusters scorching the earth and raising a huge billow of dust. Marines carried Lamont up the rear ramp, removed the body from the litter, and gently placed it on the cold metal floorboards.

"For Christ's sake," the crew chief yelled, "leave the litter so we can strap him in."

"I'm keeping it," Doyle shouted back. "We may need it before we get back to base."

While Doyle folded up the litter, Cruz radioed for the fire teams to pull back in. Binns kept his head down and didn't try to take back control of the patrol. Returning by another route, Wolfe led the patrol across a dozen fields empty of laborers. He detoured three times in response to beeps from the metal detector. At the rear of the column, Eagan occasionally stopped to place his monster rifle on its tripod and scan to the rear. The returning patrol received no incoming fire.

24

No Gaps in My Lines

It was early afternoon when Cruz, still in battle rattle, followed Barnes into Coffman's office. In a dozen sentences, Cruz summarized the fight. When he finished, Coffman seemed doleful.

"Did Lamont suffer?" he said softly.

The question startled Cruz. *Suffer? He fucking died! He was too scared to feel pain.* When you're blown up, the body goes numb. You know parts of you are missing. Fear grips the mind.

"He held on for a while, sir," Cruz said, "but he was in shock. The corpsman gave him two morphine shots."

Coffman's tone suddenly changed.

"And whose fault was it?" he snapped. "Was there negligence out there, Captain? Think before you answer."

Standing off to one side, Barnes pursed his lips together, signaling Cruz to tread cautiously. While returning to base, Cruz had thought about what to say. Lamont shouldn't have veered outside the Silly

String. But blaming him wouldn't change what happened and would cause his parents more pain.

"It was a judgment call, sir," Cruz said. "He was moving forward to help Ashford when he tripped the IED."

"That's your story? That it was an accident? An act of God? No one made a mistake out there?"

"The area was laced with IEDs, sir. Lamont moved a few feet the wrong way and…"

Coffman was mulling how he would phrase his after-action report. There had to be someone to blame.

"He tripped the IED *after* you were in contact?" he said. "Why was he moving at all? You could have launched Scorpion to locate those bastards!"

"We didn't need a second drone, sir," Cruz said. "Once the muj opened fire, we had an fix on them. Solid ISR."

"Five enemy killed, you're sure?"

"Yes, sir. Sergeant Ashford put down one. Eagan smoked four with his wonder gun. We recovered a few papers from the bodies. We have photos and DNA. That CIA team knows its stuff."

Coffman had forgotten that CIA was part of the patrol.

"This isn't about them," he said. "You were in charge. How many weapons recovered?"

"We didn't bring any back, sir. They were extra weight. We broke them up and scattered the ammo in the ditches."

"That was my decision to make!" Coffman said. "What the hell can I show to the press? Goddamn it, we'll look foolish, like we're back in Vietnam, claiming enemy kills that never happened."

"Yes, sir," Cruz replied evenly.

"No, it's not '*yes, sir,*'" Coffman said sarcastically. "It's an error in judgment on your part."

Coffman was fed up with Cruz. *So what if he'd fought in Fallujah and Sangin? He couldn't take out a local patrol without fouling up.*

"Major Barnes, interview all the patrol members," he said. "I want a complete account in forty-eight hours. Every statement signed. "

Barnes was startled.

"Sir, uh, we don't have the authority to interview CIA," he said.

Coffman quickly backtracked.

"All right, we'll put that aside for now," he said. "You both know how disappointed I am, and sorry about Sergeant Lamont. That will be all."

Once he was alone, Coffman carefully wrote his report. Then he called General Killian.

"I don't want word of this getting out prematurely," Killian said. "Worst thing would be a mother hearing about this by rumor."

"We're buttoned down, sir. The troops have no cell phones, no access to internet."

"OK. What happened?"

"The ANA provided only one understrength platoon. I had to send out my own patrol. Hit an IED."

"Shit luck," Killian said. "What about the operation? You on schedule?"

"We've delivered every fire request, sir. But I'm disappointed in Colonel Ishaq. The ANA are the slow movers. We're more than holding up our end."

"Hal, I never doubted that," Killian said.

Emboldened by the softer tone, Coffman tried to make Killian part of the operation.

"The UAVs," he said, "are providing continuous video. If we stay inside the wire, we can avoid those damn IEDs. But that leaves us open to snipers."

Killian didn't rise to the bait.

"We've been over this, Hal," Killian said. "I'm not your direct boss over there. I'll keep you informed, but how you protect your lines is up to you. Or you can call Gretman in Kabul and he'll work it out for you."

Coffman felt his cheeks flush. The reprimand stung. He should have known Killian would respond like an old-school grunt, expecting the commander on the ground to make the hard decisions without turning to his superiors. He adapted instantly.

"Aye-aye, sir," Coffman said. "I'll patrol as necessary until the ANA get up to strength. There'll be no gaps in my lines."

25

Do Your Best

When Cruz walked into the platoon tent, Binns was finishing the debrief. Most of the Marines were sitting cross-legged on the tarp spread across the dirt floor. Some were sprawled against their rucks. The CIA team was standing in the shadows in the rear with the platoon sergeant, Staff Sergeant Sullivan.

"Tough day out there, devil dogs," Cruz said. "But we can handle it, right?"

The Marines shifted uneasily. Two casualties on two patrols weren't good odds. A hand shot up.

"We going out again, sir?"

"That's not decided," Cruz said. "But 2nd Squad's on deck and should hold a rehearsal."

"Agreed," Sergeant McGowan said. "It's time to nut up and pay those bastards back."

Wolfe shyly raised his hand and tapped his chest.

"Wolfe, that's appreciated," Cruz said. "If we do go out, we need you at point."

Doyle was frantically waving his arm.

"Sir, I can operate all the systems," he said, "and I got the joint qual card."

"OK," Cruz said. "Mad Dog, you're my systems operator and you control fires."

A husky Marine, nervously shaking a few pebbles in his hand, spoke up.

"Shit, sir, why not declare a no-entry zone? Any muj within rifle range of our firebase gets pounded?"

Cruz looked down at the name stitched on the right breast pocket.

"We don't know who's a Tango until he opens fire, Corporal Kirkland," Cruz said. "We're not driving farmers off their land."

Face taut with anger, Kirkland didn't back off.

"They're part of this. They know where the muj planted the IED that killed Lamont."

There it was, the direct challenge Cruz had been expecting. He had thought about how to phrase it, how to reassure them without blaming Lamont for making a fatal mistake.

"We have the edge. We're better trained. The Tangos lost people today. They'll stand farther off. So set your BZs at four hundred meters. Wolfe knows his job. Stay inside the markings and think before acting, every minute and every step."

Cruz looked from face to face, hoping to break the soggy mood. After a few seconds of silence, Kirkland spoke up again.

"I donno, sir, you've kind of taken over. You have your shit together, but we don't know you."

Best to have this out now, Cruz thought. *Stop this spiral.*

"You don't have to know me. When I was a squad leader in Fallujah, I went through three platoon commanders in thirty days. I didn't get to know them. Focus on your job, not how well you know me."

Kirkland kept his head down, fidgeting and poking at the tarp. Cruz waited, while silence dripped like moisture down the tent walls. Finally, McGowan waved his hand.

"Yeh, well, Captain," he half shouted, "I look at this like Groundhog Day. I'm all good with wasting the stinkies. Did it on my last push, and I'll do it this time too."

"Solid attitude," Cruz said. "McGowan, you're a sergeant. I'm the captain, above me there's Colonel Coffman, above him, there's a general. How do we handle this? Simple: We're the worker bees. We do our best. I don't care what job you're given. You do your best."

He waited until another hand went up.

"Lamont was our third cas, sir. There's gonna be a lot of worried people back home."

Whenever he lost a Marine, Cruz avoided a lugubrious tone. The time for mourning was later.

"I don't want you thinking about back home," he said crisply. "This firebase depends on you. You concentrate on that. You lost a brother today. So let's share some good thoughts about Sergeant Lamont."

Again a short silence while the Marines shifted gears.

"Monty and I've been tight ever since sniper school," Ashford said. "He couldn't remember names, so he called everyone 'dude,' even the staff sergeant."

"I was feeling mellow that day," Sullivan said. "Only had him fill a hundred sandbags."

Smiles and laughter all around.

"Monty loved his woman," Ashford added.

"You got that right," Doyle said. "I never should've taken him to Tijuana."

"Mad Dog," McGowan said, "sometimes you're an asshole."

"All right," Cruz said. "Let's wrap this up before it degenerates."

"Sir?" Doyle said.

"No more from you, Sergeant."

"No, sir, I want to say a prayer."

Cruz hesitated, then slowly nodded.

"Lord," Doyle said, "please watch over my brothers, as we watch over one another. And Monty, you watch over us too. Amen."

McGowan's eyes widened.

"Mad Dog," he said, "where'd you learn that?"

26

The War Is Over

Within hours, every echelon in the chain of command had been notified of Sergeant Lamont's death. The Marine component at the Central Command in Tampa informed the battalion in Pendleton. The battalion's casualty assistance call officer, or CACO, and the chaplain were awakened at four in the morning. Two hours later, a sergeant was driving them up I-5 to Newport Beach.

They grimly studied the instructions set out in a thorough Marine Corps order. The chaplain, Navy Commander Paul Higgins, was wearing his dark blue uniform, and company commander Captain Ward Miller was in starched khakis with a stack of ribbons across his left chest.

"This is my first run as CACO, Father," Miller said. "Any tips?"

Higgins was a slender friar, Order of Franciscan Minor, with a slight paunch, soft features, and a friendly manner.

"Beyond the prescribed steps," Higgins said, "I try to stick to patience and silence. It's such a shock. What counts is that we're there. Don't say much."

"Lamont's the first KIA," Miller said. "But there were two mede-vacs before him. This'll upset a lot of parents."

"Many of the troops married?"

"About twenty in that platoon," Higgins said. "I hope to hell I don't have to call on any wife."

"You don't think this was an oddity?"

Miller snorted.

"An IED hit? That means the grunts are patrolling and the Tangos are on the prowl. No, I don't think this was a one-off."

"If we're not asked," Higgins said, "don't mention the closed casket. There'll be time for that later."

They arrived shortly after eight at a small bungalow on a quiet side street. After they knocked, a slight, pleasant-looking woman in her fifties opened the door. When they introduced themselves in subdued voices, Mary Lamont sagged, grasping the door for support.

"It's Brian, isn't it?"

It wasn't a question.

"Well, I can't leave you standing there," she added. "Please come in."

She gestured them into the small living room, overstuffed with a thick divan and a heavy leather chair facing a huge TV screen that dominated the room. As the two men sank into the couch, she sat on the edge of a straight-back chair and began talking. Her last defense was a torrent of jumbled words.

"Tim, my husband, loves football," she said. "So does Brian. They watch it together. Can I get you some coffee? Are you sure this isn't a mistake? Tim's on his way to work. He never remembers to take his cell phone. I don't watch much television myself."

She stopped talking, drew in a breath, and waited.

"Mrs. Lamont," Captain Miller said softly, "it is with the deepest regret that I must inform you that your son, Brian, died yesterday from hostile fire—an explosion—while serving with his unit in Afghanistan. The Secretary of the Navy extends his deepest sympathies."

Miller said nothing more, letting the room absorb the silence. Mrs. Lamont dipped her head as her tears flowed. Higgins offered his handkerchief as she grasped for a box of Kleenex and dabbed her cheeks. After a while, she gathered herself.

"I have to call Tim's office. Oh, dear, I should call Amy, Brian's girl. They had some silly spat before he left. They're practically engaged."

She put her hand to her lips.

"I don't know what to say to her."

"Why don't you wait until your husband is here," Father Higgins said gently. "You can talk it out together."

"Were there others?" she said. "Is his friend, Colin Ashford, all right? He and Brian were going surfing when they came home next week."

"I'll check and let you know," Miller said.

"I hope," she said, "no one else was hurt."

She looked at both of them, unsure what else to say or what would come next.

"Your son, uh, Brian's casket arrives in Dover, Delaware, the day after tomorrow," Miller said. "If you wish to be there, the government of course will take care of all expenses. I'll look after everything personally and go with you. The, uh, transfer ceremony will be brief and dignified."

"How do we get him home?" she asked softly.

"I'll take care of that," Miller said. "A brother Marine will accompany your son at all times. He won't ever be alone."

She sat upright, twisting a tissue, her face bewildered.

"Brian wasn't staying in the Marines," she said. "I mean, why did he die? The war is over."

Remembering the priest's advice that silence can be solace, Miller did not reply.

27

A Political Vise

It was a humid afternoon in Washington—approaching twilight back at Firebase Bastion—when an angry Senator Hank Grayson of California called Towns. Liberal in social policy and conservative in security matters, Grayson was a persistent critic of the administration. He chaired the Defense appropriations subcommittee and took himself seriously, lashing out at any perceived slight.

"Mr. Secretary, I've been informed about the death of Sergeant Lamont," he said. "The Lamonts are my constituents. Let me cut to the chase: What the hell's going on in Helmand?"

Towns felt uneasy. A vast hierarchy separated him from the corporals pulling the lanyards a continent away. He was as ignorant of the details of the fight as was Grayson.

"Senator, we have a small artillery unit providing temporary support," he said. "As you know, we have several of these deployed. It's standard procedure not to reveal publicly the exact location. That helps the enemy."

"That's damn nonsense," Grayson said. "The enemy obviously knows where that unit is! I want to know why it's there. You've already cut a deal to get out of Afghanistan. What's this all about?"

"Senator, the Pentagon isn't part of the negotiations," Towns said. "But the Taliban have been increasing their attacks, after promising not to do so. In any deal, you can't be pushed around."

"I don't buy that rationale, Mr. Secretary," Grayson said. "Our soldiers aren't bargaining chips. To quote your own president, fighting not to win is obscene. Yet it sounds like you're doing exactly that. To put it bluntly, you're fighting the wrong war. My committee wants a public hearing of what's going on."

"I'll get back to you on that, Senator."

AFTER HANGING UP, Towns called Armsted to fill him in. The National Security Advisor was sitting in his small office in the West Wing with Diane Baxter, the White House press secretary.

"Mike, it's a shame about that soldier," Armsted said. "I have Diane on the line with us. She's, ah, a bit concerned."

Diane Baxter had a congenial, relaxed style that played well with the press corps. She knew when to be serious and candid and when to duck a pointed question with a smile and a vague remark.

"Hi, Mike," she said. "The press will put this on the front page for a day. We have to make sure this story doesn't grow legs. I'm concerned about you appearing before a Senate hearing."

"Grayson was insistent," Towns said. "He can hold up our budget."

"Buy time," Armsted said. "Maybe tell your contacts at *WaPo* we'll be out of there in a few days?"

Clever bastard, Towns thought, *insinuating I leak to the press and setting me up if anything else bad happens.*

"That might encourage the Taliban," he said, "and undercut the operation. I think it's best to say nothing and let this blow over."

Armsted didn't hide his disappointment.

"When POTUS steps off Air Force One," he said, "he'll be steamed. I'll try to keep things calm, but I can't promise."

The phone call ended with Towns sensing he was caught in a political vise. He knew that doing nothing weakened his standing with President Dinard, who didn't fully trust him in the first place. Towns didn't care that his mannerisms—sparse comments in White House meetings and the lack of a flattering smile—conveyed aloofness. He had joined the administration to give back, at the same time telling himself that he had the wealth and self-confidence to leave anytime he wanted. He liked to believe that he was secure in himself.

Sitting at his nine-foot nineteenth-century mahogany desk, he pulled out a sheet of stationery embossed with the seal of a golden eagle. This was his fifth condolence letter in nine months, and he was modest enough to appreciate the lightness of his burden. Previous Secretaries of Defense had signed thousands of letters. He picked up his pen and wrote carefully to avoid a spelling mistake. Lamont, not LaMont or Lamonte. In his neat, tiny penmanship, he labored over each sentence to convey his heartfelt tone.

His sorrow was as genuine as his gnawing sense of unease. It was easy—too easy—to rationalize that he couldn't dwell over one fatality in a military that numbered over one million. But was he leading or merely presiding over a giant machine? How much difference did his presence as Secretary of Defense make? He imagined the owner of a football team, sitting so far above the stadium that he could scarcely see the field of strife, much less hear the jarring collisions of the competitors. He thought of asking some probing questions of the Chairman, then decided against it. Admiral Michaels and the other brass had recommended the deployment. This wasn't the time to second-guess or go wobbly.

28

Zealots

While Towns was writing his consolation letter, Mullah Akhim Sadr was driving through the dense evening traffic in the city of Quetta. As the leader of the Quetta shura, or high council, his devotion to the Taliban cause was absolute. At the age of sixty, Sadr was a hard man, convinced that tens of thousands—no, hundreds of thousands if need be—must embrace martyrdom so that the just and global rule of Allah could be restored, with Jerusalem again its caliphate. With his approval—*with his joy!*—two of his five sons and his only daughter had gone to paradise as suicide bombers.

Inside the Pakistani air base, Colonel Balroop was waiting in an abandoned hangar. After Sadr was escorted inside, they exchanged perfunctory courtesies without smiling. Balroop intended to place the Taliban emir on the defensive.

"Your representatives are negotiating with the Americans," he said. "You are close to victory. Yet you attacked Lashkar Gah, when I asked you not to."

"The American president was stalling," Sadr said. "We had to keep up pressure."

"But he didn't fold, did he?" Balroop said. "You embarrassed him when you cut off the city. He has thrown it in your face by sending back Marines."

After decades of battle, Sadr was not impressed by a few artillery tubes.

"A tiny base," he said dismissively. "We will drive them out."

Balroop's eyes grew wide with surprise and disbelief.

"Like this morning?" Balroop said. "Zar's fighters were wiped out! I listened to the villagers on their ICOMs."

"Farmers don't know what they're talking about," Sadr said.

"They're burying five mujahideen as we speak," Balroop said. "Five! Your locals are overmatched. That American base threatens our lab."

"Zar has put out many mines," Sadr said. "And I have assurances that only *askars* operate to the west."

"What if a drone detects the firepits?" Balroop said. "What then? The Americans must be forced to leave, and Zar doesn't have the brains to do that alone."

By combining guile with an iron will, Emir Sadr led the most powerful Taliban shura in Pakistan. He resented a lecture from a Punjabi.

"You went behind my back yesterday," he said calmly. "You reached an agreement with the Persian without telling us."

"I consulted with you beforehand," Balroop said.

"No, you told me you had a plan," Sadr said. "You take too much for granted. Helmand is our land. You don't decide for us."

Balroop ignored the rebuke. Sadr, like most of the elder Taliban, suffered from several maladies. Without ISI aid, he would be living in a hovel, wracked with arthritis and hacking up phlegm and blood. He would let the old Pashtun complain, as long as he agreed in the end.

"The Persian provided the money for the poppy," Balroop said, "not your shura. I made a swap with him, a few missiles for the Asians. They are on their way now."

"We don't need them. I have my own plan. I have brought a *fidayeen* for Zar to use."

Balroop was surprised that Sadr had acted so quickly.

"A good idea, if you can get him in position," he said. "My plan does not depend on chance. A front is already forming in the Gulf. You must do your part when the weather changes."

Sadr stroked his beard, as if lost in thought.

"How much did the Persian charge for the missiles?" he said.

This was the question Balroop had dreaded. The Taliban controlled the lab and counted every bag. There was no room for evasion.

"The first twenty-five million from the sale," he said.

"The shura must receive the same," Sadr said.

Balroop didn't hide his exasperation.

"Ridiculous. The heroin comes out through Baluchistan," he said. "Without the ISI, you have nothing—no money, no shelter, and no future. You know that!"

"And you know that after our *fidayeen* strikes," Sadr said, "the Americans will pull out. Then there is no need for the Asians you paid for. You made a bad choice."

They haggled for half an hour before agreeing the shura would receive ten million, if the *fidayeen* succeeded. Balroop was now committed to paying to others the first thirty-five million of the estimated one hundred million. He knew how his general would react. Either the *fidayeen* or the Asians succeeded, or he would be fired.

Both attacks depended upon Zar. To keep his composure, Balroop rubbed his forehead before speaking in a slow, cadenced tone.

"Zar will be here shortly," he said. "His temper, those beheadings…a rabid dog cannot kill a bear. He will fail if left on his own."

Sadr held up his hand in reassurance.

"Zar will do his part," Sadr said. "He owes obedience to the emir."

When Zar arrived shortly later, he was in a foul mood, having ridden for hours in a ten-year-old Toyota with sagging springs. Balroop and Sadr waited politely while he gulped down sugary tea.

"How's the struggle going?" Sadr began.

"Fine, Qaed Sadr," Zar said. "I've put out many mines. This morning, we killed six americanis. But still they ran toward our bullets. We lost two mujahideen, praise to Allah."

Sadr expected Balroop to challenge the lies. Instead, the Pakistani colonel changed the subject.

"You're taking good care of Mullah Khan?" Balroop said.

"The Persian enjoys our grapes," Zar said. "He has a few more farms to contact."

"So the harvest is not complete," Balroop said. "And what about our shipments?"

"With the americanis digging in next to us," Zar said, "we can't move the product."

Balroop gauged Zar, calculating how far to provoke his pride.

"Are you afraid to attack their base?"

Zar burst out a torrent of Pashto curses. Balroop let him run down, then spoke softly.

"How many mujahideen can you gather in one day?"

"Ha! Thirty, perhaps forty."

Balroop looked at Sadr, who nodded in agreement.

"I will leave the brave mujahideen to talk privately," Balroop said.

He walked outside to the parking lot. A small, thin teenager, barely past puberty, was standing next to Zar's Toyota. He shyly adjusted his *shemagh*, tucking in a stray strand. A few feet away, two Pakistani sentries were smiling sadly. When Balroop approached, the senior corporal saluted and stood at attention. Balroop frowned, waiting for an explanation.

"The boy brought with him his teacup from the *madrassa*, Colonel," the soldier said. "That's all he has. He asked for a Coca-Cola, with ice."

Several minutes later, Sadr came out of the hangar, followed by a scowling Zar. Without saying goodbye, Zar roughly pushed the boy into the worn-out Toyota and left. Balroop looked at Sadr.

"Zar thinks too much of himself," Balroop said.

"If the *fidayeen* fails," Sadr said, "I have ordered him to use the Asians."

"Too much depends on him," Balroop said.

Sadr nervously fingered his prayer beads.

"Zar is angry, but will do as instructed," he said. "He believes he is the sword of Allah. It is written in the Qu'ran, 'Soon shall we cast terror into the hearts of the unbelievers.'"

After Sadr had left, Balroop reflected on their conversation. He distrusted the two true believers. Both zealots flaunted their piety. Sadr scented his body with musk, and Zar cleaned his teeth with a pine twig. Balroop believed men who embraced medieval ablutions had medieval minds. He hoped his next duty station would be in Islamabad among civilized Punjabis, far from these Pashtun Islamists with their fantasy of establishing a caliphate, after they had slaughtered all unbelievers.

Day 4

APRIL 9

29

Martyr or Murderer

Feeling unappreciated, Zar brooded during the return drive. He was a warrior of Allah, not a schemer like the Pakistani colonel. When the Marines had come years ago, the mujahideen had fought them with mines and small ambushes, inflicting tiny cuts until the *kafirs* tired and went home. This time, after one ambush that had not gone well, Mullah Sadr had summoned him. He resented how the emir had instructed him as though he were a child, how to lure the Americani to the *fidayeen* and how to obey the Asians if that failed.

Zar drummed his fingers and looked out at the hillsides devoid of trees or brush, dreary even in the soft pinkish hues of twilight. He hated all things in Pakistan, except cricket and scotch. He glanced at the boy sitting to his left, face pressed against the window. He wondered how often the boy had been debased inside that Pakistani madrassa. He felt a slight erection, or was it that he wanted to be distracted?

"Give the *halek* a Coke," he said.

They reached Nantush's compound in the middle of the night. He waited outside, mulling over his instructions from Sadr, until Tulus drove up in a Hilux.

"You have them?" he said.

"Two mortars, six shells," Tulus said.

"Turn on your headlights," Zar said.

With the Americani only a few kilometers away, Tulus knew this was foolish but kept his mouth shut. Both vehicles, with headlights on, drove into the courtyard.

"Put those tubes in a shed," Zar said. "Then go back to the mosque."

Lights from kerosene lanterns, candles, and a few fluorescent bulbs shone from several buildings. In the main house, a cluster of sobbing, ululating women attended Ala's body, scrubbed clean and wrapped in a white cotton cloth. A few older children sat dozing against the walls. In adjacent rooms, a score of toddlers slumbered fitfully. Hassan's body, also washed, lay in a smaller building alongside his dead cousin and the other two from Hassan's village. In the morning, the three bodies would be placed in a trailer behind a tractor and trundled to the nearby village cemetery. The fifth martyr had been buried in a field, unattended by mourners, the site marked by a white cloth attached to a scraggly pole.

Zar did not enter the vestibule of the dead, where the women would reproach him with tear-filled eyes. He waited outside, telling his driver to flash the headlights on and off. In a few minutes, Nantush came out, offering no greeting. Zar ignored the man's surliness and offered measured sympathy for his loss.

"You lost a son, may Allah grant him entry," Zar said. "Heaven and eternal bliss await all true martyrs. Like them, it is our duty to drive out the infidels!"

Zar waited for a response, but none came. Nantush seemed listless, lost in his grief.

"My men have stored a few arms here," Zar continued. "They are not your concern."

Grasping Nantush by his shoulders, he changed his tone to one of sympathy.

"Elder brother, I share your sorrow," he said. "I know Ala was your heir. I saw how you smiled upon him and how brave he acted. I am in your debt. If you need me, I will drop everything to be at your side. The Qur'an says, 'Those who believe in Allah are united as brothers.'"

Nantush brightened slightly. Zar had not spoken so warmly before.

"*To Allah we belong,*" Nantush said ritually, "*and to him we shall return.*"

"Exactly," Zar said softly. "Older brother, your son was mujahideen. No one who believes in Allah can be excused from jihad."

Nantush grasped the message; he was about to be used.

"What do you want of me?" Nantush said.

"The *halek* I brought with me has volunteered for martyrdom," Zar said. "You must prepare the boy and feed him these capsules. In the morning, the infidels will come, and you point him toward them."

He handed three brown capsules to Nantush, who nodded dully.

"What if the infidels do not come?" Nantush said.

Zar wanted to slap him for his truculence, but held back.

"Oh, they will come," Zar said.

He left the compound and walked toward his car. He pulled the boy out, held him by his thin shoulder, and spoke in a firm, encouraging tone.

"You have been chosen for greatness," Zar said. "Your family will be taken care of. To defend Islam, you must deceive and kill. Death is not blackness. You will enjoy heaven with Allah, forever!"

After pushing the boy toward Nantush, Zar got in the car. Once outside the walls, he had his driver flick the headlights on and off to be sure the drone somewhere overhead recorded the location.

Inside the compound, Nantush gave the boy one of the heroin capsules. A half hour later, he and his wife took him into an empty room.

"I am following the book of Allah," the boy recited. "*Ummah* resides in me."

He sat half dozing, his face placid. The woman knelt before the boy and washed his limbs before applying lipstick and black mascara to his soft face.

"At the *madrassa*, they will praise my name," he said dreamily. "I will be seen on YouTube. May I watch my martyrdom from heaven?"

AT FOUR IN THE MORNING, the watch chief in the ops center awakened Barnes, who in turn alerted Coffman. In rapid succession, Barnes showed him a series of images on the video screen.

"Yesterday afternoon, sir, we saw these jugs unloaded at this compound," he said. "Last night, five bodies were brought there. An hour ago, a Hilux unloaded two mortar tubes."

"Distance?" Coffman said.

"The compound's on our side of the canal, sir. About a click east from here."

Coffman silently cursed the ANA. This was their responsibility, but they were patrolling to the west. He couldn't launch an artillery strike that was certain to kill women and children. Yet if he stayed buttoned up and did nothing, the Taliban would lob a few more mortar shells. They had failed the first time, but if they got lucky General Killian wouldn't be forgiving.

"Right," Coffman said. "Dispatch a patrol to search that compound."

AN HOUR BEFORE LIGHT, Sergeant McGowan moved 2nd Squad into position at the wire, where Cruz and the CIA team were waiting. Before stepping off, McGowan strapped a tourniquet above each knee.

"Take them off," Cruz said.

"Sir?" McGowan said. "I'm making it easier for my men. If I get blown up, doc doesn't have to crawl to me."

"You're hard, Sergeant," Cruz said. "I'll give you that. But you'll rattle your troops. It'll get in their heads. Unstrap the quets. If you're hit, take deep breaths. That slows the bleeding."

"RT, you're all heart," McGowan said.

"I don't want to hear that RT shit again," Cruz said. "Get your herd on the move."

In the thin light, they left the wire. Walking point, Wolfe held to a deliberate pace, avoiding the obvious openings between fields as he swept his metal detector back and forth. Whenever the needle quivered, he paused to hover over the suspicious spot like a setter sniffing for pheasant. Ashford guarded him, alternating between squinting through his rifle scope and squirting Silly String to mark the path. Eagan was third in line, much to Ashford's relief.

The patrol was twenty minutes out before Wolfe registered the first solid *ping!* After McGowan and Cruz marked the location on their tablets, Wolfe adjusted the route and they proceeded forward. In all directions, the terrain had a sameness, wide fields with orderly rows of startling bright poppy bulbs separated at straight angles by the green lines of scrub trees and thick tangles of bush and vines that grew along the banks of the irrigation ditches. The patrol was never out of sight of one or two compounds, each protected from its neighbors by high mud walls compressed hard as rock by decades under a searing sun. Tribal shuras and Taliban judges settled the constant disputes about the property lines. Most compounds were built on sites chosen by forbearers a century ago. One might be constructed alongside a canal, another near some tractor path, and a third in the shelter of an oak stand. Every compound served as an enemy observation post. So Cruz wasn't surprised by the radio burst in his earpiece.

"Wolf Six, we got dickers to the east giving us the evil eye," Ashford said. "They're on bikes on the other side of a canal, some with balaclavas wrapped around their faces."

Cruz was accustomed to seeing Taliban hovering at a distance. They reminded him of Western movies where the cavalry ride along, nervously eyeing the Comanche keeping pace on the ridgeline. The watchers, well inside kill range, knew they were safe. With no weapons visible and no uniforms, the presumption of innocence provided them sanctuary.

Eagan, several feet in front of Cruz, zoomed in on the group.

"Those are nice wheels," he said. "That's a command group. Smudgy with the sun behind them, but the one with the wild beard might be that commander, Zar. I can drop him."

"Not a sound idea," Cruz said. "Every muj has a wild beard. So do a few farmers."

"Target of opportunity," Eagan said. "That's all I'm saying."

"No," Cruz said. "That's all I'm saying."

ZAR HAD ASSUMED A CASUAL POSE, one leg draped across the saddle of his glistening black Kawasaki Ninja. He propped his elbows on the handlebars and looked through his binoculars at the infidels. Zar loved motorcycle flicks. His flash drives included Brando in *The Wild One*, McQueen in *The Great Escape*, and Gibson in *Mad Max*. His companions were shifting uneasily, aware of the Marines glassing them through their rifle scopes.

"They won't fire," Zar said confidently. "I can see their leader giving orders, the short, thick one with the antenna sticking up. And…"

The sudden jabbering and yelps of the others cut him off. He swung his binoculars and focused in on a bare, ugly white ass shining across the fields at him. Before he could react, one of his companions hopped off his bike and returned the moon.

"Enough!" Zar shouted, upset at humanizing the enemy.

He eased the bike into gear and his party slowly trundled down the slight rise into the tree line where their camera crew was hidden.

CRUZ WAITED TOLERANTLY while Mad Dog Doyle pulled up his trousers amidst cheers from his comrades.

"Dial it down, devil dogs," Cruz said, "and lock in. Sooner or later, we'll make contact."

They continued on in file and were within a field's length of the compound when the funeral procession emerged. A shrouded body lay on a rope bed carried on the shoulders of six males dressed in clean cotton trousers, loose shirts, and rough sandals. A few younger boys scampered alongside, while what appeared to be the family walked behind the bier.

Wolfe paused and pressed his throat mic.

"Six, we still going to search the compound?"

"Affirmative," Cruz said. "Wait until the body passes."

THE WOMEN IN FULL BLACK *CHADORS*, sobbing but no longer wailing, had said goodbye at the gate. Once at the cemetery, the men would dig the grave, lower the corpse, fill in the dirt, heap on rocks to prevent scavenging animals, string colored cloths on rope lines, kiss Nantush on his right cheek, and disperse to work in the fields. The presence of the *halek* from the *madrassa* frightened them all. Nantush had promised they would not be harmed, but none fully believed him. Still, what choice did they have, with Zar somewhere out there watching them?

Trailing a few feet behind Nantush, the boy felt calm, sleepy, tired. When he saw the Marines, they looked as big as giants. Through his heroin haze he knew enough to be scared. He tugged at Nantush's hand.

"God is with me, isn't he?" he whispered.

An agitated Nantush pried loose his hand.

"Yes, yes, Allah awaits you," he said. "Do as I say."

The pace of the procession was faltering.

"Keep moving," Nantush urged the pallbearers.

He shifted his gaze between the ground and the Marines, gauging the distance, measuring the space. Then he lost his nerve. He grabbed the boy by the shoulder and shoved him forward.

"Go," he whispered urgently, "go now. Press the button when you reach the first *kafir*."

The boy lurched off the path and hesitated, looking toward the Marines. He paused among the poppy flowers, unsure.

"Go," Nantush hissed. "Go!"

"HEY, TIC," ASHFORD SHOUTED DOWN THE FILE, "what's the word for a cross dresser?"

"*Bacha bazi*," Tic said. "Why?"

Ashford pointed at the boy slowly approaching the Marines.

"Check the lipstick on this kid," he shouted.

The boy's red lips looked like a gaping sword wound as he picked his way through rows of pink and white poppies, softly chanting, "Allahu Akbar, Allahu Akbar."

"Shoot!" Tic screamed. "Shoot that fucker! Now! Now!"

The mourners had dropped the casket and were scattering, providing Ashford with a clear field of fire. He paused before taking the shot. Kill a boy?

Eagan had no hesitation. He took one step out of line and placed a round in the boy's chest. No delay, no thinking, done in a blink. The impact drove the boy back and he tottered drunkenly, his right hand extending the kill switch toward the Marines, as if offering communion.

"Down!" Tic yelled. "Down!"

The Marines reacted instantly, diving down. The earth seemed to sneeze, a deep snort as the explosive belt ripped apart the boy's body. A pink dust cloud erupted, the brown dirt mixing with the red flesh. Three seconds and one breath later, Cruz and a few others had scrambled to their hands and knees, scanning for enemy.

"Up! Up!" Cruz yelled into his mic. "Form a three sixty. McGowan, give me a cas count!"

The Marines popped up into kneeling positions, rifles on shoulders, sweeping back and forth. McGowan took a quick count.

"All good!" he shouted.

Ashford was scoping in every direction, trying to avoid Tic, who was glaring at him.

"I couldn't shoot," Ashford said. "He looked like a scared kid."

"When I yell, you fire!" Tic said. "That kid was infected. He'd kill us all and smile about it. I know these people. He was a fucking murderer!"

30

It's War, Doc

The lipstick boy had evaporated. A black smudge, surprisingly small, marked the blast site, and only few body parts lay scattered about—a pale white foot, a slab of red thigh meat, a few innards that looked like uncooked sausage. Back down the path, Ala's abandoned corpse lay in the dirt, still secure in its white shroud. Cruz smelled the familiar sweet, nauseous mix of cordite, smoke, and broiled meat.

Farther off, the mourners had fearfully clustered around Nantush, kneeling and crouching, waving their hands in front of their faces, silently beseeching the Marines not to shoot. A shriek of pain came from the bushes, followed by high-pitched wails. Nantush bolted upright and, flapping his hands toward the Marines, ran a short way up the path and knelt down. When he stood back up, he was holding in his arms a small, screeching boy. He looked toward the Marines, shaking his head, indicating he didn't know what to do.

The boy's wails took on an anapest rhythm, sob, sob, scream, sob, sob, scream, over and over. His left foot and shin were dangling by a flap of skin, the kneecap shorn off and blood spurting out in rhythm with the boy's jagged breathing. His eyes bulged from the shock and fear of the unbelievable, his face so pale his tears could scarcely be seen.

"Doc, check out the kid," Cruz said.

HM3 Bushnell rushed up and cinched a thick black tourniquet strap around the boy's thigh, evoking a howl and sealing off the artery. Next he tore the wrapping from a three-centimeter needle, grasped the boy's other thigh, and leaned forward. Then he hesitated.

"Fifteen milligrams," he said. "His breathing's ragged. If I stick him, his heart might stop. I gotta talk to Commander Zarest."

"All right," Cruz said. "McGowan, send a fire team to search the compound."

Stovell and Richards were standing off to one side with Tic.

"Skipper," Richards said, "OK if we ask a few questions?"

When Cruz nodded, Tic strode forward, took Nantush by the arm, and half dragged him into a cluster of bushes. Legs crossed, Tic sat across from him and in perfect Pashto asked his name. Then Tic leaned forward gravely until their heads almost touched.

"Nantush, I am Ahmed," Tic lied. "Like you, I am Alikozai, from Kandahar."

Nantush accepted the words as true. The americani routinely hired locals to translate. He anxiously glanced back to see who was tending to his son. Tic grabbed his shoulders and pointed at the black smudge.

"Nantush, you caused this tragedy," he said. "You directed the bomber."

"No, no! He is *hitsok,* with a teacup from the Quetta *madrassa.* I can show you."

They were interrupted by wails and shrieks from the compound as frightened women and children poured out the gate.

"You will find no *asbaab* in my home," Nantush protested.

"That's because you moved the mortars into the fields," Tic said. "You think I'm stupid? I ask again: how did the *affindi* arrive at your compound?"

A panicked Nantush knew he was dead if he mentioned Zar.

"I, I don't know, it was dark. I was washing the body of my son."

"Liar. Your compound lights were on last night. I saw you push the *affindi* toward us."

"He was drugged. I wanted him to blow himself up away from everyone."

"Drugged? Show me the pills."

Nantush reached inside his tunic and handed over two faded brown capsules.

"Who gave you these?"

Realizing his mistake, Nantush pretended not to hear.

"He was *faqir*, not one of us," he mumbled. "We are not *kuni*. Ask them."

"Your relatives can't help you," Tic said. "The angry americani don't care if the boy was an outsider. So what if you didn't abuse him? You are old, *akaa*, but they will send you to Guantanamo, blow up your compound, sell your lands, and drive off your family."

Only two days ago, Nantush had been content, relaxed, happily bidding up the harvest price, dreaming of a flat-screen TV, a new Samsung refrigerator, a Deere tractor, and enough money for his pilgrimage to the hajj. Now his favorite son was dead, his youngest son lay dying, and he was going to the americani hell. He was ruined, his family torn apart.

Tic didn't speak for a few seconds, letting Nantush grasp the fullness of his devastation. Then he dribbled out a morsel of hope.

"You are my *bandi*. You have no rights, but I can speak to the *kafir* for you. They trust me."

Nantush snapped at the offering.

"I've paid all my workers," he said eagerly. "I have three thousand left, in dollars."

Tic waved his hand, brushing aside the words. Nantush raised the offer.

"I've sold only half my harvest," he hastened on. "I have five more *jeribs* to be lanced. I can give you six thousand dollars in a few days."

"You're lying. *Kharaab*. No one pays that much."

"No, no, the buyer is a foreigner, a *Paarsi*."

Tic glanced furtively around.

"I don't care if an Iranian pays you a few thousand dollars," Tic hissed. "I'm not risking my job for a farmer's wages. I want three bags of heroin. One kilo each, sealed well."

Nantush felt light-headed. For that, he would have to ask Zar, who would demand all his crop in exchange. He would be left with crumbs. His life lay in shambles, no matter what choice he made. His hands were shaking.

"I can't do that," he stammered. "I would be in debt. He, he…"

Tic looked anxiously toward the Marines.

"Enough!" he said. "We have no more time. I will tell the *kafirs* to destroy your compound. Now!"

"I am not Taliban!"

"You are if I say you are," Tic said. "Last chance: You have three bags when I next visit?"

"Yes, yes! When will that be?"

"Tomorrow."

NANTUSH SCURRIED BACK TO HIS WAILING SON. Tic walked back and pulled Richards off to one side. When they finished talking, Richards joined Cruz.

"Tic came up empty," Richards said. "No mortars in the shed, and the farmer's too scared to talk."

"Let's bring him in with us," Cruz said. "Sergeant Ahmed might pick up something."

"We won't gain anything by that, Skipper," Richards said. "The Tango who brought the suicide bomber is gone. That farmer won't dime him out. If he did, he'd be butchered by dawn. Tic thinks there'll be a squirter, though, when we leave. Can you vector a drone to track him?"

Cruz felt his jaw tighten in anger. The CIA team chief was holding something back. Still, Eagan had shot the suicide bomber when the Marines had hesitated. Now wasn't the time to push for answers.

"All right, Mr. Richards," Cruz said. "You got it."

He walked over to Doc Bushnell, who was tending to the injured boy. The tourniquet had staunched the dark red blood gushing from the black gnarl that had been a knee. Tiny pink bubbles formed a froth line around the edges of the seared flesh. The boy's right tibia was peppered with bits of burnt blue cloth, and his toeless foot lay at an impossible angle, as if it wanted to run away, but was attached by a stubborn skein of sizzled tendrils and fried ligaments. The kid looked like he was four, maybe five. For a second, Cruz remembered Josh clinging to his knee back in San Diego. *Was that only four days ago?*

"Sir, the trauma bandage has enough superglue to check the arterial bleeding," Bushnell said. "I gave him ten cc's of morphine. Commander Zarest might be able to stabilize him, once we get to base."

On Cruz's first tour, commanders had called in helicopters to fly wounded civilians to hospitals where skilled doctors with sterilized tools rendered aid. Year by year, disillusion and cost awareness—jeopardize a $40-million helicopter and an American crew for a wounded civilian?—had set in. On his second tour, Cruz had left the wounded for the farmers to care.

"His family can take him to Lash," Cruz said.

"Sir, he'll never make it," Bushnell said, half pleading. "Why not bring him back? Put his family out in front of us. They know where the IEDs are. That way we're protected and the kid might survive."

Good for you, Doc, Cruz thought. *You have the balls to bargain with me to save a five-year-old.*

"Doc, we're a Marine firebase," Cruz said, "not a hospital. If we bring the boy with us, tomorrow there'll be a dozen at our wire. And one of them will be another suicide bomber."

The corpsman looked hurt. He hadn't expected this from Cruz.

"So that's how it is, sir?" he said tonelessly. "We leave him?"

Cruz nodded, his face blank. "It's war, Doc," Cruz said. "We're not running a shelter."

He knew Coffman wouldn't permit bringing the boy back. But he hadn't even radioed in the request, and he didn't like himself for not doing so. Had he become too hardened, or was he too worried about his fitrep, or both?

The Marines were sorting themselves into a long file. Bushnell packed up his med kit and shuffled into his assigned space. McGowan finished his head count and looked at Cruz.

"Beat feet, sir?"

Cruz waved his arm and the Marines walked away. Only the rear guard looked back. Nantush was gently placing his dying son in a wheelbarrow.

31

Assigning Blame

Inside the ops center, Coffman squinted at the bright overhead video showing a line of troops fording a creek.

"The patrol's heading back, sir," Sergeant Ahmed said. "The CIA team has asked for surveillance on that compound."

"Permission granted," Coffman said.

He opened his notebook, checked his watch, and wrote a short entry. It would help to record how he had helped the spooks. Details, always attend to the details. He was never without his schedule.

0600: Two laps around base. Wave to sentries and cannoneers.

0700: Morning brief.

0800–1100: Emails and telcons with General Gretman and staff in Kabul.

1100–1200: Visit crews in gun pits.

1200–1300: Daily ops update.

1300–1400: Telcon with ANA Colonel Ishaq.

1400–1700: Prepare daily summary for General Gretman, copy to General Killian.

Coffman labored three hours to write three hundred words, crafting each sentence to convey the right tone. He knew Killian savored gritty particulars—range to target, firing conditions, enemy casualties inflicted, etc. Coffman made sure to include a quote or a comical quip from some lance corporal to illustrate that he was close to his troops. Now he had to report a suicide bomber. How would he phrase that to emphasize the positive?

Cruz and Richards came into his office with sweat pouring down their faces, cammies muddy, shaking packets of sugared tea into water bottles and guzzling it down. Major Barnes stood behind them.

"Good you all made it back," Coffman said. "No casualties?"

"An Afghan kid was torn up, sir," Cruz said. "No Marines were hit."

"They must have been waiting for you," Coffman said, "when you left the wire."

"That's standard MO for jihadists, sir," Barnes interjected. "They knew we'd send out security patrols."

Coffman rubbed his chin.

"Thank you, XO," he said dryly, "for pointing out the obvious. Did you find mortars at the compound, Captain?"

"No, sir," Cruz said.

"So the mission wasn't accomplished," Coffman said, "and the patrol was endangered. Do you think that's an acceptable outcome, Captain?"

Cruz felt a chill as his chances for a solid fitrep dropped.

"No, sir," he said. "But I think we covered our east flank."

Coffman offered no praise.

"That's the responsibility of the Afghan army," he said. "I'm working on that. Are your sentry posts tied in? Is the LADAR working?"

Cruz never responded quickly in intellectual combat. Put on the defensive, he needed time to couch a reply. He failed to think of a sensible rebuttal.

"Yes, sir," he said lamely.

Satisfied he had brought Cruz to heel, Coffman waved for him to leave and shifted his to Richards.

"I want to help your team," he said. "I authorized overhead surveillance. But it's too dangerous for you to wander around looking for clues. I'm suspending further patrols."

With a curt nod, Richards left the tiny office. Once outside the revetment, he turned to Cruz.

"Your colonel's too risk averse," Richards said. "We have to find another work-around."

Cruz swung up his jaw, the way he did when angered.

"What's this 'we'?" he said. "You're too one-way. That bullshit you gave me out there about finding nothing, then asking for a drone to trail a squirter? I'm not running any more errands for you. Once with Barnes was enough."

Richards didn't back off.

"We're narrowing in on our target," Richards said. "Tic's playing that farmer. That's all I can share for now."

"Earth to CIA," Cruz said, "your black op almost got us killed!"

Richards was tired. Under the noon sun, the wrinkles in his face cut so deep they cast shadows.

"You're the target, not us," he said. "No one knows my team's here. Those headlights in the middle of the night at that compound? You were suckered in. That suicide kid was meant for you. Your base has pissed off someone with heavy clout."

"You didn't tell that to the colonel," Cruz said. "You didn't say a word."

"Don't dump on me," Richards said. "I was waiting for you to speak up. You know your shit outside the wire. But when Coffman braced you, you didn't offer squat. I don't get that about you."

He turned away, his tone of disappointment lingering with the sweat on Cruz. Over the past three days, Cruz had been averaging four hours sleep. Years ago, he had learned to snatch a quick nap whenever the battlefield tempo allowed. Still smarting from Richards's remark, he curled up in a corner of the platoon tent.

In his exhausted sleep, he first saw the ashen face of Sergeant Lamont, cradling his sniper rifle. He briefly opened his eyes, forcing his mind to stop taking inventory of the fallen. When again he dozed off, though, other images crept in from prior deployments. His mind flickered from the pleading eyes of the skinny kid in Ramadi with the blood and shit spilling from his ass, to the spider spinning its web across the black hole that had been the face of a taxi driver in Fallujah, to the dust popping from the shirt of the too-trusting water truck driver as the bullets struck him. He had flashes from Sangin of a charred boy with holes in the center of his upturned feet, and a woman and baby hanging upside down in a smoldering car. Then he drifted back to the suicide bomber and the four year-old with his right shin dangling by a tendril. Somehow he knew where the dream was going. He was standing outside of himself, watching a final, terrible image. There were Jennifer and Josh clinging to each other, two more civilians he had failed to protect.

Petrified, he struggled to escape from the nightmare, to reach the surface, to leave behind the fright of sleep. He snapped awake, sat up, and sipped tepid water. He looked at the canvas walls, fighting to drive away his fear of the costs of failure.

32

The Dog That Didn't Bark

Inside the intel section of the ops center, Stovell had taken a seat next to Sergeant Ahmed. Both were looking at a satellite photo that displayed the district broken into sectors measuring five hundred meters on a side. Each square was labeled with an alphanumeric, like R6T or Q9Y. Every compound within the squares was numbered.

"You asked us to watch for squirters," Ahmed said. "After your patrol left that compound, one dude on a motorbike hauled ass going north. We had eyes on him for a click. Lost him in the bush up in Q5F."

"Any ELINT cuts from that sector?" Stovell said.

"Routine transmissions," Ahmed said. "The only structures are a *madrassa* for juvenile Talibs and a mosque with five internet connections. It's a hike to get up there for prayers. Totally isolated."

"But no calls for jihad?"

"Not a peep."

"Any firefights?"

Ahmed pointed over to the artillery fire control section.

"Check with the gunny," he said.

Stovell picked up his folding chair and plopped it down next to Gunnery Sergeant Maxwell, the artillery ops chief. Captain Lasswell put aside her laptop and joined them. The map on the electronic screen was speckled with the orange dots of on-call fire missions.

"Looks like you two," she said genially, "are communing with AFATIDS. Can I help?"

The program called Advanced Field Artillery Tactical Data System recorded data about every fire mission conducted by any US unit in Afghanistan.

"I don't see any activity in Q5F," Stovell said. "Can you pull up all the missions fired since you landed?"

Maxwell, balding and tending toward a potbelly, grinned, glad to show off his skills. In response to three keystrokes, several dozen small crosses popped up, scattered on either side of Route 11 leading to Lashkar Gah.

"The ANA call in five to eight missions a day," he said. "Three shells here, ten there. To get to Lash, they're clearing by fire, mostly blind."

"Careful, Gunny," Lasswell said. "Let's not speak ill of our ally. Those *askars* have a reason to avoid a real fight. If they're killed, their families are cut adrift."

She abruptly stopped. Stovell was regarding her with mild amusement.

"Oops," she said. "Sorry, Mr. Stovell. I forgot that you know ten times more about this stuff."

"Nonsense," Stovell said. "It's good you haven't lost your empathy. I'm called Stovell, by the way, never *Mister* Stovell."

He pointed at the Q5F sector.

"Do you have any historical data? Old patterns?"

Lasswell hesitated, knowing she should ask the XO before proceeding. But she wanted to impress Stovell. She looked at the ops chief.

"What do you think, Gunny? Will Hal object?"

"We'll get some bitching, ma'am," Maxwell said.

"Hal is our pet name for higher headquarters in Kabul," Lasswell explained. "They monitor us twenty-four seven. Confirm this, tell us that, blah, blah."

Maxwell had been busy at the keyboard. When he hit Enter, they looked at a screen with a few crosses.

"No missions in Q5F in the past year," Maxwell said. "Not a single one."

In the chat box on the screen, a message was flashing: WHAT ARE YOU DOING?

"That's Hal," Lasswell said. "Some bored watch officer four hundred miles away asking an inane question. We'll ignore him."

"How far back can you trace the data?" Stovell said.

"MARCENT in Tampa," Lasswell said, "has the records. I have a friend there."

She swiftly opened a classified internet chat room. After ten minutes of back-and-forth, the locations of 3,845 fire missions sparkled like red embers across the black-and-white photomap of Helmand.

"That's the entire laydown for 2014," Lasswell said, "the year we pulled out."

A few mouse clicks brought into focus the canals, ditches, tree lines, paths, and compounds in the four square miles surrounding the firebase.

"Look at those red crosses in Q5F," Maxwell said. "That sector was smoking hot."

Lasswell placed the cursor on a cross, clicked, and scanned the format.

"Troops in contact," she read.

She shifted to another cross and clicked.

"Another TIC. HIMARS and fixed-wing," she said. "April, 2014. One Marine KIA."

Maxwell squinted at the sitrep.

"There's cross-talk about not hitting that mosque," he said.

"That place been checked out?" Stovell said.

Lasswell glanced around before shaking her head.

"That's out of our lane," she said.

"Easy fix, ma'am," Maxwell said.

He called over to the sergeant controlling the Common Operational Picture displayed on a blown-up photomap.

"Bro," Maxwell said, "can you pull up the Afghan patrol routes?"

A young sergeant tapped a few keys, and a dozen squiggly blue lines popped up.

"That shows their GPS tracks," Maxwell said. "No ANA patrol has gone into Q5F."

From behind them, the watch officer loudly cleared his throat. Coffman had stridden out of his office, red-faced.

"Kabul just called," he yelled. "Who the hell's searching through back files?"

Lasswell raised her hand.

"My bad, sir," she said. "I got a little sidetracked."

Noticing that Stovell was in the room, Coffman decided to play it deftly, administering a measured reprimand to show that he was a hands-on executive.

"Well, no harm done this time, Captain," he said in a paternal tone. "But let's remember we're a firebase, not a library."

Stovell spoke up an amiable tone, clear enough for the staff to hear.

"The fault lies with me, Colonel," he said. "I regret if I've offended you. It's been my experience that research pays off."

Coffman's face lost color. Stovell's challenge caught him off guard. He thought of saying, *This is my command.* But that would wreck any future with Stovell Industries.

"We each have a mission, Mr. Stovell," he said formally. "Unfortunately, I also have to deal with Kabul. Let's try not to rile up higher headquarters."

He forced a smile and headed to his office. The staff turned back to their duties, murmuring among themselves. Maxwell looked at Lasswell.

"He's a cool dude," he whispered, "backing the colonel down like that."

Stovell had resumed studying the photomap.

"Q5F is as quiet as a tomb," he said. "The ANA avoid the sector, and the mullah at that mosque is not railing against us infidels. Why do you suppose that is?"

"The dog that didn't bark?" Lasswell said.

"Bravo, Captain," Stovell said. "I'd have missed it if the gunny and you hadn't checked the records. Did I hear you're going to business school?"

"Yes, sir. Stanford."

"One of my companies is in Palo Alto," Stovell said. "I'm thinking of moving out of there, though. It's an odd culture, with its post-nationalist world view."

He handed her a business card.

"You have command experience," he said. "I have a few managerial slots you'd find challenging."

"Thanks, sir," she said. "Can I say how weird it is meeting you? I mean, one wrong step out here and it's all over."

Stovell smiled tolerantly.

"Owning Apple," he said, "didn't prevent Steve Jobs from dying at fifty-six. Life should be an adventure, not a catered safari."

"Well, I guess your perspective is different, sir, having been in Force Recon and all..."

Stovell laughed.

"I was never in Force. I was a misplaced 6800 clerk! Eagan and Richards saved me on that op. If you're puzzled about my presence here, remember your Eliot: 'The end of our exploring is to arrive where we started and know the place for the first time.'"

33

The Sappers

When the suicide boy had detonated his belt of explosives that morning, Zar was hiding in a copse of trees six hundred meters away. Kneeling next to him, a Taliban camera crew recorded the blast and quickly headed to Lashkar Gah to distribute the video.

Zar and his gang drove a few kilometers north, dismounting twice to push their bikes across narrow footbridges. Under the overhang of trees along a canal bank near the mosque, Zar turned off to the right. His four companions continued straight ahead, walking their bikes across a field laced with deep furrows. When they reached the mosque, they parked their bikes in the courtyard.

Zar pushed his Kawasaki down a steep gully, pulled back the green netting over a cave entrance, and puttered down a dank tunnel supported by thick wooden beams. He parked in the center of a cavernous dirt cellar beneath the mosque. On a sturdy bench were heaped hundreds of zip-locked plastic bags, each filled with a kilo of black tar heroin. The lab was a mess of dented barrels, sliced-open sacks, soggy tubs, open jugs of precursor chemicals, sweaty laborers, dirty shovels, slushy wheelbarrows, a press machine, twisted hoses, bare light bulbs, and a sputtering generator. The actual conversion of the wet opium into heroin was done outside in vats heated by propane-fueled fires.

The Persian was waiting in the cave. Since his youth, he had been overweight, unathletic, fanciful in dress, and plodding in his studies of the Qu'ran. He had advanced by choosing a career in accounting. No man, no matter how ferocious, could bend the truth of numbers. A kilo of heroin, costing him $3,000, would sell for $12,000 to middlemen in Iran. After all payouts, he calculated his uncle and the Republican Guard would net at least $40 million for investing $15 million. The ISI and the Taliban would split about $45 million. His commission might be as high as $4 million. There was one step to go—moving the product out of the lab, despite the drones overhead.

The Persian greeted Zar by gesturing at the bulging pile of plastic bags.

"Three hundred kilos," he said, "and you bring four riders on motorcycles. With this much on their backs, they'll look like camels. It's impossible!"

Zar pretended indifference, as if the problem was easily solved.

"No motorbikes. I've decided to put forty kilos in an old car," he said. "It will go first, followed by a pickup with the rest. If anything goes wrong, we lose only the car, a small loss."

"A small loss?" the Persian said. "You're putting tens of millions in two vehicles? This is insane! Emir Sadr promised dozens of couriers, with no package over ten kilos."

"I have to keep my mujahideen here to fight the infidels," Zar said. "They can't be sent off carrying a few kilos."

"Each kilo is worth more than two of your fighters," the Persian said. "You are risking too much!"

When Zar did not reply, the Persian pushed further, delighted to have his tormentor at a disadvantage.

"You promised the farmers would cooperate," he said, "but some are still holding out. I have one million yet to spend!"

Zar tried to push off blame.

"The Baloch are telling the farmers that you will run away," he said, "because you fear the americanis."

The Persian looked from the muddy floorboards to the crusted tubs and the careless piles of his precious heroin sacks. He rubbed his forehead. Disorder depressed him.

"That's nonsense," he said. "Emir Sadr assured me that you would drive out the infidels."

Zar stood erect, inflating his chest.

"I will, *inshallah*."

Exasperated by Zar's excuses, the Persian pointed up at the wooden beams above them.

"They've arrived."

"Good. I hope they prove worth it," Zar said.

He pushed open a trap door and emerged into the prayer room of the mosque. Spread on top of the polished mahogany floor were dozens of brightly colored prayer rugs. AKs, PKMs, RPGs, sandals, Skechers, boots, and a few pairs of dress shoes lay scattered about. To the Persian, this was evidence of more disorder, caused by sloppy minds.

At one end of the room, a dozen Taliban, in *shalwar kameez* and turbans, sat barefoot, sipping tea. At the other end, Tulus was talking to a slender Asian in black pajamas. Behind him squatted his two companions, similarly dressed with black bandanas around their foreheads.

"This is all the shura sent?" Zar said.

"They know what to do," Tulus said. "Their leader Quat speaks some Americani and no Pashto."

Zar looked at Quat's battered face. The other two were in their twenties, but Quat was over forty, with a broken nose and black eyes appraising as a hawk. Pointing at Zar's face, Quat frowned and spoke softly, pausing between each word.

"Your beard," he said, "not work in the bush."

Quat ran his palm over his bald head and down his hairless cheek, making a slithering movement with his fingers. In the jungle, a hunter must glide like a tiger, with no beard to be caught in the vines. Zar took this as an insult.

"A movie ninja," Zar said in Pashto, drawing back his arm to slap the insolent little man.

Quat, slender as a bamboo shoot, dropped into a fighter's crouch. Zar hesitated. With his mujahideen watching, he wanted to strike the insolent Asian. Yet the man stood there composed, almost contemptuous.

Tulus put his hand to his swollen lip. Good, he would enjoy seeing Zar beaten. But he had his orders from the shura. He stepped forward and spoke in English to Quat, who quickly responded.

"He wants to recon the base," Tulus said. "And he needs to know the weather, day and night."

"All right, I'll show it to him," Zar said. "The other two stay here."

Tulus spoke briefly with Quat.

"His men will not sleep indoors," Tulus said. "He will find them a place by the canal and return."

Taking their sneakers and AKs, the sappers left. The Persian remained in the background, scarcely noticed. Tulus kept his head down, tapping a toe on a soft rug.

"What else?" Zar snapped.

"The journalists in Lashkar Gah are circulating the video," Tulus said. "Soon the internet will show the martyr, may Allah welcome him. As you instructed, we announced he killed four infidels."

He waited until Zar sensed there was more and nodded for him to continue.

"Nantush called," Tulus said.

"Here? You talked to him from here?"

Tulus was unfazed by the angry tone. Low-level Taliban weren't on the americani watch list.

"Don't worry. Every day there are many calls at the mosque," Tulus said. "Nantush lost a second son in the martyr's bombing."

The news brought Zar up short. He frowned as he reflected back.

"I saw confusion after the bomb went off," he said. "He's upset. It will pass. May Allah welcome his son. Don't answer if he calls again. It's a waste of your time."

"Nantush, uh, needs three kilos of heroin," Tulus said reluctantly. "Otherwise, the *takfir* working for the infidels will arrest him. In return, Nantush is offering you the harvest from five *jeribs*."

"That stupid farmer asks too much," Zar said.

Tulus glanced at the Persian, who grimaced. Zar couldn't move the heroin he had, and yet he was ranting against Nantush, who had helped him.

"We come out far ahead," the Persian said. "His *jeribs* will yield six kilos of heroin and you're giving him only three."

Zar was embarrassed to be bargaining about a farmer.

"Give him one kilo," he said, "provided he blames the americani for the boy's death and arranges for the press to view his son's body."

Tulus pawed at his lip to remind Zar of the slap.

"He is my uncle," he said. "He works hard and worships Allah. Only one kilo?"

Zar waved his hand impatiently.

"I have no time for this," he said. "Your job right now is to ride with us and tell me what the Asian says."

34

The Second Death

Tulus followed Zar outside, where Quat and two Taliban were sitting astride motorcycles. Only the Vietnamese wrapped a balaclava around his face to conceal his features. The five crossed the canal and drove a kilometer south to the knoll where earlier that day Zar had watched Cruz's patrol. It was now midafternoon, and the sun's low angle clearly silhouetted the outline of the firebase to the west. Quat heard the mosquito whine of a drone circling above them.

"They see us," he said, "but do not shoot?"

"We are safe," Tulus said. "No weapons."

"A strange way to fight," Quat said. "Can you stir them up?"

Zar considered the request. Amongst the harvesters in the fields, he had stationed a few armed teams. He knew he would be placing them in danger, but he wanted to show off. The Taliban shura in Quetta had paid dearly to hire this strange Asian. He estimated it would take the drone ten minutes to locate any shooters. Zar turned to Tulus.

"Call Habullah, Abdul Salam, and Rasha," he said. "Tell them their teams are to fire a few bullets at the base. Then hide the weapons and leave quickly."

Tulus punched in one of the hundred channels on his ICOM.

"Three ducks fly over the field," he radioed. "They lay fifty eggs and leave quickly."

AT THE FIREBASE, Sergeant Ahmed's intel section intercepted the childlike code and ignored it. Over their ICOMs, the Talibs regularly conversed with farmers, exchanged curses with Afghan soldiers, and talked in senseless riddles to mask an occasional genuine order.

THE FIRST GANG OF FOUR TALIBS, particularly bold, waded up an irrigation ditch to within three hundred meters of the firebase. The foliage from the overhanging trees screened them from the drone circling at five thousand feet. A hundred meters behind them, the second gang hid along the edge of a field while the laborers, who had been scraping opium teardrops onto their flat putty knives, skittered away. The third gang was hiding still farther back in a tree line.

Among the three groups, they had two RPGs, a half-dozen AKs, and one Russian PKM machine gun. Because the laborers walked where they pleased, the range to the base from these three firing positions had been paced off. This allowed the RPGs to be elevated at the correct angle to hit the base. Still, the Marine artillery crews were sheltered behind heavy earth berms, and the sentries on the perimeter were standing watch from inside deep bunkers. There were no obvious targets, and the shooters were aiming into the afternoon sun.

Habullah's gang, nearest the base, braced the stocks of their AKs into the dirt and pushed the barrels into the air. As soon as the first rocket was fired, the riflemen squeezed off a few bursts that quickly emptied their twenty-round magazines. The PKM crew aimed at the artillery tubes. The heavy slugs fired at a slow cyclic rate that sounded like hammers beating on iron pipes. After a few seconds, the other two gangs joined in. The shooting lasted less than twenty seconds, followed by the usual hoots of "Allahu Akbar" as the shooters slipped away. The attack was over before the sirens on the base sounded a warning.

THE FUSILLADE WAS AMATEURISH, a shoot-and-scoot tactic applied with bravado and without discipline or accuracy. Only a few dozen bullets and one rocket struck inside the firebase. Such trivial harassing fire did not merit a one-line entry in the daily log of a combat unit. Historians have determined that in battle, four thousand bullets are fired for every soldier hit. Thousands of lethal slivers of molten lead hit only leaves and dirt.

Corporal Thomas Compton was leaning over to pick up a ninety-pound 155mm shell when the PKM slug ricocheted off the firing breech and smashed into the right side of his neck. Compton lifted weights daily, so his thick muscles absorbed some of the bullet's force. But the burning iron tip slashed deep enough to sever his carotid artery. He staggered drunkenly, clasping his left hand to his neck. His gun mates grabbed him, forcing him down and pulling his hand away. The blood spurted in their faces. They desperately pushed a sweaty towel against the wound while screaming at the top of their lungs, "Corpsman up! Corpsman!"

In seconds, compression bandages were torn open and shoved under the dripping towel. When Compton tried to rip at the wound, they pinned his powerful arms and hugged him. Commander Zarest was at his side in less than a minute, swiftly applying a ligature even while knowing the wound was too deep.

Coffman had rushed from his back office into the ops center when the shooting began.

"Where are they?" he yelled at the watch officer. "Who has a visual?"

The operator controlling the drone's camera had zoomed in on the fields to the east. Clusters of harvesters—men, women, and children—were fleeing in all directions. No one was carrying a weapon. Out on the perimeter, none of the sentries had seen any muzzle flashes, but several had heard the enemy rounds snapping overhead. They focused their scopes on likely tree lines and radioed back each azimuth and distance. These wild-ass guesses were called "target locations" and circled in red on the photomap on the Common Operational Picture screen.

Less than five hectic minutes had passed when Major Barnes, his helmet and armored vest on, rushed through the door.

"We've lost a Marine, sir," he whispered. "We have one angel."

Coffman felt fear, anger, and helplessness. For the second day in a row, his command had lost a Marine. He knew this would hurt his career, and he was ashamed of that thought. Perhaps he should leave the ops center to pay his respects to the body. No, he'd do that later. Some young devil dog had been struck down, and the bastards who'd done it were laughing. Firebase Bastion wasn't there just to help the Afghan army. They were Marines, and Marines fought back. In prior wars, in Vietnam or World War II, the artillery would be blasting away.

"Hit their firing points," Coffman said. "Open sheaf, whatever you need. Friggin' obliterate them!"

He was calculating even as he spoke. Those in the ops center would later joke about "friggin'," a quaint phrase uttered by their bird colonel, an eagle proud of his perch and protective of his young. But Coffman's order was vague. Someone had to spell out a real fire mission, specifying the target, grid coordinates, number of shells, etc.

Gunny Maxwell, the artillery ops chief, kept his head down, eyes on his screen. Out in the poppy fields, harvesters were scattering helter-skelter. He would enter the firing data, but damned if he'd be tagged as the one who had ordered it. Some of those women and kids would be scythed down. How many would die? One, five, ten? Captain Lasswell was off somewhere, probably with the KIA. He'd wait until the colonel ordered him to fire at a specific set of coordinates. This wasn't going to be on him.

Cruz was standing in a corner, battle rattle on. Coffman pointed at him.

"What are you waiting for, Captain?"

"Aye-aye, sir," Cruz said. "With your permission, I'll take the QRF—"

"Oh, for God's sake, they'll be long gone," Coffman snapped. "I want you to take them under mortar fire *now!*"

Cruz was caught off guard. The red circles on the map held no validity.

"We don't have confirmed targets, sir."

"That didn't stop you from calling fire a few days ago," Coffman said.

"I was evacuating a wounded, sir. Right now, we—"

Coffman cut him off.

"Right now, Captain," he said sharply, "you're in charge of security for this base!"

The firing had ceased minutes ago. Cruz assumed the shooters had moved off, as they always did.

"I'll have the sentries confirm the coordinates, sir."

"Damn it, stop giving me semantics, Captain. The enemy is escaping! Get on with it!"

Cruz felt there were two of him. The strong one—how he had always viewed himself—was holding his ground, not saying a word, refusing to move. Yet a vaporous wraith fragile as glass was walking toward the ops chief. Again he was rolling over for the colonel. *What was he doing? This was wrong.* But before he could give the order to fire, Gunny Maxwell shook his head.

"Kabul's monitoring the net, Captain," he said loudly. "Rules of engagement don't permit terrain interdiction fires. Kabul requests your authenticating number."

As he listened, Coffman knew the gunny had trapped him. A dozen Marines had heard him order Cruz to open fire. If Afghan officials reported civilian casualties, the investigation would lead right back to him. He reversed course.

"You're right, Gunny," he said. "Kabul will slow us down too long. Captain, after you cancel your fire mission, make sure you check the lines."

Across the canal a kilometer to the east, Quat was studying the base through his binoculars. Notebook in hand, he walked over to where Tulus and Zar sat on their bikes. He held up his rough sketch.

"There," he said. "Bring me there tonight."

He was pointing at the Xs marking the very edge of the firebase.

Angry with himself, Cruz left the ops center. Outside, next to a sandbagged tent, he saw Lasswell, hands on hips, looking at the pink and orange colors of twilight. She nodded grimly and scuffed at the dirt.

"A few hours ago," she said, "I was feeling on top of my game, on my way to business school, with a connection to Stovell Industries. Whoopee for me. Damn, how could I be that shallow?"

"Don't take too much on yourself," Cruz said. "We all volunteered."

"Wow, that makes me feel better," she said. "I talked with Corporal Compton's wife at our predeployment party only a week ago. She's pregnant."

"Put that aside," Cruz said. "Visit the gun pits, share a few stories about Compton or a short prayer. Keep them focused on the mission."

"Great words. Well, what did I expect from RT? You might be Rolling Thunder, but most of us mortals care about dying. Has '*the mission*' always been your God?"

Cruz didn't reply. After a few seconds, Lasswell gave him a small smile.

"You give me advice like a brother," she said, "and I snap at you. That's my bad. Thanks for reminding me I'm the commander."

Cruz did not reply as she walked away. His mind had gone elsewhere. *Rolling Thunder?* he thought. *All I do is roll over for Coffman.*

35

Temptation

At the mosque in Q5F, the mujahideen were eating dinner, white rice and fresh, warm flat bread dipped into a cucumber sauce. The Persian had come over from the guesthouse, carrying his tan camel-skin valise. Quat had demanded 150,000 americani dollars. The mujahideen crowded around the Persian as he doled out the packs of money. They had never seen anyone paid such large sums, let alone three skinny little Asians.

"What you do," Tulus said, "with all this money?"

"Green cards to go to America," Quat said. "My cousin say good shrimping in Baton Rouge. We get other half after attack."

The Persian and the Taliban shura had agreed to this. Zar intensely disliked the arrogant Asian but was conscious of Emir Sadr's warning: "Oh, you who believe! Obey God and obey the Messenger and those among you who are in authority." Quat carried the authority of the shura.

"You have man," Quat said, "take me close to base?"

To guide the Asian, Zar had chosen Habullah. The old man had lost three fingers to a faulty blasting cap, but no one was better at sneaking through scant undergrowth, breaking cover for only a few seconds to set in an IED, then escaping. He had proven himself again only a few hours ago, shooting at the base and slipping away.

Quat handed Habullah a sheet of aluminum that looked like a flimsy rain poncho.

"Put this on," he said. "Thermal no see."

It was after sunset before Quat and Habullah, with the thin aluminum ponchos draped over them, left the mosque.

Zar drove back to his own compound. His wife, Abra, was watching a Pakistani soap. He grunted a greeting, walked into the bedroom, and flopped into bed. He was forty-two, getting old. Every morning he woke with a stiff back, listening to roosters and cows. So piercing was his pain that, in his predawn prayers, he had to lie on his stomach to touch his forehead toward Mecca.

As he dozed off, his mind wandered back to the Persian handing out stacks of dollars like mounds of fresh bread. He drowsily murmured his favorite verse from the Qu'ran: *Jihad is the duty of all true Muslims. Some prepare the food, while others plow the fields. Greatest are the mujahideen who slay the unbelievers. Allah will reward them.* Emir Sadr and the shura lived in air-conditioned houses in Quetta, sipping whiskey and watching cricket matches. What was his reward?

36

Heat

Less than three hours after Compton's death, Senator Grayson called Towns at the Pentagon.

"Mr. Secretary," Grayson said, "I've been informed of a second fatality at that base. What the hell's going on?"

"Senator," Towns said, "I don't like to use the expression 'bad luck,' but that's what we've run into. I've been assured there's no pattern to this. The two tragic occurrences aren't related to each other."

"Mr. Secretary, that sounds hollow," Grayson said. "Two in two days! How do you expect us to authorize your budget, when you won't tell us what's going on?"

"Senator, I'm not holding anything back," Towns said. "I can provide a classified briefing for your committee."

"No, that shields the White House from the public eye," Grayson said. "I'm requesting a public briefing before my committee votes on your budget. The White House has been secretly negotiating with the

Taliban. I want to know how your operation ties into that. The Senate hasn't endorsed a secret war."

"Our goal hasn't changed," Towns said. "We won't let Afghanistan become a terrorist sanctuary."

Grayson's tone expressed his frustration.

"The Pentagon's been saying that for twenty years," he said. "I want to know what's happening at that base right now."

"Senator, I'll get back to you," Towns said. "But I won't disclose details in public."

AN HOUR LATER, Towns was sitting in the small Situation Room in the White House, together with the Chairman of the Joint Chiefs, Director of the CIA, and the White House press secretary. A grim President Dinard walked in, followed by his National Security Advisor.

"The president has to fly to Houston," Armsted said, "so let's be brief. DCI, what's the intel picture?"

Director of Central Intelligence Webster looked down at his notes.

"This morning," he said in his squeaky voice, "the jihadist nets posted video of a boy blowing himself up near a Marine patrol, with the usual false claim of multiple American deaths. Plus, there's increased chatter from the Taliban shura in Quetta. We conclude that the firebase will remain under pressure."

Armsted gestured toward a televideo screen.

"General, what's it look like from Kabul?" he said.

Army General Hal Gretman, commander of US Forces Afghanistan (USFORA), looked owlish behind his Army-issue eyeglasses. He chose his words carefully. By avoiding hard calls, he had advanced his career and gained the confidence of Afghan officials.

"Sir, President Bashir has authorized more soldiers to protect the firebase," Gretman said. "Unfortunately, the press here in Kabul is showing the body of a boy allegedly killed by the Marines. Bashir is upset."

"I don't care about his feelings," Dinard broke in. "What the hell's happening down there?"

A second televideo screen showed Air Force General Bruce Laird, commander of the Central Command, located in Tampa. Laird's ruddy complexion contrasted with the dark blue of his uniform.

"Mr. President, the Marine fatality was a random event, almost an accident," Laird said. "I've ordered an investigation."

The exasperated White House press secretary, Diane Baxter, was tapping her pen on the table. Dinard gestured for her to speak.

"Generals," she said, "should we expect to hear more bad news?"

"I hope not," Gretman said. "I have Afghan soldiers waiting on the pad at Kandahar."

"Then get them moving!" Dinard said.

"Helmand's eight hours in front of Washington time, sir," Gretman said. "It's a few more hours until it's full dark down there. The helos have to fly a hundred miles over Taliban territory. We can't do that in daylight."

"I've heard enough," Dinard said abruptly. "Thank you, gentlemen."

He signaled for the televideo to be turned off.

"Those two generals wasted my time," Dinard said. "One's in Tampa and the other's in Kabul. Professor, your chain of command is too long. When I'm building a hotel, I talk with the project manager. Why aren't I talking to the colonel in charge on that damn base?"

"You'd upset him, sir," Towns said, "throw him off stride."

"Hell, the press praises you for going directly to the source. Why can't I?"

Towns frequently plucked a report off his desk and walked into some windowless back office to talk to the author. It was good for morale, and he learned facts not written down. Before he could answer, the Chairman intervened.

"You can call the firebase commander, sir," Admiral Michaels said. "But the conversation will be recorded, and it might leak out."

"We definitely don't want that!" the press secretary said. "That would be a total foul-up."

Dinard gave her a tight smile. When no one else offered comment, he peered over their heads as though looking for the television cameras.

"You're all doing the best you can," he mused. "OK, carry on."

As they were leaving, he gestured for the National Security Advisor to stay behind.

"Did you see how the military closed ranks?" Dinard said. "They don't care that I'm fighting for my political life. How can they allow one death, and then another?"

"Maybe it'll blow over," Armsted said.

"How did I let them talk me into this?" Dinard said. "The Pentagon has no idea what real heat is."

POTUS slouched in his chair, fingers beating on the desk. Then he leaned slightly to his right to look at the dark iron bust of Winston Churchill on a side table. He sat up straight and spoke to Winston.

"Grayson has the liberal vote," he said. "Now he wants to peel off the independents by labeling me as pro-war. Me, of all people! I hate those stupid wars the goddamned establishment types started. I'm not going to put up with it!"

Having won over Churchill, he pivoted back to Armsted.

"That deal we talked about? Fly over there and sound them out. If they're hard-assed, drop it."

"State's been doing the negotiating," Armsted warned.

"I'll handle State. You know how to deliver. Get going."

Day 5

APRIL 10

37

Friction

As the White House meeting was ending, it was close to midnight at Firebase Bastion and the medevac bird was on final approach. To render honors to Corporal Compton, fifty Marines were drawn up in ranks outside the ops center. Coffman had written out two paragraphs about duty, courage, and commitment. When the bird was inbound, he gestured Lasswell to stand beside him next to the flag-draped improvised coffin.

He had scarcely begun to read when the roar of the V-22 in vertical descent drowned his words out. Instead of a slow, orderly march to the LZ, the coffin bearers shuffled forward at a fast clip into the billowing dust. Whatever message Coffman had intended was never delivered.

His ceremony in shambles, he rendered a quixotic salute as the coffin was carried up the ramp. Minutes later, covered with grit and picking dirt out of his ears, he stormed back into his office. Hours earlier, he had called General Gretman in Kabul. In a level voice, the general had asked about security procedures. He had seemed satisfied, but distant. Now the phone call Coffman was dreading came from General Killian.

"Hal, I've read the sitreps and talked to Gretman," Killian said without preamble. "You didn't have a patrol out when the attack occurred?"

"No, sir," Coffman said tersely. "We hadn't been taking fire. The KIA was one chance in a thousand, a random shooting. I'm not trying to excuse it."

From somewhere on the perimeter came the sound of a few bursts of an M240 machine gun. *Shit!* Coffman wondered if Killian heard that.

"The ANA on schedule?" Killian said.

"Their colonel's slippery," Coffman said. "He's promised to pick up the pace. But we have a weather front coming, and he might use that as an excuse to hunker down."

"I'll ask Gretman to stay on him," Killian said. "There's…uncertainty about you, Hal. It extends to the top, if you get my meaning. You understand what that means."

"Aye-aye, sir," Coffman said. "More ANA arrive tonight."

"Umm," Killian said. "Maybe that'll help. You gotta keep them off you."

After hanging up, Coffman mulled over Killian's unspoken message: provide an active defense of the firebase. He called Barnes into his office.

"Major, get Cruz ready to set in the ANA reinforcements and—"

He stopped when he heard a brief flurry of shots.

"What the hell? Get after them!"

Barnes was caught off guard. Thermal cameras at night quickly picked out temperature anomalies such as hot rifle barrels. So a Taliban would fire off a burst, then smother the barrel in dirt and wait a few hours before shooting again, if at all.

"No rounds hit inside the base, sir," Barnes said. "But it'd be hard to avoid IEDs if we go searching for them in the dark."

"Then damn it," Coffman said, "as soon as it's light, I want a thorough sweep. All the ANA and Cruz's people too. I'm sick of this."

After Barnes left, Coffman rubbed his forehead and forced himself to think rationally. Lashing out at an absent Cruz was like kicking a rock. That damn captain thought he was the only war fighter. In his eyes, everyone else was a REMF, a rear-echelon motherfucker. Killian had the same attitude.

Yes, that was it! Go out with the patrol. Why not? As task force commander, he had the right—no, the duty—to see for himself what was going on. He thought of the movie *Patton*, where George C. Scott, three stars on his shoulders, had personally directed traffic to get his soldiers moving. By God, Patton knew how to command! *Be seen with the troops!* Hell, old Killian would smile when he heard about it.

SHORTLY AFTER THE V-22 TOOK OFF, two CH-53s landed and forty Afghan soldiers trotted down the ramps. Cruz had decided to post them outside the wire to the southeast. Setting them in proceeded smoothly, with the new Afghan lieutenant taking his cues from Lt. Ibril. For the patrols in the morning, Cruz assigned the southern sector to the new ANA unit, while Ibril covered to the northwest.

When Cruz returned to the op center, he called together the platoon NCOs, the CIA team, and 3rd Squad.

"XO wants us to sweep clean the perimeter to the east at first light," he said. "Sergeant Binns, your squad's up. Our job is to clear down to the canal. Think of the symbol of the Olympics—those five interconnected rings? That's us, looping back and forth. We want the muj, the dickers, the field workers, everyone to see us searching everywhere. Got it? Now let's hear from intel."

Sergeant Ahmed walked in front of the large photomap and clicked on his laser pointer.

"Stovell and I composited this overlay for your tablets. We used overhead video and the returns from the pressure plates Stovell put in. These blue dots trace where the workers walk to avoid the IEDs. You follow those dots, you're safe."

Wolfe wagged his forefinger.

"Solid hus, Sergeant," he said.

Ahmed smiled.

"Appreciated. You'll have a drone overhead, but we can't see through trees."

He stood back to let Cruz take over the briefing.

"How many of you," Cruz said, "qualified expert with those scopes on your M27s?"

Most raised their hands.

"Good. We might spook a muj or two today. He won't pose for you. It's like seeing a rat at the dump. One thousand one, one thousand two, and the rat is gone. So be fast. Take the snap shot and put him down."

"Oorah!"

Cruz allowed a small smile.

"We'll hold a steady pace," he said, "and designate a new rally point every thirty mikes. The Talibs stash their weapons in the fields, so there's no sense searching compounds."

Ashford, who was standing in the rear, raised his hand.

"Sir, me and Eagan been talking," he said. "The muj may pop up after the patrol has gone by. How about if the sniper team trails behind?"

Cruz noticed that Ashford and two other Marines had, like Eagan, painted their faces with green tiger stripes. Eagan wasn't wearing a helmet or armored vest.

"You going out naked?" Cruz said.

"Armor makes too much noise," Eagan said, "and with a helmet on, I can't hear in the bush."

Ashford was silently asking to do the same. Cruz compromised.

"You Marines on that team can take off your helmets," he said. "But wear armor."

As the meeting was breaking up, Richards approached Cruz.

"Could the patrol swing by the compound where the suicide bomber was?" he said. "It's important I get Tic back there."

Cruz hesitated, trying to think of a reason to refuse. He didn't want to return to where he had left that dying boy. And Richards had stung him for not standing up to the colonel. Still, Eagan had proven twice how deadly the CIA team was.

"All right," Cruz said. "Have Wolfe plug the compound in as a waypoint."

Binns had been watching. After Richards left, he walked up to Cruz.

"Sir, I don't like this," he said. "The snipers trailing us on their own, that spook team doing their thing—too many moving parts."

"Sergeant, work up the patrol order," Cruz said. "I'll take care of the other parts."

"Sir, you coming with me again?"

Cruz was impatient with Binns's testy tone.

"No, Sergeant, you're coming with me again."

Binns didn't reply, shaking his head at this sorry way of doing business.

IN A PREDAWN GRAY AS FUZZY AS FOG, the Marines stood in column, checking their weapons and testing their radios. When Coffman strode up in battle rattle, Cruz thought he was going to say a few rah-rah words to the patrol. Instead, he spoke quietly.

"I'm tagging along, Captain," he said. "I want to see the terrain."

"Aye-aye, sir," Cruz said.

He wasn't completely surprised. On his previous tours, senior NCOs and staff officers had joined patrols, because a single enemy shot qualified everyone as "directly engaging the enemy." For the rest of their careers, they wore the yellow-and-green Combat Action Ribbon, marking them as *combat Marines*. Cruz disliked the ribbon. Combat was episodic, flaring up in some years and absent in most. The CAR defined no one as a better Marine.

As Coffman ever so casually stepped into the center of the file, Cruz walked toward the rear for one final check. He heard a Marine snigger about "the colonel getting his CAR." Cruz stopped and spoke in a low voice.

"Someone bitching about a superior officer? Step forward, so I can ship your ass out on the next resupply chopper."

He waited five seconds, letting the Marines shift uneasily.

"Do your jobs," Cruz said, "and don't criticize others. We clear?"

He turned his head sideways, listening.

"Clear, sir," came a mumbled reply.

Cruz nodded briskly.

"Get your heads in the game," he said. "The muj want to kill you, and you're playing on their home turf."

QUAT AND HABULLAH WERE HIDING in a tree line a few hundred meters from the firebase. They watched carefully as the patrol exited in a precise Z-shaped pattern, turning left, right, and then left again. In his notebook, Quat sketched three arrows, indicating which way the Marines had pulled back the barbed wire at each turn.

Pleased with his work, he smiled at Habullah, who responded by swallowing two pills. Quat frowned, disliking the casual way in which Zar's men smoked hashish and popped uppers. More than a bit high, Habullah then decided not to retrace their route back to the mosque. Instead, he slipped through the bushes parallel to the American patrol. Quat had no choice but to follow behind him. *Foolish fellow*, he thought, *showing off by trailing the Americans.*

AS THE MARINES HEADED TOWARD THE CANAL, they were facing directly into the bright sun and had to shade their eyes even after putting on their Oakleys. There was no wind, and tendrils of mist curled up lazily from the irrigation ditches. The harvesters were slicing open poppy bulbs. The women ignored the Marines, the boys looked at them with unsmiling curiosity, and the men glared. The grunts returned the stares and ground their boot heels hard into the plants, leaving a muddy trail behind them.

Wolfe was sweeping the mine detector in rhythmic arcs. The rest walked in single file, following the dabs of Silly String. Head hunched down, Wolfe watched for changes in the color of the dirt, warily skirting around any light, turned-up patch of earth among the poppy rows. Whenever he increased his speed over ground packed too firm to conceal an IED, Binns would stubbornly cling to a measured pace, forcing those behind him to do the same. When Wolfe looked back, Binns would signal palm-down to him to take it slow.

Binns didn't think he was acting spitefully. He knew his job and wanted to impress the colonel. It was his squad, not Cruz's. He resented the presence of the spooks, and the sniper team trailing behind was another worry. What if they opened fire without asking him first? All these hangers-on weighed down his squad, his Marines.

When Wolfe reached a long tree line, he clicked on his throat mic.

"Wolf Three, I'll cut around to the north," he said. "It'll take too long to hack through that bush."

"Hold one," Binns said. "Let me think this over."

Cruz pushed forward and spoke quietly to Binns.

"We have to pick up the pace," Cruz said.

Binns straightened, hoping to catch the attention of the colonel. "I'm no boot, sir. If we rush, we invite trouble."

His petulance angered Cruz.

"You're falling behind schedule, Sergeant. We have a lot to turf to cover."

"Sir, I know what I'm doing, really I do. We both can't be in charge of this patrol. That didn't work out the last time."

Cruz grasped it then. He should have seen this coming. Binns blamed him for Lamont's death.

"You're right," Cruz said. "We're not both in charge. You obey my orders. If you don't like that, fall in at the back of the line."

Binns had blurted out his feelings without thinking it through. He had acted on instinct, sensing that the colonel's presence worked to his advantage. Now he was startled and uncertain.

"Sir, I'm thinking of my men. My job is to get them all home in one piece."

Cruz cut him off.

"Sergeant, your job is the mission. This conversation is over."

After gesturing at Wolfe to proceed, Binns let out a theatrical sigh. As he walked to his place in line, Coffman gave him an encouraging pat on the shoulder. Trailing behind, the sniper team had also stopped. Through his scope, Ashford watched the interaction.

"Wish they'd make up their minds who's running the show," he said. "We're wasting time."

38

Extortion

When they reached the field bordering Nantush's compound, the squad set up a defensive position. Tic walked through the open gate of the compound, followed by Richards and two alert Marines. Seeing this, Coffman beckoned to Cruz.

"Since when does the CIA run a Marine patrol?"

Cruz pointed to the white flags slightly flapping on the walls of several other compounds.

"Those are Talib flags, sir," he said. "Usually there's a few, but not one on every compound. The terp, Tic, is smart. He might get a line on what's going on."

When Coffman moved off, Cruz radioed the sniper team.

"Winmag, this is Wolf Six. Got anything?"

"Wolf Six, we're glassing dickers on compound walls," Ashford said. "No weapons visible."

Trailed by Sergeant Doyle, Cruz walked over to Stovell, who had unzipped his square backpack. He was squinting at a computer screen showing the spectrograph of radio lines, head cocked to listen to his earphone.

"Ahmed says there's no traffic about the sniper team," Stovell said. "They haven't been spotted yet."

Doyle looked from the Marines to the laborers in the field not a stone's throw away. He idly snapped off a vermillion poppy bulb and juggled it in his hand.

"I used to chop tobacco leaves," he said. "Made thirty dollars a day and upchucked at night. These Afghans are even dumber than me, collecting tiny gumdrops all day."

Stovell shook his head.

"Sergeant, this land's worth a million dollars an acre. You're looking at fields of gold."

"I'm looking at fucking cemeteries, loaded with IEDs."

"What do you expect? You're bad for commerce."

"Yeh, and those fucks work their kids like slave labor."

Stovell smiled.

"There's an old painting called *Cranberry Season*," he said. "It shows women and children on their knees, pawing for berries."

"That's what I mean. We were starving back then."

Stovell laughed.

"See those canals? Built by American engineers in the '50s, part of our foreign aid program," he said. "You can grow anything here. Wheat, corn, melons, sunflowers, tomatoes, you name it."

"What's your point?"

"The children in that old painting weren't starving. They were gathering cranberries as a treat. No one is starving in Helmand. Here, opium is the treat. It buys TVs, motorcycles, shopping trips to Doha. Don't feel sorry for them."

"This is fucked up," Doyle said. "What'd he die for then?"

Stovell looked puzzled.

"Lamont," Doyle said. "Everyone says you're super smart. You think maybe he went someplace special?"

Stovell answered with care.

"You're like most Marines, Sergeant," Stovell said. "You believe there's another side. It's even written in your hymn, that stanza about Marines *'guarding the streets of heaven.'*

"What about you?"

"Some claim the universe started with a big bang," Stovell said. "That sounds scientific, doesn't it? But what caused the bang?"

"You're jerking me around."

"No, I'm saying you can argue the case one way or another."

"I feel like Brian's out there somewhere," Doyle said.

"Hang on to what you believe, Sergeant. Scientists know no more about God than you do."

Doyle gestured at the laborers bent over in the fields.

"I'd be bored out of my mind doing that day after day," he said. "I wonder what they think about."

"The answer to that is simple," Stovell said. "They're thinking how to kill you,"

INSIDE THE COMPOUND, Nantush brought Tic to his modest *hujra*, or guesthouse. Once they were alone, he reached into his tunic and handed over a packet of black heroin. Tic tossed it lightly in his hand, opened the bag, and stirred the tan, coarse powder. He placed a sliver on his tongue.

"And for this you traded how much opium?"

"The harvest from five *jeribs*. Twenty-five kilos of poppy."

Tic tossed the bag back to Nantush.

"I want three bags, like I told you."

Nantush was fumbling with his prayer beads, hoping Allah would intervene.

"I asked," he said. "They gave me only one. No more!"

Tic shrugged.

"That's your problem. You do business with *ghlaa*, thieves who cheat you."

Trembling with rage and grief. Nantush pointed a shaking finger at Tic. His voice sounded scratchy, as if the words were strangling him.

"I have lost two sons," he said. "Yes, you can kill me. No one can stop you but God. You, a Kandahari, work for the invaders. Leave me alone! You are *takfir*, cast out by Allah."

That broke it for Tic, who lashed back.

"How can you speak of Allah? Think back, old man. Do you remember when your *hazra* lied about Noora, an honest camel trader from Kandahar? Were you there when the Taliban killed him?"

Nantush scrambled to remember, but Tic gave him no time. He dusted off his hands and turned to leave.

"God is great and merciful, old man," he said. "I am not merciful. I don't care about your family or your lands. Do not be *dalaal*. Three kilos, not less. Or Guantanamo."

Once back among the Marines, Tic handed a folded tissue to Stovell. "This enough?"

Stovell looked at the powder.

"This is what we need," he said. "Why the scowl? Any problems?"

"Fucking tribal memories," Tic said. "That farmer thinks I'm the second coming of Attila. Good thing my family's in Omaha. Anyway, he's broken. He'll make the call."

Tic turned to the knapsack, checked the computer settings, put on his earpiece, and held a finger up to be quiet while he listened.

NANTUSH WAITED UNTIL THE INFIDELS HAD LEFT, then retrieved his cell phone from under a stone and pressed a number. As soon as Tulus answered, Nantush began to plead, his voice trembling.

"Nephew," Nantush said, "I need two more melons. My family, please, my family."

Tulus had anticipated the call. He knew one kilo wouldn't satisfy the *takfir* traitor working for the Americanis. Tulus thought he knew how to persuade Zar to part with two more kilos.

"Uncle, melons are heavy to lift and collect," he said. "When the laborers are finished, can you provide them water and shade?"

"Yes, yes!" Nantush yelled in relief. "I have much room! I can arrange all!"

Tic TRANSLATED THE MESSAGE to Richards and Stovell.

"That seals it," Tic said. "The mosque is the lab. The farmer's getting his heroin. In return, he promised support for some job."

"Bravo!" Stovell said. "Tic, you have a future in extortion. You should consider law school."

39

The Third to Fall

After leaving Nantush's compound, the patrol headed north a few hundred meters, then south toward the canal and, after a slight hesitation, north again. It was now eight in the morning, the sun was blazing, and the ops center estimated there were two hundred laborers in the poppy fields. The white flags of the Taliban dangled limply from poles and tree limbs. On the bank of an irrigation ditch adjacent to a footbridge, Wolfe detected the day's first IED.

Cruz switched to his encrypted handheld and called the sniper team.

"Winmag, this is Wolf Six, we have an IED at our pos," Cruz said. "One hundred meters east of Compound 172."

Ashford was in command of the four-man sniper team, although he checked with Eagan before making any critical decisions.

"Wolf Six, we have eyes on," Ashford replied. "We've copied the GPS mark."

Wolfe cut around the IED, following the squishy hoofprints of sheep while monitoring the route on his iPad. He turned onto a dirt trail packed hard as concrete that led uphill next to a feeble stream. The slight elevation provided shelter from floodwaters for a dozen homes tucked behind stout walls. As the Marines warily climbed the incline, Cruz didn't see a single hole hacked out of a wall, not one murder hole to conceal a rifle barrel. This told him that in the seven years since the Marines had left, no Afghan soldiers had ventured this far into the Green Zone.

Chickens and roosters set up their usual clatter, and mangy watchdogs strained at their chains, growling and barking. As the Marines ducked under drooping electric lines leading to satellite dishes, they heard a few tinny voices before the TVs were turned off. No waifs begged for candy or pens, and no women in *chadors* and veils peeked from doorways. The Americans were the enemy, the godless unbelievers who delivered death from the sky swift as a falcon, unheard and unseen.

On the crest of the hill, a donkey hitched to a paddle wheel plodded in an eternal circle. Shallow ditches from outhouses emptied into the stream. The soiled water nourished both the poppies and watermelons whose porous skins absorbed the bacteria from the feces. This caused local bouts of mountain cholera that ran their course as unremarkable—and unreported—as snakebites.

Back at the ops center, Ahmed and his intel crew were listening to the ICOM traffic from dickers perched on roofs and walls, exchanging ridiculous code words like "two turnips," "seven cows," and "Hugulu." When the Marines raised their rifles to observe through their telescopic sights, some watchers ducked down. Others stood their ground and one gave the Italian salute to the Marines, who laughed.

Shortly before ten, Tic slid into line behind Cruz and spoke in a low voice.

"Captain, dickers have made the sniper team."

"You think the team's too exposed?" Cruz said. "Call them in?"

Tic laughed.

"Hell no, Skipper, not after the other day," he said. "The locals are calling them *kapesksa*—goblins. They're scared the goblins will pop them."

A moderate breeze had sprung up, and drab-colored kites were flying over several compounds. Tic gestured toward them.

"They're signaling where we are."

Cruz looked at his tablet. A blue dot showed the sniper team in over-watch in a thicket to his right front. He radioed to Ashford.

"Dickers have spotted you. We're pushing to our next checkpoint."

"Wolf Six, roger. We have a kid with an ICOM ducking up and down a few hundred meters to our south. OK to throw a few rounds near him?"

With the ops center listening on the net, Cruz wished Ashford hadn't been so direct.

"Negative," he said.

QUAT, WHO WAS WATCHING THE PATROL, didn't like his situation. He had concluded that his guide had lost part of his brain as well as three fingers on his right hand. A few times he had grinned at Quat and pointed at the Marines, mimicking with his hands as though a mine would soon explode. He held up his AK, indicating that after the IED went off, he would shoot at the infidels.

Quat thought this was stupid. The Americans didn't seem anxious or afraid. They didn't head in any straight direction. Twice they had doubled back, and each time their point team had disappeared into the undergrowth. Occasionally a bird-size drone that sounded like an angry bee had hovered close to where he and Habullah were hiding. Quat knew the camera couldn't see through the leaves, but he didn't like how this was unfolding. The Americans were acting like they were the hunters.

Now, Habullah was talking on his ICOM. Even if his low voice didn't reach to the Americans, his tactics were sloppy. The old man turned to Quat, his forefinger and thumb forming a circle around his right eye. He pointed to his ICOM and squeezed his finger a few times. *Warning: snipers somewhere out there.*

That broke it for Quat. His father, having endured eight years in a North Vietnamese "reeducation camp", had taught him never to trust his life to any cause or man. To prosper, one must first survive. This Taliban idiot and his foolish game would get him killed.

They were almost at the end of the tree line that concealed them. Beyond that, there was an open patch of scrub growth, and then dense thickets. If they ran fast, Quat thought they could make it across at an angle out of sight of the patrol. But the drone might pick them up. He needed a distraction. Some other Talibs had to shoot at the patrol. Gripping Habullah's arm, he gestured at their escape route, then pantomimed shooting at the patrol. His mute fury frightened the old mujahideen, who nodded and hissed instructions over the ICOM. They knelt down and waited.

BACK AT THE OPS CENTER, Sergeant Ahmed heard the feverish tones in the ICOM exchange and alerted the patrol.

"They could be jerking us around," Ahmed said. "But you may have a few stray rounds coming your way."

Coffman was monitoring both the intra-patrol and the ops center radio nets. He heard the warning and paid it no special attention. He wasn't daydreaming, but he had lost interest in patrol techniques. After two hours, the reel was repeating itself, wending inside the Silly String through field after field, avoiding paths and bridges, veering into dense brush to wade across muddy streams, sloshing along until plunging into the next irrigation ditch. Being twelfth in line was boring. The young Marines in front of and behind him had scarcely spoken, fearing to look unprofessional. Not once had anyone requested his judgment about anything. He'd learned enough. He hadn't planned to stay out all day anyway. When their next loop brought them near the firebase, he'd hop off.

He had his head down, studying his notepad, when the first bullet cracked overhead. Startled, he dropped the pad and as he bent over, three more rounds snapped by, one so close it made a zinging sound. Along with the other Marines, he went flat. For a few seconds, he felt sheer excitement, convinced he was the target. An enemy had sighted in and shot, intending to kill him. And the bullet had missed!

It never occurred to Coffman that the shots were random, a few wild bursts intended to distract the Marines. No, those bullets were meant for him. He'd heard them snapping over his head. The Taliban knew he was the leader, the commander of the task force, a full colonel with the black metal eagle pinned on the center of his armored vest. At last, after twenty-five years, he was in combat!

Now what? He hadn't seen a single shooter, and he had only a vague sense of where the shots had come from. On every side, the field was lined with trees, green vines, and shrubs. The Marines lying down near him seemed as bewildered as he was. Each had a sector to cover and despite much shouting back and forth, he hadn't heard anyone point where to shoot. A Marine blindly let loose a burst of three or four rounds. As the red arc of a tracer flashed toward a tree line, four more M27s cut loose. Cruz's voice came over the intra-squad radio.

"Cease fire, goddamn it! We got friendlies on bearing zero niner five."

Coffman poked up his head. No more incoming, and no return fire. Anxious to know what was happening, he worked his way forward, careful not to step outside the cleared path. Cruz and Doyle, on their knees studying the photomap, paid him no attention. Irritated, Coffman stood erect and looked around, as though he did this sort of thing every day.

And there they were, in the opposite direction from where the shots had come. He had never seen an enemy before, and now he was looking at two! One was wearing black, like in those ninja movies. Hunched over, they were running across a soggy field, rifles clearly visible, water spurting up around their feet as they sprinted at incredible speed. Live targets, not three hundred meters away! How the hell could they move so fast? The open patch was small, and they were almost at the thickets on the far side. The Marines, lying prone, hadn't seen them and now they were getting away! Coffman pointed, banging Cruz on the top of his helmet.

"Get those bastards!" he yelled. "Get them!"

Cruz leaped up and looked around. Get what? Shoot at what? The muj were gone, out of sight, safe in the greenery. In five seconds, it was over. The grunts were looking at each other, uncertain what had happened or what they were supposed to be doing. Cruz was not moving. Binns and Doyle looked equally confused. Coffman was having none of it. He took charge.

"Two! Right over there!" Coffman shouted. "Work up a fire mission!"

Cruz thought lobbing a few shells into the bush was a preposterously long shot. The odds of hitting any muj inside that tree line were one in a thousand. Coffman had butted in, but he was the task force commander. Cruz didn't believe any civilians were hiding in the bushes. So why not? He nodded to Doyle, who spoke into his throat mic.

"Badger Six, this is Badger Two, fire mission," he said. "Two enemy running northeast. Request an open sheaf of six rounds at 436 898. Danger close. Friendly troops at 434 890 and 435 880."

The fire direction center had been tracking the GPS positions of the patrol and the sniper team. The computer immediately calculated the firing data, and 81mm mortar crews leveled the bubbles on the tubes and placed the propellant bags between the fins of the shells. Within a minute, four shells were in the air.

★ ★ ★

THE FIVE-MAN SNIPER TEAM was two hundred meters south of the target. Ashford and Eagan were standing together, their rifle scopes resting on branches as they searched the bush on the far side of the opening. They had eyes on the patrol and were monitoring the radio traffic. But they hadn't seen the two muj. They heard the shells leaving the tubes with dull metallic clunks at the same time they received the warning from the ops center.

"Shot out," Ashford said. "Heads down!"

All four lay down. Twelve seconds later, Ashford, listening on his 153, shouted, "Splash!" He heard a sound like a newspaper being ripped in half, followed by a slight shudder in the ground; three quick, dull crumps; and one sharp crack. In a blink, the packed explosives shattered their forged steel casings, hurling thousands of molten slivers in all directions.

PFC Tommy Beal was to the front, slightly behind Corporal Tim Byrne, the engineer with the metal detector. Byrne was lying flat, the left side of his face on the ground. He thought he saw Beal lift his head up just as the earth shuddered with the explosions. A tiny lapse in judgment.

"Umph!" A cry of pain and shock, an expulsion of breath, as if struck hard in the stomach. Beal jerked to his knees, holding the left side of his neck. He fell backward, writhing from side to side, the heels of his boots kicking at the dirt.

Byrne immediately crawled to him. Ashford ran forward, followed by Eagan, who was on the radio shouting, "Check fire! Check fire!" Ashford had to use all his strength to pull Beal's hand back to inspect the wound. When he did, blood spurted into his face.

"Hold him down!"

He clamped two hands on the spouting wound as Byrne grabbed Beal's shoulders to stop him from bucking. Eagan was ripping open compression and hemostatic field dressings. He shoved Ashford aside and stuffed in the gauze. Ashford had ripped his bandage open and Eagan plugged that on top of the others. In a second, the compresses were sopping red. Eagan pushed down harder with both hands. Beal, eyes bulging with terror, jerked and fought to get loose.

"Fucking hurts," he gurgled.

Ashford pinned his arms, while Eagan pressed down harder. Wolfe was sweeping a path for the patrol to reach them, and Cruz was calling for a critic medevac. Corpsman Bushnell worked his way to the front of the file and took charge. He packed on more gauze and pressed firmly down. Beal was no longer struggling, and his head had lolled to one side. His armor was sopped through, and a puddle the color of rust had collected around his left shoulder. Doc Bushnell felt the blood seep through the fresh bandages and trickle down his fingers. He knelt there for another minute, losing his first Marine.

They unfolded the field stretcher and strapped in Beal's body. There was little talk. Coffman stayed off to one side. Binns took a knee in silent prayer, then stood back passively, as though he were an onlooker. Cruz told Byrne, the engineer, to sweep a path to a nearby irrigation ditch. The corpsman and the sniper team followed behind him. They rubbed their hands in the mud and splashed the brown water on their faces. They returned dripping with mud and blood, looking more like ogres than Marines.

Cruz told the op center they were returning with one angel and read off Beal's initials and the last four digits of his Social Security number. Sergeant Doyle sat numbly in the dirt, staring at his digital tablet. Had he sent the wrong position? Hell no! Besides, the ops center checked the GPS position and knew exactly where the sniper team was, well off the gun-target line. So did a mortar crew bungle when leveling the bubbles or attaching the powder bags? No, every step was checked twice. Then he remembered a whanging sound he'd never heard before. Had one shell hit a boulder and ricocheted crazily before exploding? Bewildered, he looked up at Cruz.

"I don't know how it happened, sir," he said. "I've called hundreds of missions."

Four Marines picked up the collapsible litter. A fresh team would rotate every ten minutes. Wolfe figured they'd reach the wire within half an hour. The trip back was less a patrol than a funeral procession, carrying a body without a shroud and with mourners lost in their own thoughts.

Head down, Doyle tagged along in the column, going over the details again and again. Farther back in the column, Coffman forced himself to think calmly and logically. When the patrol came under fire, he had to take charge because Cruz hadn't taken action. He had to order the fire mission to protect the patrol. That was logical, wasn't it? The tragedy wasn't due to error on his part. Still, he dreaded the phone call from General Killian. PFC Beal was the third to fall. *Shit.*

Binns was walking with his back erect, glancing to neither side, almost stomping, signaling that he hadn't caused this disaster. He was smoldering, stoking his grudge, thinking that Cruz had pushed his way in, then screwed up royally.

Once inside the wire, a casualty detail placed a poncho over the body. Coffman was standing with his hand on Beal's blood-soaked shoulder, as if to reassure the dead nineteen year-old that things would be all right. Binns paused next to Coffman.

"Beal should still be alive, sir," Binns said softly. "Captain Cruz told him not to wear his helmet."

It took Coffman a few seconds to grasp the accusation. Then he felt a surge of relief. *Of course! I had nothing to do with Beal's death. It was Cruz who lacked judgment! Thank God for the common sense of snuffies like Binns.*

"You lost a good man, Sergeant," he said. "Damn shame. I'll have Major Barnes take your statement."

40

Counterpunch

As Binns headed to the platoon tent for the debrief, Barnes and Ahmed nervously approached the colonel.

"We're picking up buzz, sir," Barnes said. "The muj saw the stretcher. They're psyched, whipping everybody up. Sergeant Ahmed thinks we'll take incoming if we don't push back out."

Coffman was caught off guard.

"What about the ANA? Can't they do it?"

"They're still patrolling where we sent them, sir," Ahmed said.

Coffman got it. Only the Marine patrol had returned to base, leaving a sector unprotected. He couldn't hole up like a scared hedgehog. How would he explain that? He had no choice. This was Cruz's fault, so he'd have to deal with it.

"Tell Cruz to get after it," he said.

★ ★ ★

CRUZ CALLED OUT McGOWAN'S SQUAD that was standing by as the Quick Reaction Force. While the Marines loaded the waypoints into their GPS watches and tablets, Ahmed gave a brief intel update.

"Everyone's squawking on ICOMs and cell phones," he said. "They're happy out there, all jacked. Bottom line: you'll make contact."

The Marines nodded, pumped and hard. It was their fourth day, and every one of them had been outside the wire at least once. Half of them under twenty, seasoned enough to be lethal and impulsive enough to do wrong.

"Devil dogs, I want fire discipline out there," Cruz said, "not The Wild Bunch. We lost a brother. We'll get some, the right way."

The agency team was also going back out, and Wolfe was staying at point. Cruz took Doyle aside.

"That fire mission was on me, not you," Cruz said. "When I get back in, I'll see to it."

"No, sir," Doyle said. "I called it in. I can't stay here. I gotta go too."

If Doyle was left behind, his gloom would affect all who saw him.

"All right," Cruz said. "Fall in behind me."

The sniper team was standing off to one side, talking in low voices among themselves.

"Two fucking days," Ashford said, "and three brothers dead."

Eagan reacted angrily.

"There's no such animal as a one-way war," he said. "They lose people, and so do we. You die here when you're twenty or fifty when a heart attack kills you in the States. The difference is that you chose to be here. So suck it up."

"I was just talking," Ashford said. "I'm ready."

QUAT ESTIMATED THEY WERE HALFWAY BACK to the mosque when he saw four unarmed Afghans on Hondas slowly wending their way along a serpentine path. Habullah, who had been jabbering on his ICOM, put down his AK and rushed out of the bush to welcome them. Recognizing Tulus, Quat too left the tree line.

"No! No!" Tulus yelled. "Hide rifle!"

Puzzled, Quat placed his AK in the reeds and walked forward. Tulus pointed upward.

"Eye in the sky," he said, "very bad. But a dead American, very good! All fight now!"

Quat looked at Tulus. The man's cheeks were flushed and he was nodding, beating softly on the handlebars. Allahu Akbar! Tulus patted the rear seat, indicating he'd drive Quat back to the mosque. Quat climbed on and looked up at the sky—somewhere a drone was watching.

Americans tolerate their enemies, he thought. *A foolish people.*

THE PATROL WAS SCARCELY BEYOND SIGHT of the wire when a group of workers bolted from a field to their east.

"Winmag, we're headed to that field," Cruz radioed. "Stand by for us to take fire."

"Wolf Six, we're tracking on your south flank," Ashford replied.

Wolfe found a cut through the undergrowth. Reaching the field where the workers had been, he veered left so that the Marines were walking parallel to a tree line about a hundred meters away. The patrol was in the open when the first AK bullets cracked over their heads. Immediately some flopped down, while others knelt to see above the poppies.

"Willkes, return fire at seventy degrees!" Sergeant McGowan shouted at the machine gun crew.

After three short bursts, he signaled to stop. For the next minute, there was no return fire. Then a few more AK rounds passed high over the Marines, followed by the short, deep bark of a PKM machine gun. There were no tracers, but McGowan thought the firing sounded slightly north of the previous shots. As the M240 responded with a long *ratatatat*, Cruz knelt down next to McGowan.

"I think the shots came from northeast," he said. "They're trying to lure us in. Probably IEDs waiting for us."

The tree line was as long as a football field, a tangle of thin poplar trees, thick undergrowth, and Andean vines thin and strong as fishing lines, coiled around branches and anchored under rocks, waiting to trip the unwary.

Cruz tugged the 153 handheld out of a breast pocket and called the ops center.

"Eagle Three, you watching this?" he radioed. "Have Big Bird zoom in on the field on the east side of the tree line. Let me know if you see any squirters."

Over the speakers inside the ops center, Cruz's voice sounded loud and firm. Barnes, as the watch officer, nodded to the corporal controlling the drone. Coffman, listening in the rear, did not interfere.

"Winmag, this is Wolf Six. I want to cut those shooters off," Cruz radioed. "Move into the tree line from the south."

This was an unusual tactic for a sniper team, but they were grunts before they became HOGs.

Cruz turned back to McGowan.

"I'll stay here with the 240," he said. "You take two teams and move straight north. Let me know when you can see the field on the far side of that tree line."

On their tablets, McGowan, Ashford, and Cruz watched the blue blips that marked their three separate groups of friendlies. At point, Wolfe followed a yellow teleprompter line that traced the footsteps of the workers who had fled minutes before. Big Bird's two-hundred-power telescope was zoomed in, allowing a half-dozen Marines in the ops center to examine each tiny open space in the foliage and to scan the poppy rows that provided escape routes for the Talibs.

Cruz toggled his 153.

"Eagle Three, this is Wolf Six," he said. "How about dropping a closed sheaf of 81s in the field on the east side of the tree line?"

Barnes winced at the request. He stole a nervous glance at Coffman. A few of the operators were smiling and rolling their eyes. Rolling Thunder at work. Barnes tried to provide Cruz with an out.

"Wolf Six, the dust will obscure Big Bird's view. Over."

Cruz wasn't buying it.

"Eagle Three, understood. I want to block them in."

Typical, Barnes thought. *In the field, Cruz doesn't know how to back off. Coffman's blaming him for Beal, and three hours later he's calling a fire mission?*

"Wolf Six, that's a solid negative," Barnes said. "Friendlies are too close. Remember? Out."

Barnes intended his reprimand to sting. Instead, it angered Cruz. Barnes was using Beal as his excuse not to fire. The mortars would hit a hundred meters away from the nearest Marines. Take some risk. Don't allow the Talibs to hunker down so close to the base.

Cruz knew it was futile to argue. He waited as McGowan moved north. Fifteen minutes passed with no more shots from the tree line. Cruz looked inquiringly at Tic, who had earphones on and was turning the channel settings on his intercept box.

"Can't find those shooters talking on any channel, Skipper," Tic said. "Neither can Ahmed. Lots of other chatter, but they're staying off the net, probably waiting for us to push on."

Cruz turned to Corporal Juan Fuentes, the squad's systems operator, who had taken off his pack and was adjusting a four-bladed drone the size of a thick book.

"Sweep just above the treetops," Cruz said. "What's the flying time?"

"Fresh battery, sir," Fuentes said. "Tinker Bell's good for thirty mikes."

"That'll do. Hover over different spots, like you're checking something out."

Fuentes unfolded the rotor blades and launched the drone toward the tree line, watching the video return on his handheld tablet. Each time he twisted a knob on his control mechanism, the pitch of the tiny motor changed. The drone climbed and dove like an angry bee, the sounds floating across the fields. It darted back and forth, dipping and hovering. Fuentes, peering at the small video screen, shook his head in frustration. With the camera bouncing and jiggling, he could see only leaves and foliage.

Inside the tree line, the engineer with the sniper team was sweeping as best he could. But as he ducked and twisted through the undergrowth, his detector missed many spots. It was a calculated risk. Cruz knew the Taliban rarely buried IEDs far back in the tree lines amidst the root tangles and vines. Concealing the wires was too tricky, and the chances were too remote of any *takfir* blundering past.

On his tablet, Cruz looked at the blue dot marking the snipers. It would take another half hour for them to complete their search. Altogether, he was spending a full hour on one tree line less than a quarter mile from the base. If he came up empty, it would be a long night. On the other hand, if they killed some Tangos here, the others would likely pull back to decide their next move.

"Give me a sitrep. Over." Cruz radioed.

"Wolf Six, this stuff is thick," Ashford said. "I'd need a machete to hack my way through. Plus, we're making way too much noise."

"Understood. Make as much noise as you can. Over."

"Wolf Six, say again your last."

"Make more noise. Shout back and forth."

There was a pause. Then from somewhere back in the tree line off to his right, Cruz heard a clear "Hello!" followed by, "Can you hear me now?"

"This is Wolf Six. Louder. Break, break. Wolf Two, sitrep. Over."

McGowan's team had advanced beyond the northern end of the tree line.

"Wolf Six, this is Wolf Two. We've got eyes on the field on the other side of the tree line," Mac radioed. "What now?"

"Stop and go 360," Cruz replied. "Stay alert for any muj running east from the bush."

McGowan signaled to Wolfe to take a knee. Behind him, Lance Corporal George Adler, the platoon's Designated Marksman, did the same. Though a notch below Ashford's status as a sniper, Adler's performance on the snap-shooting course had won him rave reviews. He scoped the field on the far side of the tree line and focused on the swaying purple-and-white poppy bulbs.

Pop, pop, pop, he thought. *Gotcha. Three for three.*

INSIDE THE TREE LINE, Mustafa Benjab was crouching in a small ditch alongside his two companions when he heard the americanis shout back and forth. One thing after another had gone wrong, and his head hurt. Zar had told them to shoot to help the Asian escape, then join the workers in the field. *Ha!* The workers had fled before the firing. So he had waited and these americanis had come. Fine. His men took a few shots at them and then waited. But that drone was now circling like a giant mosquito. He gestured to his two companions to stay hidden and wait for the *kafirs* to move off. Only instead, some americanis were shouting from inside the tree line. Time to pull out. He stood up and gestured at the field to their east. Run across, fast!

ADLER HAD TAKEN A KNEE, his butt resting on his right ankle, left elbow dug into his left thigh, both eyes open, right pupil dilated from constantly peering through the seven-power Bausch scope. Wolfe was squatting next to him, leisurely sipping sugared tea through the tube attached to his CamelBak.

"Give that scope a rest, bro," Wolfe said. "You'll get cross-eyed doing that so long."

"Sergeant Mac assigned me the prime shooting spot," Adler said. "Gonna get some."

"Yeah, well," Wolfe said, "Sergeant Mac's gungy. But shit, no hajji's going to tear ass across your personal three hundred range. All those sneaky bastards do is plant their IEDs and ditty-bob by us, carrying their fucking and shovels. I—"

Bang, bang, bang! Wolfe fell back on his ass as Adler squeezed off fast shots. A few hundred meters away, three men in dusky *kameez* were sprinting through the poppies. The one in the lead, hit twice, was stumbling. The other two tried to support him, and then all three dropped out of sight. Wolfe scrambled to grab his M27 but before he could get to his knees, three more M27s had joined in. Every rifle had a noise suppressor, enabling Mac's shouts to be heard over the din.

"Cease fire, damn it! Give me a pos rep!"

"Three! Three at two o'clock!" Adler yelled, pointing to his right. "I got one, maybe two."

"See any weapons?"

"I think so. They were carrying something. I mean, why else were they running?"

"OK. Listen up! Adler, you and Wolfe shoot where you saw them. Everyone else, watch their impact area and then hose the shit out of it. One mag each!"

Adler stood up, aimed in carefully, and fired three more rounds. Wolfe got off a burst that included a tracer. Seven other rifles joined in for several furious seconds.

"That's enough!" Mac yelled. "But if anyone sees movement out there, shoot first and inform me later."

McGowan radioed the situation to Cruz.

"Wolf Two, copy all," Cruz said. "Move to where you saw them. Tinker Bell will recon."

Thirty seconds later, the tiny drone was hovering twenty feet above the spot. On Fuentes's tablet, the video showed one man sprawled on his stomach. A second man was lying on his side in a fetal position, knees tucked close to his stomach. The drone rose to thirty feet for a wider camera angle. Farther away, a third man, dragging a PKM machine gun, was crawling on his hands and knees between two rows of poppy. The operator tilted his tiny joystick, and the screeching drone dove and hovered a few feet over his head. Whether panicked or brave or both, the man leaped to his feet and swung the PKM upward, firing madly at his tormentor. At least five Marines, delighted to see a live target, responded immediately and the man danced spastically for a few seconds, twitching as dozens of bullets beat the dust out of his *kameez* and the blood out of his body.

When the shooting stopped, recon by the drone confirmed three men down and no others in the vicinity. Cruz called in the sniper team and the drone was retrieved. Within ten minutes, all the Marines were together at the defensive perimeter McGowan had set in near the dead men. Holding the PKM across his chest, a grinning Adler was posing for pictures and Wolfe was waving an AK.

Two rounds from an M27 coughed out, sounding like burps. A Marine, rifle muzzle pointing down, was standing over one of the crumbled bodies. Cruz glared at him.

"Delivered a hammer pair, sir," the grunt said. "Dead check."

"You mean brain dead," Cruz said. "You wanted to shoot someone, so you shot a dead man. Give me your weapon."

Cruz removed the magazine, ejected the round in the chamber, and roughly handed the M27 back.

"For the rest of this patrol," he said, "you carry a club, unless your squad leader decides otherwise."

McGowan pointed a finger at the Marine.

"Meet Terminal Lance Corporal Merrill, sir," he said, "my perpetual motard fuckup."

"Merrill," Cruz said, "you disappoint me."

The Marines briskly searched the bodies, finding little of interest. Tic had stripped an ICOM from one of the dead.

"Do they know we have it?" Stovell said.

Tic shook his head.

"No. There's no coordinator on this net," he said. "It'll be a few hours before they know we zapped these three. I can screw with them big time."

Stovell turned to Cruz.

"If we confuse the Talibs," he said, "we deflect their attention from the base. When Tic is finished, they won't know what to think or believe."

Cruz hesitated, wary of being manipulated. The CIA team was relentless, doling out information only when it suited them. Still, time and again Eagan's shooting skills had proven valuable. And while Stovell behaved as though his brilliance meant little, he was obviously the strategist.

"All right, Stovell," he said. "I'll let Barnes know."

As the patrol returned to base, Tic keyed the ICOM, alternately speaking in Pashto and Dari. With the volume turned up, he was laughing at the torrent of replies.

"Hey, bro," McGowan said. "Don't keep it to yourself."

"They all watch TV," Tic yelled. "They know the virus killed lots of people. They're afraid of it. So I tell them Marines are bringing a new plague."

He was gleefully shaking his fist.

"They believe it!" he shouted. "The stupid fuckers!"

Cruz looked quizzically at Stovell.

"Why's he laughing?"

"Tic's father bought a dozen camels at auction in this district," Stovell said. "The local council claimed the rich outsider was a spy. The Taliban hanged him and the locals divided up his money. Tic's indulging in payback."

"You didn't bring him to settle a personal grudge," Cruz said. "Isn't this over the top?"

"Actually, I suggested it," Stovell said. "I hired Tic for this mission. We're not here to win friends. We want them afraid. The unknown rattles them, so I'm sowing fear. It may not pay off, but the cost is negligible."

THE SNIPER TEAM WAS LAGGING BEHIND the patrol, hoping for a shot. Their chance came when Ashford scoped a compound wall seven hundred meters to the south. A thin man with a full beard and AK over his shoulder was putting out of the gate on a motorbike, balancing a young boy on the handlebars. An older boy sat behind the driver, shielding his back.

"A bad dude," Ashford said. "Can you spill him?"

Eagan adjusted the tripod under his Heckler rifle, dialed in the scope, and read the tracking numbers.

"Negative," he said. "Bike's bouncing too much."

"What sorry-ass father," Ashford said, "sends his kids out as shields?"

They set off again. Once within sight of the wire, some older boys began to walk parallel to the patrol, pointing and laughing at the grim giants. A gang of little ones popped up, skittering behind the older ones. To show off, a skinny teenager threw a small stone at the Marines. A second, then a third stone followed.

Eagan stopped and extended his tripod, bringing his rifle to bear. Ashford felt a tingling feeling in his neck. *Would Eagan shoot? Should he say something?* Seeing the monster rifle swinging toward them, the older kids ran away. Satisfied, Eagan folded up the tripod, put aside his rifle, opened his rucksack, took out a fistful of thin sticks, and threw them away.

After he moved on, the little kids darted forward to pick up the sticks.

★ ★ ★

ONCE INSIDE THE LINES, Cruz went to the ops center, where Barnes listened intently to his debrief.

"Well done," Barnes said. "The bird for PFC Beal is inbound. No ceremony this time. Better check security at the LZ, and after that, check your own six."

"Meaning the C.O.?"

"Worse. Binns submitted a statement," Barnes said. "He's a true blue falcon. He blames you because Beal wasn't wearing a helmet. It's bullshit. Beal was hit in the neck, not the head. But it'll look bad in the investigation."

"No, it'll look good," Cruz said. "It takes the heat off Sergeant Doyle."

41

Ambition Dashed

By late afternoon, Coffman had twice rehearsed his talking points, the index cards carefully arranged on his desk. His report, sent to Kabul and the States hours earlier, had been crisp, thorough, and exonerative. For his televideo appearance, he remained in his soiled, sweat-stained cammies, leaving a smudge of dried mud on his left cheek.

The first call came from General Hal Gretman in Kabul. He led Coffman through a review of the written report without indicating approval or disapproval.

"Looks like you have a front moving in, Colonel," he concluded. "Once that weather passes, I'm coming down to see where things stand."

A few minutes later, General Killian called, wasting no time on preliminaries.

"Your base still under pressure, Hal?"

"No, sir. We've swept the area," Coffman said, launching into his first talking point. "In fact, we killed three of the bastards, captured a PKM and…"

Killian brushed that aside.

"What's this about friendly fire maybe causing the fatality?"

"The corporal wasn't wearing a helmet, sir. A squad leader wants to bring charges against the patrol leader, Captain Cruz."

Killian's face hardened. Coffman's manner irritated him, sitting there in dirty cammies, pretending to be a snuffy yet not defending his junior officer.

"Back here, Colonel, no one's interested in some platoon commander," he said. "According to your report, you were out there too."

"Yes, sir," he said. "I wanted to see why simple patrols were going wrong. The corporal was in the sniper team, not the group I was with."

"We'll sort that out later," he said. "How's the agency team working out?"

Thrown slightly off stride, Coffman chose a noncommittal answer.

"No hiccups, sir. They pitch in occasionally."

"They may be onto something big," Killian said. "Now, what about your mission?"

Coffman was ready with his second talking point.

"We're pumping out a dozen fire missions a day, sir. The cannoneers are outstanding, putting a hundred shells a day downrange. We're giving solid support."

Killian was out of patience with the glib responses.

"That's not how it's playing," he said. "The task force is under a microscope in Kabul and Washington. It's results that count, Colonel. You're behind schedule, with another KIA."

The harsh rebuke hit Coffman like a hammer. He felt his hands trembling. Blood seemed to be rushing from his body. His face paled.

"Sir, I didn't mean…"

Killian saw the tremor. The last thing he needed was a commander afraid to make decisions. He softened his tone.

"The Chairman will calm Gretman down," he said. "I'm flying to Pendleton to meet with the families. Your job is to finish strong. The Talibs are tough bastards. Not every command works out the way we hoped. Good night, Hal."

Coffman turned off the televideo, the dim screen reflecting his sinking chances for promotion.

42

A Daring Enemy Plan

On his ICOM, Zar had listened to Tic's taunts and the shrill responses from the frightened farmers. Throughout the late afternoon and evening, he had ridden at a fast clip, jouncing along the hard-packed paths next to the canals, crossing at foot bridges and occasionally dismounting to pull the bike through shallow ditches or tug it up muddy banks. Before full dark, he had visited dozens of compounds, urging the farmers to collect more poppy sap tomorrow, before the weather changed.

Satisfied, he called Emir Sadr in Quetta. They kept the conversation brief to hide among the thousands of intercepts the americanis collected daily between Afghanistan and Pakistan.

"That new pack of coyotes," Zar said, "continues to yip. I will kill them all."

"I sent you an esteemed coyote hunter," Sadr said. "Let him lead you."

Zar bristled at the reference to Quat but did not reply.

"May Allah guide you," Sadr concluded, "as you collect your sheep and bring them to market."

Zar hung up and pitched the burner phone into the canal. He resented Sadr's orders to buy more poppy and to ship more heroin packets. That sniffling Persian must have complained to the shura.

Long after dark, he arrived at the mosque and turned off the headlight. He could barely see the building. Usually the stars lit the ground like a million tiny flashlight beams. Now a cover of skittering clouds was blocking out all light. Yet the wind was faint, barely stirring. Good. It would be another day before the storm hit.

Inside the prayer hall, Tulus, the Persian, and a few others were sitting cross-legged on rich, wide carpets, their backs propped against thick pillows. Quat and another Vietnamese were squatting near Tulus, sipping tea. Zar slipped off his boots and sat down opposite the Persian. As he had promised his wife, he spoke quietly and politely.

"*Salaam alaikum,*" he said. "Did the shipment go well today?"

"As you directed," the Persian said. "Three thousand kilos in one truck and one car, with three bike escorts."

His unhappiness at risking so much in so few vehicles was plain.

"Then why is Emir Sadr," Zar said, "upset with me?"

For once, the Persian didn't wince. Numbers were his forte and Zar's weakness.

"I called Tehran," he said, "with my weekly tally. Tehran may have called your shura in Quetta. We're short of our quota, and this storm will sweep away the poppies not yet harvested."

"I have ordered the farmers to harvest all they can tomorrow!" Zar shouted.

His response to any problem was to take action. The Persian had to grant him that.

"You are Allah's true servant," the Persian said. "But some are hoarding, hoping for the price to rise."

"How many do you suspect?"

"I have about twenty on my list."

"Tulus and I will visit ten each. If we offer double the price, how much will we get?"

The Persian quickly calculated.

"Double? After we process their poppy," he said, "we'd net two million in American dollars. But next year, everyone will demand that price."

Zar snorted.

"No, next year I'll take twice as many farmers from the Baloch," he said. "Bring the money to distribute."

As the Persian reluctantly got to his feet, he tried again.

"This will hurt our long-term bargaining," he said morosely. "We're undercutting ourselves. Tehran will be upset."

Zar dismissed him. Tehran was the Persian's problem. Zar was confident he could buy the poppy and still put aside $20,000 for his own family. His wife would be happy and, with the ongoing battle against the invaders, no one would track the exact accounts. Besides, this was Persian money. The Taliban shura wouldn't care.

Zar felt momentarily pleased with himself. Then he saw Quat glowering at him.

"Tulus, why is the Asian angry?" Zar said. "Did you make him walk back to the mosque this afternoon?"

Tulus hesitated. Because Zar exploded so suddenly, it was best to choose with care each word.

"The shooting today," Tulus said, "has upset him."

"An invader was killed!" Zar said. "Mustafa and the two other mujahideen gave their souls to God. They have entered paradise. Why is he afraid? He escaped unharmed."

Instead of translating, Tulus gestured at Quat to speak.

"When tiger in jungle," Quat said, shaking his finger, "do not..."

Unable to think of an English word, Quat mockingly slapped his own cheek.

"The infidels are like a tiger," Tulus translated. "Too strong to attack in small numbers."

"I saw that slap," Zar snapped. "He thinks he is smarter than me. He was paid to attack, yet he sits here."

After Tulus translated, Quat pointed at a television in the corner. "Weather," he said. "Wait."

"No!" Zar said. "I want to know his plan now! Call in my mujahideen. Together we will judge what the shura paid so much money for."

Within a few minutes, a dozen bearded fighters in *shalwar kameez* had clustered behind Zar. Tulus gestured at Quat to explain. The Vietnamese waved his hand in front of his face as if brushing aside the air. He blinked his eyes, pretending he could not see.

"When wind comes," Quat said, "we attack."

On a rug, he placed a white cardboard map of Firebase Bastion, with the fields from Nantush's compound seven hundred meters west to the barbed wire laid out in exact proportion. Quat had drawn two lines of dots, one leading toward the wire. The other trail led northeast, ending in a series of perpendicular dots that showed where the mujahideen would launch a diversionary attack. Two larger dots represented where the PKMs would be laid, with tiny slashes indicating where aiming stakes would be driven into the ground to prevent the guns from pivoting and hitting the assault force. Zar did not have to ask a single question.

On a separate cardboard, Quat had drawn a scale model of the firebase. The bottom edge of the drawing showed the assault force at the line of departure. In front of the force were circled the numbers 1 through 3. Quat pointed and held up three fingers; he was sapper number 3. With a bamboo pointer, he tapped at the drawing of the barbed wire, slowly wiggling the pointer to pantomime the sappers working their way through the strands of wire. He held up six fingers once, then a second time. He finished by pushing down the palms of his hands, gesturing for silence.

"He says to get through the barbed wire will take one hour, maybe two," Tulus said. "During that time, our mujahideen must not shoot, even if the infidels open fire."

"Two hours to crawl thirty meters," a swarthy mujahideen scoffed. "A turtle moves faster."

As the other fighters laughed, Tulus translated the remark. Quat nodded pleasantly.

"Please ask," he said, "how many times has thick-beard man crawled under barbed wire?"

When Tulus translated the sarcasm, the insulted fighter scowled. "Allahu Akbar!" he shouted.

Zar drew a deep breath, rapped for silence, and pointed at Quat to continue. The diagram showed the position of the sentry posts along the perimeter. Quat tapped two adjoining bunkers and clapped his hands, indicating explosions. *BLAM!* He pointed at Zar and his fighters and pantomimed, *Now all of you rush in!*

Amongst a chorus of appreciative murmurs, Zar nodded approval and spoke to his men.

"Good," he said. "Now go back to your homes. Tomorrow we visit many compounds. No farmer is permitted to store away his poppy. We buy everything."

After most of the fighters left, Quat remained behind. He held up one finger, indicating he wasn't finished. He held his fists in front of his stomach, elbows akimbo, as if balancing a heavy wheelbarrow. Then he tapped the diagram, pointing to Nantush's compound. Organize the farmers to carry back the fallen. There will be many. *Tap, tap, tap, tap.*

Tulus seized the opening to aid his uncle. Looking at Zar, he spoke offhandedly, as if delivering a message already agreed upon.

"Nantush will organize the women and his workers," Tulus said. "In return, I agreed to give him two more kilos of heroin."

"Two?" Zar shouted. "That wasn't necessary. Nantush deserved only one! Jihad is the sacred duty of all Muslims. *'O Prophet! Strive hard against the infidels.'*"

Not for the first time, Tulus thought that Zar was a man with a sharp knife and a small brain.

43

The Game Changes

During the stand-to at twilight, most of Cruz's platoon deployed along the perimeter. Following that, the platoon secured the landing zone for the V-22. Beal's body was respectfully carried on board and the plane departed.

The agency team had remained in their small tent, where Stovell had unpacked a compact gas chromatograph. He was examining the powder Tic had pinched that morning from Nantush's kilo bag of heroin.

"This has the same properties," Stovell said, "as the capsule we took from the suicide bomber. Tic, did the guy talking from the mosque have a Pakistani accent?"

"No," Tic said. "He was Pashtun. He called the farmer his uncle. What're you driving at?"

"I'm trying to get a fix on who brought that suicide kid from Pakistan."

"We got multiple cuts of Talibs talking to their shura in Quetta," Tic said. "All ordinary stuff."

"Dispatching a suicide bomber that fast is not ordinary," Stovell said.

"Let's not get sidetracked," Richards said. "Our job is locating the Iranian buyer."

"Eight kilos of opium are boiled to produce one kilo of heroin," Stovell said. "Where do you think that happens? The Marines slugged it out in that sector for years. Now Afghan soldiers don't patrol there because some commander is on the take. Conclusion? That mosque is the lab."

"So what?" Richards said.

"So that's the logical headquarters for the Iranian," Stovell said. "Overhead video shows guards outside the guesthouse."

"Too speculative," Richards said. "I need more to request a raid."

Tic had listened to the back and forth.

"You're missing something," Tic said. "The *haroum* will bring an end to the harvest season. The Iranian will close shop and leave. Why don't we check the mosque out ourselves?"

"Because if he's there," Richards said, "we might end up killing him. Not a good idea."

"Actually, Tic's idea has merit," Stovell said. "The Iranian doesn't know we're looking for him. He's a businessman, not a fighter. He'll pass himself off as another mullah."

Where Tic was intuitive, Stovell was logical. Richards hesitated. He looked at Eagan, who was shaking his head.

"We need Cruz to cover us," he said, "and that's not happening."

Stovell looked surprised.

"Cruz is solid," he said. "I trust him."

"Your year in a cemetery," Eagan said, "is showing again."

"Seminary," Stovell said.

"Same difference," Eagan said. "You're inclined to trust. Cruz's gungy, but the colonel hates him. That's rubbed off on others. I watched Binns. He's a sullen asshole. I don't want us out there with reluctant grunts, while Cruz is left in the rear."

"Coffman's a bumptious suck-up," Stovell said. "He reacts to what helps him. We might not find the Iranian, but a move into Q5F could throw the Talibs off their game. That helps Coffman."

"Wasn't he sniffing around about a job?" Richards said.

"He wasn't not subtle about it," Stovell said.

"OK, Stovell, we ask for a meeting and you troll this," Richards said. "If he doesn't bite, we drop it."

"You'll check with Kabul?" Tic said.

The question amused Richards.

"At the right time," he said.

By early evening at the mosque, Quat and Tulus had gone over the assault plan for a fourth time with the seven mujahideen Zar had selected. Each would lead five others through the wire tomorrow night. Zar considered and rejected holding a fifth walk-through. They were too tired to pay attention.

"Go home," he said. "Tomorrow afternoon, gather your men and weapons. But don't start for Nantush's farm until after dark."

Over the next half hour, they left by ones and twos. Zar chose a guide to lead the Vietnamese to Nantush's compound, where they would sleep outside in the bamboo thickets. After posting a few guards, Zar was the only one to take the underground exit from the lab, pushing his bike through the tunnel and up the path hidden by poplars and undergrowth.

When the agency team entered the ops center, Coffman had gathered his staff at the folding table. Sitting at the end of the table,

Cruz kept his eyes locked on his coffee cup. Still smarting from his talk with Killian, Coffman looked churlish. He'd agreed to meet only because he wanted Stovell's goodwill.

"Colonel," Richards said, "thanks for meeting with us. Bottom line: Q5F is probably the location for the Taliban who're attacking you. Power emissions from the mosque indicate four or five internet connections, way too many for a local mullah. Stovell thinks our target may be hiding there."

Stovell laid out the evidence in a few crisp sentences.

"The mosque is definitely a heroin lab," he concluded. "In the past three days, calls were placed to Quetta, Tehran, and Zabol, the hometown of our target."

"That's not much," Coffman said.

"We extracted the IMEI number from the cell phone of a farmer buying heroin," Stovell said. "The network's primitive, but the recipient was inside Q5F."

"I give it a seventy percent chance our quarry is there," Richards said. "That's not high enough to launch a raid. Still, we gave it a good try. I'll recommend a letter of commendation for your task force."

Coffman rose to the bait. The White House wanted this target. A letter of commendation? No, his task force merited more.

"This goes much higher than Kabul," he said.

"It does," Richards said slowly, encouraged that Coffman had snapped out of his funk.

"How important is this lab?"

"It provides," Stovell said, "at least ten percent of the Taliban budget."

"And it's the command post for the attacks on my base?"

"Yes. But once this *haroum* moves through," Richards said, "our target will leave. Regardless, I'll put in a good word for your task force. You tried your best."

Coffman's mind was racing, calculating risks versus opportunities.

"Major Barnes," he said, "how many Taliban at that mosque?"

"In the past hour, sir, a meeting broke up," Barnes said. "About two dozen males drove off in different directions."

Barnes glanced toward Sergeant Ahmed.

"At most five to ten are still there, sir," Ahmed said.

Coffman weighed the odds.

"IEDs?" he said.

"We have a video track of the main route in," Barnes said. "It's safe, used by the locals every day."

Coffman, still hesitant, turned back to Richards.

"You're not sure your target is there," Coffman said. "And if he is, he may leave. That's too many maybes."

Richards gestured at Stovell to weigh in.

"Colonel, in both our lines of work, we never have complete information," he said. "That's why we promote people who take initiative. I believe General Marshall wrote, 'When reports are uncertain, never hesitate to attack.'"

Coffman wavered, unwilling to antagonize Stovell.

"Yes, I remember that quote," Coffman lied. "Of course I prize initiative. An attack, however, is beyond the scope of my mission."

"We're proposing only a recon," Stovell said, "to reduce our uncertainty. It has the added benefit of throwing the Talibs off balance."

Coffman's excitement grew. If the target was captured, it increased his dimmed chances of making general. If he was passed over, Stovell would remember he had helped. And regardless, he was acting to protect his Marines.

"A recon has merit," he said. "But mosques are out of bounds to Americans. I'll run this by General Gretman."

Stovell quickly leaped in.

"I think you misunderstood," Stovell said. "Our objective is the guesthouse. Of course, if any recon is too much…"

Coffman straightened his spine, projecting the decisive, intelligent commander, aggressive but not impulsive. This could work!

"All right," he said. "Major Barnes, you're mission commander. Include Mr. Richards in your planning."

Barnes's mouth dropped open.

"Sir," he said, "I'm not an 03. I mean, I'm happy to assist. But Captain Cruz is—"

"I'm not going to repeat myself," Coffman snapped.

Coffman beckoned to Barnes to accompany him to his office. Once they were out of earshot, the colonel whirled around.

"Major, don't ever contradict me in front of others," he said. "You're in charge of this recon, not Cruz, not after Binns's testimony. He can tag along as your subordinate. I don't want to hear his voice on the command net."

THE PERSIAN HAD RETIRED to his comfortable bedroom in the guest-house. As he sipped black tea heaped with sugar, he went over the sums. He had reluctantly given $200,000 each to Tulus and Zar to buy more poppy tomorrow at double the standard price. That was a minor irritant. Altogether, he had purchased sixteen thousand kilos of opium. Once boiled down into heroin and shipped, the Republican Guard would collect at least thirty million and he would receive a million dollars for his deal making.

He turned out his reading light and lay back on the soft mattress. The incessant murmurings of the two sentries on the compound wall annoyed him. But as a guest, he didn't want to shout at them through the open window. He rolled over and took a deep breath, inhaling the sweet, pungent odor of hashish. He smiled slightly. Scattered elsewhere dozens of mujahideen were preparing for battle, while he remained safely behind.

44

Mowing the Grass

Before planning the mission, Richards and Cruz walked over to the platoon tent to brief Sullivan. When they pushed through the double flap, Cruz was surprised to see the platoon sergeant sitting with the other sergeants.

"Kind of an NCO meeting, sir," Sullivan said.

The Marines looked uneasy, none smiling. Cruz sensed the divide. They were the platoon and he was the outsider.

"Anything to share?" he said.

Sullivan looked at the dirt for a few seconds before replying.

"The men are beat, sir," Sullivan said. "They patrol all day, stand watch all night, the 155s bang them out of their sleep, the families are upset, no internet, no cell phones."

Cruz looked around the tent.

"I know everyone's tired," he said. "Grunts are always run ragged. And yes, your families are worried, but we have a mission."

He opened his hand, inviting comment. Binns got to his feet and looked levelly at him.

"Every time we leave the wire, we lose someone, sir," he said. "We're not getting anywhere. I mean, it's like all we're doing is mowing the grass."

There it was, doubt breaking into the open, surly but not unreasonable.

"The Commandant hasn't consulted me lately, Sergeant," Cruz said. "But you're right. A cop arresting criminals doesn't stop crime. He's doing his job, mowing the grass in the States. We mow it overseas, wherever we're told to go. Why? Because we volunteered for this job."

Binns remained standing, not satisfied with the answer.

"A few years ago, I watched a flick about a Danish platoon stationed here in Helmand," Cruz went on. "They had lost a soldier and morale had dropped. So the platoon commander excused those who didn't want to join the next patrol."

"No one's asking to be excused, sir," Binns said. "It's just that—"

Cruz raised a hand and cut him off.

"I'm not finished," he said. "Know what had gone wrong? That platoon commander had assumed all the responsibility. That's not happening here. It isn't the colonel's mission, or my mission. It's *our* mission, all of us, together. You're sergeants. If you bitch, that rubs off on your men. Lamont's gone. Beal's gone. Compton's gone. If you're worried about leaving the wire, your fire teams will sense that. You have to be all in, or you're not leading your squads. Are we clear?"

Cruz paused, knowing he hadn't won Binns over. The tension lingered like the moisture on the tent flaps. Ashford glanced uneasily around and then made a show of rustling through his notebook.

"Lima Charlie, sir," he said with a slow grin. "But I got a heavy question for Mr. Richards here."

When Richards stepped forward, everyone brightened, happy to be distracted.

"Some of us saw Eagan giving sticks to some kids," Ashford said. "I asked him what tracking device he was setting in. He said I wasn't cleared to know."

Richards smiled.

"Those sticks were Tinker Toys," he said. "He brings some on every deployment. Fun for any kid in any country."

For a moment, no one had anything to say.

"Eagan?" Ashford said. "The snuff man? That's crazy shit."

"You're free to tell him that," Richards said.

"I ain't suicidal," Ashford said.

Laughter rippled through the tent.

"You all admire Eagan," Cruz said. "He's the professional. But don't sell yourselves short. When you get back home from here, you'll be the ones who went through fire."

McGowan nodded, thumping a fist into the dirt.

"Sergeant," Cruz barked, "belay the theatrics."

The squad leader looked up, grinning through tobacco-stained teeth.

"No, sir," he said. "I was just wondering if you're older than Eagan."

A few grunts hooted and others applauded. McGowan took a mock bow. Cruz kept a neutral expression.

"Let's move on," he said. "Sergeant Denton, how's your knee?"

Denton had fashioned a crutch to hobble about, staying out of the sight of Commander Zarest. The pain was tolerable, except when he tripped.

"I'm fine, sir," he said. "I'll take care of the lines."

"Good. Sergeant McGowan, Wolf Two's up tomorrow."

"Semper Gumby, sir," McGowan said. "Time to get some back."

The meeting ended, with Sullivan hanging back.

"What's bothering you, Staff Sergeant?" Cruz said.

"McGowan doesn't think before he acts," Sullivan said. "Binns is wicked smart, a 134 GCT score. I'm putting him in for the officer program."

"Staff Sergeant, if I tell McGowan to take the hill," Cruz said, "he charges. Binns would ask, 'Should I take the hill?' Sometimes being smart isn't the right answer. McGowan is my choice."

WHEN THEY WALKED INTO THE OPS CENTER, Barnes made no effort to hide his relief at seeing Cruz. Knowing he was out of his depth, he had been stalling.

"We have to launch first thing in the morning," he said. "The front will start hitting in the afternoon."

Cruz joined the others in front of the colored photomap of Q5F that filled the ninety-inch flat screen. The Helmand River ran through the one-kilometer-square sector at an angle from north to south. A canal sliced southeast from the river. The mosque was at the tip of the land between the river and the canal. A thick jumble of poplars and undergrowth lay to the east, with a wide windrow to the west formed by the river's flotsam.

"Without choppers," Cruz said, "the only way in is from the south."

On an adjoining screen, thermal video from Big Bird showed two sentries at the mosque and two others at the guesthouse, fifty meters to the east.

"Encouraging," Stovell said. "Someone worth guarding is still there."

Cruz decided they would approach with two columns, one focused on the mosque and the other on the guesthouse. Each could act as a base of fire for the other, while the sniper team would hang back, with clear fields of fire down the center. The mortars would be on call.

Cruz looked toward Sullivan. He should stay behind. But he looked so eager that Cruz decided to include him.

"Once we're on the objective," Cruz said, "you take one team while I move with the other."

An elated Sullivan raised a clenched fist.

"We split into two breaching teams?" McGowan asked.

"No!" Barnes said. "The colonel authorized a recon. If we hit anything heavy, we back off."

"The sergeant meant that we may have to enter," Cruz said mildly, "through a wall. Safer that way."

"Well, OK," Barnes said. "But remember, this is a highly sensitive mission."

McGowan looked sideways at Doyle, rolled his eyes, and placed his index finger and thumb close together to indicate a tiny space— a normal, routine patrol. Then he spread his hands wide apart and silently pantomimed the words *White House!*

After sorting out the details, they took a coffee break. Richards pulled Barnes and Cruz aside.

"Our target may squirt to the mosque," Richards said. "That's off limits to Americans. We need some ANA, without telling them where we're going."

Barnes began to object.

"You told the colonel it was only the guesthouse…"

When both Richards and Cruz glared at him, Barnes stopped talking.

"I'll call Golstern," Cruz said. "He'll arrange for us to bump into one of Ibril's patrols."

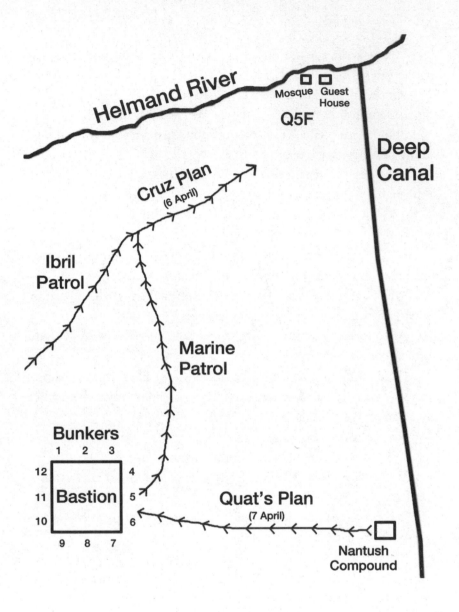

Day 6

APRIL 11

45

We Help You, You Help Us

At four in the morning, the muezzin's ululating call awoke the Persian inside the *hujra*. He knelt on his prayer rug and, not fully awake, ritually performed his ablutions. When he did not hear the usual belching, farting, and braying of Zar's men, he remembered most had left during the night. Gratefully he crawled back into his comfortable bed and slept soundly until seven. After washing, he sat down at the aromatic cedar table covered with a clean white cotton sheaf and leisurely ate his soft-boiled egg, served with melon and yogurt. The local mullah was a thoughtful host, and the Persian appreciated his civilized gestures. The air was warm, and a steady breeze carried in the calls of birds in the thickets.

The Persian idly tapped his porcelain spoon and thought about the coming day. He expected a last-minute influx of poppy. He would stash it rather than risk lighting fires to refine it. Besides, the caves were already bulging with heroin. Fortunately, the Vietnamese seemed quite professional. Once the base was breached and the Americans badly hurt, they would pull out.

IN THE PREDAWN GLOOM, the patrol left the wire. Few of the men had gotten much sleep after rumor spread that the president had personally ordered this ultrasecret raid. A "recon" with Rolling Thunder and Eagan in the lead? No, there'd be a gunfight. Maybe Osama bin Laden hadn't been killed in Pakistan and they were going after him? Or a kidnapped USO troupe, with some hot babes? After the rescue, they'd be invited to a ceremony in the Rose Garden, wearing their blues.

With Wolfe at point, the twenty-two-man column wended its way northwest. Near the front, Cruz was watching on his tablet the slow northerly path of Lieutenant Ibril's patrol, about six hundred meters to the west. Gradually, Cruz steered toward the ANA. Around seven, with the sun blazing behind a veil of wispy clouds, the patrols were within waving distance of each other. Cruz radioed to Barnes, who was near the rear of the column.

"Eagle Five, we're in position for Eagle Six to make his call," he said.

The Marines took a knee and Wolfe, Cruz, and Tic walked toward the ANA patrol. Ibril beckoned to the interpreter Mohamed and they came forward. Cruz thought Ibril looked burnt out. His face seemed too small for his sagging skin, and his eyes drooped as he passively awaited an order from yet another americani.

BACK AT THE OPS CENTER, on cue Coffman called Colonel Ishaq and Golstern, telling them Big Bird had eyes on four Taliban at the mosque. Since both the ANA and Marine patrols were close by,

Coffman recommended they push forward jointly. Ishaq paused before answering and glared at Golstern.

"Q5F is my sector," he said.

"The Marines do everything to support you," Golstern said. "It will look bad if you don't help them."

Ishaq knew he couldn't directly refuse. A complaint from Coffman would rocket straight to Kabul.

"I cannot respond blindly," he said. "This decision is up to my patrol leader."

Ishaq called Ibril on a cell phone and spoke in a fast, clipped Tajik dialect.

STANDING NEAR CRUZ, Ibril listened to Ishaq's instructions. Then he held the phone away from him as if it were a live grenade and shook his head, making no effort to conceal his anger. Gesturing at Mohamed not to accompany him, Ibril rejoined his men at the edge of the field.

"What's that about?" Cruz said.

"Ishaq was chewing on him," Mohamed said, "telling Ibril to say no. That's all I got. They use Bukhori to shut me out. The *askars* bitch that I'm an americani. Fuck yes! For three years, I'm an SF terp. Fuck those Tajiks."

"What'd you pick up, Tic?" Cruz said.

"I don't do Bukhori either," Tic said. "That colonel sounded real pissed. I'm guessing Ibril tells us to shove it."

Ibril and his *askars* were shouting back and forth, gesturing from the Marines to the far tree lines. Some were pointing in the air, a reference to Big Bird watching them. After several minutes, Ibril walked back to Cruz and looked vaguely around, not certain what to say.

"Mosque is bad, very bad," Ibril said. "If we help you, you help us?"

Cruz glanced at Tic and Mohamed. Both shrugged blankly.

"Of course," Cruz replied. "We work together."

That seemed to satisfy Ibril, although both knew they were talking past each other. He waved at his six *askars* to come forward. The two groups moved on parallel paths toward Q5F, less than a kilometer to the north. They had barely started when the local ICOM and cell phone nets lit up. Cruz switched to the task force net.

"We're monitoring all kinds of warnings," Ahmed radioed, "that you're headed to the mosque. I judge contact imminent."

ZAR WAS FIVE KILOMETERS TO THE SOUTH, buying poppy from a farmer delighted at the price, when the watchers called. Their cover phrases were alarming, "goats in the flower beds" and "many foreign herders." The infidels were approaching the mosque in large numbers.

Zar was caught out of position. Calling over the ICOMs for reinforcements would be suicidal. He knew the Americans had tuned in their direction finders and were watching overhead, eager to call an air strike on any armed convoy headed toward the mosque. And now was not the time to seek guidance from Emir Sadr. The Taliban shura had a firm rule: when under pressure, do not call blindly and risk electronic intercept. Wait for instructions.

46

The Smell of Vinegar

The mosque was a large single-story concrete building, stubby and square, without a cupola or prayer turret. It sat on a slightly elevated patch of bare ground that sloped on the west side down to a gravel wash next to the river. To the east was the two-story guesthouse fronted by a trellis of grape vines.

The Marine and ANA columns were four hundred meters southeast of the mosque when the first shots cracked by. Inside a minute, the shooting increased to ragged volleys, too wild to be dangerous. *Bat, bat, bat.* Silence. *Bat, bat, bat.* So erratic were the aim points that the Marines heard only a few pops as bullets broke the sound barrier several meters over their heads. Over the task force net, Ahmed reported that Big Bird had picked up two men running from the guesthouse into the mosque.

Tic was paying no attention to the shooting, absorbed in listening to the headset attached to the pack on his shoulders.

"Yes, our target's there!" he yelled. "He's panicked, screaming for help over his cell!"

When the Marines were still two fields away from the mosque, the snaps of the bullets came closer. The Marines flopped down and advanced by bounds, each four-man fire team running forward while the others provided a base of fire. With the suppressors on their M27s and protective ear cups in their helmets, the Marines could talk to each other without screaming and could concentrate their fire.

Next to the guesthouse were two smaller dwellings for the help. A wooden sentry shack sat atop the compound wall in front of the house, a white Taliban flag fluttering in the steady breeze. Chunks of the wall had torn loose, and there was no gate. On the river side, the wall was badly crumbled. After years of peace, there had been no reason to maintain it.

A guard in the shack had propped the barrel of his AK against the window shelf and was peering out, firing ragged bursts. From seven hundred meters away, Eagan shot him in the head. Two Taliban lugged a PKM out of the mosque and lay down behind it. They got off ten rounds before the laser dots of five M27s converged on them. Small wisps of dust puffed from their gray *shalwar kameez* as a dozen 6.5mm bullets tore into them. Two mangy dogs, loosed of their chains and big as wolves, tore snarling across the field. Bursts of bullets shattered their knobby forelegs and tore through their stout chests, and they tumbled for a few feet before quivering in death.

In less than a minute, the Marines and *askars* had reached the ditches outside the guesthouse. Tic yelled in Pashto for anyone inside the *hiraj* to come out. When there was no response, an engineer crawled up to a wall, slapped on a two-pound C-4 gummy charge, popped the fuse, and sprinted back to the ditch. After the explosion blew out part of the wall in a large billow of gray dust, four Marines rushed inside. Others quickly followed. Two servants cowering in a back room were herded outside. Inside two minutes, the guesthouse was secure. The Persian was not there.

Frightened voices of women and children were coming from two smaller abodes. After Tic shouted a few commands, a throng of women and children flocked into the courtyard. Clinging to each other, they obeyed Tic's order to stay out of the way. A hasty search found no one hiding inside the buildings. While Barnes stayed with McGowan to set up a defensive perimeter, the agency team ran across the courtyard to join Cruz outside the mosque.

"Our target's probably hiding in the mosque," Richards said. "I don't want a corpse. No shooting if you can avoid it!"

Shouts were coming faintly from the mosque.

"Guy inside claims he's a mullah," Mohamed said. "Local dialect. He says no Taliban inside."

"Tell everyone to come out," Cruz said, "through the front door."

Crouching in the ditch, Ibril and Tic were yelling at each other, almost on the verge of blows.

"Ibril wants to assault with his *askars*," Tic said. "He's gone crazy."

Cruz slid along the ditch until he was upslope a few feet above Ibril. Putting down his M27, he pointed an accusing finger at the lieutenant and his excited *askars*.

"Tic, tell him if his men fire one shot," he shouted, "I'll disarm them and file charges. Tell him not to fuck with me."

Face contorted with anger, Cruz's voice had risen an octave. Reacting instinctively, McGowan and several Marines had shifted around so that their weapons, muzzles down, faced toward the *askars*.

"OK!" Ibril yelled, "OK! OK!"

The front door opened and a plump mullah dressed in black nervously stepped out, followed by three other men. In response to Tic's shouts, they stripped off their clothes at a safe distance. Satisfied they had no hidden explosives, the Marines beckoned them to advance to the ditch. After redressing, they were flex-cuffed, blindfolded, and separated. When Barnes rushed up, a frustrated Ibril kept pointing at the mosque, insisting he be allowed to enter.

"All right, Lieutenant," Barnes said. "You go in first."

Ibril and his *askars* rushed forward, their tactics sound but hurried. A Marine search team followed at a cautious pace. The long rectangular room was cluttered with cots, blankets, cushions, faded prayer rugs, lanterns, candles, dirty clothing, small washing bowls, chipped enamel cups, tea kettles, loose cartridges, discarded sandals, and pages ripped from magazines.

"Damn, they trashed their quarters," McGowan said. "These muj have a piss-poor platoon sergeant."

"Guess you don't have to be neat to pray," Wolfe said.

McGowan kicked at a small cardboard box with small red apples printed on the cover. Tic picked up the box and plucked out a pill.

"Uppers, tramadol," he said. "In Africa, they feed them to the cattle so they'll plow the fields. After a Tango pops two of these, he'll walk through fire."

"How do you put down a dude that fucked up?" McGowan said.

"Two to the head," Tic said.

Watching the dial on what looked like a handheld calculator, Stovell had zeroed in on a pile of junk.

"Stingray's locked on," he said.

He kicked aside a few blankets, rummaged through a crumpled carton, and plucked out a cell phone. Tic poked a bit farther and drew out a crumpled, dirty notebook. After thumbing through a dozen pages, he grinned.

"It's an account book," he said. "Listen to this: Mullah Nastah, 12,000 rupees. Nantush, 16,000. Verben, 20,000. He's the district chief. Terbol, 7,000. He collects the water tax."

Stovell took the notebook.

"What we have here," he said, "is the midrash of Helmand."

McGowan jumped back.

"A rash? Drop that thing!"

Stovell smiled.

"The paper's not infected, Sergeant," he said. "The people are. This is their holy book of greed. These are payments to government officials, mullahs, farmers, middlemen, the whole community. They all share from the poppy."

He held up the captured cell phone.

"I'll check this out," he said.

The *askars* were tapping at the walls, looking for hiding places.

"Stinks in here," McGowan said. "They cook with vinegar?"

"That's raw heroin," Richards said.

He sniffed and poked around, trying to locate the source of the smell. He looked down and stamped his feet.

"Stomping out bugs?" McGowan said.

Richards pointed at the floor.

"Look at those boards," he said. "Cedar joists all tied in, solid, no give to them."

The terp Mohamed was jerking loose rugs, sending kettles and cups clanging. When he uncovered a trap door, the Marines and *askars* backed away, wary that shooters were lurking in the cellar beneath them. Once all were outside, Richards pointed at the bosky terrain, the thick scrubs and tough poplars entangled in green leaves.

"If they're hiding below," he said, "they're certain to have an escape hatch."

Cruz turned to the waiting Marines.

"McGowan, search all the way to the river," he said. "Take Tic and a few *askars* with you."

A dozen Marines formed a skirmish line, the stiffening east wind blotting out their sounds as they broke through the brush. Within minutes, McGowan radioed back.

"Wolf Six, we've found a sink hole," he said, "so deep we can't see the bottom."

"That's a *karez*," Mohamed said. "Wells dug by the farmers. Taliban use them all the time."

Five more minutes passed before Cruz heard the pop-pop-pop of an M4, followed by McGowan's husky voice.

"Wolf Six, an *askar* lit up a guy breaking cover. There's a road back here!"

Leaving Sullivan to cover the mosque, Cruz and Richards moved north through the undergrowth. They found McGowan crouched on a steep slope under a tangle of low-hanging branches. Directly beneath him, two *askars* and a Marine were peering into the black mouth of a tunnel wide enough to accommodate a small truck. Several feet away a body lay facedown. Ibril was squatting next to the opening, shouting for anyone inside to surrender. There was silence from the tunnel, no shooting and no voices.

Cruz looked at McGowan.

"Who's your best fire team for this job?" he said.

McGowan considered.

"I'll call up Brannon."

47

One Hundred Million Dollars

In the courtyard, Tic and Stovell were questioning the three prisoners from the mosque. The plump mullah rattled off the names of his two wives and five children. With no hesitation, he added the names of the district chief and the *mirab* who settled water disputes. And no, he did not know the name of any Taliban.

The second captive was wearing a soiled *kameez* and tattered flip-flops. He had a shriveled left arm and limped heavily. His scarred face was twisted into a perpetual sneer, and he tangled his words. He seemed bewildered by simple questions, insisting he cleaned the mosque and made tea for the mullah and his guests. And no Taliban or *dussmen* ever visited the mosque. They were not welcome.

The third captive wore a clean gray *shalwar*, Asolo hiking boots, and a black cotton turban. His beard was neatly trimmed, and in his breast pocket Tic found a pair of wraparound Oakleys.

"You speak with a Persian accent," Tic said in Pashto.

"I am Pashtun," the Persian replied, "from Farah Province. We trade with Iranians every day."

"Why are you here?"

"Mullah al-Aqeeda is my father's third cousin. I am hoping to export his corn and melons."

Tic laughed lightly and nodded at Stovell.

The Persian didn't care if his story sounded absurd. The americani could only hold him for a day. Once turned over to the Afghan National Police, he would be released. Losing the heroin was not his fault. That idiot Zar would take the blame. For now, all he had to do was remain vague and not admit anything. He lowered his face, signaling that he wouldn't answer any more questions. There was a tug on his beard and as his mouth dropped open, he felt a dab of cotton brush against his inner cheek.

Placing the cotton tip in a zip bag, Stovell picked up his backpack and moved away. Opening his portable DNA kit, he compared the swab with a sample lifted from a teacup in Zabol months earlier. It was a match.

He smiled at Tic as he sent the confirmation code to Langley.

Cruz was waiting alongside McGowan when Corporal Ted Brannon slid down the slope to join them. Brannon, who had played center on his high school basketball team, seemed too tall for the job. *He could stumble and trip a wire in there*, Cruz thought.

"You've practiced this, Corporal," he said. "If you sense something's wrong, back out. I'm good with whatever you decide. This is your show."

Cruz felt like a coach giving instructions before sending his star player into the game.

"Good to go, sir," Brannon said gravely.

He crawled over to his team, and they adjusted their night-vision goggles and tested the Sidewinder flashlights secured on the rails of their M27s. At Cruz's signal, they fired a few bursts down the tunnel and ducked back. There was no return fire. After waiting a minute, they fired three more bursts. Again, no return fire.

The team slipped into the tunnel, two Marines hugging each wall. After flipping down their infrared two-tubed goggles, they duck-walked forward. The tunnel was as high as a man, with timbers shoring up the sides. The greenish beams of their IR lights bounced off barrels, wheelbarrows, and sacks at the far end of the passage. Alerted by a tinny scraping sound, the team stopped and their four lights gradually centered on a man squatting next to the dirt wall, an AK propped against his knees. He looked like a wax dummy in a carnival fun house. For perhaps a second, the scene was frozen. Then a dozen rounds slammed into him, pounding chunks of his flesh into the dirt wall.

From deeper in the tunnel, an AK fired, the red flashes dazzling and the sound cascading down the shaft. Again the IR lights converged. The panicky shooter was running away, his back to the Marines. The first round hit the back of his thigh, shoving him forward and he sprawled face-first into the damp dirt. In an instant, the Marines were on top of him, hurling aside his AK, roughly flex-cuffing him before moving past.

Another fifteen seconds and their lights were bouncing off an open wooden door at the end of the chamber.

"Three, you good?" McGowan said over his handheld.

"We're secure," Brannon replied. "Got a big room here."

"OK, we're coming in."

Eight Marines were soon in the room, green IR beams dancing in all directions. Overhead, heavy timbers laid horizontally supported the floorboards of the mosque. Upstairs, enthusiastic *askars* had run back into the building. They opened the trap door and climbed down. Poking around, one found a light switch. In the harsh glare of several bare hundred-watt bulbs, the size of the lab was impressive.

Several dozen fifty-gallon barrels of precursor chemicals, including acetic anhydride from Pakistan, were stacked along one wall. Next to them were large aluminum tubs and long-handled shovels for mixing the chemicals with the bulging sacks of opium pitch heaped against the opposite wall. At the end of the room nearest the tunnel sat an industrial-strength stove, vented by twin tin chimneys, for heating a few vats. A quarter of the cave was taken up by hundreds of wrapped plastic bags looking like small loaves of uncut black bread.

HM3 Bushnell was tending to the wounded Taliban, whose right leg had ballooned up like a boiled sausage. The man was whimpering, looking at his gargantuan leg with wide, disbelieving eyes. Doc glanced at Cruz and shook his head.

"Artery's been cut," he said. "Only thing holding the blood in is his skin."

McGowan grabbed Brannon by his web gear.

"I don't want blood spilling all over the place," McGowan said. "Move him outside."

"Why my team? We did the clearing!"

"Yeh, the kills are yours," McGowan said. "Now clean this up."

As the dying man was dragged out, Stovell was taking photos of the heroin stash.

"This shit looks like it came out of my ass," McGowan says. "And it stinks. I've seen the flicks. Good heroin is white and soft like flour."

Stovell laughed, picked up a plastic bag, and tossed it in his hand.

"Sergeant, heroin turns white when it's cut with strychnine," Stovell said. "You're looking at pure HCL heroin. This bag sells for two hundred K on the streets in Europe."

Barnes had climbed down the ladder and was eagerly looking around.

"Can I tell Eagle Six," Barnes said, "mission accomplished?"

Richards looked at Stovell, who shook his head. The Marines had no need to know.

"Report that you took down a top-level heroin lab," Richards said. "Don't mention my team. After you call in, I have a favor to ask."

Minutes later, the cave was empty except for the CIA team and the Iranian mullah. They turned off the lights, placed the Persian alone in front of the heroin stash, removed his blindfold, and took several pictures as he blinked at the camera flashes.

"Perfect," Stovell said. "The president will love it. Catnip for the press."

They walked out of the tunnel and joined Cruz, who was tracking several blue dots on his tablet.

"I have teams looking for other caves," he said.

A few rifle shots followed by high-pitched babbling in Tajik came from a thick tangle of bush off to the west. The command group moved in that direction, with Tic shouting at the *askars* not to shoot them. After ten minutes of breaking through brush, they reached an *askar* standing next to another *karez*. A man in a torn *shalwar* was lying on his side, his wrists flex cuffed behind his back.

"They captured this Tango," Tic said. "Ibril's gone down that hole with a couple of his guys."

"That's stupid," Cruz said. "He doesn't have the right gear or training. He'll get his ass killed."

Tic started to reply, then thought better of it. Instead, he knelt at the cave entrance and shouted loudly in Pashto. Ibril yelled back and slowly climbed up a sturdy wooden ladder, followed by three *askars*.

"Much down there," Ibril said.

Cruz, followed by Stovell and Barnes, climbed down. The small cave was well ventilated, with a solid roof and a backup generator. Used solely for storage, the stacked shelves held over a thousand one-kilo bags of heroin.

"Gentlemen, you've found the Amazon warehouse of Helmand Province," Stovell said. "You've busted one hundred million dollars of black tar heroin."

Barnes grinned, his eyes wide with excitement.

"That's a Bravo Zulu!" he said. "The colonel won't believe this!"

They climbed back up the ladder, and Barnes rushed off to call Coffman.

"Blast it," Cruz said.

The Marines placed ten pounds of C-4 inside, set the fuse for five minutes, and backed off. The explosion collapsed the cave, grinding the heroin into the dirt.

It was approaching noon. They had been on the objective for an hour, and the wind was increasing.

"Major Barnes," Cruz said, "we should move out before the Tangos swarm in. I'll send Ibril back to his sector."

"OK," Barnes said, "but I have to ask permission to destroy the mosque."

"If you do," Richards said, "the colonel has to ask Kabul. We'll be stuck here all afternoon."

Barnes hesitated. The speed and success of the operation had delighted him. This was likely to be the only field operation in his career, and he was grateful for their expertise. He waited for a suggestion.

"Mosques are Afghan business," Cruz said.

He looked over at Ibril, who was chatting with his *askars*.

"Lieutenant Ibril," he shouted, "we destroy mosque?"

Ibril frowned and flapped his hand. It was none of his business what the americanis did.

"What's bothering him?" Cruz said. "A few minutes ago, we couldn't hold him back."

"You asked him in front of others," Tic said. "If he burns their mosque, the Pashtuns will track down his family."

"My bad," Cruz said.

"Ibril's not good or bad," Tic said. "He's Tajik."

"I can't call an air strike on the mosque," Barnes said, "not with women and kids here."

"We can burn it," Stovell said. "Opium melts like wax. They'll salvage some, not much."

For the past hour, Barnes had been on the net with Eagle Six, who had nitpicked every move. With his self-confidence surging, he now made his own command decision.

"Do it," Barnes said. "I'll tell the colonel later. Light it and let's get the hell out of here."

Each squad was carrying two TH3 incendiary grenades with eight hundred grams of thermite filler that burned for forty seconds. McGowan climbed down into the cavern beneath the mosque, smashed open several barrels of the precursor chemicals, and wedged in two grenades. He removed the safety latches, straightened the cotter pins, and pulled. As the grenades popped in white fizzling flashes, he climbed back up the ladder. Within seconds, the iron oxide reached four thousand degrees Fahrenheit and the melting began.

On the cedar floor above, the Marines had heaped rugs and other combustibles into piles. Once they heard the pops from the cellar, they set off their own incendiaries. As the trash flared up, they strolled outside. McGowan had seized an inscribed white Taliban flag that he whipped back and forth, celebrating the bonfire.

"Burn, you mother!" McGowan yelled playfully. "Burn!"

"Stop!" Tic shouted. "Give me the flag."

McGowan stood back, dropping the flag into the dirt.

"What's your problem, bro?" he said.

"The flag say Muhammad is the messenger of Allah," Tic said. "What you do is *shahada*."

"I don't give a fuck if it's whahada," McGowan said. "I'm bringing this rag home."

"No!" Tic said. "That will cause big trouble."

McGowan glanced at Cruz.

"Tic has a point," Cruz said. "Leave it."

"An enemy flag is sacred?" McGowan said. "This is one messed-up war, sir."

278

"Your strategic insight is duly noted, Sergeant," Cruz said. "Now get into formation. We're OTM. Ibril takes the Talib prisoner. The two mullahs come with us."

As THEY WALKED AWAY from the compound, thick gray smoke was pouring from the mosque. The servant with the stunted left arm and scarred face was standing in the courtyard, waving his cane for the women and children to hurl buckets of water at the flames. Once the Marines were beyond the wall, he ducked around the corner of the guesthouse, took out his ICOM, and called Zar.

"The coyotes have slaughtered your sheep," Tulus said. "All of them. The shepherd was taken."

Zar, five kilometers away, did not reply. All the heroin? *All?* He turned off his ICOM and struggled to clear his mind. This wasn't his fault. The shura had assured him that the mosque wasn't in the americani zone. He hadn't been warned the *kafirs* were coming. Someone had betrayed the brave mujahideen. But who, and why? Every year, Emir Sadr paid seven percent to the Afghan puppet officials. Their colonel had been paid. So why had *askars* come? It made no sense. And the Persian taken alive! Thank Allah the americanis did not know who he was.

Zar squatted down on the side of the canal. The strengthening wind was blowing the gray smoke and the vinegar stink toward him. Across the district, the local phone nets had lit up. Every farmer had a question or a comment about the raid. There was no sense visiting any more farms, and Zar was too experienced to try to ambush the patrol returning to base. The americani could be tricked by clever planning, but only a fool rushed into battle against them. Their eye in the sky was too keen, and they listened for code words in all ICOM conversations.

It would take the shura in Quetta a day to assess the damage. In the meantime, he was on his own. The attack against the americani base had to succeed. Zar forced his mind to concentrate upon the coming assault. It was the only way to make amends. Surely Allah would reward him.

48

No Right Decision

The *askars* had moved away from the Marines and were standing in a loose column, with the captured Taliban in the center. Off to one side, Ibril was shaking his finger at Mohamed. As Mohamed turned away, a tall *askar* wearing Army-green wool mittens slapped at him with the butt of his PKM. Mohamed staggered slightly, retaliated with a short kick, and walked over to Cruz.

"I want out, sir," he said. "I'm going back to Captain Golstern. Let the fucking Tajiks and Pashtuns kill each other."

"Mohamed, you can't walk off," Cruz said. "Ibril needs a terp."

In the distance, Ibril was waving scornfully at Mohamed.

"Sir, Ibril speaks English good enough," Mohamed said. "He was with Tenth Mountain in the Korengal. He doesn't want me talking about his shit. The SF are my real brothers, not those crazy fuckers."

Barnes and Tic had hurried back from the front of the column.

"I'm picking up a lot of chatter," Tic added. "We've pissed off the neighborhood. Not good to stay here."

"Ops center's reporting some bikers off to the east," Barnes said. "We have to move. What's the holdup?"

"Ibril's in a pout," Cruz said. "I'll settle with him later. Mohamed, you stay with us. Now let's step."

Ibril was leading his men through the crumbling compound wall. The *askars* were looking back toward Cruz and giggling nervously, like students concealing something from the teacher. As the Taliban prisoner, arms bound behind him, struggled through the wall, he slipped and fell. His guards jerked him to his feet and kicked him. He stood tottering, then suddenly bolted across the wash toward the Marines. The *askar* with the mittens raised his PKM and fired a three-round burst, striking the man in the back. He sprawled on his face, twitched, and lay still.

"What the fuck?" Cruz yelled.

Ibril strode to the *askar* and slapped the killer. He gestured toward Cruz with his palms up, indicating he was dealing with an idiot.

Tic exchanged a glance with Mohamed.

"They were going to kill him," Mohamed said. "They didn't want him talking."

"What the hell," Cruz said, "are you holding back from me?"

Tic spoke up to support Mohamed.

"You got the wrong target, Captain," he said, pointing at the *askars*. "They're the ones carrying. Inside that cave, each grabbed three or four kilos. That's why they rushed into the mosque. They wanted to score."

Tic had extended his finger directly at Ibril, who stiffened and glared back. His *askars* grew defensive, shifting to face the Marines. The Marines turned, weapons half raised. Between the two groups, the dead prisoner lay in the scree, the blood-splashed pebbles glistening like rubies. Eagan stepped off to one side to have a clear angle of fire.

"Hey, Tic," Eagan shouted, "tell Mittens over there, don't twitch."

Tic didn't have to translate. The *askar* with the PKM had the sense to remain frozen. This wasn't a two-sided standoff. Every *askar* knew he would die inside a few seconds.

Richards and Stovell didn't speak. This was a matter for the Marines to work out. Barnes didn't know what to do. His mind was blank as he watched the blood from the dead man ooze into the dirt. Everyone silently deferred to Cruz.

"Drop your packs," Cruz said, pointing at Ibril and the *askars*.

His tone was as neutral as death. Ibril sensed his doom. Americanis were rigid about things they didn't understand. It was insane to challenge them. With no way out, he exploded in anger.

"CIA got prisoners!" he shouted. "We helped you!"

Ibril had participated in enough spec ops missions to know that Richards and Stovell were CIA. He was bargaining, demanding payment for services rendered. Cruz kept his face firm and unyielding. He pulled his handheld from a vest pocket and pointed it at Ibril.

"I'm calling Captain Golstern," he said. "When you get back, you'll be searched. You have no choice. Drop those packs."

Ibril didn't back off. He was enraged, his face turning purple.

"Why Colonel Ishaq say no go to mosque?" he shouted. "Everyone take. My men are poor. What we get, huh? What we get?"

There it was, direct and unapologetic, the great wheel of commerce revolving in its immanent tribal circle from farmer to drug lord to the Taliban to the ANA colonel, each receiving payment and none facing punishment. Why shouldn't one skinny, burnt-out lieutenant steal a sliver of drug money for his castaway platoon? The heroin would reach the addicts regardless of who sold it.

Cruz looked at Richards, standing there beside him, blank as a telephone pole.

"Tic told you Ibril came for that powder," Cruz said, "and you didn't tell me? You let him steal it?"

"I didn't want you dealing with a mess," Richards said. "If you call this in now, Ibril's finished. Ishaq will cut his balls off and sell the powder himself. Who gains from that? Let this go!"

Barnes was listening, unable to think of a solution. A few feet away, the dead Taliban was leaking out. Whether he was murdered or executed depended on one's point of view. And the enraged Ibril, was he an ally or a thief? Barnes didn't know. He did know he was standing with his mouth open like a beached fish. He had to say something.

"We don't have proof," Barnes said. "We can't strip-search our fucking allies!"

It was more a plea than an order. The decision rested with Cruz. His parents had ingrained rectitude into him. Though he hadn't attended church since enlisting, Christianity had shaped him. The Corps wasn't a God substitute, but like most Marines, Cruz believed in its dogma. *"First to fight for right and freedom, and to keep our honor clean."* To Cruz, that hymnal verse was real. It molded and stamped him. All of his training—the rigid discipline and sense of order accumulated over sixteen years, his unquestioned assumptions about right and wrong—told him tthis was wrong. If he didn't search the *askars* or call in a report, they'd hide their stash before returning to base. But without Ibril, they couldn't have entered the mosque. Without Ibril, the mission wouldn't have succeeded.

Barnes was impatient. The comm net was loaded with Tango intercepts, and he didn't want to tarry.

"This isn't our business," he murmured. "We have what we want. Let's get out of here."

Cruz could think of no better decision.

"Aye-aye, sir," he said.

Staring at Ibril, Cruz slowly slid his 153 handheld back into a breast pocket. Ibril nodded and gestured for his *askars* to move out. Cruz watched them go, then turned away, feeling he had left part of himself behind. Stovell read the turbulence in his face.

"This isn't a country," Stovell said. "It's a pathology. Don't fight what you can't correct."

In a dispersed column, the Marines walked warily back to base, pestered only by a few desultory shots from tree lines rustling and bending under the stiffening wind.

49

Solace

As the successful patrol was returning to base, Secretary of Defense Towns was getting off a helicopter at Dover Air Force Base. The morning newspapers and TV shows had featured Senator Grayson's blistering press conference about a "secret war." He ignored the shouted questions from a gaggle of reporters and TV crews. Several minutes later, a C-130 touched down, carrying the body of Sergeant Brian Lamont packed in ice inside a sealed aluminum casket covered with the American flag. Tomorrow, Corporal Compton's body would arrive, and PFC Beal's the day after. The public had long forgotten Afghanistan. Now, three fatalities had occurred on one tiny base in the middle of nowhere. Towns felt it was his duty was to show the families that their sons were not whimsically sent off to some far-flung pile of rocks, forgotten by those at the top.

Standing on the tarmac were Lamont's parents, flanked by the casualty assistance officers and Lieutenant General Paul Killian. Towns remained unobtrusively in the background during the transfer of the coffin to the Air Force mortuary. Upon conclusion, the assistance officers escorted the family to a private room. Towns followed behind with Killian.

"Admiral Michaels speaks highly of you, General," Towns said.

"Thank you, sir," Killian said. "The Chairman and I served together on two deployments."

Both squared their shoulders as they entered the room. Mary Lamont looked wraithlike in a somber gray dress, her face almost as white as the string of pearls around her frail neck. Tim Lamont, a stout man wearing cowboy boots and a stern expression, was holding her hand, his eyes fixed in space to fight back the tears. After extending his sympathies and offer to help in any way, Towns stopped talking to let them express their feelings. He braced himself, prepared to accept bitterness without lurching into excuses.

"I did four years in Army artillery, sir," Tim Lamont said. "Brian was proud that he qualified as a Marine sniper. He always was a good shot. It's hard, though. Mary and me, we're not sure Brian's death changed anything."

"Believe me, if there was an easier way," Towns said softly, "I'd find it. If we don't stop them there, they'll come here. Brian helped us hold the line."

As he spoke, he placed a hand on Tim Lamont's shoulder. The Lamonts exchanged a look indicating they had expected to hear something like that.

"What were they doing there, sir?" Tim Lamont said.

"Helping the Afghan Army protect their city," Towns said. "It's a provincial capital, important for keeping the country together."

The face of Tim Lamont hardened.

"Isn't it time they protected their own damn cities?" he said.

Mary Lamont squeezed her husband's hand, shushing him gently.

"I know you and the generals are only doing your duty," Mary Lamont said, "like Brian did."

Her tone expressed resignation rather than accusation. Towns gently patted her arm. Killian stepped forward. He had been through this hour of sorrow too many times before.

"I wish," he said, "I could have been out there with Brian. That's where us old farts belong."

He thought his words would mean little. The strain in his voice and the three small silver stars on his collars, though, might bring a dollop of solace.

After ten minutes, no one could think of anything more to say. The casualty assistance officers escorted the grieving parents from the room, leaving Towns alone with Killian.

"This is my second time here, General," Towns said. "It's rough. Have you lost many?"

"Fifty-seven, sir."

"My God!"

"At different levels of command, I pulled three tours in Iraq and Helmand."

Both looked out the window at the TV trucks driving away.

"The press will be back tomorrow," Towns said. "The Chairman is coming. He told me he keeps you informed."

"Yes, sir, but I'm not interfering with General Gretman."

"No worries. Personal contacts help in tight circumstances," Towns said. "How have the deaths affected the unit at Pendleton?"

"The support system is strong, sir," Killian said. "But everyone's shaken."

"When the task force gets back," Towns said, "I'll fly out to congratulate them. The CIA captured their man. And General Gretman thinks the Afghan brigade will soon reach Lash. We assured the president we could do this in a week, and we've done it."

When Killian nodded without enthusiasm, Towns smiled wryly.

"This is the two of us talking," he said. "Let's hear it."

Killian admired the Secretary, but thought he was too self-assured and too removed. He picked his words and spoke in a respectful tone.

"On my last push, we cleared the Green Zone, sir," he said, "and the Afghan Army gave it up when we left. I hope that doesn't repeat."

"So in your tours, General," he said, "you didn't see much progress."

Killian avoided a direct answer that might contradict Admiral Michaels.

"I didn't intend to be my remarks as negative, sir. We always do our job and carry out the mission."

Towns controlled his irritation. He didn't understand generals. One minute they were candid, and in the next, they closed ranks. They were their own union, promoted inside a closed system through the ranks to the top. Every mission was "can do," even when it could not be done. He had embraced the strategy of the top brass, who spoke as a chorus. Yet here was one of their key deputies, in an oblique manner offering a contrary view. *Where*, he thought, *did truth reside?*

"In your personal judgment, General, what's going on down there?"

Invited to be candid, Killian didn't hold back.

"Mr. Secretary, I sent a genuine hardass captain to guard that base," he said. "That wasn't good enough. Three Marines have died, fighting tribes from another century. Pakistan shelters the Taliban, and the elite in Kabul stay alive through a system of payoffs."

Towns felt a jolt of conscience. His day was broken into fifteen minutes segments of meetings and calls, an udersectretary, a senator, the White House, a major news outlet. The demands for his time never slackened. He hadn't spent even an hour trying to understand this bygone war. When General Gretman and Admiral Michaels had recommended the task force, he had agreed. His job was too big and his rank too high to focus on a small part of a small war, barely a skirmish. Still, he felt unease. What had been gained by Brian Lamont's death?

50

Coffman Takes Charge

While Towns was flying back to the Pentagon, Coffman was soaking in praise. The classified internet chat room in the ops center was cluttered with attaboys from various commands. General Gretman called to congratulate him on "an aggressive display of mission command," meaning he had allowed his subordinates to take the initiative. Coffman seized the moment to advance his personal standing.

"General, we should be in Lash by now," Coffman said. "Colonel Ishaq is all field and no hit. I'd like to motivate him, Marine-style."

Gretman laughed.

"Go get 'em, devil dog," he said. "If he doesn't pick up the pace, let me know and I'll pay a visit to the palace."

Coffman was glowing. In a day or two, he'd be waving alongside Ishaq at the cheering residents of the provincial capital. His twin successes—capturing the Iranian drug lord and liberating the city—guaranteed a note of praise from the White House to the selection board for brigadier general.

He quickly called Captain Golstern for an update.

"Ishaq's acting strange, sir," Golstern said. "Usually he's all smiles, but now he's withdrawn. After he heard the lab was burned, he went to his tent. I haven't seen him since. I'm not sure I can move him."

"Well, my size-ten boot will move him," Coffman said. "Once this front pushes through, I'm coming over to motivate his lazy ass."

Once again a confident commander, Coffman strode to the concertina wire. It was midafternoon, and cobalt mares' tails were skidding across the sky. He stood with his face toward the gathering wind and warmly greeted the two dozen returning Marines, slapping the back of each grunt as he came through the wire. He exclaimed over the captured PKM machine gun and patted the heads of both prisoners, the twin totems of his sudden, spectacular success, the guarantors of his rise to brigadier general.

He waved at Barnes to follow him to his office, where he eagerly poured him a cup of coffee. Barnes launched into his carefully edited debrief, saying not a word about Lieutenant Ibril's platoon.

THE AGENCY TEAM KEPT CUSTODY of the prisoners. A backhoe had clawed a hole out of the side of the revetment that enclosed the ops center. Reinforced with a few sheets of plywood, the dugout provided a dank, dark cell for the two mullahs. Tic dragged them inside and forced them to sit.

"This is a dirt hole!" the Persian screeched. "A grave! You are *Kandarhari*. You can't leave us here. Allah demands mercy!"

Tic spat out his answer, half playing his role and half speaking from his heart.

"Don't speak to me of Allah. He grants mercy to those who show mercy. That doesn't include you. You are Iranian, a Shiite."

"No! I am Sunni!"

"You keep repeating lies. I am tired of listening."

"You must hand us over to the Afghan police," the Persian said. "It is forbidden for americanis to keep us."

"It is death that will keep you," Tic said. "Remember those swabs I stuck in your mouths? I infected you with the virus. When the fever comes, your lungs will fill with yellow crud and you will slowly suffocate. It takes about a day."

Both mullahs mumbled incoherent prayers. Tic shone his flashlight on the two needles he was holding.

"This vaccine will save you," he said. "Tell the truth, or die here, with your bodies buried under a ton of earth, unclaimed forever."

When the Persian didn't respond, Tic shrugged and left. Once outside, he huddled with Richards and Stovell.

"By tomorrow afternoon," Richards said, "we have to fly the Iranian out."

"He'll break before then,"Tic said, "and give up his network. He's not a true *salif.*"

Richards turned to the sentry standing a few feet away.

"Thanks for standing guard," Richards said. "You can bar that door for the night."

"You're not coming back," the sentry said, "with food or a shit bucket?"

"Not until morning," Richards said. "If they start screaming, ignore them."

★ ★ ★

INSIDE THE PLATOON TENT, Sullivan, cheeks flushed with excitement, was conducting the after-action debrief. He looked up when Cruz walked in.

"OK if the men crap out here when I'm finished, sir?" Sullivan said.

Everyone was worn down, and most had lost between five and ten pounds during the week. If they dispersed now to their bunkers, they'd spend the next few hours sharing their adventure with those who hadn't been there. When it was their turn to stand watch, they'd be exhausted.

"Affirmative, Staff Sergeant," Cruz said. "Four hours' rack time. Bravo Zulu, devil dogs!"

Grins all around. Cruz paused, then shifted gears.

"Let's focus on our next task," he said. "Tonight's storm will be heavy. The GPS might malfunction. I want the squad leaders to memorize the compass heading and number of steps to each bunker. What's the password tonight, Staff Sergeant?"

"Semper, sir."

Cruz raised his right arm like a conductor before an orchestra and cocked his left hand to his ear.

"Fidelis!" the Marines shouted in unison.

After glancing at his watch, Cruz gestured at Denton, who was sitting in the rear. Once they were outside, Cruz took out his lensatic compass.

"Sergeant, while it's still light," he said, "let's walk the lines."

"Think it'll get bad, sir?"

"Back in '03, I was a snuffy turret gunner on the march up to Baghdad," Cruz said. "A dust storm hit us, and I felt like I was locked in a closet with no light. Let's be ready."

With compass in hand and Denton hobbling beside him, Cruz set out to inspect the perimeter. He stopped first at Bunker Five on the east side, nearest the ops center. He was amused to see the sentry crouched behind the neck-high parapet, staring fixedly through his binoculars.

"Anything to report, Delgado?" he said lightly.

The surprised teenager looked up, then flushed.

"The workers are leaving the fields early, sir. Maybe we're going to get hit."

In the distance, a few workers were climbing onto a rusty tractor. The wind was pushing the incandescent poppy plants sideways. In the thinning light, the bulbs looked like strings of Christmas lights, dancing and jiggling.

"I wouldn't leap to that conclusion," Cruz said. "Wind's too high to lance poppy, so the workers are going home. How long you been on watch?"

"Since zero six, sir, when the patrol left. Guess I wasn't good enough to be selected."

Jealous and hurt, he had blurted out his frustration. Then, realizing how it sounded, he rushed on.

"The private didn't mean that, sir," he said.

"Delgado, this isn't the recruit depot," Cruz said. "I'm not going to chew on you. Look, the patrol was chosen by rotation. If there's another patrol, you're next up. Every Marine does his part."

Delgado brightened.

"Cool, sir. Is it true we're getting the CAR?"

"What, you think the Taliban are selective? You've all been shot at. You all get the Combat Action Ribbon and can spin bullshit combat stories for the rest of your lives."

"We're wrapping up soon, sir?"

"Only a few more clicks to Lash. Stay alert."

Cruz rapped a pleased Delgado on his helmet and moved on. He took his time getting to the next bunker, sixty meters away. Denton was using two rough crutches, putting little weight on his left leg.

"McGowan was right about you, Sergeant," Cruz said. "You are a horse. But remember, they shoot crippled horses."

Denton laughed.

"Your sympathy is appreciated, Honorable Captain, sir."

Cruz smiled. The NCOs had come around, except for Binns.

Recording each compass heading and the number of steps, they walked from post to post, spending ten to fifteen minutes in each bunker. When they reached the west side, Cruz stopped at the gate leading to Ibril's position on the far side of the wire. After a few minutes Ibril walked up, his face blank. In the fading light, the wind was blowing flecks of dirt and straw.

"Tonight will be bad," Cruz said, brushing at his face.

"*Dussmen* stay inside in bad weather," Ibril said. "My soldiers stay awake."

"Good. See you tomorrow."

Ibril's eyes widened. The face-off was behind them.

"*Shukran*," Ibril said.

Cruz headed toward the next post.

"Ibril's squared away," Denton said.

"I'm not passing out roses," Cruz said. "He'll probably keep a few sentries up, but don't count on them. You're in charge of this sector."

It was early evening when Cruz returned to the squad tent. Sullivan had roused the sleeping Marines and sent them back to their bunkers. Cruz poked through a stack of MRE leftovers, settling on beef enchilada with refried beans. He kneaded and mashed the package to mix the meal. Once it was heated, he walked over to the ops center. Lasswell and Gunny Maxwell were holding their nightly ops chat with Golstern. As he listened, Cruz poked a plastic fork into the soggy mess.

"Hey, Matt," Lasswell said over the radio, "RT's joined us, smelling ripe."

"Solid hit today, brother!" Golstern said. "That dust storm coming in? The *askars* call it a *hamoun*, one big mother."

"I've been caught in one," Cruz said. "It's a bitch."

"We're staying open for business," Lasswell said. "Colonel Coffman wants to wrap up this op."

"He told me to light a fire under Ishaq," Golstern said. "You'll fill your quota tonight. Stay safe."

After Golstern signed off, Cruz turned to Lasswell.

"Quota?"

"Ishaq has his people call in a fire mission every two or three hours," Lasswell said. "We've killed all the Tangos in this district three times over. Pure theater on Ishaq's part."

"You won't be pulling lanyards tonight," Cruz said. "I don't trust radar in this storm. Can you give me thirty of your people to help man the lines?"

Lasswell looked at her ops chief.

"The captain has a point," Maxwell said. "We're expecting winds of seventy miles an hour. Our radar has a sixteen kilohertz pulse. It'll signal that every bush is attacking us. Thirty troops? We can accommodate that."

"That's a tough call," Lasswell said. "I'm in, but we have to brief Major Barnes."

They walked over to the intel section where Barnes and Ahmed were editing the overhead video of the raid on the mosque. Barnes was bubbling.

"The colonel's sending this video to Washington," Barnes said. "SecDef will watch it, maybe even the White House. Seven enemy KIA, not one friendly cas, two high value prisoners, and a hundred million in heroin burned. Damn, we're good! What've you got?"

After Cruz stated his request, Barnes looked at Lasswell, who deferred to her ops chief.

"I'll stand down two guns, sir," Maxwell said. "Their crews can catch up on sleep in the morning. We'll have all guns back on line by afternoon."

Barnes's good cheer sagged as he looked at Cruz.

"Do you really, really have to ask for this?" he said.

"My people are dragging," he said. "Our posts are spread far apart."

Barnes shook his head. "You lost that argument when we first arrived. But if you insist, let's ask the colonel."

The meeting was short. Coffman looked perplexed.

"Major, why didn't you inform me the Taliban are likely to attack?" he said.

"We have no indications of that, sir," Barnes said.

"When did the Taliban last assault an American position?"

"Uh, I think that was in 2012, sir."

Coffman widened his eyes for theatrical effect.

"That's ancient history, Major, not actionable intelligence," he said. "I ordered Colonel Ishaq to get his ass in gear. I'm not giving him the excuse that I took two of my guns off the line."

Barnes hastened to make amends.

"Understood, sir," he said.

Coffman rose and looked in turn at each of his subordinates.

"Major, provide a list of all the precautions we've taken," he said. "Captain Cruz, can you spare me a few minutes?"

After the others left, Coffman sighed for dramatic effect, fingers tapping the desk, and spoke in a paternal tone.

"Captain, your job is to stand guard," he said. "The cannoneers' job is to support a final push by Ishaq. I'll give you an extra generator for the radar. That should do it."

Cruz felt his face reddening. Time and again, he had backed down from Coffman.

"I've been through a *hamoun*, sir," Cruz said. "That's why I'm asking for more men."

"In that previous storm, how many casualties did you take?"

"None, sir. There was no attack. Everyone was hunkered down."

Instead of yelling, Coffman wearily shook his head.

"Precisely my point," he said. "The storm will drive everyone to shelter. We'll be picking sand out of our ears for a week. There's no evidence of a pending attack. Hell, you tore them up at that mosque! You do understand that, don't you?"

"Yes, sir," Cruz said, "but…"

Coffman waved his hand to cut him off.

"Good, we agree on the basic assumption," he said. "There's no ev-i-dence. You did well today. Let's leave it at that."

51

The Storm Gathers

When Cruz entered the platoon tent after dark, the air felt clammy. The tent sides were usually rolled up a few feet to allow air to circulate. With wind gusts now buffeting the tent, the sides were pegged down and Cruz found it hard to breathe. Sullivan was sitting with his back against a tent pole, staring at a laptop computer. Blue dots numbered Bunkers One through Twelve were shining brightly in a clockwise square.

"Solid reads and good comms with all bunkers, sir," Sullivan said.

Binns was responsible for Bunkers One through Four to the north, and McGowan for Bunkers Five through Eight to the east. To the west, Denton had Bunkers Nine through Twelve.

"We'll stand the normal watch in the ops center," Cruz said. "Staff Sergeant, you're first up. I'll monitor from here."

Sullivan nodded and headed for the center. Through the NCO channels, he'd heard about friction with the colonel. It made sense for the captain to stay out of Coffman's sight.

Richards and Stovell were studying the blue bunker dots on the laptop.

"Pressure's dropping," Stovell said. "It'll be sixty knots after midnight. Debris is sure to distort the GPS signals."

Cruz looked at Doyle sitting off to one side with Eagan, Ashford, and two other Marines.

"Sergeant Doyle," he said, "you're in charge of the snipers as the Quick Reaction Force. If I call you out, follow your damn compass."

Cruz's tone was sharp, fatigue having worn down his body and Coffman having soured his mood. Doyle gave him a surprised look.

"Fresh intel, skipper?"

Cruz shook his head.

"Negative. The muj are quiet."

By 10:00 p.m., forty Taliban had gathered in the lee of the trees in Nantush's pomegranate orchard, their backs to the wind pelting them with pebbles and twigs. Most had wrapped *kufiyas* around their faces and were wearing boots or Skechers instead of sandals. All had covered the receivers of their weapons. Some were adjusting skiing or welder's goggles and, to Quat's amusement, one old man was wearing sunglasses to protect his eyes.

The three Vietnamese had slipped into thin body-length black swimsuits, complete with hoods and swimming goggles. Each carried a vest containing an ICOM, wire cutters, heavy gloves, and cyalume sticks. Quat watched as Zar doled out pills to his fighters, who received them like a religious sacrament. In his eyes, they were Mongols, the ignorant descendants of Genghis Khan. He didn't care how these bearded illiterates found their courage.

He was paid to guide them through the wire. After that, what happened was up to these bearded believers who seemed willing to die. Zar had issued no orders for withdrawal, and farmers were lining up wheelbarrows for the fallen. Quat was glad he wouldn't be joining them in the assault wave. They'd need more than pills to protect them from the beefy Marines.

Zar was solemn as he inspected the four suicide bombers. Each had a bodyguard, and all were dressed in Afghan Army uniforms. The bodyguards, equally committed to martyrdom, provided a second set of eyes and sense of direction in the storm. The pack of each bomber contained three kilos of C-4, enough to obliterate a small house. He patted their shoulders, murmuring encouragement.

Next he unfurled his black battle flag, the symbol of total war. In the dark, none could see the color of the flag, but the flapping of the cloth stirred the mujahideen. Satisfied all was ready, he gestured at Hamullah to leave. The three-fingered old man grinned and headed north with a PKM machine gun and an RPG crew. Zar led his thirty fighters in single file west through the orchard to their jumping-off point at the edge of the foliage.

By midnight, all the pieces for the assault were in place. To reach the firebase, they had to get through both coiled and straight strands of barbed wire strung across sixty meters of open ground where the americanis had hacked down all undergrowth. Having rehearsed the movement, Quat calculated his team could slither forward, snipping one strand of wire after another, at a rate of one meter per minute. He had doubled that estimate and told Zar to be ready to assault at two in the morning.

The sharp wind was blowing westerly toward the firebase, whipping Quat's back with broken branches. He grabbed Zar by the elbow and held up two fingers. Zar tapped his watch in agreement. The three sappers lay down on their stomachs and wiggled out from the bushes. Quat had snaked forward less than five meters before he grinned. The screaming wind was blasting past his ears. His face wasn't eight inches off the ground and still the dust was so thick he could barely read the luminous needle on the lensatic compass he was holding in front of his nose. Perfect cover! One meter a minute.

Day 7

APRIL 12

52

Broken Arrow

Quat knew the Afghans lacked tactical patience. Once he gave the signal, they would rush forward wildly, yelling, "Allahu Akbar," too frenzied to think. He was compensating for that by opening a wide gap in the wire all the way up to the bunkers, following the path he had watched the Marines use. It had three zigzags, meaning more wire to cut than if he took a straight path. But it was clear of mines, acoustic sensors, and trip flares.

When he reached the first coil, his companion snipped the wire, pushed it two feet to the right, and tied it back. Quat pulled the other strand the same distance to the left, cinched it off, and anchored it with a short bamboo stake. He dug a shallow hole with his knife and took a cyalume stick from his pack. After snapping it to ignite the chemical, he placed it in the hole. Good. One wire breached, leaving a four-foot opening. Two dozen to go.

After ninety minutes, the three sappers had cleared a lane from the tree line across the sixty meters of open space leading to Bunker Five. Once near the bunker, they cut the final coils of wire and peeled back a five-foot section. Satisfied they had opened a path through all the barriers, Quat gestured to his two assistants to go back and bring up the four suicide bombers and their bodyguards. Only after hearing the suicide explosions would Zar lead the assault wave of his holy warriors.

Squatting alone inside the wire in the raging wind, Quat felt a pang of anxiety. Had he measured correctly in the blackness? If so, Bunker Five lay close by to his right, several meters north. On his hands and knees, he crawled in that direction. In the wind and dust, he couldn't hear or see, but in less than a minute he felt the steep upward slope of the bunker's revetment. Relieved, he clawed at the dirt, scooped out a hole, snapped a cyalume, and placed it in upright. A final touch. Now even a doped-up zombie could see where to hurl his body and disintegrate the Marines. That done, Quat crawled back the ten meters to the cut in the wire. His companions had returned with the four suicide teams. They all lay down to wait for the diversion.

Zar had confidence in three-fingered Habullah. Yes, he panted and pawed for his daily Captagon pill from Lebanon, costing much more than the tomato pills from Africa. Zar supported his five-dollar-a-day habit because the old man was steady. He hadn't backed down from the Asian, and he knew where to cross the canals. Zar wasn't surprised when the call came promptly at 2:00 a.m.

"The water is cold," Habullah radioed. "Allahu Akbar."

When he finished his brief radio message, Habullah did as instructed and left his ICOM on. The Americani would focus their radio direction finding toward Habullah, adding to the diversion. The old man and his four mujahideen were lying in an irrigation ditch four hundred meters to the north, facing the Marine bunkers farthest from the ops center. Habullah leaned over and tapped the PKM machine gunner on the shoulder.

"Begin firing!" he shouted.

INSIDE BUNKER ONE AT THE NORTH END of the perimeter, Binns sat hunched against the deafening wind, a towel wrapped around his neck, peering through his goggles at a greenish maelstrom of twigs and flecks. He heard the slow bark of a PKM, sounding like a hammer beating against a pipe, so loud the gunner had to be within a few hundred meters of the wire. Binns thought the gunner was an idiot. A complete, total waste of rounds. He knew better than to fire back in the remote chance of revealing where he was. His two comrades had popped up and were peering forward, unable to see any rifle flashes. Seconds later, the deep clapping bang of an RPG caused Binns to instinctively duck before hearing the rocket explode near the piss tubes off to his left. He crouched down out of the wind to report in.

WHEN HE HEARD THE BARK OF THE PKM and the thump of the RPG explosion, Quat pulled the first suicide team to their feet, aligned them in the direction of the ops center, and gave them a shove. They stumbled forward with the wind pushing them. Quat oriented the second and third teams toward the artillery pits. That left the fourth team. They had to take out Bunker Five to allow Zar's assault wave to rush past without encountering fire. He grabbed the tunic of the fourth bomber and dragged him a few meters forward so that he could see the glowing green marker at the foot of bunker.

He patted him on the back and crawled back to his two companions. He gestured at them to go back and bring up Zar's force. He would remain at the cut in the wire to point them in the right direction as they entered the base.

★ ★ ★

INSIDE BUNKER FIVE, Lance Corporal Henry Delgado was still standing watch. It had been five hours since Cruz had visited him. When his two bunker mates had returned from the patrol, he had insisted they get some added rest. They were curled womblike in their ponchos, breathing through bandanas clutched in front of their mouths, occasionally spitting out a swish of bottled water.

Whenever he peered out, sand whipped and lashed his face. It felt like sandpaper was scouring his body, pricking at every capillary, flaying him inch by inch, scraping raw every inch of exposed skin. He tried to think of home, but there was no past, no parents, no girls, no parties, no warm memories. Only stings, bites, and nips, the wind screeching and his flesh peeling.

It was shortly after two in the morning when Delgado heard the RPG explosion. He snapped alert, tugged down his helmet-mounted goggles, and peered through the infrared intensifier. A million black dots collided against the artificial green backdrop. He shook his head and flipped to thermal. A zillion bright green particles of dust, pebbles, straw, and twigs swirled around like a child's kaleidoscope. He had no field of vision and no notion whether he was looking at the sky, the horizon, or the ground.

He switched off the night vision aids and peered out through clear plastic goggles. It looked like he was swimming with his eyes open under muddy waters. Not able to see a thing, he tucked the handheld close to his left ear and listened to the traffic on the net. As he hunched forward, he heard someone scrambling up the revetment. He looked out. A dust-caked face with a shaggy beard and small goggles was staring back at him. He saw a brilliant white flash.

Inside the platoon tent, Cruz was looking at his laptop when the pressure wave cracked through like a lightning bolt. He lurched sideways, falling on his right shoulder. He scrambled to his feet, head ringing, and pressed his handheld to his ear. The platoon net was flooded with the voices of excited Marines. He waited for a break in the frantic transmissions and pushed the talk button.

"This is Wolf Six. Everyone shut up! If any Marine has real info about that explosion, speak up now."

"This is Wolf Three" McGowan said. "I think it came from Bunker Five. Bunker Five, answer up!"

Silence on the net.

"Break, break. Wolf Six, this is Wolf Three again. Request permission to go to Bunker Five. Over."

"Wolf Three, this is Six. That is a negative! All bunkers, hold your pos! I want each bunker to report in, starting with Bunker One. Give your bunker number and sign off."

★ ★ ★

Yusef, the first suicide bomber through the cut in the wire, knew his target was the ops center. He felt no fear and was alert, but his brain was functioning on automatic. Two hours earlier, he had swallowed two tramadol pills. Now he had no real sense of where he was and didn't care. His mind was racing through past images, sitting on a camel in a dry desert, his glum father leaving him at the *madrassa*, praise from the mullah with the bad breath, the mujahideen treating him with respect, Zar bowing before him, the sweet purple grapes at the mosque.

His bodyguard was holding his hand to guide him. Suddenly the hand squeezed hard and released. A tall infidel in a helmet and goggles was standing right in front of them, guarding a door. The infidel raised his rifle. Yusef heard a slight coughing above the shrieking wind as his guard grabbed his stomach and fell to his knees. Yusef didn't hesitate. Lunging forward, he squeezed his kill switch.

OVER THE RADIO, CRUZ HAD CHECKED on three bunkers when the second shock wave knocked him sideways. He fell to one knee, shook his head, and pushed himself up, fumbling for a water bottle to wash out his eyes. He was breathing in dust, and all around him Marines were coughing and spitting, trying to clear their throats.

"Everyone get outside!" Cruz yelled. "In the lee! Go to the west of the tent!"

In less than a minute, they had gathered in the downwind side. The canvas had collapsed, providing a partial bulwark against the screeching wind. Cruz flicked on the miner's light strapped to his helmet. Other Marines did the same and quickly responded to a ragged roster call. Everyone was accounted for. Cruz fumbled for his handheld and called the ops center.

"Eagle Three, this is Wolf Six, over."

Only static and a few garbled words came back.

Cruz switched to the platoon net.

"This is Wolf Six," he said. "All bunkers! Enemy inside the wire. Stay in place and watch your six at every bunker!"

Cruz grabbed Doyle and Richards by the shoulders and shouted at them over the howling wind.

"I'll check the ops center," Cruz said. "Wait for my orders."

"My team will go with you," Richards said. "We can't do anything here."

"All right!" Cruz said. "Doyle, send one man with me as a runner. If I can't establish comms, I'll send him back with instructions."

"Take Ashford," Doyle said. "He's got a good sense of direction."

Cruz took a bearing with his compass and started out, followed by the CIA team and Ashford. When they reached the ops center, they had to crawl over the crumbled revetment. The tent top had snapped off, with sections blown away and remnants the size of living room rugs flapping crazily. Marines were running about in the dust and smoke, some screaming for order and making the chaos worse, others carrying bodies to the aid station. One Marine on a stretcher was groaning and holding his dark-stained stomach. Cruz wondered how the medics would ever get the dust and sand out of his intestines. He saw Sullivan being helped out, his left leg dangling at a crooked angle.

Pawing his way from group to group, Cruz found Barnes sitting on the ground, back resting on an upturned table. Lasswell was down on one knee, shining a light in his blood-smeared face. Barnes pointed a trembling finger at Cruz.

"Muj all over the place!" Barnes yelled. "Fire the FPF!"

"We got no targets, no Tangos!" Cruz said.

He peered at Barnes, who hadn't been wearing a helmet when the shock wave hit the ops center. Cruz looked at Lasswell, who grimaced and shook her head.

"I just got here," she said. "The colonel's concussed, barely conscious. Said for us to wait for his orders. Barnes isn't any better. He's not making sense."

"We called in broken arrow!" Barnes yelled. "We're going under!"

Cruz looked at a Marine with a handset who was hunched next to Barnes. The radio operator nodded.

"I sent it," the operator shouted. "We have comms with Captain Golstern. He says there's no shooting in the Afghan sector."

"Fuck the Afghans!" Barnes yelled. "We're the ones in the shit!"

Promptly at 6:00 p.m., President Dinard heard the heavy chugging of Marine One as it landed at the far end of the West Lawn. He was looking forward to his weekend in Florida, especially tomorrow's round with Tom Barrow, a two-time winner of the Masters. He walked quickly outside, where his wife and a few aides were waiting. His buoyant mood vanished when he saw his National Security Advisor walking hurriedly toward him.

"Sorry, sir," Armsted said. "It's about that base in Helmand. We have word of a broken arrow. That's the emergency code for a unit's that's being overrun."

"Shit! They're fighting enemy inside the base?" POTUS said. "What orders do I give?"

"None, sir. Everyone's poised to help, but there's a huge storm down there. No aviation can get in."

"Terrible, terrible," he said. "Keep me updated."

POTUS turned back toward Marine One. Armsted, looking uncomfortable, didn't move.

"I recommend you stay here, sir. To be, ah, playing golf when this breaks in the press...the optics would look bad."

Dinard didn't hide his frustration.

"The damn press always pounds me for other people's mistakes," he said. "What's the next move?"

"The Chairman and Towns are on their way over," Armsted said. "Diane will take pictures of all of you in the sit room."

"Like the one of Obama watching the raid that bumped off Bin Laden," Barnum said, "with everyone around the commander in chief?"

"We have no video to watch, Mr. President," Armsted said. "The photo op will make you look presidential. But those Marines are on their own."

53

The Tipping Point

Inside the wrecked ops center, Barnes was struggling to stand, legs twitching. Cruz turned to see Coffman standing behind him, blood trickling from his nose, dilated eyes popping out of his dirt-caked face. He was swaying, but he brushed aside Cruz's outstretched hand.

"Cruz, this is your fault," he said, slurring the words. "Barnes, you're the watch officer. You take over security."

He stumbled back, confused that troops were moving around him as if he didn't exist, tending to others and shouting to each other. Over the din, he pointed at Cruz.

"Report to me in my office!" he yelled.

He staggered drunkenly away, barely keeping his balance. Barnes was now on his feet, supported by Lasswell and Richards. Cruz looked at them and shook his head. The operations center wasn't functioning. No officer had taken charge or was giving sensible directions. No one had a solid fix on where anyone was. The GPS signal couldn't cut through the swirling dust. Every bunker, sleeping tent, and gun pit was on its own. In his mind's eye, he pictured the Taliban swarming through the cut at Bunker Five. He shook Barnes by his shoulders.

"Disperse everyone!" he yelled. "Muj are loose with satchel charges!"

Barnes looked confused.

"The colonel said," he began, "you're not supposed to…"

Cruz pushed past him and grabbed the arm of the radio operator.

"Get on the net," he said. "Order everyone out of the tents. NCOs are to form their people in 360s. Stay prone in wagon wheel formations and for God's sake, no one shoots unless he's looking at a muj with a beard!"

Cruz turned to Richards.

"Sullivan's down," he said. "Can you run comms with the bunkers? Tell the squad leaders to fire only to their front, and check the wire between bunkers. I'm heading to Bunker Five with the QRF. Tell McGowan not to fucking shoot me!"

Barnes tried to intervene.

"You need permission from the colonel," he said. "You're disobeying—"

"I'm checking the lines!" Cruz yelled. "You restore order here!"

Cruz left the bedlam of the ops center. Lasswell too didn't wait for Barnes to recover.

"I'm going back to my sector," she said. "I'm evacuating all tents."

The wind whipped away her words as she adjusted her goggles. Stovell looked at Richards.

"Eagan should go with her," he said.

Hearing this, Lasswell looked relieved.

"Be glad of the company," she said.

"No!" Richards said. "Eagan stays with you."

"I'm not helping here," Stovell said. "Eagan and I will go together."

"You're not trained for this!" Richards shouted over the storm. "Make sure Eagan leads!"

★ ★ ★

Across the base, everyone was on the move. Within minutes, 319 Marines and 27 Navy medical staff were forming into groups of five to twelve, grabbing ropes or cords, or simply holding hands, and stepping out into the screeching void of whirling dust. Some shuffled into the lee of the revetments, while others wandered short distances before plopping down and forming defensive circles, lying shoulder to shoulder, unable to see, the wind shrieking, imaginations running wild.

At the north end of the perimeter, Binns was standing watch with Corporal Gordon, who had been brooding since he'd watched Beal die. Gordon's wife was expecting, and he was upset that he couldn't call to reassure her. The third grunt in the bunker, PFC Josh Byram, had joined the platoon a week before the deployment.

Binns resented the order to check the wire. *Can't see shit*, he thought. *Fucking Cruz, why doesn't he do it himself?* Still, he knew the order made sense. To hunker down was to die. But he wasn't going out there by himself.

"Byram, you hold here," Binns said. "Gordon, let's check the wire."

"I got to?" Gordon said.

"Yeah, you got to," Binns said. "Byram's the newbie. I need you at my six."

Gordon patted his armored vest, feeling for his notebook. He knew he wouldn't be coming back. He had to write something for Carol. Couldn't leave her wondering why he hadn't come back. She…

Binns was jerking a rope around him, slapping at his hands.

"Stop fucking around! Tie in! Let's go!"

Gordon cinched the rope, picked up his M27, and followed Binns out of the bunker.

At least he didn't whine about his wife, Binns thought. *Shit, I'm starting to think like Cruz!*

He radioed to Bunker Two that he was coming down the wire and be damn careful about shooting. Followed by Gordon, he stumbled from the bunker down the slight slope to the wire. A ten-foot rope, attached by slipknots, linked the two Marines. Binns flipped down his NVG and clicked the SureFire illuminator on the rail of his M27. In the halo of greenish light, thousands of dust and sand particles swirled like a snow blizzard. He couldn't see beyond the front sight. He shuffled forward, poking tentatively, until his rifle barrel pinged against a coil of barbed wire.

Still strung tight! No break here. He stopped momentarily to let his heartbeat subside. *Thank you, Lord!* He turned right, hunched over, and duck-walked south with his head down, pebbles and twigs pelting his face. He held his rifle in his left hand, like a blind man with a cane, tapping the wire as he moved toward Bunker Two. Holding the rope taut, Gordon followed behind, his face feeling sandblasted.

NOT TEN METERS AWAY, a suicide bombing team was staggering toward them. Abdul Quaz, with three tramadols racing through his system and his synapses misfiring, clutched his kill switch as he blundered blindly along. His target was an artillery pit, but the wind had pushed him sideways toward the perimeter.

His bodyguard, Natiz, could offer no guidance. He had refused the pills. He didn't need them to numb his brain; he was confident Allah would welcome him. But this was foolish. Four minutes had passed since the Asian had pushed them through the cut in the wire, and they were wandering aimlessly. Natiz had no idea where he was.

He was bumbling along, fighting the impulse to turn back, when Abdul tripped. Startled, Natiz jerked back. Abdul was yelping and flailing, fighting some monster that was pulling him down from behind. Natiz reached out a hand and felt a sharp sting. Abdul had tripped over a coil of barbed wire. He was struggling to pull free, both arms stretched out. His writhing entangled him more. Desperate for help, he appealed to his companion.

"*Dalta raasha!*" Abdul yelled. "Help me!"

Frightened at being blown to bits, Natiz backed away.

BINNS HAD HIS HAND ON THE WIRE, puzzled that it was vibrating, when he heard the shout. He straightened and looked back. Gordon was pointing ahead with his M27. Without exchanging a word, they advanced side by side, rifles at the ready. They hadn't walked a dozen feet before they dimly saw a figure pinned against the wire, tugging and straining to pull himself free.

BOTH MARINES AIMED IN. Neither glimpsed Natiz, who was standing farther back. Recovering from his shock, he opened fire without raising the AK to his shoulder. Four of the five bullets hit the Marines in their armored vests, staggering but not putting them down. Both returned fire on automatic, the rounds ripping through the Afghan's stomach and chest.

NATIZ'S FIFTH BULLET HAD PLOWED INTO Binns's right thigh, shattering the femur and femoral artery. Binns tottered, then collapsed, his back catching in the wire, rifle barrel pointed at the suicide bomber, who was struggling to reach his kill switch. Binns shoved the barrel into the Afghan's side and fired fifteen rounds, emptying his magazine. Gordon rushed over and put a final bullet in the bomber's head.

"Call it in," Binns wheezed. "Get help from Bunker Two."

He felt Gordon patting him, trying to find the wound, struggling to open his vest.

"Where you hit?" Gordon was yelling. "Where you hit?"

With each breath, Binns felt his blood spurting out. He'd done his best, and wished Cruz had been there to watch him. He felt cold and started to shiver. In the distance, a light was faintly glowing, becoming brighter as it approached. That was strange. He thought death was a black curtain.

AFTER LEAVING THE SHATTERED OPS CENTER, Cruz had set out for Bunker Five, with Doyle and the QRF behind him. Compass in hand, he walked slowly, counting each pace. When he reached the wire by bumping into it, he backed off and turned to Doyle.

"The bunker's right around here," he shouted. "Take four Marines and search north. I'll take Ashford and two others south. Stay in touch on the net."

He hadn't made a dozen steps before he was stumbling up a large mound of dirt and kicking aside Bunker Five's broken boards, some with flapping strips of canvas attached. The mound wasn't higher than Cruz's chest, and it dipped into a concave bowl where the grunts had eaten, slept, and stood watch. Ashford tripped over a body and called out. The others rushed up and, digging with their hands, pulled out a half-buried Marine. He was unconscious and his head lolled. Ashford placed his thumb and finger under the dirt-caked chin.

"I feel a pulse!"

"He was blasted and buried!" Cruz yelled. "He's gone. Let's go!"

"You don't know that for sure!" Ashford shouted back.

Another body was found, leading to more frantic efforts. Cruz grabbed Ashford.

"We have to find the cut wire," Cruz shouted. "They're getting through! Leave one Marine here. The rest come with me!"

Cruz slid out of the collapsed bunker. Ashford didn't follow immediately, pausing to pull dirt from the mouth of the lifeless Marine. Without looking back, Cruz plunged into the blizzard of dust. As Binns had done, he kept his face down, rifle in his left hand to check the tautness of the wire.

QUAT WAS CROUCHING NEXT TO A STEEL STAKE that anchored the wire. While waiting for Zar to bring up the assault wave, he had pulled the broken coils farther apart so that two Taliban could rush through abreast. Four minutes had passed since he had sent Nguyen and Trao back to act as guides. Where were they? Was that idiot Zar waiting for more detonations by the suicide bombers? The man had the brain of a monkey. Weren't two explosions enough to get him moving? A minute ago, Quat heard one burst from an AK a short distance to his north, but no third explosion. That wasn't good. Come on! Come on!

What was that? He looked up, the dust pelting his goggles. A monster was standing not a foot away, peering down at him. Quat reached to bring up his AK. Not able to swing his rifle around, Cruz charged forward, smashing into the Vietnamese. Quat's slight body bounced backward and his rifle went flying. He felt the barbed wire slash into his back. Adrenaline surging, he wrenched free with no sense of pain.

Then the American was on him, heavy arms around him, picking him up to slam him into the ground. Quat spun and ducked low, instincts honed by years of training. He was halfway loose when Cruz sensed his escape and lunged after him, using his weight to bear down. Quat fell and twisted onto his stomach, Cruz's arms locked around his thighs. Quat squirmed and wriggled, digging his hands into the dirt, his rubber body suit slipping from Cruz's grasp. Quat rolled onto his back, drew up his right leg, and drove his heel forward like a piston.

Cruz felt a jolt of pain and saw a jagged flash of lightning as his left cheekbone shattered. Instead of backing away, he dove forward, flopping on top of Quat before the Vietnamese could deliver another kick. He wrapped his arms around Quat's lower ribs and pulled the Vietnamese on top of him, locking his hands and squeezing with all his might.

Quat felt the American's thick arms tightening their vise grip. He dug his heels and elbows into the dirt and arched his back, straining to gain an inch of separation from Cruz's chest, twisting and turning to open enough space to slip free before the breath was squeezed out of him. Cruz hugged him in a bear's embrace for five seconds, seven, ten. Then Quat had to breathe. When he did, Cruz pulled harder and a rib broke. The pain exploded through Quat's body. His muscles went into spasms and his heels and elbows momentarily lost their grip in the dirt. He banged the back of his head against Cruz's face, trying to deliver a hammer blow. He felt the American's teeth bite down on his hair and tear at his scalp, trapping his head before he could deliver a second blow.

When he next tried to inhale, Cruz again squeezed and a second rib fractured. Quat was no longer fully conscious. Cruz knew he had to keep applying full pressure until the Vietnamese passed out, but his muscles were tiring. Quat felt a slight slackening and gathered himself. When he next heaved himself up, he would roll to his right, pinning the American's arm. Once he squirmed loose, he'd deliver fast kicks to the face.

Then Ashford was there, down on one knee, peering from Cruz to the Vietnamese as though the referee at a wrestling match.

"Fuck!" Ashford said.

"Knife," Cruz grunted.

Ashford drew out his Ka-Bar, pressed the tip against Quat's windpipe, and shoved hard. Quat's head jerked up, his blood spraying Cruz's face.

54

We Hold Here

Cruz pushed the body away as two more Marines rushed up. He pointed a few feet to the east where the broken wire, unseen in swirling dust, stretched across the flat ground. Unable to fully open his mouth, his words sounded garbled.

"Grazing fire," he said. "Short bursts, knee high, spray."

Ashford loosed a burst into the black void of the gale. Two seconds later, they heard several cracks as AK rounds broke the sound barrier above their heads. That told Cruz what he needed to know. Bunker Five, ripped apart, was the critical hole in the perimeter and the enemy assault force was somewhere out there, closing toward them. But in the wind and dust, the Taliban had to crawl blindly toward the waiting Marines.

"We hold here," Cruz said.

He ripped the Velcro cover from his handheld and radioed to Doyle.

"Wolf Four, this is Six. I need your 320 here! My pos is on the wire ten meters south of Bunker Five. Feel your way along the wire."

Inside a minute, Doyle had groped his way to them. A grenadier followed him with a grenade launcher that looked like a flare gun pistol attached to the underside of his M27 rifle barrel. Cruz pointed vaguely east.

"Plaster our front," he mumbled.

Each 40mm shell had a burst radius of four meters.

"I can't see shit!" the grenadier yelled.

"You don't have to!" Cruz said. "How many rounds you got?"

The pouches on the Marine's vest bulged with explosives the size of oversize shotgun shells.

"Forty!"

"Pump out one every ten seconds, right in front of us!"

"How far out?"

"Put 'em in the wire!"

The grenadier tilted his rifle barrel vertical, pulled the trigger, and the first shell thunked out.

THIRTY METERS DOWNSLOPE and midway through the dozen bands of barbed wire, Zar was kneeling next to his Vietnamese guide when the first 40mm shell exploded with a sharp bang. He dropped flat. Behind him thirty fighters were lying in a long row. Dimly he heard the cracks of bullets overhead.

What? Had the Vietnamese failed to cut the wire? The infidels were firing from somewhere close, and that idiot Quat was not answering the ICOM. He looked at his watch. 0215. Fifteen minutes since the assault had begun. Too long, too long! They had to get inside the base before the americanis could rush up reinforcements.

Another burst of bullets, so close he instinctively flinched. No sound of the rifles, just *crack! crack!* as the bullets snapped overhead.

He jabbed at the Vietnamese next to him. Go on, get up there. The Asian shook his head.

"We cut wire," he hissed. "You fight!"

Zar knew it was suicidal to crawl blindly forward with bullets cracking over his head and the enemy waiting. He rolled over and tugged at the mujahideen lying behind him.

"Pitai," he yelled. "Get Pitai!"

Pitai, a slight Pashtun with a wild beard, crawled up, dragging his RPG. Pointing at the flickering green cyalume to his front, Zar gestured to him to move forward to a firing position. Pitai immediately obeyed, pushing past Zar before steadying himself on one knee and raising the RPG to his shoulder. Zar rolled away from the recoil area as he fired. Following the sharp whack of the back blast, Zar strained to listen. Four full seconds passed before he heard the rocket explode. Too far away, a clear miss.

LYING PRONE AT THE BLASTED ENTRY GATE, Cruz saw the red flash a millisecond before he heard the rocket grenade sizzle past. He snapped the safety clip off an M67 grenade, straightened the pin, rose to one knee, and hurled it. The fourteen-ounce bomb carried sixty feet through the air, bounced, rolled, and exploded. *WHAM!*

PITAI WAS LOADING A SECOND ROCKET when a white-hot shard whizzed through his cheeks, splattering teeth fragments and blood across Zar's goggles. Shattered mouth agape, Pitai stood up and staggered blindly, his brain a dazzle of white, searing stars. Four silent bullets hit him. He lurched sideways and pitched headlong into the wire, the fierce wind blowing his body back and forth like a puppet.

The two Vietnamese guides looked at each other. One pointed toward the tree line and both low-crawled toward the rear.

Zar heard a few more snaps overhead, but again there was no sound of shooting. The *kafirs* were near, very near, using rifles with suppressors. He needed Quat to point out where the enemy was. He grabbed Bacha, next in line behind him. The man's face was wrapped in a balaclava, and he was wearing sunglasses to ward off the stinging sand and grit. Zar jerked off the sunglasses and shouted into his face.

"Crawl forward! Follow the green sticks to the Asian. Bring him here!"

Bacha squinted at him, raising his hand to shield his eyes.

"I can't see," he protested, making no effort to move up.

Zar yelled to bring up a PKM. Seconds later, the heavy barrel of a PKM machine gun glanced off his shoulder. Good! At least Sial was willing to fight. Zar pointed into the stinging wind.

"Shoot!"

Sial stood erect, braced himself against the wind, and, holding the weapon waist-high, fired wildly. Five Marines returned fire on full automatic, aiming in the direction of the PKM sound. Hit four times, Sial lost his balance and the wind pushed him backward into the wire.

Staying flat on the ground, Zar was trying to tug the body loose when another 40mm shell exploded. He felt a thousand hot needles puncture his upraised arm.

BOTH SIDES WERE SHOOTING BLINDLY. Cruz heard the sharp *crack!* as a bullet snapped by his left ear. As he turned to check on the others, Doyle leaned against his right shoulder. Without looking around, Cruz tried to shrug him off.

"Damn it, Mad Dog," he shouted. "Give me firing room!"

Doyle didn't budge. The rim of his helmet seemed stuck inside the collar of Cruz's armored vest. Cruz felt hot liquid on his neck.

He wrenched around and looked at the bloody pulp that had been Doyle's face. A heavy slug from the PKM had smashed through his forehead and shattered his skull. Cruz held the sergeant in an embrace for a second before lowering the body face down into the dirt.

Ashford was kneeling a few feet away, focused toward the wire, oblivious to Doyle's death. Cruz grabbed him by the elbow and jerked him flat.

"Stay prone! Shoot low!" Cruz yelled. "Short bursts."

Six Marines were now lying prone across and on both sides of the gap in the wire. He crawled from one to another, repeating the message. First one sent a few rounds downrange, then the next, and the next. Occasionally the grenadier popped another 40mm shell.

ZAR REMAINED FLAT, flinching as bullets cracked and snapped over his head. Gradually the pain in his arm subsided. He knew he had to crawl forward. The three Asians were gone, but he didn't need them. He could see the green cyalume beckoning a few meters in front of him. Move! Once he dragged himself up to it, he would see another. And there would be one after that. Move!

Courage is not constant. Even the stoutest warriors need encouragement. When there is the hand of no other warrior to grasp, and your eyes see only black, and your face is pelted with dirt stinging like needles and no encouraging voice is heard over the deafening wind, then courage ebbs and blind rage cools. Zar had reached his moral limit. With one arm numb, he made a feeble effort to crawl forward and then stopped. His zeal, anger, and belief in Allah could propel him no farther. He laid his cheek in the dirt and breathed heavily. He would rest for a few seconds.

A searing white flash and a close clap of thunder shook the ground, followed by lashing rain. Then the ice pebbles came, hitting him on the head and bouncing off the ground around him. He grabbed a fistful. Through his glove, they felt like cold marbles. Hail like this had fallen only twice during his lifetime, and both times the frozen rain drops had proved to him that Allah's heaven existed. Now the pounding hail, whipped almost vertical by the wind, was beating on his back, punishing him for hesitating.

This freak of nature swept by in less than a minute, leaving Zar shivering in the mud. He hunkered there, cursing the elements, unable to summon the grit to rush forward. He had lost the conviction to assault. When the moment counted most, he was no longer a leader or a believer. His men couldn't continue to lie inside the wire in single file, while the infidels shot and threw bombs at them. They would be slaughtered when light came.

"Turn around," he said to Bacha. "We have to go back."

THE ATTACK HAD FAILED. In fact, the assault had never taken place. The mujahideen crawled away from the caldera of six frightened, angry Marines defending a four-meter cut in the wire. As the Marines took turns loosing three-round bursts, they received scant return fire. The wind had decreased, but they still could see no targets. Peering through their night vision goggles, they swept their infrared aiming dots back and forth in the swirling maelstrom, unable to lock on a single target.

CRAWLING THROUGH THE MUCK back to the shelter of the tree line, Zar tried to assure himself that he had done the right thing. The assault had failed because of the Asians and the freakish weather. No one could blame him. Four martyrs with satchel charges had penetrated the American base. Dozens of infidels had surely been killed, maybe more than one hundred. News of his victory would spread around the world.

★ ★ ★

AT 0220, TWENTY MINUTES AFTER Bunker Five had been obliterated, Cruz called the ops center.

"Wolf Five Acting, this is Wolf Six. We've plugged the hole. No incoming, repeat, no incoming. Over."

"Six, this is Five," Richards replied. "All bunkers have reported in. No other points of entry. One angel at Bunker Two. I think there's Tangos still inside the perimeter. Over."

"Five, this is Six. Understand all. Wolf Three, come forward to my pos. Five, I will come to your pos once Three relieves me here."

McGowan, who had been listening inside Bunker Seven, squeezed hard on the push-to-talk button.

"Six, this is Three. Copy. Am moving to your pos."

He turned to his two companions.

"It's about fucking time! You devil dogs monitor the net and stay alert."

Stay alert? He knew that sounded stupid, as if they might fall asleep in the middle of a wild storm with suicide bombers wandering around. Alone, he slid down to the wire and, tapping it with his right glove, slowly duck-walked his way north. He was counting his thirty-ninth step when he bumped into an Afghan soldier.

The *askar* was bent over, facing into the wind, peering forward over the wire as though trying to see something in the void. Mac's knee hit his shoulder and the soldier sprawled forward. Mac lurched back.

"Sorry, man," he blurted out. "I didn't see—"

The *askar* was scrambling to his feet when Mac's brain snapped into gear. *An ANA here inside the wire?* He brought up his M27, still hesitant to shoot. The soldier responded by raising an AK. From three feet away, Mac fired on automatic. The bullets hit the armored vest of the mujahideen, staggering him. Mac swung the muzzle up and fired again, hitting the man in the throat, with two bullets ricocheting off his helmet and zipping past Mac's face.

The Taliban fell thrashing, feet kicking convulsively. Mac swiveled, making a full circle, tense, straining to see. *Damn,* he thought, *I almost shot myself!* The wind was keening and the gravel was pelting his cheeks He took a knee and waited for a few seconds. He peered down at the corpse.

"*Tashakor,* motherfucker."

He grasped the wire and warily continued north, soon linking up with Cruz.

55

The DNA of Warrior Ants

In that howling black, there was no functioning chain of command, only an instinct forged by training and tradition, a sense that others had fought through much worse. The Marines had the DNA of warrior ants. Kill one or one thousand and the result was the same: the survivors swarmed into the breach. They knitted together, opened their incisors, and continued to attack. Remove one leader and another stepped forward.

Every component looked out for its own. The security platoon guarding the perimeter plugged the gap and held on. With both Coffman and Barnes barely coherent, the sergeants at the ops center cleared the casualties and connected the comms. The aid station had a working generator, and Commander Zarest and his Navy medics were working feverishly to stabilize a dozen severely wounded. The artillery NCOs had evacuated all tents and set up circular defenses inside the four revetments holding the 155s.

Lasswell knew her duty was to check on each revetment. Accompanied by one Marine at point and another at the rear, she set out into the storm. The Marines carried their M27s, while Lasswell cradled a lensatic compass and behind her Stovell and Eagan held SIG Sauer pistols.

After checking one revetment, they headed toward the next. In the open space between the two, the wind was pushing so much dirt they had to cover their mouths to breathe. They stopped while Lasswell adjusted her headlamp to read the compass.

THREE SUICIDE BOMBERS WERE DEAD. The fourth was wandering aimlessly inside the artillery compound. He had broken his goggles, and his bodyguard was leading him by the hand. Utterly lost, they had agreed to blow themselves up as soon as they stumbled upon an infidel, any infidel. With his head down, the bodyguard walked straight into Stovell.

Jolted by pure terror, both men jumped back, with Stovell stumbling into Lasswell. The bodyguard recovered first, dropping the bomber's hand and swinging up his AK. Stovell shoved hard with his left hand, sending Lasswell sprawling out of harm's way. Only then did he raise his pistol. But he had lost three seconds. He saw the muzzle of the AK flash brightly and he felt a hammer hit him in the throat. The pain shocked his nerve system and he stood stock still, paralyzed.

Eagan took one step forward, firing as he advanced. His first bullet caught the shooter in the shoulder. With his second step, Eagan had closed the short distance. He shoved the pistol barrel against the Taliban's face and squeezed the trigger. Pistol extended, he swung to his left. Before the suicide bomber could react, Eagan shot him in the cheek. As the man staggered back, Eagan placed the muzzle against the man's temple and blew out his neural circuitry. The gunfight had lasted six seconds.

Stovell was down on one knee. He tried to stand, but his legs wouldn't work. The pistol slipped from his hand and he slowly pitched forward. Lasswell rushed over and rolled him onto his back. Blood was pumping out the right side of his neck. She was trying to stanch it with her hand when Eagan pushed her aside and grasped Stovell by his vest. He hugged him, squeezing his forearms against Stovell's neck, as if that could dam the gushing. Stovell's head lolled forward as the blood spurts lessened and his heart fluttered to a stop.

On either side of them, the two Marines were in semicrouches, M27s leveled, peering outboard into the dirt-filled void. Eagan stood and flipped the body onto his back in a fireman's carry, the blood from the cavernous wound splashing across his face. His ruck tore open and Tinker Toys spilled out, whipped away by the wind.

Lasswell screamed into his ear.

"Let him go! We got to check the gun pits!"

Eagan dully nodded and unslung the body. Lasswell took a compass reading and they moved off, leaving Stovell behind.

AT THE OPS CENTER, the NCOs were trying to restore a sense of order. Coffman, still woozy, pretended to assume the role of senior officer and brushed aside several offers of medical aid. His nose bled whenever he moved his head too rapidly, and he had a remorseless headache throbbing in rhythm with his pulse. Golstern kept calling, apologetically explaining that Kabul and Washington were demanding updates every minute. Coffman kept replying that the battle was continuing, while adding no details

He hadn't said or done anything that affected the outcome. He knew Wolf Six was heavily engaged somewhere. Yet he vaguely recalled he had told Cruz to stand down. After all, his carelessness had caused the whole mess. With the wind howling and the hard dirt pelting him, Coffman wandered about in a semidaze, ignored by the others.

Battery-powered lanterns provided light, and a paper drawing of the perimeter was spread on the ground, heavily anchored at all four corners against the wind ripping through the shattered tent. Coffman had the sense not to challenge or distract Richards, who was coordinating updates from the bunkers along the perimeter. As radio reports came in, the numbers and rough locations of the scattered units were filled in.

Several feet away, Gunny Maxwell received a call from Lasswell. He walked over and put his hand on Richards's shoulder.

"There was a fight at Gun Pit One. Stovell's KIA. Eagan is staying with Captain Lasswell. Sorry, bro."

Richards nodded and pushed the news out of his consciousness. He squinted at the diagram of the perimeter. With a Magic Marker, he drew a large X at Gun Pit One. Similar Xs showed the locations of the other fights—Binns near Bunker Two, Cruz at Bunker Five, McGowan at Bunker Seven.

Coffman wobbled up and looked down at the Xs.

"Four contacts, Colonel, all to the east," Richards said. "Cruz has plugged the break at Bunker Five. Don't know how many muj are inside the wire."

Coffman tried to focus. He squinted toward Barnes, who was standing behind Ahmed and Tic. They were listening to intercepts of ICOM and cell phones.

"Barnes," Coffman barked, "what's your take?"

"Heavy ICOM traffic from the farmers," Barnes said. "They're evacuating wounded from the wire. Our 320s have them piss scared. Sounds like the attack has stalled out."

Coffman was slowly regaining his senses.

"Could be a deception to throw us off guard," he said. "You're sure the farmers are working with the Taliban?"

Tic and Ahmed exchanged a glance.

"We're sure, sir," Ahmed said. "We're not picking up any attack orders. They're definitely confused out there."

Less than half an hour had passed since Coffman had been knocked off his feet. The wind had dropped to thirty knots but was still whipping up a thick blanket of dust. Did he dare hope it was over?

Cruz came in, looked around, and headed over to talk to Barnes. Coffman didn't recognize him. He looked like a bear that had been rooting in a garbage pit, his red, blinking eyes the only human feature. In a slurred voice, he assured Barnes that no more muj could get through the cut.

"I'm out of men," Cruz said. "I need at least five Marines standing by as QRF. If called, I'll lead them out."

Coffman listened with a splitting head and a stomach on the verge of vomiting. He wanted to do something to show he was in command. He pushed forward between Barnes and Cruz.

"Holding the line isn't enough," he said. "We have to flush out the bastards inside the wire. I want killer teams spread out across the base, now!"

Barnes didn't reply, leaving it up to Cruz.

"I can't see my hand in front of my face out there, sir," Cruz said. "If you send out combat patrols, they'll shoot each other. We hold our positions, stay flat, and let the muj come to us. Once the storm passes, we finish off any stragglers, not now."

"I agree, sir," Barnes said.

Coffman didn't let go. He wanted Kabul and Washington to know he was on top of things, that he hadn't choked or lost his nerve. He had to do something. *Take charge!*

"You agree?" he said. "I didn't ask for your opinion. I'm giving an order."

Unnoticed, Richards had gotten to his feet. He spoke in a low growl, his frustration and sense of loss over Stovell spilling out.

"You want to blunder around blind, Colonel?" he said. "OK, I'll go with you. One dumbass colonel and one dumbass paramilitary operative. And after we shoot Lance Corporal Shit-For-Luck, we'll be famous. Hoorah for us. You ready? Let's go."

Coffman was too shocked to react. He'd underestimated Richards. The man was challenging him in front of his staff in the middle of a battle.

Barnes quickly intervened.

"I don't have the people to send out, sir," he said. "It'll take a while to get any search organized."

Coffman had the dim sense to accept the exit.

"Well, inform me when you're organized, Major," he said.

In the pre-dawn hours, no Marines were sent out to wander around blindly.

56

Control the Narrative

As the ops center was sorting out the confusion of battle, Towns and Michaels were entering the Oval Office. POTUS, flanked by Armsted, was watching the 6:00 p.m. news; Diane Baxter was looking at her notes; and Dick Deo, the White House lawyer, was sitting unobtrusively next to the grandfather clock.

"Nothing on the news yet," Dinard said. "What've you got, Admiral?"

"Sir, it's three in the morning at the firebase," Michaels said. "Communications are spotty, but the base seems to be holding."

"Shit, it isn't over?" Dinard said. "You're telling me they can still be overrun?"

"No way of knowing, sir. It's a fast-moving storm, so conditions should improve by daybreak over there, about three hours from now."

"I want them given all help, you understand?" Dinard said loudly. "Don't hold anything back! Make sure they get everything, everything."

Deo dutifully scribbled a legal note for the record.

"General Gretman has Rangers on strip alert at Kandahar, sir," Michaels said. "As soon as the dust lifts, they launch."

"Admiral, what do we know about casualties?" Diane Baxter said.

"Preliminary reports indicate several fatalities," Michaels said, "with others critically wounded."

The lawyer spoke up in a soft voice.

"Admiral, can you copy me on your execute order about sending help?" Deo said.

Caught off guard, Towns glared at Deo.

"That order," he said, "went from me as SecDef to the Chairman an hour ago. That's the proper chain of command."

After glancing at POTUS, the lawyer replied in a neutral tone.

"I'm not suggesting anything irregular, Mr. Secretary," he said. "My job is to dot the i's, to provide a legal audit trail, so to speak. Our political adversaries are sure to accuse us of not helping the task force."

"And I can assure you," Towns said, "that we're doing all we can."

Dinard wearily gestured for them all to leave.

Towns and Michaels returned to the National Military Command Center inside the Pentagon, where televideo linked them to General Gretman in Kabul, CENTCOM General Laird in Tampa, and his Marine deputy, Killian. There were no video images from Firebase Bastion, where it was 4:00 a.m. on a black, dust-clogged morning. Golstern, four kilometers away from the firebase, was relaying voice information to the NMCC. Over the next two hours, the generals learned that the perimeter at Bastion was secure and the wind had decreased. By 6:00 a.m., visibility on the base had improved to thirty feet, allowing a slow search by small hunter-killer teams.

"Sorry the info flow is so choppy, sir," Gretman said.

Towns looked at the video screen where a parabolic map showed which parts of Helmand were visible from which satellite feeds. He gestured around the room, where dozens of officers were tending to the phones, computers, and weather reports.

"I was thinking what historians might write about this," he said. "All these generals, satellites, and computers focused on garbled radio reports from an exhausted Special Forces captain in a bunker seven thousand miles away…"

"If we go home, the watch officers here will breathe a sigh of relief," Michaels said jokingly.

"Yes, and the press will kill us," Towns said. "We have to stay, but let's not pester that captain."

AT BASTION, THE FIGHTING HAD CEASED. No Taliban outside the wire was shooting randomly into the thick haze. Richards had drawn a detailed sketch of where the Marine groups were hunkered down. Via radio, a roster of all personnel was tallied. Having stabilized the wounded and relieved their pain with ketamine and morphine, Commander Zarest was fretfully waiting for tacevac. After a sweep, the firebase and the landing zone were declared secure at 0700.

Coffman had retreated to his wrecked office. He popped six aspirin for his splitting headache. After ordering a heavy canvas draped over the entrance, he called in Barnes.

"What's the latest on casualties?"

"Nine angels, sir. Twenty-seven wounded, two critic. Birds are inbound."

Coffman glanced down at his checklist, straining to concentrate. Unconsciously he nipped at the crust from his bloody nose, loosing a stream of red.

"Sir, maybe you should go over to med…"

Coffman dismissively waved his hand.

"The doctor's busy enough," he said. "What about the terrorists? Severe losses, I expect?"

"Five bodies found on base, sir."

"Five? That all? Impossible."

"Some blew themselves to bits, sir," Barnes said carefully. "Those outside the wire, well, the farmers are body snatchers. They clean everything up."

"Bull shit! We fired thousands of rounds! We killed dozens!"

"The dust will prevent overhead video for a couple of days, sir. The muj will be buried by then."

As Coffman continued to glare, Barnes hastened to calm him down.

"The one killed at Bunker Five was wearing a rubber suit and carrying wire cutters. Looks Chinese, no beard."

Coffman scribbled a note. Maybe he could use that. He reached down and picked up an American flag folded inside a plastic sheaf.

"Rig a pole and run up this flag. Scatter those bodies near it, close enough for photos."

An exhausted Barnes was slow on the uptake.

"Sir, there's a reg prohibiting pictures of enemy dead."

"We're not taking pictures, Major," Coffman said. "The press is. I want the reporters to see Bastion in our hands. It's our home, our turf. When terrorists attack us here, they're fucking with America, and they die. That's the photo I want—our flag and their dead."

In the background, the throb of incoming choppers could be heard.

"Got it, sir," Barnes said. "We've spliced the cables for the PRC-132. Comms are back up. I'll tell Captain Golstern we'll handle it from here."

The steady thump-thump of rotor blades was increasing. Coffman was unconsciously drumming his fingers in beat with the chopper noise. He stopped, stared into space, picked up his notebook, and began to write quickly.

"Excuse me, sir, maybe I wasn't clear," Barnes said. "We can connect you by voice to Kabul."

A pulse of anger drove through Coffman's head.

"This battle isn't over, Major. The winner is the one who controls the narrative. I'll release a message only after our wounded arrive safely in Kandahar. We hold off talking from Bastion until that's done."

Outside, there was no real daybreak. The blackness ebbed into a deep, sultry orange. In feats of magnificent flying with zero visibility and no sense of depth, two Army 47s and two Marine CH-53s touched down in massive billows of dust. The wounded and dead were swiftly carried on board and the choppers took off for Kandahar.

When the choppers touched down forty minutes later at the sprawling airfield, a long row of ambulances and military vehicles was waiting. Several hundred American and Afghan servicemen and civilians had gathered, standing respectfully on both sides of the line of vehicles. The CH-53 carrying the dead, wrapped in black body bags and blankets, was shielded from view when it landed a hundred meters distant. The other helicopters touched down near the ambulances. First to be unloaded were the stretchers holding the severely wounded, intravenous bags on poles fluttering like banners. The mass of onlookers stood silently. The only sounds were the camera shutters on hundreds of cell phones clicking and clicking.

Next came two-dozen walking wounded, gently helped down the ramps. Some wobbled, others limped, and a few hobbled, leaning on torn strips of boards in place of crutches. All were coated with dust, their features scarcely human, their uniforms caked with layers of grime. They weren't badly injured, but they looked like the dazed survivors of a death march. Their appearance shocked the sympathetic crowd. Gradually the clicking stopped and the clapping began. As it swelled, BBC and Sky News TV crews swept their cameras back and forth, capturing the faltering steps of the filthy, exhausted Marines.

PRESIDENT DINARD WAS IMPATIENT with the written word. Briefing papers bored him. They didn't capture what he considered to be the essence of decision-making, sizing up the other players. Newspapers too he threw aside. They were full of gossip about how unfit he was for the Oval Office, or any other office. In Dinard's opinion, the followers of those papers were lemmings, as mindless as the fake news they consumed.

He preferred television. It was up-to-date, quick, and relevant. He could see the event or interview and decide for himself its importance. When he saw the Marines at Kandahar on the 10:00 p.m. news, he spilled his Diet Coke as he lunged for the phone. Within minutes, Armsted had hastened upstairs to the living quarters. His face sherbet red, Dinard was standing in front of two sixty-five-inch TVs, clicking back and forth. His next click practically broke the remote.

"A disaster! Those soldiers look like they were just freed from Auschwitz!"

Armsted watched the scenes, the shambling Marines, the grimy uniforms, the stretchers and ambulances, the crowd, some clapping, others with hands clasped to mouths in disbelief.

"Give me a minute to calm down," Dinard said. "What's the Pentagon doing?"

"Rangers are set to fly in," Armsted said, "as soon as the weather clears."

"No, goddamn it, no! The military's going the wrong way! We're finished there. Get them out, now. O-U-T!"

Armsted had anticipated the anger. This needed calibration.

"Admiral Michaels is sure to object," he said. "It'll look like we ran away."

"He's my military adviser, not my boss. He'll do as he's told. You do agree, don't you?"

"I agree Michaels will go along," Armsted said. "Generals don't resign. Your real problem is Towns."

Dinard frowned.

"What're you driving at? You came back with a good deal."

"He's going to be pissed we didn't consult him about that. Plus, this fight throws a wrench into the gears. He might resign on principle."

Dinard looked puzzled.

"What principle? He has a cushy job and the press loves him. I increased his defense budget, for God's sake. What more does he want?"

"He sent them into Helmand, and you're pulling them out."

"He and Michaels sprang that on me. They would've leaked to the press that I was weak if I'd told them no. Well, turnabout's fair play. I make the hard decisions, not Towns."

Armsted didn't back off. He knew when to stand against Dinard's impulsiveness.

"You don't want anyone quitting," he said. "Senator Grayson will leap on that. You need consensus in the cabinet."

Though exasperated to hear the truth, Dinard wasn't foolish.

"Fine," he snapped. "Bring them in and we'll wrap it up."

"SecState's in Brussels."

"He'll go along," POTUS said. "Alert the others. And by the way, you look like shit."

"Haggling with smug Pakistanis has that effect."

Dinard pretended to applaud.

"My sympathies," he said. "But you're probably right about Towns. He can be stubborn. Soften him up before we meet. Do some wet work."

OVER AT THE NMCC, the 11:00 p.m. news was showing the wounded at Kandahar when the carefully crafted message from Coffman arrived. The normally diplomatic General Gretman, on the televideo link from Kabul, made no effort to conceal his anger.

"Sirs, I'm sorry this update got directly to you," he said. "Colonel Coffman should've gone through me first."

"He's under stress, Hal," Michaels said. "He cc'd the standard chain of command."

"The colonel's a vivid writer," Towns said. "Sounds like a great victory. He writes, 'The press will be impressed with the heroism.' Are there reporters at the firebase?"

"Not that I know of, sir," Gretman said.

"Don't send any," Towns said. "We haven't heard how the White House plans to handle this. And Admiral, we don't need messages like this floating around. Let's tone down the self-congratulation."

Michaels looked at Gretman on the screen.

"Hal, you'll be conducting the investigation of the broken arrow," he said. "We don't want lawyers later claiming prejudice. Before you meet with the colonel, it's best if General Killian counsels him."

As the lower-ranking three-star, Killian was surprised the Chairman had noticed him sitting in the background. He looked up at the televideo screen.

"Aye-aye, sir."

57

The Reckoning

After Coffman sent his sitrep, he walked outside. With visibility slightly increasing, repairs were in full swing. The artillery tubes had been scrubbed and the sentry posts were manned. But the troops looked wretched, their cammies and faces covered with grime. Without showers, there was little he could do to spruce up their appearance for the press. Good. It showed they'd won a tough fight.

He was back in his office when the first call from higher up came in. He assumed it would be Gretman, but it was Killian's grim face that popped up on the televideo. Killian was leaning forward, almost glaring, on the verge of giving a lecture. Coffman hastened to speak first.

"Good morning, General," Coffman said. "Oh, I forgot, it's midnight on the East Coast."

He'd left the blood smears on his face and had his notes ready. He'd focus not on how the attack started, but on how it had ended, with his Marines the winners.

"It was a hellava fight, sir, no vis—even fucking hail!—hand-to-hand stuff. The troops were superb!"

Killian ignored the enthusiasm.

"They're Marines," he said flatly. "They did their job, as expected."

Coffman wasn't thrown off course.

"Of course, sir. Still, when the press gets here, the devil dogs have a hellacious story to tell, complete with muj bodies we haven't finished policing up."

"No press is coming," Killian said. "And hand over any bodies to the locals to bury. We're not ghouls."

The rebuke jolted Coffman. He had expected some bonding, some mutual tie now that he too had tasted combat. Instead, Killian had adjusted his bifocals and was looking down.

"Here's what you wrote in your sitrep," he said. "During an intense dust storm, a vicious assault fell upon the dispersed bunkers along the perimeter...blah, blah, blah."

Killian put down his glasses and slowly looked up.

"What kind of CYA crap is this?" he said. "Nine KIA, Colonel, nine!"

"General, I was providing context. The attack didn't happen in a vacuum. In fact, foreign mercenaries were involved, maybe from China. It..."

On the screen, Killian raised a warning finger.

"Colonel, this isn't a TV detective show. You're not listening. Remember that disaster in Somalia called *Black Hawk Down*? Let me read the first sentence of the report by that commanding officer: '*The authority and responsibility for what happened rest with me, the task force commander.*'"

Killian stopped talking and waited. Coffman immediately shifted gears.

"Aye-aye, sir," he said. "The responsibility is mine."

"Correct," Killian said.

"Once we get to Lash, well, being in the provincial capital will change things. I'm prepared to continue…"

Killian held up his hand and paused to let Coffman compose himself.

"Colonel, Fire Base Bastion is playing in the press as a catastrophe," Killian said. "You're not going to Lash. Your mission is terminated. General Gretman is preparing the order."

Coffman looked so stricken that Killian softened his tone.

"Hal, did you take precautions before the storm?"

"Yes, sir. I have a list…"

"That's not enough. Gretman's prepared to relieve you on the spot. You need someone to back you up and support any list you have. That's all I have. Wash your face. You look shitty."

The televideo switched off.

COFFMAN SAT STOCK STILL, feeling cold and empty. Yesterday, his future had looked promising. A heroin lab destroyed, an Iranian prisoner wanted by the White House, his chances of making brigadier sky-high and Stovell perhaps offering a civilian job. Twelve hours later, the prisoner had been vaporized, Stovell and nine Marines were dead, and his career was over.

He moved past that. The worst thing—*the very worst*—was to be relieved of command and flown back to the States in disgrace, his picture on cable news hour after hour, day after day as the bodies were returned through Dover.

Shaking slightly, he tapped the 9mm strapped to his hip and for a full twenty seconds thought about ending it. But he had the instincts of a survivor, not a brooder. No! He had taken all necessary steps before the storm! He was sure of it. All he needed was the right officer to back him up. He wiped the blood from his face and called Barnes into his office.

"Major," he began, "last night you performed with remarkable courage. Let's go over what we did. We don't want higher headquarters to act on false information. So let's, ah, write down the true facts, beginning with how we prepared."

An exhausted Barnes was befuddled.

"Sir, I was kinda knocked out. The real fight was on the lines. It was Cruz…"

Coffman's memory was hazy. It took him a few seconds to recall Cruz stumbling into the ops center, filthy and baleful, reporting that the perimeter was holding. *Cruz?* he thought. *Yes! Killian's pet, prior combat. He'd make a much better witness than Barnes.*

"Of course, I remember," Coffman said. "Have him to report to me immediately."

Cruz was catching a catnap in the platoon tent when Barnes shook him awake.

"Sorry, bro, but the colonel wants you," Barnes said. "He needs a statement that our defenses were prepared the right way. He's acting kind of loopy."

Cruz walked over to Coffman's office, too groggy to think about what Barnes had told him. Coffman had his talking points ready when Cruz sat down.

"Hellava battle last night, Captain," he said. "I'm letting everyone up the chain of command know what a magnificent job you did."

Cruz had no reaction. His fractured cheek was throbbing too much to bother replying to an irrelevant remark. His thoughts were on the moment.

"Captain Lasswell has loaned me thirty cannoneers to stand guard, sir," he said. "My men needed sleep."

"Fine. Good to see everyone helping," Coffman said. "In fact, there's something you can help with. Or maybe we can help each other."

He gave a tentative smile. Much as it grated him, he knew he had to mollify this insubordinate captain.

"Before I get to that," he said, "I want to clear up the matter regarding PFC Beal. He wasn't wearing a helmet when he was killed, and that upset Sergeant Binns. But in my judgment, the mortars were registered improperly."

Cruz snapped out of his mental fog.

"Sir, are you saying that Sergeant Doyle called a bad mission?" Cruz said.

"I'm not assigning blame for Beal's death. In fact, there won't be an investigation of you or anyone, if I contradict Binns's statement."

"I trust Doyle, sir," Cruz said. "The fire direction center confirms every fire mission. You can check the log."

The retort sounded like a challenge. Coffman suppressed an angry reply and kept his voice level and matter-of-fact.

"I'm stating what I recollect," he said. "Neither of us gains by having a debate. In fact, you're reinforcing my point. None of us will ever know what caused that tragedy. That's why I'm inclined to close the matter, not prolong it."

He waited for some expression of gratitude, but Cruz didn't respond. Coffman thought that strange. After all, he was salvaging Cruz's career, while his own was over. At this point, all he wanted was a graceful retirement, with a small band playing and his headquarters company of admin and computer specialists marching past in review. He would salute smartly and walk away with dignity.

"Captain, here's where your recollection will help. We'll be questioned about last night, and we don't want accidental contradictions. As I remember it, you and I took all possible precautions. In fact, I went beyond that and provided you with another generator. As for your actions, well, they deserve my highest praise."

Coffman believed he was being reasonable. He was offering Cruz a superb fitness report. Hell, he'd throw in a medal, maybe the Silver Star. All he wanted in exchange were a few words about precautions duly taken. In their prior confrontations, Cruz had backed down. It wasn't in him to stand up to a high-ranking officer. No reason this wouldn't work out to both their benefits.

Cruz was tired and hurt. He couldn't keep his head up. Each time his jaw sagged, a bolt of pain cracked through his broken cheek bone.

"No, sir," he said.

Cruz wasn't sure why he had said it. He was too spent to feel anger and yet his rage at Coffman, so long smothered, was growing by the second. He sensed the fleeting presence of Jenny cheering him on. It felt good not to care what Coffman said or wrote about him. Following his duty came as a release, not a burden.

"What did you say, Captain?" Coffman said. "Perhaps you didn't hear me correctly. I simply said that we took all reasonable precautions."

"That's not true, sir," Cruz said. "You refused to reinforce the perimeter. I'm not laying it all on you. I didn't argue hard enough against your decision. We didn't take the necessary precautions. That's on both of us."

Coffman remembered insisting that the artillery crews remain at their gun stations. That was sensible in light of the mission. He felt no culpability about the perimeter. That was Cruz's job. Because he was the overall commander when the attack occurred, he accepted that his career was over. But he didn't accept that he personally could have done more.

"Captain, you asked to take cannoneers away from their primary mission," Coffman said. "You had no hard intelligence to back you up. How did you expect me to agree?"

"Because I needed them, sir," Cruz said.

The defiance surprised Coffman. He had never taken the time or had the interest to discuss anything with the captain. He hadn't built up the trust to turn Cruz aside by applying logic. For seven days, he had simply given orders to the captain and that had sufficed. Now Cruz was declaring what he would not do and Coffman could think of no rebuttal. He needed a few minutes alone to collect himself.

"Well, Captain," he said, "it seems we have agreed to disagree. Let's hope our differences are not as stark as you make them out to be. You better get on back to your men. Ask Major Barnes to step in, would you?"

Neither offered to shake hands. They would never see each other again.

★ ★ ★

SEVERAL MINUTES LATER, Barnes walked from Coffman's office back into the ops center, where Cruz was jotting notes. Barnes gestured to him to step outside. Together they stumbled over the collapsed berm and stood in the gloom where they couldn't be heard.

"Looks like a golf ball inside your cheek," Barnes said.

"I'm sucking on an orange," Cruz said. "What's up?"

"Coffman's worried shitless," Barnes said, "that he's going to be fired by General Gretman. He says you'll testify against him."

Cruz snorted.

"He sent you running after me, like you're his errand boy? He refused to reinforce the lines. What's he expect I'll say? He's worthless."

Barnes gazed at the charred ground, thinking how to phrase his next words.

"That's too harsh," he said carefully. "He put together this task force, he wrote the plan, he drilled us so that we meshed as a team. We've responded to every request for artillery support. The Afghans didn't do their part, not Coffman. I'm not taking his side. I'm just trying to work out what's best for everybody."

Cruz shook his head. Each throb of his cheek felt like a hammer chipping at his brain. His resentment of Coffman flared.

"Best? Doyle did his best. So did Binns," he said. "The colonel didn't do his best. That's how I see it."

Barnes rubbed his forehead, unsure whether he was disappointed or proud of this stubborn Marine.

"Fuck, RT," he said, "this isn't the time to get all moral. You're not thinking straight because you're pissed at yourself."

Cruz reacted angrily.

"Meaning I should have stood up to Coffman from the start?" he said. "That I wimped out?"

Barnes swung right back.

"Now that you mention it, yes. We all saw you wanted to do your job," he said, "but without pissing Coffman off. I didn't know which side of you would win until you came through last night."

"Came through? I failed! I didn't get more troops before the storm hit."

"That wasn't your decision," Barnes said. "He's your commanding officer! This is the Marine Corps, not a debating corps. And suppose you had more troops, would that have changed things?"

The question set Cruz back. He rubbed his forehead and thought before answering.

"No, probably not. We were screwed once the bunker was blown."

"Then why place all this on Coffman?"

"Because he's a one-way asshole," Cruz said. "I'll dispute anything bad about Sergeant Doyle."

"I'll handle that."

"Fine. And tell the good colonel I said, 'Fuck you, Colonel.'"

Barnes stared at him, willing Cruz to push aside pain and think clearly.

"You don't see what's happening here," Barnes said. "You've been like this from the start. The first day we landed, you fronted for Richards to put pressure on me for using a cell phone. You were subtle as a rock, set on patrolling your way. Coffman was clueless about you. That's why you're called *Rolling Thunder,* isn't it? You keep rolling forward until every muj is killed and you're the king of the hill. Once you focus in, you don't think of anything or anyone else."

The accusation confused Cruz. He thought it sounded like something Jenny had said last week. His head throbbed and tiny jangles of lightning were flashing across the edge of his vision.

"Barnes, you've only been in one firefight," he said. "Don't judge what you don't know. I take care of my people."

Barnes shook his head and scoffed.

"Care of your people?" he said. "No, you're taking care of your pride. You're consumed with going mano-a-mano against Coffman. Suppose he is relieved now, while we're still here. Know what follows? The press makes this all about Coffman, with the Marines cast as helpless, miserable victims. You saved lives last night, but now you're killing the dead. 'Rolling Thunder' suits you. You don't think in front of your nose."

Cruz hadn't expected Barnes to attack him. He wished he could talk to Jennifer. He knew what she would say, but wanted to hear it from her. He didn't like hearing it from Barnes.

"For a staff weenie," Cruz said, "that was one hell of a speech. You've been building up to that, haven't you?"

"Yeah, I have," Barnes said. "You're feeling guilt that the perimeter was breached. But this fuck-up isn't all about you. How does your ego help the troops? I'm trying to turn the spotlight on how they fought. You're keeping it pointed at Coffman."

Having blurted out his version of truth, Barnes was spent. Throwing up his hands, he turned to leave.

"Hold on," Cruz said. "Maybe you have a point. What if I say Coffman took reasonable precautions? Then once the storm cut vis to zero, what more could he do? Does that take care of it?"

Before Cruz could reconsider, Barnes agreed.

"You took your time getting there," he said, "but that covers it. I'll inform Gretman's staff. It's enough to keep Coffman from being fired on the spot. He's finished anyway once we're back at Pendleton. I'll make sure the report is about how our troops fought."

Cruz put on his best stone face and nodded gravely.

"Let's shoot the bastard and have done with it."

Barnes burst out laughing.

"At last Rolling Thunder sees the irony, Coffman bailed out by Cruz."

58

A Cauliflower Death

As the firebase was being torn down during the morning, Zar received a cryptic call from the shura. In simple prearranged code, an anonymous voice told him to come to Quetta, bringing the Asians as well as the funds and records of the Persian.

"One of the three melons was crushed," Zar replied. "All the grapes were destroyed in a fire."

One Asian had been killed and all of the Persian's money had burned inside the mosque. There was a moment's silence on the cell phone. Zar thought he heard the murmur of Emir Sadr in the background. The caller came back on the line.

"Leave your sheep in the hands of the digger," he said in harsh Pashto. "Bring the two melons and one hundred kilos of cauliflower."

After hanging up, Zar stood motionless while the anger surged through him. The useless Quat lay dead somewhere. But he was ordered to drive the two Asians, who had failed, to freedom. They didn't deserve it. And why did the shura direct that he leave Tulus in charge? It would take weeks to dig a tunnel under the americani base. A stupid plan. He would tell the shura to give him more mujahideen and he would assault again.

He threw the burner phone into an irrigation ditch and walked back inside the compound. Nantush had done a good job of policing the battlefield. Ten dead mujahideen were hidden in the trunks of cars and under hay in the beds of pickup trucks, to be buried that afternoon in four separate cemeteries. Of the five seriously wounded, Zar had sent the two most likely to survive to the government hospital in Lashkar Gah. That had cost $500 in bribes. The others would have to languish. He would spend no more cash.

Tulus was waiting for him in the guesthouse.

"The shura has summoned me," Zar said. "Put the Asians in my pickup. Pack a hundred kilos of cauliflower on the roof. This trip I'm to be a farmer. I'm leaving you in charge."

Tulus tried to look surprised.

"I'm a cripple," he protested, "not a renowned warrior of Allah like you."

Brimming with shame and anger, Zar glared at him.

"I was poised to kill the infidels," he said. "The Asians did not guide me. They are cowards. I'll be back with more holy warriors to finish this."

"How much do you think the Persian has told the infidels?"

Zar felt a chill.

"That's not our worry," he said. "The fool got himself captured."

He scrambled into the front seat of the Hilux next to the driver, with the two Vietnamese in the rear. In a side pouch of the SUV, he'd shoved the cash left after purchasing some harvests yesterday, maybe $20,000. If the shura didn't ask about such a small leftover amount, he'd give it to his wife. His family deserved something for all he did for Allah.

As he drove off, Nantush approached Tulus.

"There goes the great Zar," Nantush said bitterly. "My sons are dead, the infidels remain, and still the shura favors him."

"Uncle, the shura knows more about Zar's actions than you think," Tulus said. "Allah will reward you with justice. Be patient a while."

THE LATE AFTERNOON SKY WAS CLEAR when Zar reached the border crossing at Chaman. A steady southerly wind had blown the dust toward Zhob, far to the east. Zar kept on the air-conditioning to avoid choking from the fumes of a hundred lorries queued up for inspection and the payment of small bribes. He hated waiting in lines, and it always irritated him to see the blue highway sign written in English, WELCOME TO PAKISTAN. *English! Not Pashto or even Punjabi! The Pakistanis had no pride.*

His driver dodged around overloaded trucks and stopped in front of the customs office. Zar handed over their forged credentials, with one hundred dollars in crisp rupees folded inside. The young *fauji* corporal gave the documents to his mustachioed sergeant, who took them inside the building. Zar wasn't concerned; this sometimes happened. He counted out more rupees when the sergeant walked back to the Hilux.

"Wait over there," the sergeant said, pointing to a parking lot.

Knowing better than to make a public scene, an irritated Zar complied. Within ten minutes, he was fiddling with his worry beads. Ten minutes later, he was opening and closing the passenger door, trying to hold his temper. After thirty minutes, he was worried. During the four-hour drive to the border, he had replayed the failed assault again and again. Once in Quetta, he would explain that the Asians had run away.

But what if others were talking against him while these stupid border guards treated him like a common truck driver? He leaned forward so he could not be clearly seen, took out a cell phone, and called the cutout for the shura. No one picked up. Much as he hated asking for a favor of any Punjabi, he had to call the ISI. He punched in the emergency number and was surprised when Colonel Balroop personally answered.

"I am late for dinner," Zar said. "I'm detained at the intersection."

"I'll take care of it," Balroop said. "Are the cauliflowers on the roof?"

To a sleep-deprived Zar, the question seemed a normal cover to deceive the NSA programs sifting through big data sets.

"Yes, and I brought the two melons."

"Take the old road," Balroop said. "It is faster."

Another hour passed before the sergeant handed back Zar's documents, without the rupees. As the driver took the turnoff up the old mountain road, Zar saw no trucks in front of them. Good, they would make up the lost time. Behind him, the border guards had again stopped traffic. With the weight of the cauliflowers, the Hilux was taking the upgrade at a slow pace. To avoid overheating the engine, the driver turned off the air-conditioning. In the back seat, the two Vietnamese were jabbering in their singsong voices.

Through the open window, Zar breathed in the clean air and admired the vista. They were three thousand feet above the dusty valley floor, and the twisting road to their front was free of traffic. Zar began to relax. Emir Sadr would understand. No one won every battle. Tomorrow he would return, perhaps with another young martyr from the *madrassa*.

AT BAGRAM AIR FORCE BASE four hundred miles to the north, Air Force Master Sergeant Todd Swanson adjusted the reticle on the nose of the six-foot-long Hellfire missile. For the past ten minutes, he had flown the Predator UAV in a large loop around the mountain road. Now the target stood out sharply, with no other vehicle within half a kilometer. No donkeys, kids, or jingle trucks to worry about. After 176 missions and 55 kill shots, this was too easy. No sweating collateral damage. What a setup. How could he miss the SUV with vegetables on its roof? He laid on the crosshairs and pressed the red button on top of the joystick.

ZAR WAS DOZING OFF when he heard *zissst!* The hair on the back of his head sprang up in instinctive animal fear a half second before the white flash of obliteration.

"THAT'S SHACK!" SWANSON SAID over his voice mic. "Behold the lotus death blossom, all those lovely petals floating skyward. A beautiful secondary."

"Bagram Four-Zulu, this is Phantom Three," a wry voice replied. "Control your enthusiasm. Those white petals are cauliflower heads."

"Phantom Three, thanks for spoiling my dinner."

59

You Held the Line

By late afternoon, the orange haze had thinned to the viscosity of Los Angeles smog, with visibility improving to several hundred meters. Relieved that he had not been publicly fired, Coffman retreated to his office, leaving the evacuation details to Barnes. At the staff meeting, everyone was hacking up balls of phlegm and tapping their fingers. They all knew the drill. So Barnes kept his remarks brief.

"Artillery lifts out first," he said, "followed by the task force staff. The security platoon will be the last out."

"I'll set 0400 for my final chalk," Cruz said.

Barnes gathered himself and spoke with a determined finality in his tone.

"Your cheek is badly infected," he said. "Commander Zarest says you're risking disfigurement for life. You're to take the next bird out. That's a direct order, not open for discussion. You've done all you can, RT, and not one of us will ever fucking forget it."

The swelling had swollen shut Cruz's left eye, and his cheek bulged with dry, black blood. Lasswell nodded firmly at him, making clear her agreement with Barnes.

"Gotta inform the squad leaders," Cruz mumbled.

After he angrily left, the meeting broke up. Lasswell lingered to talk with Richards.

"I don't feel right about Stovell," she said. "I should have reacted, done something…"

"That's not on you," Richards said. "He'd be disappointed to hear you say that. He knew the score."

"Wife? Kids?"

"Short marriage, divorced, no kids. Maybe that's partly why he was out here. I'll miss him. You should take him up on his offer. I'll clear it with his chief operating officer."

"No, thanks," Lasswell said. "His corporation's too tied in with you guys. When I finish school, I'm going in a different direction."

"Why?"

"Why? Because I have to talk to Corporal Compton's family and two others, and I don't know what to say. For you, this is a career. For me, five years was enough. I'm proud of the Corps, but it's time to push on."

CRUZ HAD WALKED OVER TO WHAT REMAINED of the platoon tent, a flap of shapeless canvas the size of living room rug. The squad leaders were waiting.

"I'm ordered out on medevac," Cruz said. "Chances are I won't see you all again. So, uh, let's wrap up a few things. First, there'll be funeral ceremonies, but every family needs a personal letter. I'll do Mad Dog Doyle and Binns. I knew them well enough. Sergeant McGowan, you write to the Delgados and the two corporals in Bunker Five."

McGowan shook his head.

"I can't write stuff like that," he said. "I can't even print straight."

"The subject's not open for debate," Cruz said. "The platoon'll help you."

"You mean my squad."

"I mean your platoon," Cruz said. "Staff Sergeant Sullivan's evaced with a broken leg. As of now, you're the acting platoon commander."

He waited for the chorus of yelps and groans to subside.

"No way that's happening, sir," McGowan said. "I'm a mud Marine, two NJPs. I can't handle that responsibility shit, having to think, going to meetings. This is fucked up. No way."

Cruz let him wind down.

"Noted, Sergeant," he said. "I'll inform the Green Machine about your midlife crisis. In the meantime, suck it up."

"You're all heart, sir," McGowan said. "Ever wonder why they call you RT?"

The NCOs laughed.

"All right, let's flesh out the evac plan," Cruz said.

After they had finished, he invited any final questions.

"Our families are sure to be spazzing out, sir," Denton said. "Can we call home?"

"I know every family's going through hell, Sergeant," Cruz said. "But notifying next-of-kin comes first. Once you're back at Kandahar, you can call."

Corporal Gordon, who had taken over 2nd Squad after Binns was killed, spoke up next.

"We hear the press is claiming we got our asses kicked. My squad is pissed about that."

"I don't see no reporters out here," McGowan said. "Fuck them."

The NCOs bobbed their heads in agreement.

"Yut!" Gordon drawled.

Cruz looked at their tired faces. He knew from prior tours how deaths and subsequent investigations sucked the spirit out of the kids.

"Wrong approach," Cruz said. "Sullivan's gone, I'm gone. You're the NCOs. If you think negative, it'll infect the whole platoon. Hold it together on a strong, positive note."

With his face down, McGowan was doodling in the dirt. The other NCOs were fidgeting. Cruz knew he had to keep going. He had to get a message across they could hold on to.

"I won't have the chance to say goodbye to each grunt," he said. "When your people get off watch, you deliver this message for me. I've served in five platoons in two wars, and I have never been prouder of any group of devil dogs."

That touched them. McGowan was now looking at him, Denton was nodding, and Gordon's mouth was open, as though he was inhaling every word. Cruz found his rhythm. He knew what he wanted to say, what image he wanted to leave them.

"Last night tested every one of you," he said. "When the enemy came among you, not one of you could see or hear them. You were blind and alone. But you held the line, each and every single one of you. You tell your men to post that thought in their brains for the rest of their lives—when the world was black and howling, you held the line."

60

First, Get Elected

Seven thousand miles west of the platoon tent, Towns and Michaels were walking down a thick beige carpet past nineteenth-century classic paintings of American landscapes. Mixing architectural understatement with sophisticated taste, the West Wing exuded majesty and tradition. The corridor leading to the Oval Office imposed upon every visitor, no matter how important he was in his own mind, a sense of humility.

When summoned by the world's most powerful leader to a sudden meeting on Saturday morning, common sense dictated reviewing how to respond to pointed questions.

"Not to nitpick, Admiral," Towns said, "but you're sure there's no change?"

"No fighting in the past twelve hours, Mr. Secretary," the Chairman said. "Visibility has improved, and the Taliban have dispersed."

"He could be golfing," Towns said. "Instead, we're here, with no agenda."

Without stopping, they exchanged a glance. As they passed the office of the National Security Advisor, Armsted stepped out.

"Admiral," he said pleasantly, "mind if I have a word with the Secretary?"

As soon as the Chairman left, Armsted spoke in a husky, confiding whisper.

"Nine dead! It's really bad. POTUS is being pressured to let you go."

Towns felt like kicking himself. He had been so wrapped up in following the fight he hadn't seen this coming. Yet it was so obvious. Someone had to be blamed, and maybe he deserved it.

"If he wants my resignation," he said, "all he has to do is ask."

Armsted was surprised. He thought Towns, a corporate CEO with a Christmas tree up his ass and fifty million in bonds, had a better grasp of real power.

"Resign? It's too late to run for that cover," he said. "You recommended the task force. Dinard wants to fire you for incompetence. The public elected him, not you or me. We're the hired help, remember?"

"Why are you telling me this?"

"You're not the only one who cares about the troops," Armsted said. "I'm working on something important for them. You being kicked out now would complicate that. Don't fall on your sword and spoil things. Listen to POTUS with an open mind, OK?"

Together they walked into the Oval Office. Webster and Michaels were sitting on the sofa. The White House lawyer and the press secretary were absent. A solemn Dinard did not rise from his enormous desk. After a few idle taps of his pen, he opened the meeting.

"Broken arrow," he said. "Goddamn, I never want to hear those words again. The way our soldiers looked on TV, covered with dust and crap, heads down, beaten, so, so un-Marine like."

With his phobia about dirt, Dinard couldn't imagine those battle-worn grunts were the same chiseled young men with perfect posture and razor-creased trousers who rendered sharp salutes whenever he walked by.

Michaels had a grim, fixed expression.

"The investigation will be thorough, sir," he said. "General Gret-man may recommend relieving the colonel in charge of the task force."

Dinard looked across at Armsted, inviting him to speak.

"Admiral, that's your business," Armsted said. "But doing that right now would create a major distraction."

Michaels offered a sensible compromise.

"The task force is being disbanded," he said, "and the investigation will take a month. So dealing with the colonel can wait until then. But regardless, there's no excuse for enemy getting through the wire."

Webster thrust his head forward, his round owl eyes magnified by his bifocals. As usual, the others paid deference to the CIA Director. He spoke sparingly in a giggling, self-embarrassed tone.

"May I amend the admiral?" he said. "Though hard to imagine, I was once a lieutenant in Vietnam, where my own lines were breached. The Vietnamese are the world's best sappers. They possess infinite patience. What happened last night was partially my fault."

When Michaels started to protest, Webster reached out and patted his arm.

"Yes, Admiral," the DCI said, "we did alert the Pentagon that a few Vietnamese were training Haqqani's terrorists. But we didn't trace their movement to Helmand. That was our lapse."

"Vietnamese!" Dinard said. "Well, Hanoi can kiss goodbye to selling us any more T-shirts and socks."

"Actually, Hanoi alerted us," Webster said. "These sappers were *nguoi*, outcasts from society because their fathers had served as South Vietnamese soldiers. I don't think we want that circulated."

"Why not?" Dinard said. "I'm doing Hanoi a favor by not slapping a tariff on their cheap goods."

"Back in 1975, we, uh, left the South Vietnamese soldiers in a bad way, with no ammo to fight. This could be seen as revenge for having abandoned them."

"Let's not give the media that opening," Armsted said. "We'll treat any mention of Asians as rumor. Thank God we didn't bring back any bodies."

"Speaking of bodies," Dinard said, "what happened to that drug buyer from Iran?"

"Not a spoon of him left, sir," Webster said. "We have a photo of him inside the heroin lab, but that's too thin to use publicly."

"The *Journal* has reported the death of Stovell," Armsted said. "He's well known in business circles. How do we—"

Dinard interrupted.

"He was at a meeting I had with some CEOs a month ago," he said. "Was he a donor? Did he give to my campaign?"

Webster concealed his distaste.

"I don't know," he said. "We discussed technical things. Stovell—no one used his first name—was quite gifted."

"What was he doing out there?"

"He held patents on some detection devices," Webster said. "And he was a close friend of our ops chief."

"How will you handle it?" Dinard said.

"Officially, he was a contractor testing equipment," Webster said. "In a private ceremony, we'll add a star to our wall for him."

Dinard looked at his watch. In four hours, he could be teeing off in Palm Beach.

"This is tragic, a true catastrophe," he said. "It gives Grayson an opening. Know what Kissinger once told me?"

He affected a deep German accent.

"Zee first rule of foreign policy, Meester President, is to get reelected."

He waited while Armsted guffawed and the others gave slight smiles.

"OK, no more politics," Dinard continued. "Let's talk about Afghanistan. I've decided to change direction. I called Duncan. Our wonderful Secretary of State is doing a terrific job at that summit in Brussels. He agrees with the change."

POTUS gestured at Armsted to take over. Armsted tried to look sheepish, as though none of the credit was his.

"Well, I've been logging the air miles. The president wanted a secret back channel. The result is a breakthrough. Congratulations, Mr. President."

POTUS beamed.

"Lay it out," he said.

"All parties agree that Helmand will be a neutral zone," Armsted said, "with the capital off-limits to armed combatants. This provides a venue for the Taliban and Kabul to reconcile. The Afghan troops will fall back."

Towns and Michaels looked at each other in stunned surprise.

"I haven't heard anything from General Gretman," Michaels said. "Did the palace agree?"

Dinard squinted over his pen at Armsted.

"Security Advisor, I don't want blowback," Dinard said. "You're certain Kabul's on board?"

"The president was reluctant, sir. I told him your patience had run out. He'll go along."

"Damn right he will. He needs us a hell of a lot more than we need him. When you discussed this, did he look like he was having a nervous breakdown?"

"No, sir," Armsted said. "I got the feeling he's glad we had made the tough decision for him."

"You actually negotiated with the Taliban shura?" Webster said.

"A few discreet meetings in Quetta," Armsted said. "I went through the ISI."

"That explains why an ISI colonel tipped us off," Webster continued. "A few hours ago, we droned Zar, the leader of the attack on the firebase. He was tied into that heroin lab, a very expensive loss for our Pakistani friends."

"So the Pakistanis set him up?" Admiral Michaels said.

"It appears to be a gesture to us, after our losses at the base," Webster said. "Of course, someone has undoubtedly replaced him. Rich, what have you offered Pakistan?"

"We take them off the terrorist watch list and restore aid," Armsted said.

Webster shook his head.

"That's a billion-dollar gamble," he said. "The Pakistanis live in a world of self-deception, an incurable affliction. They can't be trusted."

Armsted understood this, but it exasperated him to hear it.

"This is a transaction, not an alliance," Armsted said. "Quid pro quo. If they renege, we cut them off again."

Dinard rapped his pen like a teacher calling students to pay attention.

"Hey, I get it! Pakistan plays both sides. Let's get back to Afghanistan," he said. "Admiral, suppose things fall apart over the next year. It won't end like Saigon, will it? That looked terrible, terrible."

"No, sir," Michaels said. "The Taliban don't have the vehicles or armor to take the major cities. In the worst case, the country reverts to warlords."

Since entering the room, Towns hadn't said a word. Dinard now gestured at him to speak up. Towns was seething at being blindsided. POTUS had exploited the deaths of the Marines to accelerate America's withdrawal from Afghanistan.

"Sir, I'm concerned we're walking into a strategic defeat," he said, "based on a tactical setback."

"Tactical? We got plastered last night!" Dinard said. "All those dead and wounded, soldiers wobbling, looking like shit. The public saw that. So did Grayson and everyone in Congress."

POTUS had slipped back into domestic politics. Armsted leaped in before Towns could object.

"President Reagan pulled out of Lebanon after our barracks were bombed," he said. "Clinton did the same in Somalia. They knew when to cut their losses. After last night, the public won't stand for our troops staying exposed."

"You're not just pulling back," Towns replied. "You're carving up a country. Afghanistan won't hold together!"

"Oh, for God's sake, Mike," Armsted said, "this isn't Munich. Kabul never controlled Helmand. We're not abandoning what we or Kabul never had."

Towns ignored Armsted and appealed to the president.

"It's about unraveling, sir," Towns said. "If we flinch, the crazies become emboldened. The Taliban will share Helmand with al-Qaeda."

There was silence as each participant weighed what to add. They had exhausted all their standard lines. Dinard drummed his fingers on the heavy oak of the *Resolute* desk. When no one spoke up, he finally pointed at Webster.

"What does the CIA think?"

Aware of the stakes, Webster replied cautiously.

"Helmand's drug industry is worth five hundred million to a billion dollars," Webster said. "Al-Qaeda will try to muscle in. That will throw the province into chaos."

"Agreed," Towns said. "We're handing back a safe haven to al-Qaeda."

Webster glanced almost sorrowfully at Towns.

"Actually, chaos works in our favor," Webster said. "The Taliban are Pashtuns and al-Qaeda are Arabs. Friction is inevitable. We have a deep bench of informers. We can bomb as we please."

"We're conceding territory to the Taliban," Towns said. "We can't whitewash that."

Armsted had anticipated that objection.

"Mike, we already have a written deal with them," he said. "A neutral Helmand fits inside of that."

Before Towns could respond, Webster put forward his closing argument.

"The Taliban want to rule Afghanistan and shut out the world," he said. "They're a cancer inside an isolated country, not a global pandemic."

Armsted vigorously nodded, agreeing with his unexpected ally. Dinard too was happily surprised. The DCI had provided the ending he needed.

"Reagan and Clinton knew when to pull back. So do I," Dinard said. "We're going ahead. Security Advisor, coordinate the details with State and Defense."

As they got up to leave, Dinard called to Towns.

"Mike," he said, "can you stay for a minute?"

Despite calling him Mike, Dinard's tone held no warmth. He didn't ask Towns to sit down. Instead, POTUS walked out from behind the desk, stood a few feet away, and paused before speaking, conveying the gravity of what he was about to say.

"Let's clear the air between us," he said. "If you stay silent, the press will assume you're opposed. I'd like you to stay on, but I can't have that."

The president's candor hit home. Towns had intended to avoid saying anything to the press, the dodge he employed whenever he disagreed with his commander in chief. He enjoyed his taciturn reputation, detached from the White House out of concern for the larger common good. He hesitated, unsure how to respond.

"Keep killing terrorists. Drop all the bombs you want," Dinard continued, "but no more troops. Those wounded kids looked awful, all banged up and bloody. That was the last task force."

Towns didn't reply. His mind was whirling. His pride at being one of the most powerful men in the world was struggling with his fear of being fired for a disaster over which he had no control. Unsettled by his own indecision, he kept his face neutral.

Dinard stepped closer, bearing in.

"I have to know," he said quietly, "are you with me?"

Towns wasn't conceited enough to view their disagreement as a moral drama between good and evil. He considered Dinard a narcissist and Armsted an opportunist. But neither would deliberately put American soldiers in an untenable position. He responded in a level tone.

"Yes, sir. I will fully and publicly support your decision."

The president dismissed him with a patronizing pat on the back.

"You're a good man, Mike!"

Towns walked out, upset with himself. *Was he a good man?* Like five Secretaries of Defense before him, he had failed to come to grips with Afghanistan. For two decades, the generals had claimed the war could be won, plodding ahead despite the vacillations of three commanders in chief. Towns had gone along first with Admiral Michaels, who wanted to trudge on, and now with President Dinard, who wanted to get out. In his own mind, he hadn't decided which one was right.

He dreaded his next trip to Dover to console the families. Why had their loved ones died to protect Helmand, heroin supplier to the world?

61

Don't Blame the Dirt

Shortly after the NCOs left the platoon tent, Cruz heard the chugging of incoming choppers. He popped five Motrin, shouldered his ruck, and strode to the landing zone, where Richards was standing with a few others.

"We're out on the same bird," Richards said. "End of a long week."

"Tic going with you?"

"Only to Kandahar. After that, he's off to LA. Stovell set him up at USC. Full ride."

"Who is he, really?"

Richards took him aside.

"You know I won't answer that," he said softly.

"He's a pro. I'll give him that," Cruz said. "All you spooks are. You almost pulled it off."

"We caught one break," Richards said. "If that Marine hadn't been guarding our prisoner, the suicide bomber would've waltzed right into the ops center. I don't want to think about that carnage."

"We still got our asses handed to us," Cruz said.

His cheek was throbbing and he slurred the words.

"Yes, we did," Richards said. "I assume Dr. Zarest gave you a shot?"

Cruz looked at him blankly.

"No, of course not," Richards continued. "You're too stubborn to block out pain. Well, take a final look, cowboy. Say goodbye to Helmand. No more rodeos. You commanded the last platoon."

All around them, ragged, filthy Marines were breaking down structures, dragging howitzers into liftoff zones, and queueing up into chalks.

"What're you going to do," Richards said, "once your face is plastered together again?"

"I'm wrapping up my tour at the recruit depot," Cruz said. "After that, it's back to the fleet, maybe a company command."

Richards pointed toward a group of Marines.

"A command? Sounds impressive," he said. "Look at Barnes, collecting statements. He thinks that'll help you. Busy beaver."

"He didn't clear that with me," Cruz said.

When he started toward Barnes, Richards stopped him.

"Let him be. It makes him feel good," he said. "Won't help you, though."

"You're one hell of a motivator."

"Coffman's finished," Richards said. "When he goes down, he's sure to throw shit on you. Add in this broken arrow, and you're carrying too much baggage to snag a command."

"I've thought about that," Cruz said. "I'm working on my teaching cert. If the worst happens, I can step into a classroom, teach algebra, and coach wrestling. Maybe art on the side."

Richards burst out laughing.

"Right, your credentials are sterling," he said. "You're the first guy I ever met who strangled someone. The teachers union will send you to a school for headhunters in Pago Pago. Earth to Cruz: you are not a model instructor for the safe space generation."

For an hour, Cruz had been imagining he had a fallback if he was forced out of the Corps. In one sentence, Richards had popped that daydream.

"Even if you stay in," Richards continued, "you're too old to ever do it again."

"Do what?"

"Lead from the front. Shape your younger brothers. Take care of them. Watch over them. Stovell saw that in you right away. He was smarter than me."

"Doesn't seem right that he's gone," Cruz said. "He's the one who didn't have to be here."

"A long time ago, I saved his ass," Richards said. "He never forgot. I'll miss him every day. He treated life as an adventure."

Cruz nodded.

"You going back to Kabul?"

"For a few months," Richards said. "Then I'm slated for a cushy stateside posting, with sunshine and sea breezes. Eagan's coming along. There's a few billets open in our Special Operations Group. Good pay, interesting work, a sound pension. You're welcome to join us."

The offer caught Cruz off guard.

"I'm a slow learner, not completely crazy," Cruz said. "I'm having a long talk with my wife before I jump off another bridge."

"Job's one world and family's another," Richards said. "I have a solid home life, a terrific wife and two daughters. You can balance both. You've deployed enough to know that."

"I'll think about it."

"She's on the staff of the 3rd Fleet, right? Easy to get a transfer so you'll stay together."

Cruz didn't know whether to be interested or irritated.

"How do you know about my wife?"

Richards shook his head like a teacher disappointed in a star student.

"After Stovell recommended you," he said, "Langley ran a background check."

"I'm sure as hell not a substitute for him."

"No, you're not. But I need someone fluent in Spanish."

"I'm not trained for what you do."

"You forget I was a jarhead?" Richards said. "What does the Corps do? It protects civilians who lack the sense to get out of the rain. My outfit does the same thing. What have you been doing for the past seventeen years?"

"Mowing the grass," Cruz said.

Richards laughed.

"Good description. If you cut grass short enough, snakes don't have a place to hide. You'll fit in with us, and we have fewer Coffmans to foul things up. We both love the Corps, but it's time for you to move on."

"I don't know. That's a lot to digest. This fight and all will come as a surprise to Jenny."

Richards looked sharply at him.

"You haven't talked with her?"

Cruz looked into middle space. His jaw was throbbing, with jolts of pain flashing through his head.

"I told my platoon," Cruz mumbled, "that calls had to wait until we were out of here."

"The wounded are supposed to call home!" Richards said. "What, you think your wife doesn't assume that Rolling Thunder wasn't in the thick of it? She has to be worried sick."

He extended a cell phone.

"Sometimes you're dumb stubborn," he said tightly. "Here, reassure her. Hell, if you want, tell her you have a job offer."

Cruz took the phone and walked a few feet away. Jenny picked up on the first ring.

"Hi, Babe, I—"

Jenny immediately cut him off.

"Thank God you're alive! How bad are you hit? Tell me the truth. I'll know if you're lying to me!"

She knew the protocol that wounded called after a fight.

"Fractured jaw," Cruz said, trying to sound normal. "I got off easy. How are you and Josh?"

"We're fine. Don't try to divert me. You're really in one piece?"

"Yes, I swear."

He listened to her sobs of relief.

"This is the second time!" she said. "Two Purple Hearts! I don't think we could cope if you were gone."

"We lost twelve angels, Jen," Cruz said quietly, "on my watch."

"Honey, I'm just grateful you're alive," she said. "But my heart breaks for those poor families. I'm on my way now to the Support Center."

"I should have done more," Cruz said. "The mothers, the wives...I..."

"Stop!" she said. "Don't take everything on yourself."

Cruz hesitated, then decided to tell her.

"It's not about me, Jen, it's about them," he said. "There's no going back. The investigation will hammer me. But I may have a job. Kind of an interpreter, somewhere nice in the States. We'd be together."

"Oh?" she said softly. "Well, that's worth talking about when you get back."

After hanging up, Cruz returned the cell phone to Richards, who snapped it in two and shoved the pieces into his pocket.

"Once we're out of here," Cruz said, "maybe we can continue our conversation."

"Good," Richards said. "Working with us beats supervising recruits on a rifle range."

Richards had wound down. It had taken considerable effort for him to be so open. Cruz too felt numb and exhausted. Together they listened to the throb of the approaching helicopters. The *nishtgar* workers were scouring the nearby fields for any surviving poppy bulbs.

They acted as though all the Marines had left and life had resumed its normal tedium. Sunlight filtering through the billions of dust particles suspended in the air bathed the landscape in a baleful orange that glowed like a molten furnace.

"Hell's the right color for this place," Richards said. "Hope I never see it again."

They watched as a teenaged Marine, sweat pouring down his grimy face, filled in the gaping hole that had been Bunker Five. With each stroke, he smacked the earth harder with the flat side of the shovel. Gradually, he picked up the pace until he was swinging with all his might. Cruz walked over and took hold of his arm.

"Easy there, devil dog," Cruz said. "Don't beat dirt for being what it is."

Glossary

81s: 81mm mortars, effective out to a range of four thousand meters

152: a handheld radio providing crypto and a UHF/VHF line of sight with a nominal range of ten miles

153: a handheld radio without crypto with forty-nine channels

(A platoon commander or a patrol leader might carry both a 152 and a 153. He would talk to the ops center on the 152 and to the squad leaders and fire team leaders on the 153. In this novel, all patrol members talk to one another over the 153s.)

(Note: There is also a PRC-117, a more powerful and heavier radio. In this scenario, the distances are short and it is not needed, except for calling in an air medevac. A JTAC or JTO might have a 152, a 117, and a digital tablet to pull ISR feeds from aircraft and drones, while a sniper team would have at least the 152 and 153.)

AK: the Kalashnikov, a gas-operated 7.62mm assault rifle developed in the Soviet Union

Akaa: old man, or uncle

ANA: Afghan National Army

Asbaab: equipment

Askar: an Afghan soldier

Bacha bazi: a boy forced to perform as a sex slave

Bandi: prisoner

Blue Falcon: buddy fucker

Bravo Zulu: well done

BZ: battlefield zero, adjusting the aiming point of the rifle scope for a certain distance, such as two hundred or four hundred meters

CACO: casualty assistance call officer

Cammies: field fatigues with camouflaged design

Check your six: Watch out for an enemy shooting you from behind

C.O.: Commanding Officer

CYA: cover your ass

Dalaal: foolish

Dawlat: rich

Devil dog: a Marine nickname attributed to the German infantry in 1918 ("Marines fight like devil dogs")

Dussmen: bandits, terrorists

ELINT: electronic intelligence; intelligence acquired by electronic or digital means

Faqir: stranger

Fauji: soldier

Fitrep: military fitness report

FO: Forward Observer to call in artillery, also called a JTAC or JTO

Fort Meade: a base in Maryland where the National Security Agency and others intercept radio and digital communications from adversaries

FPF: final protective fire. When a platoon is under heavy assault, the last defense is the FPF. Everyone in the platoon fires at the same time, throwing out a curtain of lead.

Hajj: journey to Mecca

Hajji: a Muslim who has visited Mecca

Halek: boy

Haroum: wind and dust storm

Hazra: a council of district elders

HIMARS: High Mobility Artillery Rocket System, a long-range artillery rocket system

HOG: hunter of gunmen, a sobriquet given to every sniper after he qualifies

Hus: favor

HVT: high-value target

ICOM: inexpensive VHF handheld radio used throughout Afghanistan

IED: improvised explosive device

IMEI number: a fifteen-digit code unique to each cell phone

Intel: intelligence reports

ISR: Intelligence, Surveillance, and Reconnaissance, a catchall phrase to include multiple intelligence feeds

Jarhead: slang for a Marine

Jerib: the common farm measurement system used in Afghanistan; about half an acre

JSOTF: Joint Special Operations Task Force

JTAC: Joint Tactical Air Controller, certified to call in air or artillery

JTO: Joint Tactical Observer, certified to call in artillery and limited air

Kafir: one who does not believe in Islam as the true religion

Kufiya: scarf

Khan: a respected community elder

Kharaab: bad

KIA: Killed in Action

Kuni: enjoys anal sex

LADAR: Laser Detection and Ranging. Measures distance to a target by illuminating the target with pulsed laser light and measuring the reflected pulses with a sensor.

Lancers: common Afghan term for workers who collect the opium sap from the poppy bulbs

Langley: site of the CIA in Virginia

M240 Bravo: a 7.62mm machine gun

M27: Infantry Automatic Rifle (IAR), a lightweight, magazine-fed 5.56mm select-fire weapon based on the Heckler & Koch HK416 rifle

M302: 81mm mortar

M320: the new single-shot 40mm grenade launcher system

M67: a grenade weighing fourteen ounces, with a clip to prevent the safety pin from being pulled accidentally

M777: 155mm artillery tube

Mal: male

Malik: a leader

Mirab: local officials who settle water and land disputes

MO: modus operandi, a standard way of operating

Motard: slang for highly retarded

MREs: meals, ready to eat, wrapped in plastic

Muj: short for mujahideen, or holy warrior, a common US grunt expression for any Afghan who shoots at them

Nishtgars: day laborers

NJP: nonjudicial punishment, less than a court martial

NMCC: National Military Command Center located in the Pentagon

NVG: night-vision goggles

OTM: on the move

Paarsi: a Persian

PKM: Russian machine gun

PTT: Push to Talk

Qaed: leader

Reg: regulations

Ruck: rucksack

Salaf: a believer in an extreme form of Islamic fundamentalism

SCIF: sensitive compartmented information facility

Semper Gumby: always flexible, sarcastically meaning the situation can and will change dramatically

Shahadah: the Muslim profession of faith

Shaheed: a martyr

Shalwar kameez: typical Afghan male attire: a loose shirt worn untucked over loose cotton trousers

Shemagh: turban

Shukran: thank you

Shura: a high council of Afghan elders

Snuffy: junior enlisted man

STFU: shut the fuck up

Tacevac: evacuation from the field, mainly for wounded

Takfir: a Muslim accused of apostasy, or of denying the Muslim faith

Tango: Taliban

Tashakor: thank you

Tramadol: a potent drug, an upper

TH3: incendiary grenade

TIC: troops in contact; denotes a firefight serious enough to warrant indirect fire support by air or artillery

UAV: Unmanned Aerial Vehicle; a drone

Unsat: standard military abbreviation of unsatisfactory, a damning word across all ranks

Yut: oorah!

Note with Regard to Military Chain of Command

This is a novel. It is not intended to depict literally the complexities— some would say the convolutions—of the military bureaucracy.

I streamlined the actual chain of command. Normally, in a crisis the president gives a verbal directive to the Secretary of Defense, who would direct the Chairman of the Joint Chiefs to send a digital execute order via the J3 (Operations) of the Joint Staff in the Pentagon. The recipient would be a geographic four-star combatant commander, or CCDR. Only a combatant command (COCOM) can send the message directing military operations to the appropriate subordinate command on the battlefield. In an emergency, many of these steps would be swiftly done by secure phone.

(Or they could be delayed. In the 2011 Benghazi case when our ambassador was missing during an extended firefight, the J3 was entangled in a lengthy meeting in the White House with representatives from other staffs. This delayed taking action through the military chain of command.)

For time-sensitive information, the Chairman or J3 (a three-star billet) could call the Pentagon ops center (National Military Command Center), where a one-star supervises the collection of minute-by-minute breaking news from all theaters.

As of January 2020, the four-star general in charge of the Central Command in Tampa, Florida, still had a four-star general in Kabul

(Commander, US Forces Afghanistan, or USFORA) who exercised operational command over all US forces in Afghanistan. It would be unusual, but not unheard of, for the CCDR and USFORA to permit a subcomponent command—in the novel this is the three-star general at MARCENT (Marine Corps Forces Central Command)—to call directly to a task force conducting a short-duration mission in Helmand.

★ ★ ★

Additional information about the chain of command and operational control was excerpted in 2019 from https://www.army.mil/article/38414/Understanding_OPCON/.

Combatant command (COCOM) is the authority vested only in combatant commanders by Section 164 of US Code Title 10, or as otherwise directed by the president or Secretary of Defense.

COCOM is "the authority of a combatant commander (CCDR) to perform those functions of command over assigned forces involving organizing and employing commands and forces; assigning tasks; designating objectives; and giving authoritative direction over all aspects of military operations, joint training…and logistics necessary to accomplish the missions assigned to the command. Operational control is inherent to COCOM."

OPCON "is the authority to perform those functions of command over subordinate forces involving organizing and employing commands and forces, assigning tasks, designating objectives, and giving authoritative direction necessary to accomplish the mission." Combatant commanders can delegate OPCON within their commands. In this book, CENTCOM has delegated OPCON of Task Force Joint Resolve to USFORA.

Tactical Control, or TACON, is inherent in OPCON and is delegable. TACON "provides sufficient authority for controlling and directing the application of force or tactical use of combat support assets within the assigned mission or task."

In Appreciation

This novel could not have been written without the selfless understanding and constant encouragement of my loving wife, Betsy.

For an understanding of infantry warfare and close-in battle, and for keeping me alive, I owe thanks to generations of Marine grunts. I hesitate to write some names, without mentioning a thousand others. But let me start with my uncles Walter and Tommy, platoon commanders on Guadalcanal in 1942 and Okinawa in 1945. In Vietnam, Corporal Phil Brannon (KIA) was my stalwart point man in Binh Nghia village, while Lieutenants Tom O'Rourke and Tony Monroe were my fighting comrades, along with Sergeant Orest Bishko of Force Recon and Charlie Benoit, an extraordinary man of many talents and languages. In Iraq, my son Owen carried on the family tradition as a Force Recon Marine and adviser. In Afghanistan, the 3rd Platoon of Kilo Company 3/5, commanded by Lieutenant Vic Garcia, showed me the realities of the savage firefights and tribal loyalties. Sergeants Joe Meyer and Philip McCulloch were staunch in their duties, and Corporal Colbey Yazzie unflinching at point. Dr. Bob Mazur, a surgeon with two tours in Afghanistan, reviewed my recollections from the battlefields of the trauma cases and the effects upon those hit.

For understanding the interactions between the Pentagon and the White House, my tours as Special Assistant to the Secretary of Defense and later as Assistant Secretary of Defense for International

Affairs were invaluable. So too were the wisdom and tutelage of three friends who served as Secretaries of Defense—Jim Schlesinger, Frank Carlucci, and Jim Mattis.

The United States Marine Corps has been described as the world's most lethal fighting force. It is more than that. Its culture imbues in those who serve rigorous standards that are passed down from one generation to the next, century after century.

About the Author

Over the decades, bestselling author Bing West has embedded on the battlefields with dozens of Army and Marine platoons in Vietnam, Iraq, and Afghanistan. A former assistant secretary of defense and combat Marine, he has also met repeatedly with four-star generals and secretaries of defense, and was twice awarded the Pentagon's top medal for Distinguished Public Service. He is the co-author, with Secretary of Defense Jim Mattis, of the *New York Times* #1 bestseller, *Call Sign Chaos: Learning to Lead.*

The Last Platoon is his seventh and final book about our wars in Iraq and Afghanistan. It is a story of illusion versus reality, courage versus fear, and duty versus ambition.